POISON
EVIDENCE

RACHEL
GRANT

JANUS
PUBLISHING

Books By Rachel Grant

Evidence: Under Fire

Into the Storm

Trust Me

Don't Look Back

Zero Hour

Evidence

Concrete Evidence

Body of Evidence

Withholding Evidence

Night Owl

Incriminating Evidence

Covert Evidence

Cold Evidence

Poison Evidence

Silent Evidence

Winter Hawk

Tainted Evidence

Broken Falcon

False Evidence

Fiona Carver

Dangerous Ground

Crash Site

Flashpoint

Tinderbox

Catalyst

Firestorm

Inferno

Romantic Mystery

Grave Danger

Paranormal Romance

Midnight Sun

Writing as R.S. Grant

The Buried Hours

This one is for all the brainy girls who struggle to fit in.

Chapter One

Babeldaob Island, Republic of Palau
April

Age: early thirties. Accent: American, Boston—Southie, not Harvard, and trying to hide it. Looks: handsome but forgettable. Attitude: smug. The man fixed Ivy MacLeod with what he must believe was a charming smile, when in fact everything about him spoke of condescension. "If you find the Palauan president intimidating, just remember that the country only has a population of twenty thousand. He's more like the mayor of a small suburb."

Ivy didn't let her party smile slip as she glanced over his shoulder, scanning the packed ballroom for an escape. Mark Frost seemed to think he was clever, when in fact he was merely smarmy, and she would bet her next paycheck that he hadn't crossed the packed ballroom because he wanted to give her unsolicited advice on how best to deal with Palauan politicians.

He canted his head. "But then, look who I'm talking to. Your cousin is a US senator and your husband is...was..."

His voice trailed off, then he cleared his throat as if embarrassed.

That confirmed it. He'd cornered her at the edge of the room because he wanted the ugly details of Patrick's upcoming trial.

"Ex-husband," she said, her jaw tight, then berated herself for responding at all. She took a sip of the drink she'd just gotten from the open bar and looked longingly toward the open door to the garden, which she'd been heading toward when Frost pinned her.

Ivy felt some relief when the governor of Melekeok nudged Frost to the side and held out a hand to indicate the Asian man at his side. "Ms. MacLeod, I wish to introduce you to Shiro Kimura, from the Japanese embassy."

She flashed a smile as she extended her right hand. "Mr. Kimura, it's good to meet you." She knew her effort to appear unfazed fell short. It was a shame it was necessary here, but three days ago, that damn news article had outed her. Half a world away in a tiny country in Micronesia, and her ex-husband's infamy had followed her thanks to the Internet. "I understand you have questions about my mapping of Peleliu and whether there will be any disturbance to the World War II battle site that holds wreckage and remains from both our countries."

Frost jumped into the conversation before Kimura had a chance to answer. "Tonight is for celebrating. Save the work talk for later."

She frowned at the man. He was wrong about the purpose for the evening. While the gala event was a celebration of another milestone achieved by the Compact of Free Association between the US and Palau, it was work for Ivy, her chance to connect with government officials, ease concerns, and stroke egos. And even though, as Frost had pointed out, the country was tiny, the largest employer in the

Micronesian island nation was the government. Everyone who was anyone in Palau politics was in the ballroom.

She didn't doubt that they all wanted to know the sordid details of her ex-husband's arrest and upcoming trial. But that was just too damn bad. She didn't speak about Patrick to anyone except the US attorney who was personally handling his prosecution.

Kimura cast a glare at Frost before facing Ivy. His handshake had been stiff, and while he was clearly irritated with Frost, she wouldn't be surprised if some of his hostility was directed at her. Most people greeted her with hostility once they learned her ex had been an arms trafficker who bought weapons from Russian mafiosi and sold them to Islamist terrorist groups.

She could see the accusatory question in Shiro Kimura's eyes: *How could you not have known what your husband was?* But all he said was, "How long will it take you to map the site, Ms. MacLeod?"

She took a sip of her sweet tropical drink. Passion fruit. Guava. Probably three types of rum, at least one of them coconut. Not bad. She'd have to ask the bartender what it was called again. She smiled warmly at Kimura. Or at least hoped it came out warm. Easy-breezy just like the drink. "The battle site is vast, but data collection is going well so far. I expect another week to ten days until I've mapped both the land and water wreckage."

Even now she was itching to be back in the seaplane. She was a beauty, an old de Havilland Beaver, piloted by a Palauan who never made snide comments when they were in the air. When flying with Ulai at the controls, Ivy could get lost in her work. Data points and markers. Infrared readings layered with Lidar. The colors, lines, and numbers that filled her computer screen were even more beautiful than the incredible tropical landscape they flew over. This first field test of CAM's abilities was exceeding her wildest dreams.

"I do have concerns, Ms. MacLeod," Kimura said. "I find it hard to believe you can map the ocean bottom from the air."

The damn article that mentioned her disastrous marriage had ostensibly been about the Lidar-radar interface others had theorized but she'd managed to create. Maybe Kimura hadn't read the exposé.

"I won't bore you with the technical details, Mr. Kimura. Suffice to say I've developed a system that is capable of seeing through both jungle canopy and water."

The official gave her a tight smile. "Won't bore me? Or is that a way of covering that it wasn't your invention and you don't really know how it works?" His English was very good —on par with her Spanish and better than her Japanese—but he'd had enough to drink that it showed at the edges of his speech, and now he was saying things she had to wonder if he'd utter when completely sober. Not that he wouldn't think them, just that he wouldn't say them.

It was clear he'd read the article about CAM after all, but he believed her job at MacLeod-Hill had been a token gesture, in deference to her family tree and marriage to Patrick. She'd heard the rumors: she'd claimed invention credit to keep the patent out of government hands.

In truth, she'd spent five years developing CAM at the MacLeod-Hill Exploration Institute, the organization her Grandpa Cam had founded decades prior. Her father may have had the poor judgment to invite Patrick Hill to join the institute, but she was the fool who'd married the bastard.

When Patrick was arrested for treason and the government dismantled the institute she'd been born to run, she'd dusted herself off and brought her technological baby to Mara Garrett at Naval History and Heritage Command. So the argument that she'd lied to keep her patent out of government hands was ridiculous.

"Do you have great interest in learning about how lasers can be used to transport radio signals through water?" she asked. "Because I'm more than happy to get technical. Because light waves are packed more tightly, they outperform radio waves in their ability to transmit information. They're faster, can carry more data, and even have stronger signal. For this reason, several labs have been attempting to embed radio waves *into* light waves, and with CAM, I have succeeded—are you following, or should I switch to Japanese?" She then repeated herself in his native language, to prove that she could. But instead of feeling satisfaction, she was irked with herself for rising to his bait. Kimura had been drinking too much, and she clearly hadn't been drinking enough.

Next to him, Mark Frost grinned, and his eyes lit with respect. Maybe Frost wasn't such a bad guy after all.

She took another sip. Coconut rum. Really, she should buy a bottle for an after-work cocktail now and then. Even snide comments were more tolerable when served with coconut.

"Dr. Patrick Hill is as likely to have developed CAM as you, Shiro," a man behind her said. "And you still get lost in Koror with GPS."

Kimura's face reddened, yet he hadn't flushed at Ivy's take down.

She turned to see who'd managed that feat, and a frisson of recognition ran through her. She didn't know him, but she'd seen him at the marina where Ulai and his floatplane lived. This man lived aboard a big yacht moored two slips away from Ulai's hangar and living quarters.

A sign on the dock indicated the man's boat, *Liberty*, was available for charter, but she'd ruled out hiring him for portions of the water survey because the gorgeous yacht would no doubt exceed her government budget.

Of course, she'd noticed the man as much as she noticed the yacht. While *Liberty* was sleek and luxurious, her captain was hot. Death-Valley-in-July hot. And it'd been forever since Ivy had thought along those lines about any man.

Tall and tan, with sun-kissed blond hair, he had thick brows, one of which was bisected with a scar, a wide nose, and a hard jawline. His receding hairline gave him maturity she found even more attractive. Unlike Frost, his features were distinct, imperfect, and memorable. He'd been scruffy the other day as he scrubbed his deck wearing nothing but low-slung shorts. Now he'd shaved and put on the requisite pants and shirt for this formal event. It didn't matter; he was scorching hot either with or without a beard, dressed or half-naked.

Frankly, she preferred half-naked.

She offered her hand. "Ivy MacLeod," she said with her first genuine smile since Frost had cornered her.

His warm blue eyes held hers as he lifted her knuckles to his lips. "Jack Keaton. It's nice to finally meet. Ulai said you're keeping him on his toes."

She laughed as she extracted her fingers, feeling strangely fluttery from the press of his lips. She'd been kissed on the hand before and never thought twice about it. Perhaps Jack Keaton had the power to resuscitate her long-dead libido.

It was an intriguing thought.

"Highly unlikely. I have a hard time keeping up with him, and I'm half his age."

It was his turn to laugh. "So do I."

She doubted that, given what she'd viewed of his physique.

She eyed the open double doors to the garden, seeking a breeze. Despite her light silk evening gown, she sweltered in the heat of the room. The air-conditioning in the new grand resort's ballroom couldn't keep up with the press of bodies.

She turned toward the governor, embassy employee, and…she wasn't sure what Frost was—he'd never offered up a reason for being in Palau or at this event. "I'm afraid I'm overheating. I'm going to escape into the garden." She turned to Death Valley. "Join me, Mr. Keaton?"

"Jack, please," he said and presented his arm.

She gripped his bicep, knowing it would be rock hard and thick. She'd been a shameless voyeur whenever he worked on his boat sans shirt.

The soft breeze hit her as she stepped outside, fragrant with tropical blossoms. The quiet, empty garden was a relief after the full-to-bursting ballroom.

The night was lit with tiki torches and moonlight, which reflected off the sea that stretched out beyond the low-walled garden. A mangrove swamp bordered the manicured grounds to the right, while a path to the beach curved around the garden to the left.

How tempting it would be to follow that path and escape the party. Pay homage to the turquoise Pacific that embraced the archipelago. The water here was exquisite, a scuba diver's paradise. She'd have to ground-truth several underwater wrecks to make sure CAM was as accurate as she believed. Maybe Jack was a diver?

She discarded the ridiculous notion before it could take root. He'd done nothing more than help extract her from an awkward conversation. She'd charter a legitimate dive boat and partner when the time came.

Waves splashed below, the soothing sounds faint. She had the insane urge to lean against the stranger at her side. He was tall, slightly taller than her in her three-inch heels, and she was five-nine without them.

Between his height and broad shoulders, he made her feel

downright dainty, when nothing about her was petite. She probably should stop cataloguing his attributes, but this was the most fun she'd had all night.

She'd known he was American at first glance, even though his features hinted at a northern European background. He wore his American-ness like he wore the dress shirt. His posture, the tilt of his head, even the way he smiled. He had Montana bearing—and as a cartographer and anthropologist, she fully believed there was such a thing. She was endlessly fascinated by the connection of people to place, even, at times like this, when far removed from their birthplace.

"Well, that was unpleasant," she said, breaking the quiet.

"Shiro was being a prick."

"He's not alone in his beliefs. He was just drunk enough to express them. A blogger for a well-known online scientific journal recently said—to my face—'*Hard to believe a woman designed something so technical by herself.*' When I complained to his boss, he all but said I was reading too much into the statement and being overly emotional. You know, because I was a woman and called the guy on his condescension."

"If you were a man," Death Valley said, "you'd have been called 'forceful in your beliefs,' and your strength in not backing down would have been lauded."

Her grip on his bicep tightened. He smelled good and said the right things. The party was becoming less of a chore by the minute. "Exactly. The president of Harvard once made a statement that men outperform women in math and science due to biological differences. The president. *Of Harvard*. And he was surprised by the backlash. Sexism is rampant in the sciences. It's not even a dirty little secret. It's blatant."

One reason she loved her new job with Naval History and

Heritage Command: she worked with several damn smart and strong women.

Jack paused when they reached the overlook, but instead of looking out toward the sea, he gazed at the mangrove swamp that abutted the garden. "I read your paper in *Scientific American*, detailing your use of Lidar to calculate the loss of mangroves in Indonesia due to rising sea levels. If anyone bothered to look at the research you've published, they'd know you're the real deal and were the brains at the institute."

If Jack hadn't woken her libido before, he did now. Was there anything better than having a hot man call her brainy?

She smiled. "Thank you. I'm proud of that project. It was one of the last ones I completed before MacLeod-Hill imploded." Her research had been funded by a National Institutes of Health grant and yielded solid data on the hazards of climate change. She'd miss being able to work on studies like that.

She glanced toward the nearby mangroves. The hotel developers probably wanted to take out that habitat, but mangrove swamps were vital to the ecosystem, and they were rapidly disappearing, which she'd proven in the multiyear study. That this mangrove remained, partially blocking the ocean view of the new hotel, could be, in part, thanks to her work.

"Is CAM an expansion of the technology you used for the mangrove study?"

She had to be careful how she answered. While it was public knowledge that NHHC had finally gotten the long-awaited funding to map the battlefield, only a select few knew exactly what CAM was capable of. The technology was, in all likelihood, better at gathering intelligence than the CIA and MI6 combined. But that also meant that in the wrong hands, her baby could be dangerous.

"Yes, for the most part. With a few enhancements."

Mapping the Battle of Peleliu was the perfect test for CAM: terrain known to hide tunnels—on land and underwater—with plenty of historic wreckage to pinpoint, and the ability to ground-truth the data to calibrate accuracy.

He gazed down at her, his eyes lit with interest. On another man—like Frost—the sexy stare would look rehearsed, but on Jack, it came across as natural smolder. "Is this your first visit to Palau?" he asked.

It was crazy how the simple question combined with stare made her flush with excitement.

Hello, libido. I didn't even know I missed you.

He reminded her of the actor who played Captain Kirk in the new Star Trek movies, with his blue, blue eyes. "Yes," she managed. "How long have you been here?"

"A few months."

"What brought you to Palau?"

He turned and faced the sea, his jaw tight, but then a corner of his mouth turned upward. "Do I need a reason to move to paradise?"

She frowned at his evasive answer. Evasion reminded her of Patrick and all the signs she'd missed in their four-year marriage. "Most people do."

"I suppose that's true. Either running away from something or running to it."

"And you?"

"Neither." His gaze slid to the side, just meeting hers as they faced the water. "My reason is private."

She had to respect that. The one thing she'd lacked in her life since last August was privacy.

"Are you enjoying paradise?" he asked.

"Very much," she answered, then paused. "Well, I was, before that article about CAM was published. Now everyone except Ulai looks at me differently, and often they're outright rude."

"They think you were complicit in your ex-husband's treason."

She tried to read his gaze. Did she see salacious curiosity in his eyes? Was he just like the others, only smoother?

She took a step backward. She was done fielding probing and frequently offensive questions from total strangers. No thickness of biceps or blueness of eyes could make up for the pain of insulting interrogation. "I should get back inside."

Before she could turn, he caught her arm. "Wait. I didn't mean *I* believe it—" His gaze caught on something over her shoulder. In a smooth but quick motion, he slipped a hand around her waist and pulled her close against him.

She pushed at his shoulders. Awakened libido or not, this was abrupt and as unwelcome as questions about her ex. "At least buy me a drink first."

His arm locked, a vise twisting closed, bringing her against the hard plane of his chest. Alarm shot through her, and she braced her hands against his pecs. She took a deep breath to scream.

His mouth covered hers, muffling the sound. She moved to bite him, but he pulled back just enough to say, "There are three men who've just jumped the garden wall. They're armed with adzes and machetes." He moved his lips to her neck as he continued speaking. "This is the best way to get both of us deeper into the shadows without letting them know I've seen them." He ran his lips over her jaw. "Play along."

She didn't know what to think. He'd seemed sane enough just seconds ago. Another thought slammed into her.

What if he works for Patrick's terrorist buddies?

"Bullshit." She shoved at his chest again.

"*Look,*" he said against her mouth, the sound a muted

whisper. He turned their bodies ever so slightly. "Use your peripheral vision."

She did...and saw the men, just as he'd described. They were dressed in traditional Palauan garb, but their faces were covered with latex masks that were decidedly *not* Palauan: Captain America, Ironman, and the Hulk.

The Avengers had arrived, and they were armed with razor-sharp adze blades hafted to sticks and long, vicious-looking machetes. Their choice of weapon made sense—guns were illegal in Palau—but the way they carried the tools did not. They weren't intent on carving wood or hacking vines. No, they looked intent on carving up the VIPs inside the hotel's grand ballroom.

Jack planted his lips on hers again as he twisted around so he faced the men. She did her part to make the kiss look real but had no doubt the shiver that ran through her was more fear of the Bizarro-World Avengers rather than triggered by the fake kiss from an utter stranger. No matter how hot the man was, he couldn't compete with unbridled fear.

He ended the fake kiss as he positioned her at the edge of the manicured grounds next to the mangroves. They stood just feet from the brackish water. Ten yards separated them from the open ballroom doors, but they were as far as they could get from the hotel without entering the swamp.

Her belly roiled at the idea of the men attacking the guests inside the ballroom. "I don't have my cell phone," she said. "I can't call the police."

He frowned. "Mine's in my car."

A shout sounded, followed by the crash of breaking glass.

She considered the people in the ballroom, the political officials and dignitaries, and didn't remember seeing any obvious security detail for the president. "Surely the president has a security team in plainclothes?"

He shook his head. "This is Palau." His worried gaze fixed on the ballroom. "I have to go back."

"You aren't armed."

"I was in the military. I can fight." His jaw was firm. "Wait here."

She nodded. It wasn't like she had a better plan. She hadn't served in the military and wasn't trained to fight. And, contrary to the song, it wasn't possible to blind someone with science. Well, unless you had a laser. Which, technically, she did, but they were attached to CAM.

He pressed a kiss to her temple. "I'll come back for you once it's safe." The gesture was sweet and surprising, but it made an odd sort of sense. They were strangers who'd crossed an intimate line even if it had been fake, and he was setting off to take on three armed men.

He moved through the shadows with the ease and grace of a panther, then crossed the open garden as though moving in for the kill.

She wove through the trees, the ground soft under her feet as she went deeper into the mangroves. She found an angle from which she could see into the ballroom, but remain hidden behind a sturdy tree trunk. She could just see one of the masked men holding the arms of the president of Palau while Hulk waved a machete in front of his face. She could hear voices—shouts, really—but couldn't make out the language they spoke or their words. She had no idea what the masked men demanded from the president.

A woman's shriek rose above the buzz and clicks of insects in the mangrove swamp. Both Hulk and Captain America turned in the direction of the sound.

Jack came into view. In a flash of movement, he pinned Ironman to the floor and snapped his forearm.

Hulk lunged for Jack.

Why isn't anyone helping him?

But then, a man did. Shiro Kimura took a blow to the face from Captain America but got his own punch in in the process. Jack disarmed Hulk with a spinning kick. He shoved Hulk into Cap, helping Kimura evade the swing of an adze.

Jack wasn't kidding when he said he could fight. He was like Jason Bourne, with rapid, hard jabs that showed no mercy.

Swift, smooth, and violent. It was a brutal, vicious ballet.

She dug her fingers into the tree trunk, struck by both the horror and beauty of it. Who was Jack Keaton?

Part of her was repulsed, while another part...*wasn't*.

There was so much power and strength there.

The rustle of leaves followed by a muffled curse was the first hint she wasn't alone in the grove. She turned to see Spiderman wielding a machete, coming straight for her.

Chapter Two

He had Captain America pinned prone to the floor with his knee in the man's back. Shiro was tying up the unconscious Hulk, while Ironman writhed in pain as the Palauan president and the governor of Arai bound him with their silk ties.

"Who are you?" he asked as he peeled the rubber mask from the man's face.

The man cursed in Arabic.

Dread shot down his spine. *Motherfucker*. This wasn't a group of locals with a beef over the Compact of Free Association between Palau and the US. This was bigger.

Why here, why now?

He catalogued the list of party guests. The biggest names in Palauan politics, but hardly players on the world scene.

Shit. The article about Ivy MacLeod and CAM had been published three days ago. Just enough time to send a small terrorist cell, but not enough to get weapons into the country. For that, they'd need a boat.

He'd bet one loaded with weapons was en route from Indonesia or the Philippines now.

Did these men want CAM for the same reason he did, or did they have a different agenda?

Police flooded the ballroom, and he stood and hauled the fake superhero to his feet, then shoved the man in the direction of a young officer.

He needed to get Ivy and set himself up as guard for her equipment. Odds were, CAM was no good without Ivy to operate it—the system probably had biometric security in addition to being too complex for a layman. His line of thought caused him to blanch.

Ivy.

A smart team of terrorists would send one group to disrupt the party while another hunted the woman. Terrorists who operated in foreign lands might be scum, but they were rarely stupid.

And he'd left Ivy alone in the garden.

"*Y*ou scream, I cut you," Spiderman said.

She swallowed the sound as if it were bile. Jack knew she was out here. He'd come, even without her scream for help.

She hoped.

The man shoved her forward, toward the swamp. Her feet sank in the muck and her heels caught on the viny root system that defined the mangrove tree. She fell forward, landing on her knees, her palms sinking deep into the murky silt.

"Clumsy whore!"

The flat of the machete blade struck her back, and she couldn't hold back a yelp of pain.

He yanked at her hair, exposing her throat to the blade. "I said no screaming."

She sucked in a breath and held back the sob that wanted to accompany the tears that escaped. She dug deep for anger to squelch the fear. "You hit me, asshole. It's not my fault I screamed."

He released her hair and lowered the machete. "You fell on purpose."

What accent did the man have? Was that Arabic she heard in the vowels? Or Farsi?

Definitely Middle Eastern, whatever it was.

She sat back in the muck and worked the clasp of her heels. "I fell because I'm wearing three-inch heels in a fucking mangrove swamp."

"Watch your language, infidel whore."

She was no fool. She knew exactly why this man was here. *Patrick.* "Fuck you. Your version of Islam is bullshit. You insult the Prophet by your actions and are an enemy of Islam. You will burn in Jahannam for your sins."

He slapped her, but she just smiled, taking the blow with pride. "Hurting me won't help Patrick. They don't need my testimony to convict him."

"He can rot in prison. You are the one we want now. Your husband promised us technology. We paid him well. He didn't deliver. So you will make good on his debt."

And now everything made sense. The Avengers were here for CAM. Patrick must have told them about her ongoing project. He'd *sold* her baby before it was even born. And they'd come for it in Palau, because there was no way they could steal it from the Washington Navy Yard in DC, where she now worked.

"Only I know how to operate CAM," she said. "You need me alive."

"That is why I am taking you. Now get up and walk." He smacked her shoulder with the flat of the blade.

He would hurt her, even terrorize her, but at least he knew he couldn't kill her.

She slipped the slime-covered stiletto from her foot and shifted to the other one. Fear had her in a tight grip, but she couldn't let it win. She had so many plans, a life ahead of her now that CAM was nearly complete.

"Hurry up."

She tossed a glare at the man over her shoulder. He'd been shorter than her when she wore the heels, but now when she stood, they'd be about the same height.

Her dreams for the future flashed through her mind—her career, her plans for motherhood. Patrick wouldn't steal those from her too.

She planned her motion carefully as she stood, one heel in each hand, spiked end out. He pushed at her back again, and she exaggerated her stumble, twisting to grab a tree for support but really using it for leverage as she pushed off and slashed at his face with both heels, aiming for his eyes.

His mask was cloth—like Spiderman's—not rubber like the other Avengers had worn. The fabric split and ran like cheap nylon.

He dropped the machete to protect his face and let out a scream and a curse that was definitely Arabic.

He tackled her and slammed her into the trunk, but not before she'd gouged one eye. Blood spread outward, darkening the already red material.

When science fails to blind, use a stiletto.

His hand closed on her throat, and he pressed her neck into the tree as he cut off her air. She aimed for his face with the heels again, but he knocked them away with his free hand.

She tried to gouge his wounded eye, but he held his head back, out of reach. She kneed him in the groin. He flinched but didn't release his iron grip from her windpipe.

All at once, he lurched backward and was slammed into a tree.

She took a deep, gasping breath, but hope faded as she recognized Thor. Not a savior. Another of Patrick's associates.

"We need her alive, asshole."

This accent was…*Russian*?

"Ivy!"

The shout—Jack's voice—came from the garden. A glance in that direction showed she'd been dragged quite a distance and was deep in the swamp. She waded deeper into the swamp, where the vines were so thick they concealed her. Anything to escape these men who wanted her and CAM.

The men cursed—one in Arabic, the other in Russian—and followed her into the swamp.

Jack shouted her name again, closer this time, and she waded deeper into the brackish water, angling in his direction. She wanted to shout back, but her attackers were closer and would find her first if she did.

"Shit. Let her go," the Russian said. The men slipped into the dark recesses of the mangroves.

"Ivy!" Jack said again, and she waded through the muck toward his voice, not answering until she had him in sight, in case Thor and Spiderman remained nearby.

She brushed aside a vine. "Jack! Spiderman and Thor—"

His arms circled her, pulling her to his chest. "I'm so sorry. I shouldn't have left you."

She pushed him away, rejecting the embrace. "We have to get CAM and get out of here. Now."

She broke into a run. For all she knew, Thor and Spiderman had already taken it.

She ran to a side door at the edge of the garden, bypassing the chaos in the ballroom. Inside, she took the stairs two at a time, glad she'd left the stilettos in the swamp.

She was out of breath by the time she reached her room on the fourth floor, but grateful to see the door was intact. She fished her room key from her bra and unlocked the door.

Jack, who'd followed without question, nudged her aside before she opened the door. In the blink of an eye, a gun filled his hand. Where did he get that?

She waited to ask the question until he'd entered and scanned the room.

She made a beeline for the closet where she stored CAM. "If you had a gun this whole time, why didn't you use it in the ballroom?"

"I don't believe in bringing guns to a knife fight. I'd've used it if I had to, but with so many people in the room, it would've been dangerous. Plus, given that they're illegal here, my Sig would've been confiscated."

She couldn't fault him for that.

He nodded toward the closet. "Is everything there?"

She counted the aluminum shipping containers. Six total. She picked the first one up. Heavy. The lock was intact.

She pressed her thumb to the lock pad, then punched in her four-digit PIN. The lock released. The computer and assorted hardware were present and accounted for. She locked it and opened the next one. Each box was keyed to a different finger and had a different PIN.

She'd practiced this for hours at the office and could unlock the containers blindfolded without a hitch. This was important because three mistakes in entering the code would lock the case and disable the equipment inside. After that, it could only be opened without damaging the equipment back in Washington, DC.

The Navy was serious about protecting their investment in her, and twice as serious about making sure the technology didn't fall into enemy hands. She couldn't store CAM in a vault—even if there was one she had access to in Palau—

because she needed access to the system twenty-four seven to crunch the data and refine the system. The biometric security codes and a built-in tracking beacon had been her solution to the problem. Plus only she could work CAM, and until the news article had been published three days ago, no one had known she was in Palau with her high-tech masterpiece.

Throughout the procedure, Jack didn't say a word. It took her less than five minutes to inspect all six boxes, but her work wasn't done. Moving quickly, she dumped her clothes into a backpack and grabbed the toiletries from the bathroom.

She faced Jack, a man she'd just met and knew little about except that he had a boat and had managed to beat the hell out of three armed Avengers.

In this moment, there was no one else to turn to, and she had everything to fear from staying at the hotel. "Can you take me somewhere safe? Now?"

Chapter Three

He'd be thankful for his amazing luck, except, given Ivy's bruises, it wasn't luck that had brought them here. It was a brutal assault that left her shaking even as she ensured her equipment was secure.

"I live on my boat," he said, his voice guarded even while his mind raced, considering how to reply. If he overplayed this opportunity, she'd bolt.

"I figured." She glanced down at her mud-coated skin. "Just promise me it has a shower."

The rank slime from the swamp had begun to dry. He couldn't help but notice how beautiful she was, even coated in mangrove mud, but mostly he was surprised by how rationally she responded to what must have been the most terrifying experience of her life.

"It has two," he said. He'd liberated *Liberty*—originally owned by the Pakhan of a Russian Bratva organization—from Indonesia, neatly providing himself with both housing and a job that had been the perfect cover for his search.

She arranged the aluminum boxes, locking them together in two stacks of three and extended a luggage handle from the bottom case, which had wheels. She slipped her backpack over her shoulders, then draped a purse across her chest and grabbed the handles for both stacks of equipment and headed for the door.

When he didn't follow, she stopped and glanced over her shoulder at him.

This was a delicate game. If he came across as too eager, it would raise alarm bells. "I don't know, Ivy, I—"

"Please?" She shook her head, clearly realizing she'd forgotten both her manners and to wait for his affirmative response. "I can pay you. Just for one night. I need to contact the FBI and explain the situation, but first, I need to protect CAM."

He gave a sharp nod. "One night." He reached for one of the luggage handles. "Let me help you with that."

She jerked back from him. "No. Only I touch the equipment."

He raised his hands and backed away. "Suit yourself, but you're going to find the stairs difficult. If we take the elevator, you'll be seen in the lobby. The cops will detain you and everyone will see us together. My boat won't be safe then."

"It's a good thing I know how to find the service elevator, then."

He smiled, liking this woman's cool wits in the face of terror. He'd have to remember that she didn't give in to hysterics. When she learned what he was, she'd be a cunning adversary.

*I*vy's cell phone rang on the drive to Jack's boat. She glanced at the screen. Her boss's name lit on the display. Shit. She should have called Mara the moment she and the equipment were safely tucked into the vehicle, but the first priority had been to call the police and tell them about Spiderman and Thor. She'd completed that call and had yet to catch her breath.

She pressed the phone to her ear. "Hey, Mara, I take it the party has made headlines."

"Thank God you're safe!" Mara paused. "Wait, *are* you safe?"

"Yes. And so is the equipment." She glanced sideways at Jack, then said in a soft voice that he'd hear no matter what, "I triggered the transponder. Can you make sure it's working?" Knowing the US Navy could track CAM's location was the only reason she felt safe taking off with a virtual stranger, even if she had been ogling him for the better part of a week. No way could Jack possibly know how to interrupt the embedded signal.

"Cressida opened the direct link." Mara projected her voice away from the phone. "Do you have CAM on the map?"

Ivy heard a muffled response before Mara said, "You're nearing the bridge to Koror."

A glance at the road ahead showed signs for the bridge. "Yep. I planned to report what happened once CAM and I are settled in a safe place." She then explained to Mara what happened in the swamp. "I need to talk to Aurora Ames," she added, naming the US attorney for the District of Columbia, who was personally handling Patrick's prosecution. "She can add selling CAM to the charges."

"I'll brief Curt. He'll want to send out a team of FBI investigators, but it will probably take a few days to get them out there." Curt was US Attorney General Curt Dominick, Mara's husband. If anyone could get the FBI to respond quickly, it was the head of the Justice Department. Ivy had been battling panic from the moment she heard the soft curse in the swamp. This reminder that she had powerful allies led to her first deep breath in what felt like hours.

"We need to consider bringing you home," Mara said.

Dread settled in her gut. The test of CAM was going so well. "I understand. I don't want to leave. But I understand."

"If we could ensure your security, you could complete the project, but I doubt the Navy will be willing to send a team. It's too expensive." After a pause, Mara added, "I'll see what I can do."

"Thanks, Mara. Did you have a chance to see the upload I did today?" Because of the scheduled party, she'd worked in her hotel room all day, giving Ulai the day off. She'd used her direct satellite link to upload the latest data, which she'd already compiled into GIS layers.

"It's amazing," Mara said, her voice full of awe. "I can't believe how detailed the map is of the submerged Zero. And I could swear you found a tunnel in the Peleliu jungle."

"Me too. I planned to go out there in a few days, to confirm." She closed her eyes and took a deep breath. "It would be a win for Patrick if I had to run home and hide."

"I know, Ivy," Mara said. "And I know what CAM means to you. I'll do what I can on my end. In the meantime, promise me that if you're in distress, you'll lock CAM down."

Lockdown would mean full abort of the project. Her stomach clenched at the thought. "I promise."

She'd initiated CAM's tracking signal. He wasn't sure if that was a good thing or a bad thing. No doubt she had a direct satellite uplink. He didn't have the skills to block it.

Just the idea that she'd been on the phone with Curt Dominick's wife... It brought both a shiver of fear and...

hope. The man could be an ally, but given his straight-arrow reputation, he was more likely a foe.

It was absolutely vital for him to earn Ivy's trust, or the game was over. For him and for Ivy.

Even after the assault in the swamp, she probably didn't realize exactly how much danger she was in, because she had no idea what the stakes were. He was the only one who knew.

So far she trusted him. But then, he'd been trained to be a charmer. A seducer. Part of the job description.

He wanted to believe he was a good guy, but all evidence pointed to the contrary, even if none of it was his choice.

Free will. A key trait of humanity, and the one thing he'd always lacked. He had more in common with Ivy's mapping drone than anyone knew. The day he achieved control over his choices was the day he'd both enter and leave the human race.

Ivy MacLeod was his ticket to humanity. His liberation. And eventually, his death sentence.

He couldn't fuck this up. More than his and Ivy's lives hung in the balance. The sister he hadn't seen in years and the nephew he'd never met were vulnerable. Freedom waited for them if he pulled this assignment off.

"What branch of the military were you in that you learned to fight like that?" she asked. "Were you special forces?"

The reckless side of him wanted to tell the truth, just to see her reaction. But he'd learned to curb that impulse after a few lessons at the end of a hockey stick reinforced the message of control at all times. "Major Jack Keaton, US Air Force, retired."

She glanced at him askance. "You're a little young to be retired."

"Medical retirement."

"I'd have guessed you were more the Green Beret type. Aren't they all about the hand-to-hand combat?"

"Sometimes pilots have to bail in enemy territory. It's important to know how to fight." He'd been assured Jack Keaton's military records would hold up. All he had to do was say the right thing.

He pulled into the marina parking lot. She had to let him help unload the cases from the backseat of the truck cab. "Sorry I was difficult at the hotel. You were being so great and helping me. I shouldn't have... I—I'm a bit mother-bearish about CAM."

He draped an arm around her shoulder and pressed his lips to her temple. "I get it. We're cool."

She leaned against him, and he felt her tremble. She was running on fumes.

He'd found her attractive from the first time he saw her photo, and his ego had enjoyed the way she'd stared at him when he brazenly swabbed the deck shirtless to snare her attention. But he'd never expected to actually *like* her.

However, from the moment he'd overheard her call Shiro Kimura on his bullshit—in two languages the man could understand—something had shifted.

She was obviously smart as hell, given that she'd designed, built, and coded equipment that could be a game changer in surveillance and search technology. But in the wake of the assault, he saw the strength that had carried her when her life and work had become tabloid fodder.

She'd been attacked and nearly kidnapped, and yet she'd held herself together with a razor-sharp focus on protecting her invention. It demonstrated in stark relief what her priorities were—which would be a problem down the road. But for now, he was impressed. It didn't help that he found her beautiful in spite of her exhaustion and mud coating.

It was the imperfections of her features that caught his

attention. The sharpness of her chin, the slight crook in her nose. She was tall, voluptuous, and unique.

Lying to her left a bad taste in his mouth, which was odd. He'd been lying for so long, what were a few dozen more?

But the one truth she'd never believe once the bigger lies were exposed was he'd never hurt her. No matter what happened, she was safe with him. He'd protect her—and CAM—with his life. And he had no doubt she needed his protection now.

His path had been forced upon him, and Ivy was the key to getting out of this mess, but he wouldn't sacrifice her for this assignment.

She'd already been used by one spy. Being used by a second might break her magnificent inner strength.

Chapter Four

*E*xhaustion had settled in on the drive. Ivy faced the dock to *Liberty* as if it were telescoping before her.

"I'd offer to carry you, but someone needs to carry CAM, and I can't do both," Jack said.

She cast him a wry smile. Given the impressive muscles he'd displayed, she had no doubt he could carry her the distance, and given her height and healthy appetite, she was no featherweight. "Another time, maybe."

He leaned close and said, "Count on it."

The flirtation in his tone gave her a shot of energy. Enough to push forward to *Liberty*'s slip, anyway. At last they were aboard, and Jack made a beeline for a control panel in the salon. He typed on a keypad and stared at the screen.

"We're clear. You can sleep easy," he said. "This boat is rigged with the best security available. The previous owner was...probably not on the up and up. Every window, door, and hatch is wired and monitored. No one comes in or out without me knowing about it. No one boarded while I was out tonight."

That was a relief. She'd been counting on Patrick's

buddies not knowing where she'd fled to; it was good to know that if they found her, Jack would be alerted.

He led her to the guest stateroom in the bow, then showed her how to convert the head into a shower stall. "There's plenty of hot water while we're at the dock. Take as long a shower as you need."

As exhausted and dirty as she was, she wasn't ready for that. She had no doubt she'd collapse in the bunk the moment she was clean, but she needed to decompress first, or her sleep would be far from restful.

"I've imposed enough on you already, but...you wouldn't happen to have any booze would you? I wouldn't mind sitting on the deck for a bit to get my bearing."

He smiled. "Sure. I'll join you."

He opened the liquor cabinet in the galley. "I keep a stocked bar for charter clients. What would you like?"

She studied the selection. "Vodka if you have something fruity to mix with. Otherwise, gin and tonic."

He made them both drinks with an assortment of tropical fruit juices. The end result was the color of a sunset, and when she finally settled by his side on a bench seat on the upper deck, she discovered it tasted heavenly.

"How long did you say you've lived in Palau?" she asked.

"Since December."

"Not long, then. You planning on staying?" Her feet ached from running barefoot through muck. She toed off the tennis shoes she'd donned in her hotel room and tucked her feet beneath her on the bench. The position had her leaning toward him. She stiffened as if hitting an invisible barrier.

"Not sure." He smiled and draped an arm around her shoulder, pulling her to his side.

She relaxed into him. Frankly, she could use the comfort, and it was nice of him to offer it considering she smelled like mangrove swamp. But then, she'd seen the blood splatters on his shirt. He wasn't exactly pristine either.

His arm tightened around her. "I love Palau, but the US is my home."

His voice was a low rumble against her ear, deep and masculine. She closed her eyes and could see the fight in her mind, the brutal beauty of it.

Jack Keaton was nothing like Patrick. Nothing like any man she'd ever dated. That was probably why he'd managed to wake a part of her she'd been certain was dead.

"You falling asleep on me, Ivy?"

She opened her eyes and met his gaze. His mouth was just above hers. She could so easily kiss him. "Maybe." She dropped her gaze and took a sip of the drink she held loosely in one hand. She smiled into the glass. "This is delicious." She pushed away from his side and sat straight. "I needed this. Thank you."

"I needed it too." He rolled his shoulders. "The adrenaline after a fight like that... I needed to come down."

She gazed up at the starry sky to avoid seeing the blood on his shirt. His swollen knuckles. The darkening bruise by his right eye. They were quite a pair, battered as they were and sitting on a boat a mere seven degrees above the equator.

It was a sultry, beautiful, clear night, and the stars were a map across the sky. Grandpa Cam had taught her how to navigate by the stars when she was in elementary school. For many years, she'd believed she'd study astrophysics and still harbored a crush on Neil deGrasse Tyson. But then the siren call of GIS and Lidar had caught her at the age of seventeen and she'd gone into the family business after all.

The star map here was so very different from the sky in DC, but the North Star was still there, sitting on the horizon, barely visible above a finger of Babeldaob Island that jutted into the Pacific to the north. She had her compass. Her bearing.

She took another sip of the fruity drink. As long as she had north, she could find her way.

The night had been a trial, but north remained true. She finished her drink and stood. "I think I'm ready for that shower now."

He followed her down the ladder and reset the security system while she filled her glass with water in the galley. In spite of the humid night, her throat was dry, and she downed the liquid in one long drink, then set the rubber-based container on the counter and stared out the window, seeing nothing, not even her reflection on the glass, as exhaustion won at last.

Sounds behind her told her that Jack had entered the room, but she was frozen in place, unable to even pour a glass of water for him.

An arm slid along her waist, and she felt his warm chest at her back. "C'mon, Poison. You need your shower."

She smiled instead of protesting the silly, obvious nickname. Only fair that he'd dubbed her Poison when she'd been mentally calling him Death Valley for days.

He was right about the shower. Her skin itched with dried mud, and her back ached where the machete had struck her.

"I'd blame the vodka, but I'm not usually such a lightweight."

"Adrenaline crash. I expected this twenty minutes ago. The fruit juice bought you time."

She leaned against him, looking up. He was taller than her by at least five inches, which she found comforting in her exhausted state. She remembered the feel of his smooth skin against hers when he'd kissed her, and she reached up and stroked his jaw.

Too bad that kiss hadn't been real. He was good at it, and

she could use a kiss right now. That fake kiss was her first since the divorce. She missed kissing.

She missed sex too, she realized. That was new. She hadn't really missed it before. Aloud, she said, "The mud itches." She wasn't so far gone she lacked a verbal filter.

He nodded and steered her across the galley to the head next to her stateroom. He released her and lifted the hatch in the floor to open the shower drain and pulled the curtain that would prevent the spray from hitting the toilet and the counter, then he turned on the water, leaving his hand in the spray to check the temperature.

The silk adhered to her skin, glued by the dried muck. She tried to reach the zipper at her back, but her arm was sore. The blow from the machete. She closed her eyes against the memory. "I can't...I can't get my dress off."

He nudged her into the tiny shower stall, dress and all. The dress was beyond ruined anyway. She relaxed into the hot spray. The water felt heavenly on her skin, washing away the slime and smell. Mangroves might be vital habitat, but they stank to high heaven.

Jack slipped off his shoes and emptied his pockets, removing the gun and cell phone. He then stepped into the shower with her and pulled the door closed.

He took the massage showerhead from the cradle and sprayed her down, gently washing away the mud glue. She closed her eyes, enjoying his tender touch combined with the spray. The shower was so small, her body pressed to his even as he washed her.

He replaced the wand, then unzipped the back of her dress. He spread the split wide, then let out a low grunt. "I should have hunted them down."

She must have quite a welt across her spine.

His touch was gentle as he probed the mark with his

fingers. She opened her eyes and saw his arms planted on either side of her on the wall. Not his fingers, then.

His lips. He caressed her abused skin so gently with his mouth, heat unfurled in her belly.

Exhaustion left her as adrenaline surged anew. Her body woke with the feel of his soft lips.

She didn't know this man. She shouldn't feel this way.

But it had been so *long* since she'd felt this way.

The fear that had been with her from the moment she saw the armed men entering the garden washed down the drain along with the grime of the mangroves. She felt safe with Jack Keaton.

And warm…and wonderfully alive.

She'd been struck and choked. Those men might have succeeded in abducting her, if not for the man who was now running his lips down her spine.

He'd defeated the men inside the ballroom. Then he'd raced back to the garden to find her, scaring her abductors off.

She turned to face him. The spray filled her open bodice and the narrow straps slid down her shoulders. She swept the ruined silk down her arms and stepped out of the dress, standing before him in a satin strapless bra and panties.

She pressed her nearly nude body to his wet, clothed one, and slid her hands around his neck, threading her fingers through his short hair as she pulled his head down for a very real kiss. Her tongue slid between his lips. Just one kiss. That was all she would take.

He hesitated.

For the space of a heartbeat, his body was stiff against hers and his mouth unresponsive. Then his hands slid across her wet skin, pulling her tight against his chest, as his tongue delved deeply into her mouth, stroking with a slow sensuousness that was as hot as the water that steamed up the tiny bathroom.

The kiss went on for a perfect eternity, a long exploration of mouths and nothing more. His erection grew in scale with her arousal, but he made no move to touch her beyond where his hands rested at her lower back.

She ended the kiss and pressed her forehead to his shoulder, taking a deep breath.

She should let it end there. It would be simple to push him out of the shower and wash her hair. But she didn't want it to end. Didn't want to be alone.

But she had her security clearance to consider. Sex with random strangers was…frowned upon, to say the least.

But he wasn't a *random* stranger. He'd saved a room full of politicians. Mara knew she'd bolted with Jack Keaton, and that Jack would hide her and CAM from the terrorists who'd escaped from the mangrove swamp. Curt was probably running a background check on him even now.

Her body ached with arousal. She'd forgotten this part. How it was possible to want sex so desperately, she could make excuses for anything. But then, sex in the last months of her marriage had been perfunctorily procreative, even before Patrick's cutting words destroyed her confidence in herself. She knew exactly *why* her libido had died. What she didn't understand was how Jack Keaton had managed to resurrect it.

And *that* was what she wanted to explore now. This feeling of being alive and desirable.

But still, her rational side held the reins, and she reached for the shampoo. Jack's hand covered hers, and he filled his palm with the mint-scented gel. He massaged the lather into her long hair, and she let out a soft groan at the feel of his fingers on her scalp.

He used the shower wand to rinse the suds away, then

started over with conditioner. His gentle touch was her undoing.

She'd needed this for so long…and she'd had no idea. She'd forgotten how it felt to be cared for. To be desired.

Hair rinsed, she turned and pulled his mouth to hers again, sinking into the pleasure of his touch, his kiss, his attention.

She was reclaiming a piece of herself she hadn't realized she'd lost. Her sensual side that she'd buried under pain and humiliation.

His kiss was deep, sweet, and hot, but his hands never strayed from where they'd settled on her hips. He didn't touch her breasts, which ached for attention. Nor did he leave her mouth to explore her neck or any other part of her awakened body.

She needed his lips on her neck like an addict craves a hit. Musical notes without progression to melody was like hovering on the edge of a sneeze for eternity. Sensual, with ever-ratcheting tension, but hollow. Endless waiting.

He was letting her know with his hot, stroking, magnificent tongue that he wanted her, but this would go no further if she didn't want it to.

She released his neck and began opening the buttons on his shirt. She ended the kiss and pressed her lips to his skin as she exposed him to the hot spray.

Jack let out a low groan when she stroked the wet slacks that covered his erection. In one smooth movement, he scooped her up, pulled her legs around his hips, and pinned her to the wall beneath the showerhead, grinding his erection against her center.

Yes. Oh yes.

Her libido was back, riding into town on a rush of faded adrenaline. It brought tears to her eyes to feel this intense desire again after being dormant for so long.

She purred as he kissed her. God, she wanted this. Him. Everything. She wanted him hard and fast and wild.

She wanted him to pound into her until she was sore, so the violence of their coupling overshadowed the violence of the night. She wanted to hold off on her orgasm until she was certain she'd lose her mind and her body was shaking with need. Then she wanted him to take her from behind and finish her off with his cock inside her and his fingers on her clit. There would be no cuddling afterward. She'd pass out from sexual exhaustion, and in the morning, she'd thank him for his service by going down on him while she stroked herself to orgasm.

She ended the kiss so she could tell him exactly what she needed, but he spoke first. "I don't think we should do this, Ivy."

Chapter Five

*W*hy the fuck did he say that? He wanted her. God, did he want her. Plus, this would only help him in the long game.

Yet some misguided sense of humanity stopped him. He was taking advantage. But hell, that was what he *did*. How he'd been trained. Look for an opening. Seize it. Why stop now when he could have it all? Ivy, her invention, and with it the chance to find the missing equipment.

But that might just be the problem. He could have Ivy now, but tomorrow, she'd hate him.

Well, tomorrow she'd hate him no matter what. Might as well take the hot screw while he could.

But.

Fuck. He kept coming up against that damn *but*. Using people pushed him deeper into the pit of self-loathing. It wasn't who he wanted to be.

But it was exactly who he was.

He turned off the shower. He didn't have to be that man.

"Please? I *need* this. Need you." Her breath hitched. "I—I..." She shook her head even as she held his gaze. "This just feels right. Like the prefect prescription to escape a truly awful night." Her voice was breathy, her lips wet from the shower spray.

He wanted her mouth, her touch, her tongue. Her wet heat. He wanted all that she offered and so much more.

"I don't want you to regret this in the morning." It was as close as he could get to warning her off.

"I won't. Listen, I know the deal. It's a hookup. One-time thing. I'm good with that. In fact, I prefer it."

Hours ago, he'd approached her at the party, hoping to end up in exactly this position. But there'd been a sharp detour on the way, and if he had sex with her now, she'd find it hard to believe he didn't have a role in the reroute once she learned the truth.

Her hand stroked the crotch of his wet slacks, and logic evaporated in the wake of her touch.

"Escape with me, Jack. We both need this."

She pulled his mouth to hers again. Her kiss was fierce. Hot. Hard. He slid his tongue against hers, drinking her in as he rubbed his erection against her scant satin panties. It was a good thing he still wore both slacks and boxer briefs. He was hard enough to go off on contact.

He'd tried to stop. He'd been a good guy. Sort of. It wasn't his fault she'd begged. He'd point that out to her right after she slapped him across the face when she learned the truth.

He buried his face in her neck, pressing hot openmouthed kisses to pale skin that matched the peach-colored orchids that grew in the marina garden, being careful to avoid the dark purple bruises that had developed lower on her throat. The bruises he'd failed to protect her from.

His eyes closed, and his mind filled with trampled flowers. He'd allowed that to happen. His fault. His failure. He ran his lips along her peach skin, across the line of her jaw, returning to her lips. The word "orchid" slipped out right before he delved into her mouth.

She sucked on his offering, causing him to groan. Her laugh came soft and low. "What does that mean?"

He pulled back and gave her a wry smile. "I'm not really sure. Just that you remind me of the peach moth orchids that are ubiquitous around here."

"I never knew hearing the word ubiquitous during foreplay could be such a turn-on."

He laughed. This moment of enjoying being with her, it was as pure as any he'd ever experienced.

"Condoms?" she asked. "Please tell me you have condoms."

He shoved the curtain aside and slid open the door to the storage cabinet mounted under the mirror. "I stock everything for my charter clients. Take your pick."

"I don't care, just hurry."

He chuckled and set her down, but instead of reaching for the condoms, he unhooked her bra. If they were going to do this, they'd do it right. He'd give her exactly what she wanted.

He licked a nipple, then sucked it into his mouth. She threaded her fingers through his hair and groaned. His fingers played with her other nipple as he slipped his right hand into her panties and stroked her wet clit.

She bucked against him. "Holy fuck, yes," she said with a pant. "Now do that with your cock. Or your tongue."

He smiled as he licked her nipple again. "Your language surprises me, Ivy MacLeod."

"Does it bother you?"

He dropped to his knees and pulled her panties off, then took in the scent of her wet arousal. He stroked her clit with his tongue. Her back hit the shower wall as she groaned.

"Total. Fucking. Turn-on," he said. He sampled her clit again and she let out another satisfying moan.

"Good." She gasped as he slipped a finger inside her. "It turns"—another gasp as he stroked deep—"me on too."

His tongue followed his finger, and he let out his own groan at her tangy taste.

He could do this all night and not get enough.

"Bring me to the edge," she commanded. "But don't let me come. Not until your penis is inside my vagina."

He grinned at her switch to proper anatomical terms. That was what he'd expected from brainy, scientific Ivy MacLeod. That she was comfortable with both raunchy and grammatical somehow made him even harder. And he was still fully clothed.

He released her and stood so he could strip.

She helped him, working his fly while he doffed his shirt. She nudged him back toward the head in the tiny space. She dropped to her knees while pushing his pants and briefs over his hips, past his knees, until they ended in a puddle on the shower floor and her mouth was level with his bare and ready erection.

She grinned and licked the tip, then swirled her tongue over the head, tasting his precum before she opened her mouth and took him deep.

He bucked at the sensation, caught off guard by how insanely good it felt to be in Ivy's mouth as her hand stroked his balls.

"Let's move this to my bed," he said as he slid his fingers through her long, wet dark hair.

She tightened her throat around the head, then released him with a slow suck along the shaft. She licked the tip again, then said, "No. I want you to fuck me against the shower wall."

Again her language surprised him and turned him on.

He tugged her to her feet. "Fine. My cock is yours to command." He kissed her and pushed her back against the wall, kicking aside his clothes as his hand groped for a box of condoms.

Condom acquired, he ripped open the packet. She took it from him and stroked his cock several times before rolling it down his hard length.

Sheathed and ready, he picked Ivy up and braced her against the wall. "Are you ready to get fucked, Ivy?"

"*Y essss.*" The word came out as both answer and approval as he thrust into her before she uttered the consonant.

"Is this what you want?" he asked. "A hard cock deep in your pussy?"

His words were fierce, coarse. Sexy. Exactly what she'd expect from the man who fought with such brutal grace. He drove into her again and again.

"Yes," she repeated. "This."

"God, you are so hot."

"And you are so fucking thick. You feel amazing." She kissed him, her tongue sliding along his in a delicious dance. His cock felt so glorious, slick and hot as she took him deep. This was her first sex in two years, and she wondered how she'd ever given it up. How could her libido die when sex felt this incredible? How did she manage to forget?

Pleasure built like a wave, with her riding the top.

"Come for me, Ivy."

"No. I want to savor…" She gasped when he braced one arm under her ass so he could slip a hand between their bodies and stroke her clit. She gripped his shoulders and tightened her thighs around his hips, practically dizzy with the sensation. "That's cheating."

"Come. I'll make you come again with my tongue. You can savor that orgasm. But this one is going to be fast, and it's going to be hard."

With the pressure of his thumb, she had no choice. He stroked her inside and out, and she crashed over the edge, tumbling into a hot sultry sea that left her breathless.

Orgasm achieved, Jack shifted his hands and gripped her ass. He thrust into her with all the rough heat she'd wanted from the start.

She kissed him as he came with a hard groan. They kept kissing long after he stopped thrusting. The ultimate make-out session as their heartbeats slowed.

He lifted his head even as he rocked his hips into her one more time, sending shivers of pleasure shooting through her.

"God, you're beautiful, Poison," he said, his voice reverent.

She laughed. "Beautiful poison, or beautiful, comma, Poison as in a name?"

He slipped his tongue into her mouth again, as if he couldn't get enough of tasting her. "Both," he said against her lips. "Many poisons are safe at low doses, but I have a feeling if I keep tasting, I'll be a goner."

She grinned and stroked his cheeks, still smooth from his pre-party shave, and she wondered if she'd get a chance to feel his stubble against her skin.

She barely knew this man. A meeting at a party followed by a vicious assault, and now he was deep inside her as they came down from what had to be one of the hottest screws of her life.

"Well, I may be poison, but you're Death Valley hot. And only a fool ventures into Death Valley unprepared."

"Sweetheart, right now, Death Valley is in *you*." He ground into her again with his hips.

She groaned at the joke. "I set you up for that."

He flashed a grin. "And I appreciate it."

She nibbled at his jaw. She'd never really gone for blonds, but he was an exception. Strong jawline. Prominent nose. The scarred brow. She'd guess his age around her own, mid-thirties.

Good Lord, she'd just had sex with the man and she didn't even know his age. "How old are you, Jack Keaton?"

He slipped from inside her and set her feet on the ground. "Let's get comfortable before we get to know each other." He slipped off the condom and dropped it in the trash, then turned on the shower again and rinsed the residue of semen and spermicide from his cock before taking the wand and rinsing her intimately.

The hot spray caused a quick, hard jolt of pleasure, which intensified when his fingers joined the water. She rocked on her feet and would have fallen if not for the wall at her back.

He chuckled and shut off the shower and reached for a towel from a cupboard above the head.

He wrapped the towel around her back and used it to pull her against his chest. He kissed her long and deep before saying, "I'm thirty-four."

He lifted her with an arm under her butt and one around her back and carried her out of the shower, then he boosted her over his shoulder and crossed through the galley and salon, finally reaching the captain's stateroom in the stern, where he dropped her on the bed.

She loved everything about the way he'd taken charge. She scooted back on the bed, and he followed, pinning her. "I'm a Pisces," he murmured before he sucked her nipple into his mouth. "Not that I believe in that crap." He sucked on her other nipple. "I was born in Montana. Moved to

California when I was fifteen. Joined the Air Force after college when I was twenty-one. I was a pilot and retired a major."

He slipped a hand between her legs and stroked her, and she twitched with pleasure. "Anything else you want to know?"

She touched the scar that bisected his eyebrow. "How did you get this?"

"Jumping out of a plane in a hurry. A strap wasn't secure, and when I pulled the chute, it sliced me." He widened her thighs so he could play with her clit and slip two fingers inside her. "My turn. What turns you on, Ivy?"

"Right now, you."

He grinned. "No. I mean what are your fantasies? Have you ever done this, sex with a stranger before?"

"In my early twenties. Not since—" But she wouldn't mention her marriage. Not now. Not with Jack.

"It's empowering, isn't it?"

"Yes." She breathed more than said the word as he moved and stroked her clit with his tongue. And she realized that was part of why she wanted this tonight. She couldn't control what happened in the swamp, but right this moment, she owned her body and was doing as she pleased with it.

Or rather, letting Jack do as he pleased, which pleased her very much.

She was reclaiming herself, which she'd given up in pieces during her marriage. Plus, she'd gotten lost in the empowering oblivion of sex, escaping the shock and horror of the mangrove swamp. "Thank you for fucking my brains out, Jack."

"I'm not done yet."

He slipped his tongue inside her, causing her to purr.

"That sound right there." He moved to lavish attention on her clitoris. "Drives me wild."

She made the sound again, first as a joke, then for real. He'd earned it with his clever tongue. "You're good at this."

"Thank you. Too bad it's not the sort of reference I can put on the charter website."

She laughed. "Five stars. Captain Jack fights and fucks like a champion."

How did she forget that sex could be so much fun? Not just that it felt good. She felt his laughter against her inner thighs as his body shook with it.

Then he got serious about his task, and she held her breath as another orgasm built. As promised, he held her on the edge, letting her savor it forever before he added his fingers to the task and pushed her over the precipice.

Afterward, she was drowsy and sated, but she felt like she should show him the same courtesy. He stopped her from scooting down on the bed and kissed her temple. "Get under the covers. You're beat and need to sleep."

They lay spooned together. She enjoyed the feel of his hard, muscular body against hers. Muscles he'd earned in the Air Force. He'd served in the one branch of the military she knew the least about. She knew plenty of men in the Navy and Marines through her work both at the institute and now for NHHC, and when her cousin Alec had been in the Army she'd met her share of soldiers, but she didn't think she'd ever spent time with an Air Force pilot.

"How long were you in the Air Force?" she asked.

"I thought it was my turn to ask questions."

"If you've read or watched the news in the last nine months, you probably know everything about me."

She felt him shrug. "I know a bit. Your grandfather and father were cartographers. You followed in their footsteps. You have a cousin, Alec Ravissant, who is a senator in Maryland."

He probably knew about Alec because of the damage

control necessary when Patrick was arrested. Patrick had campaigned for Alec, and everyone close to Patrick was suspect. She'd made several statements pointing out that *she* was the connection between Patrick and the campaign. She'd actually left Patrick months before the election but hadn't told Alec because she didn't want to disrupt things when his campaign had other, far bigger problems.

"Like the senator, you came from money, but your branch of the family poured their money into the institute, which was a nonprofit, and with the dissolution of the institute, the money is gone now."

She nodded and rolled to face him. "My father brought Patrick aboard because he had money and a philanthropic bent. Or so we thought." She brushed her lips over Jack's. "But that's all we're going to say about Patrick, okay?"

"Sorry."

"It's fine. I'm just—I'm happy right now. I want to keep that." How crazy was it that she could feel happy after the night she'd had? Jack was good medicine.

"Deal. Okay…what else do I know? You're fluent in Spanish and English—and, apparently, Japanese."

"Less fluent in Japanese, but getting there."

"Basically, you're smart as hell. You work for NHHC—which was in the news a lot last fall."

"You're referring to the thing that happened on the ferry in the Strait of Juan de Fuca."

He smiled. "Yeah. The *thing*. You know anything about that?"

"Not really. I've only met Undine Gray—the NHHC archaeologist who was involved—a few times when she was still working for the Underwater Archaeology Branch."

"She doesn't work there anymore?"

"She quit so she could stay in Washington. She fell in love with Luke Sevick—the guy from NOAA who"—she raised her fingers in air quotes—"*single-handedly* saved the world that night." She didn't bother to hide the sarcasm in her voice.

Jack laughed. "You don't believe the story?"

She shrugged. "The news helicopter footage from that night clearly shows two people set out on the Interceptor. There is only one logical explanation for why the Coast Guard and Navy won't reveal the identity of the second man. He must've been one of the Ukrainians. A terrorist who was then let go. Or given amnesty. Or some other bullshit deal."

"So you're one of the conspiracy theorists. What about the idea that the Coastie preferred to remain anonymous? You've seen what happened to Sevick."

"Fair point. And it's clear Sevick didn't have a choice in the matter—he was outside on the boat and reporters identified him before the Interceptor had even gone a mile." She ran her hands over the hard planes of Jack's chest, loving the smell and feel of him. Loving talking in bed. "But still, why remain anonymous when everyone in the US wanted to kiss the guy's ass?" She slipped her hands around to his butt to punctuate her words.

She'd been lonely these last few years and hadn't even realized it. Too obsessed with her work to notice she was missing human interaction. Sex. *This.*

"So you think the other guy on the boat with Sevick was Ukrainian," Jack said.

"How else would Sevick have gotten the information he needed? It sickens me that they let the guy go."

"Even if he helped save the world?"

"He had to be some sort of spy or terrorist. He should have been arrested along with the others." She had some experience dealing with traitors and wouldn't mind seeing them all punished. Severely.

"I take it you haven't asked Luke Sevick what happened that night?"

"We've never met. But he and Undine will be in DC over Memorial Day for the ceremony at Arlington. Everyone from NHHC will be there."

"I suggest not using air quotes when talking about that night. Former SEALs can be touchy."

Her laugh turned into a yawn.

He stroked her hair. "You should sleep, Ivy."

She nodded. "Thank you. For fighting the Avengers. Coming for me in the swamp. Bringing me here...and rocking my world."

He nuzzled her neck. "Thank you for rocking mine."

She rolled to her side, presenting her back to him. "And now, I think I'll pass out."

He held her snug against him and tucked his knees behind hers. She felt secure. Cared for.

"Sweet dreams, Poison."

"Good night, Death Valley."

Chapter Six

He watched Ivy sleep, hating, dreading what he was about to do. The woman was utterly captivating. He'd gotten lost in the power of her strength, humor, and brains. Lost in the seduction.

For a while there, he hadn't been playing a role. He'd been living in the moment and enjoying every breath and stroke and heartbeat.

Jack Keaton was the man Ivy had wanted, but it was Dimitri Veselov who'd delivered. And now, Dimitri would destroy that fragile, fleeting happiness. Never again would she pant his name as she came. But then, the name Jack was just another lie.

He pressed his lips to her temple, then slipped from the bed. Remorse sat in his gut, but liking Ivy MacLeod didn't change what he had to do. Relationships, love—anything beyond sex in the heat of the moment—was a luxury he couldn't afford. At least he could free his nephew from facing the same bleak life. Sophia and Yulian would be free. But to do that, he needed Ivy and CAM to find Russia's lost toy that would buy their liberation.

He dressed quickly and quietly. This would be easier if he'd deposited Ivy in the guest stateroom, but his lower brain had been in control when he brought her to his bed.

"Why are you up, Jack?" she murmured.

He leaned down and kissed her forehead. "I'm going to move us to a different marina. In case someone saw you with me. They won't know where to find us." At least with this excuse, she wouldn't wonder at the engine noise.

"Good idea." She pushed at the covers. "Do you need me..." Her words trailed off as she drifted toward sleep again.

"No, sweetheart. I got this. Sleep. I'll be back in bed in an hour or so."

She made a soft sound of acquiescence and that was it. The last time she'd take him at his word. The last time she'd think of him in a good way.

He was losing something important here. But that was nothing new.

Maybe, when this was all over, after he was long gone, she'd come to see him as something other than a villain. He knew of one person who could tell her a story that might paint him in a lighter shade of black.

He'd also hoped the same person would watch out for Sophia and Yulian when the time came. Not because he owed Dimitri—he didn't—but because he was a good man.

Three days ago, when he'd read the article about Ivy and CAM, he'd figured others would zero in on her and her brilliant toy. After all, he wasn't the only one searching for Russia's missing tech. The waters of Palau were about to get crowded, forcing him to make a decision. But he couldn't simply *call* Luke Sevick and ask for his help.

Sevick had been lauded as a hero after that November night. He was the "Sully" Sullenberger of SEALs—the go-to man the media wanted to interview when anything remotely related to the Navy, NOAA, or SEALs made the headlines. Dimitri had no doubt that Ivy would listen to the former SEAL, even if she did believe the other man on the Interceptor that night had been a Ukrainian terrorist.

Dimitri always kept tourist cards on hand for the rare guest who wanted to send snail mail home to family instead of posting a selfie to Facebook. After reading the article on Ivy, he'd grabbed a card featuring Jellyfish Lake, the single biggest tourist attraction in Palau. The lake was in the Rock Islands—the place where all the hunters would gather.

The message he wrote on the card had to be cryptic. He couldn't simply sign it, not when it would go through scrutiny at Luke's work, and he didn't have the man's home address.

In the end, he'd decided on the one message Luke would recognize as clear as a signature. He'd written the combination of numbers they'd used to save the world on the inside of the card and slipped it into an international express envelope and mailed it.

Given the time difference, Luke might, in fact, be receiving the card right now, which wasn't a moment too soon, given that Ivy had said Thor had a Russian accent. A wild card had been thrown into this clusterfuck of a snipe hunt.

Days ago, he'd worried at the risk in bringing Luke into the loop, but after tonight, his doubts were gone. Once Ivy's predicament became clear, Luke would come to Palau. He'd be here to protect her should something happen to Dimitri.

Now he crossed the salon to the small library and game shelf. Not that his clients ever read or played games. They drank and fucked and complained. He had no problem with the first two, but when vacationing in paradise, one should at least bother to look at the scenery once in a while. Then again, he'd never tried to pull in respectable clientele.

He flipped through the cards, finding another Jellyfish

Lake image. Was a second card to Luke warranted, or would it overplay his hand?

With express mail, the card would arrive in two to three days, but from Ivy's boss's call, he knew word of what happened at the party had already made headlines across the Pacific.

Dimitri had avoided the news cameras when he hurried to the garden to find Ivy, but plenty of people in the ballroom knew Jack Keaton. That name was probably all over the news. Luke was smart. He'd receive the card and watch the news. He'd put together two and two without a second nudge.

When Luke arrived in Palau, he'd need direction. Dimitri held on to the card. He had one errand before *Liberty* could depart. He set off down the dock. When he reached the end, his gaze paused on the flower garden that edged the shoreline. Moonlight shone on the orchids, and the memory of Ivy in his arms hit him like a fist.

But what he was about to do wasn't about Ivy. It was about a four-year-old boy he'd never met, and likely never would, but whom he loved fiercely all the same.

He would see this plan through for Yulian and Sophia.

He finished his task. After that, departure was simple. He'd been prepping for this for weeks. He glanced at his dive watch—a gift from Sophia when he joined the Coast Guard, and the only item he'd retained from his life as Parker Reeves —it had been less than fifteen minutes since he'd left Ivy in his bed, and already *Liberty* was pulling out of her slip. By the time she woke, it would be too late.

*T*he dark tinted windows in the captain's stateroom couldn't compete with the bright, tropical morning. Ivy woke slowly, taking stock of her surroundings before she committed to keeping her eyes open. The bed felt lonely, and she reached toward Jack's pillow and found it empty.

Disappointing, but she smiled, thinking of ways to convince him to return to bed.

She rolled to her side. Her body was sore, both from the assault and the lovemaking. She focused on the good aches and tried to ignore the bad.

Her sleepy gaze landed on a note and a flower on Jack's side of the bed. She smiled and held the peach-colored orchid as she read the note.

Ivy –

I will never look at a peach moth orchid again without thinking of you. We need to talk about what happened at the party, but if we try to talk in my stateroom, I won't be able to keep my hands to myself. Join me for breakfast on the upper deck when you're ready.

– DV

"DV" must stand for Death Valley, which made her laugh. She was eager to see him. Eager to touch him. She'd promised him it was a one-night hookup. Was it wrong that she wanted to extend it a few days? Maybe even for the rest of the time she was in Palau?

But the Palau end date would be firm. She'd promised herself that once CAM was running, she'd attempt artificial insemination, so this was hardly the time to entertain fantasies of a relationship. No, this was about sex, pure and simple.

She found her toiletries on the shelf in the master cabin bathroom. Head, she corrected herself. On a boat, the bathroom is called the head. Cabins are staterooms. The living room is a salon, and the kitchen is called the galley. She'd thought Patrick was pedantic over boating terminology, but she'd learned he wasn't unique or even extreme. Boating people were sticklers for language.

She washed up and dressed, then took the orchid with her when she left the stateroom. The curtains in the salon were closed tight, leaving most of the room in shadow. Sunlight poured through the rectangular hatch above the steep steps that were more ladder than stairs to the upper deck.

She climbed, her bare feet silent on the treads as she emerged into the brilliant, blinding sunlight of morning in the tropics.

She blinked and squinted. A table was arranged on the aft end of the upper deck. White tablecloth. Champagne bottle, fruit juice, and a vase filled with orchids arranged in the center. Jack stood next to the table, facing her.

Warmth flooded her—entirely different from the heat of the equatorial sun that was scorching even at this early hour. Her heart fluttered just looking at him. Remembering the feel of his hands, the caress of his lips.

She grinned and stepped forward, having eyes only for him. When he didn't smile at seeing her, she faltered. Was he nervous about her morning-after reaction?

Or was this a fancy kiss-off?

She blinked again as her eyes adjusted to the light. She should have grabbed her sunglasses from her purse. She was half the distance to the table before she bothered to look left or right, to take in their surroundings. She vaguely remembered him moving the boat to another marina in the middle of the night.

She stopped short, and her breath left her in a rush. The sunrise was behind Jack, meaning he stood to the east. Nothing but blue water to the north. Blue water to the south. She spun around. The port must be behind her, to the west.

But no. There was nothing. Nothing but water stretched from *Liberty* to the horizon in all four cardinal directions and every degree on the compass in between.

For the first time in her adult memory, she had no clue where on the planet she was.

Chapter Seven

*J*ack must've guessed how debilitating it would be for her to feel...unmoored. She was a cartographer. A GIS wizard. She was like a homing pigeon. She lived and breathed compass bearings as if mag north was implanted in her brain. And now she lacked her superpower. Wonder Woman sans lasso. Thor without his hammer.

She grimaced. Best not to think of Thor. Batman was better. Yeah. Batman without his gadgets.

But really, what mattered was she lacked the one thing she knew and understood better than anything else. She was—quite literally—adrift. *Lost.*

And for her, that was unique. Unprecedented. But even worse, the man who'd stripped her of her power was the same man who'd been inside her body just hours ago.

"How could you?" she asked, her voice breaking. Dammit. She didn't want to show him hurt, didn't want to give him that satisfaction.

Bile rose in her throat. "You're one of them? One of Patrick's terrorist buddies? Was this plan A or plan B?"

Oh God. She'd fucked one of Patrick's cronies. A terrorist. A murderer.

"I'm not a terrorist."

She crossed the deck to where he stood by the table and struck him. A hard slap across his cheek that left her hand stinging even as her body began to shake. "Don't lie to me!"

He didn't react to the blow, not even to grab her hands to prevent another one. "I'm not lying. I had nothing to do with the men who attacked you and the party last night."

"You want me to believe it's a coincidence you abducted me just hours after Patrick's men tried to kidnap me? I'm not stupid. Odds are, my IQ is higher than yours."

"At a verified one sixty-six, your IQ is higher than most people's and a full eighteen points higher than mine."

"Am I supposed to be scared that you did your homework on me? Do you know my bra size and birth date too?"

"I know your bra size." He gave her a pointed look. "But your birth date escapes me."

She flushed at that. Perhaps bra size wasn't the smartest data point to use. Hard to know when she was freaking out. Fear was draining those precious IQ points. She needed to take control of this conversation. "You've screwed up in a big way. CAM is transmitting my location. The Navy knows where I am. And you can bet this odd blip of a location—wherever the hell we are—will be noted."

"I'm counting on it."

His confidence left her cold. "Is your plan to sell me and CAM back to the Navy? You know what the Navy did to the Somali pirates who demanded a ransom for Captain Philips, right?"

Before he could answer, another thought struck her. He could have unloaded CAM while she slept. Right now it could be in the hands of terrorists, and the Navy would have no more idea of where she was than she did. All the blood in her body raced to her feet. She was going to faint. Or puke. So much for her freaking high IQ.

She hadn't seen this coming. She'd never imagined Jack Keaton was the enemy.

Puking won, and she bolted for the railing and lost the meager contents of her stomach over the side. Jack touched her shoulder, and she slapped his arm away. "Don't touch me!"

"Ivy—"

She bolted down the ladder and ran to the forward stateroom where she'd stored CAM. The room that should have been her bedroom, but she'd spent the night screwing a terrorist instead.

"Ivy!" Jack shouted as he followed her. "Stop and let me explain."

But she didn't stop until she yanked open the stateroom door and saw all six cases stacked on the bed. She leaned against the sill, faint again, but this time with relief.

Jack was right behind her. "You didn't let me finish. I'm counting on the Navy tracking CAM so you'll feel safe, knowing you can call for help at any time. Odds are there's a team in Guam tracking your signal right now. I know you won't believe it, but you're safe with me. This isn't an abduction."

"Then what the hell is it?"

"A negotiation."

"And what the hell are we negotiating? Whether or not you're a liar and a terrorist? Because if I get a vote, I'm pretty sure we're deadlocked one to one. Let's forgo Robert's Rules of Order and skip to the part where I call in the Navy and they drop Hellfires on your ass."

A corner of his mouth kicked up in a smile. "You have a magnificent brain."

"Tell me something I don't know—like why the hell you kidnapped me."

He laughed outright at that, then leaned against one of the shelves that flanked the doorway. "This is a *work* negotiation. I need you and CAM to help me find something. That's all. Once we find it, I'll take you back to Koror."

"Right. You'll take me to Koror. Where a team of SEALs will be waiting to take you out for stealing top-secret high-tech equipment."

"I hope SEALs will be there to protect *you* more than CAM. The men we dealt with last night are proof you're in danger."

She took a step back, shocked by his gall. "I'm in danger from *you*."

"No, Ivy. Not from me. I need your help."

"You fucked me so you could kidnap me."

"I had sex with you because you *begged* me to. I already had you here. I had what I needed and wouldn't have touched you except you begged for it. Hell, I even warned you that you would regret it in the morning."

"So you're saying I *imagined* your lips on my back in the shower—the action that led to the rest?"

He cocked his head and frowned, then said, "Okay. I fucked you because I wanted to. Better?"

She slumped down to the floor at the foot of the triangular bed that filled the stateroom. Stupid to argue about who'd initiated sex when the man had abducted her.

She could lock down CAM. That would signal Mara that something was wrong. SEALs would come. She'd be rescued. Lockdown was simple. Enter the wrong code three times and boom. Locked out forever.

"I know what you're thinking. My IQ might not be as high as yours, but I'm no dummy either. If you lock down

CAM, I will throw all six cases overboard and hightail it away from the drop site."

Dammit. The sonofabitch could read minds. He'd certainly done his homework. He knew about her mangrove swamp study and her freaking IQ. Only one article included her high-genius numbers. She'd been embarrassed, but the journal insisted. It had been published as part of a series on women in science. She and her sisters, Hazel and Laurel, had been inter-viewed together. The article had to be at least seven years old. Given the number of far more recent articles about her and Patrick, Jack Keaton must've dug hard to find that story.

She did her best to appear unfazed. "So? If they've got a team in Guam, they'll get here fast. They'll find me. You can't have moved us *that* far in the night. We can't be more than a hundred nautical miles from Palau."

Jack shrugged. He could give lessons in appearing unfazed, while her act was unconvincing. She couldn't even stand; hence she huddled at the foot of the berth and leaned on the built-in cabinets at her back.

Damn boat. Every surface boasted storage of some sort, and the knob for the cabinet dug into her spine.

"This boat might look like a simple pleasure yacht, but her previous owner was Russian Bratva, and prior to that, the guy was KGB. He had her built to mirror the design of one of the fastest yachts in the world. *Liberty* has three gas turbines. Combined with the surface drives, she can generate upward of thirteen thousand horsepower. I've clocked her at sixty-five knots. We'll be far from the drop point by the time a SEAL team could get here. They'll never find us in the open ocean."

Holy hell, what had she done in boarding this yacht last night? Tears slid down her cheeks. "Yet you said you wouldn't hurt me."

"I won't. But that doesn't mean I won't drop you off on some remote island in Indonesia, Malaysia, or the Philippines. There are lots of uninhabited islands in the Celebes Sea."

No way had they gone all the way to the Celebes Sea. He was screwing with her, rattling her confidence.

Geography was her freaking superpower.

But that didn't mean they weren't *halfway* to Celebes. He could make good on his threat. She'd visited her share of remote places for work, but she'd always been well supplied and had a satellite phone. He'd made no such promises. "Who *are* you?"

He was silent for a long time. She could hear water splashing against the hull as they floated, dead in the water. Negotiating.

Or so he'd said.

At last, he took a deep breath and said, "My name is Dimitri Veselov, although I haven't used that name in more than a dozen years."

"Russian." So much for her ear for accents. She hadn't picked up Russian in his speech at all. Not even in bed, when adopted accents and speech patterns tended to disappear. Laurel, a linguistic anthropologist, would be so disappointed in her utter failure.

"*Da,*" he said.

One simple word in Russian and chills went up her spine. "You're a spy," she added as her belly twisted and flipped and pretty much tried to leap from her body via her throat. Holy hell, as if marrying Patrick weren't bad enough, she'd screwed *another* spy. Her career would never survive this. She could kiss her top-secret security clearance good-bye. Poof. A lifetime of work decimated by one night in bed with a man she'd believed was helping her.

It had crossed her mind last night that she was risking her clearance, but she'd discarded the thought with little consideration. He'd been the hero of the night. The man who saved the president of Palau.

She was such a fool.

Her security clearance was vital for CAM's satellite link. Sitting on the berth above her was equipment that could directly access the most advanced and highly encrypted mapping database the US military had developed. CAM was but another data supplier to the massive system.

But really, it was futile to worry about her job when her very freedom was in jeopardy. People thought she'd been complicit with Patrick, but this…this was the final nail in her coffin. She could be facing prison.

"I *was* a spy," the man she'd slept with mere hours ago said. "I'm freelance now. Sort of."

"A mercenary."

"Unwilling mercenary." He slid down the wall, joining her on the floor. "I was trying to get out of the business. I was pulled back in. Not my choice. Hell, being a spy was *never* my choice. I was selected when I was fourteen by the GRU. Do you know what the GRU is?"

"Russia's version of the CIA."

"Essentially, yes. And because of *my* high IQ, I was recruited. They called it that—recruitment—like I had a choice. But with my parents dead and no adult relatives to intervene, they just took me and began my training."

"Do you expect me to feel sorry for you?" She put as much bitterness in her tone as she could, and yet…she did feel sympathy for him. She had no reason to believe a word he said, but something about his voice, the pause before he mentioned being orphaned, had sounded like authentic pain.

But then, what did she know? Nothing. Not even the

Universal Transverse Mercator for where she was. She'd take a lat and long if she couldn't get a UTM, but all she had was the guesstimate that placed her somewhere in the Pacific but not yet in the Celebes Sea.

"I don't expect anything from you, Ivy, except your hate."

"Well, at least there I won't disappoint you."

His mouth curved in a sad smile, but his voice dropped to a lower, sexy register. "Oh, Poison, you couldn't disappoint me if you tried."

She raised her hand to slap him again, but he caught it, preventing the blow. He held her hand, his thumb caressing her palm. "I hate doing this to you. If there were any other way, I'd have left you out of it. But I can't work CAM, and I'm worried about the men who attacked the party last night. By taking you out to open sea, I'm protecting you. They won't find you here."

"Bullshit." She yanked her hand back, angry that her belly had fluttered at his touch. A reaction she couldn't control, but which shamed her nonetheless.

"The guys you met last night were probably just the first wave. Scrambled the moment they read the article about you mapping Peleliu with CAM. They were unarmed except for tools they could buy here, meaning they probably flew commercial to get here quickly. But odds are, a boat loaded with Syrian and Iraqi terrorists and a shitload of guns departed from the Philippines at the same time. By my calculations, they'll be here in a day, maybe two. You're in danger, Ivy, and I promise, I won't let those assholes find you."

He was probably right about a second wave coming, but that didn't make the freaking Russian spy her protector. "Somehow, I'd feel safer in Koror, away from the asshole who *actually* abducted me."

"That would be a mistake." He sighed. "We can go round and round on this all you want, but the facts remain the same.

You're with me. I can let you boot up CAM or not. If I let you, you'll have a chance to contact your coworkers, who have direct information on your global position. Hardly the predicament of the victim of an abduction. A defining point of abduction: no one knows where the abductee is."

She hated that he was right on that point. She might be clueless as to her particular latitude and longitude, but no less than the might and power of the US Navy knew exactly where she and her equipment were.

So was this an abduction? Or something less nefarious?

Given that the guy in control was a closet Russian, she was leaning toward the nefarious end of the continuum.

He nodded toward the aluminum cases. "I assume you have a direct satellite uplink, which means you'll be able to send and receive emails, no matter where we are on this big blue planet."

She nodded. Because of the encryption and layers of security, she could only access a heavily secured email network. It was a closed system; only people on the network could email others on the same network. But Jack—or Dimitri—didn't need to know the limits of her email access.

"You're going to let me email Mara and tell her you've abducted me?"

"No. You're going to tell her I'm protecting you and making it possible for you to finish your survey."

She swiped at tears that had started to fall again as he quibbled over the definition of abduction. "You're unbeliev-able. She's going to notice when I'm not uploading data from Peleliu."

And that was where he grinned, a full-on *gotcha* that she would have found charming mere hours ago. "But you see, that's the beauty of it. The item I'm looking for is in the Rock Islands. You can map the site *and* help me."

"So we're going to return to Peleliu and the Rock Islands

and pretend everything is hunky-dory? You can't tie me up and leave me aboard. You can't fly the mapping drone. I need to go into the jungle to ground-truth the data. You can't keep me prisoner."

"I have no intention of keeping you prisoner. We're going to work together. Listen, I'd have wined and dined you to win your trust and weasel my way into your project, but the attack last night forced my hand. I really am protecting you. And frankly, I'm worried about Ulai."

Her emotions had been in a tumble from the moment she discovered they were at sea and not in port, and now horror kicked her in the gut. How low was she that she hadn't given a thought to her pilot? He'd be the first person the terrorists would go after, and she hadn't stopped to warn him.

"We'll check on Ulai, Ivy. All you need to do is initiate CAM, email your boss and tell her you're fine, and I'm protecting you. No mention of Dimitri Veselov. They can do a background check on Major Jack Keaton. I'll pass with flying colors."

"Why did you tell me your name is Dimitri, then?"

"Because I wanted to give you power over me, something to hold on to. The name will mean nothing to the US, but there are others who might be searching for Dimitri Veselov, and if they find me, we'll have problems."

"Meaning anyone who is with you will be in danger too."

He nodded.

"That's a shitty token of power. I can't use it without it being suicidal."

He shrugged. "I didn't choose the parameters of my life. They were forced on me."

"And now they're forced on me."

"Boot up CAM. We've been in this location for too long without word."

She was neatly blocked in. She was out of options, but at

least this would buy her some time. They would be working together for days. He'd make a mistake. She could escape. She'd be spending hours on the computer as she processed the mapping data. Surely she'd be able to get one email out without him reading it. Or she could find a way to embed an SOS in the upload. He wasn't a techie. He'd never know.

Chapter Eight

*D*imitri didn't think he'd taken a deep breath from the moment Ivy had emerged at the top of the ladder. She'd been so beautiful with the morning sun glinting on her thick honey-brown hair as she held the erotic flower he'd picked on impulse the night before.

Her face had been alight, eager, but he'd known it would take only seconds for her to take in the situation. Then fear, anger, and pain would take over.

He'd had several tough missions in his life, but never before had he so thoroughly embroiled an innocent. And one thing he'd come to believe in the hours since they'd met was that Ivy MacLeod hadn't been part of her ex-husband's treason. She might not be as pure as the driven snow, but she was damn close.

And he'd tainted her with a second treason by association.

He hated his fucking job.

He helped her carry four of the cases to the upper deck. The other two contained the drone, which she would assemble later.

First she set up the satellite uplink. He watched her carefully as she positioned the mushroom-shaped external antenna and hooked it up to the transceiver. The transceiver had a phone port, and there was a landline phone in the case. He plucked the phone out of the box. "Anything special about this phone?"

Her focus was on the power pack, which had a different plug from the boat's outlets. "Not particularly, no. Do you have an adapter for the power cord, or do I need to set up the solar array?"

"I've got an adapter, but if it draws a lot, we should use the array. No shortage of sunlight." He then stepped to the side of the boat and dropped the phone overboard.

Her eyes flattened with anger. "Dammit, Jack! I don't have a stand-alone satellite phone because I had *that*. Now I won't be able to call my tech team with the specs."

"Dimitri," he corrected. He had a perverse desire to be called by his real name, even if only in anger. "And you don't get to call anyone. You can email, but I read every email coming and going."

"Fuck you, *Dimitri*."

"I'd love to. But I have a feeling that isn't what you meant."

She glared at him.

He reached toward her, not even sure what he intended. He just wanted to take the fear from her eyes. To assure her she was safe with him.

She slapped his hand away. "I told you not to touch me."

He dropped his hand to his side and held her gaze. Last night, he'd taken her against the shower wall. It had been as hot and intense as any sex he'd ever had. His cock thickened with the memory.

If she ever realized exactly how much she turned him on, he was doomed.

Her gaze flicked downward, and her body stiffened, but

she didn't step back. Her nostrils flared, and she took a deep breath.

If he had to guess, he'd say she was turned on in spite of her fear. He filed that away under facts about Ivy to be used against her.

She stepped closer to him, as if drawn like a magnet. But then she moved to knee him in the balls. He blocked her—his actions pure autopilot. In a flash, he had her pinned flat on her back on the teak deck, his body straddling hers.

Shit. What had he done? He'd cushioned her landing with a hand behind her head, but still.

She pushed at his chest, her eyes wide with fear.

He did not get off on restraining women. He rose to his knees and raised his hands to shoulder height, as if she'd pulled a gun on him.

She surprised him, and next thing he knew, he was the one on his back on the teak, and she was above him, straddling his hips.

Her breathing was heavy as she stared down at him. He kept his hands up and open. Full surrender.

His damn erection increased at the feel of her nestled against him. He willed it to go the fuck down, but then her eyes narrowed even as her nostrils flared. She didn't move from the intimate position. Instead she shifted her hips, increasing the friction.

"Well played," he said, his voice coming out hoarse. "I'm at your mercy." And he was. He wouldn't hurt her, no matter what she did to him. He needed her to know that. He didn't want her to fear him.

Light flared in her brown eyes. "You were a damn fine lay, Dimitri Veselov. It's a shame you're a dirty fucking spy."

He flashed a weak smile. "Does it help that I'm trying to reform?"

One corner of her mouth kicked up even as she took his

hands and pinned them above his head. The action brought her breasts inches from his mouth. He didn't mind that at all. "It might've if you also weren't a dumbass and abducted me. That sort of cancels the reformation out."

"Well, I'm taking you back to Palau. And you were never tied up. I never threatened you or held a gun to you. I even made you breakfast with champagne and bacon. It's not my fault you didn't eat."

"You're a regular fucking saint. And you didn't mention bacon."

He laughed. Oh, thank God her spirit hadn't left her. The last thing in the world he wanted was to break her. Seeing her cry as she sat at the foot of the guest bunk had cut deep furrows of remorse into his soul. "You say fuck a lot."

She frowned. "Huh. You know, in my regular life, I don't swear all that much. She leaned down until her lips hovered over his. The shift in position ground her crotch against his erection. He groaned at the sensation.

Her smile was pure cold wicked. "I guess you just bring out the fucks in me."

Dirty talk and her pussy pressed to his cock. His erection thickened. *Shit*.

He did *not* want her to know how she affected him.

She held his gaze. Fighting the urge to tease her clit by rocking his hips caused sweat to break out on his brow.

"What are you looking for? Why is it so important you'd kidnap me and CAM?"

Much as he appreciated her interrogation methods, he couldn't reward her with an answer. "I can't tell you."

"I'll know what it is if we find it."

"We'll cross that ocean when we come to it."

She released his hands and rocked against his cock, testing her power. And maybe her own limits. His control broke, and he reached around to cup her ass in both hands.

She peeled his hands from her body. "I said no touching." She leaned down again, her beautiful face hovered over his. Her sexy scent had a blinding effect. He just wanted to close his eyes and breathe her in.

"Here's the deal, Dimitri. I can touch you whenever I want, but you can't touch me at all. Ever."

"So you get off on torture?" Sure as hell that sounded like she intended to torture him.

"You get off on kidnapping women?"

"No."

"Well, maybe I get off on not being a victim. Right now, I'm in control. And you will obey, or all deals are off."

So much for keeping her from knowing how much power she held over him. But she was calmer now. Her breathing was easier. He should have let her pin him to the deck from the get-go. "So I never get to touch you. Not even to go down on you? I hear I'm good at it. I have a five-star review on Yelp."

She laughed at that, then sat up straight again, but rose to her knees, breaking contact between his erection and her hot center. "Ahh, dammit. Why did you have to go and ruin this by not being Jack?" Her voice was weary, pained. "I liked Jack. He was fun."

"But I was never Jack. If I'd stayed Jack, I'd be lying to you right now. Would you prefer that? Ignorance of who you're dealing with?"

"I'd prefer if you'd never lied to me to begin with." She stood and brushed off her lightweight hiking pants. "Is there a real Jack Keaton? I can't imagine he's thrilled you stole his identity."

He pushed to his feet. "I didn't steal his financial ID, just his name and military background."

"Still, he's going to be surprised when the FBI shows up at his door."

"There's no door for them to show up at. I was told he's sailing around the world. Out of touch. By the time the truth is discovered, this could all be over." He itched to smooth the lines of worry from her brow, to promise again that he'd protect her from the real threat. But she'd established the rules, and he had to follow them. "Until then, can we call a truce?"

She sighed. "This isn't a truce, but it also isn't war."

"An alliance, then?"

"I doubt it. I don't trust you. We're going to have to take this one hour at a time, but if you don't restrain me, and never threaten me again—"

"I never threatened you."

"Really? 'I will drop you on an uninhabited island in Malaysia' isn't a threat?"

He frowned, then inclined his head. "Okay, I threatened you."

"Yeah. You did. If you can avoid threatening me for the next hour, I won't initiate lockdown on CAM. Yet."

He gave her a sharp nod. That was the best he could hope for. Well, that and that she'd torture him a bit. "Email your boss. She's got to be antsy because she hasn't heard from you yet."

"I will, but first I need bacon."

She delayed the email just long enough, operating on the hope that a Navy team would come to her rescue simply due to the long silence. It would have been a win/win scenario. No CAM lockdown. No uninhabited-island stranding. Just rescue and Death Valley in custody.

"Quit stalling, Ivy, and email your boss. We need to warn Ulai."

With his promise not to threaten her, she was testing his limits, but those words brought her up short. If anything happened to Ulai, it was her fault for not having warned him.

Not surprisingly, when she logged into the closed email system, which was as bare-bones as an old DOS terminal, there were several emails from Mara, all with pleas to know Ivy's status.

Oh, Mara, if only I could tell you...

She replied quickly to the first one.

```
I'm safe. Writing up a more detailed
reply now.
```

That would ease Mara's fears and buy time for Ivy to construct a carefully worded message.

"You're going to have to lie to explain the delay in contacting her," Dimitri said. He'd positioned himself next to Ivy on the bench seat, with just a hair's breadth between their shoulders and thighs. He was keeping to the deal and not touching her while still monitoring her every keystroke. "Tell her you had a problem with the satellite uplink."

She nodded. It was the only viable excuse.

Her email was short and to the point. They'd left port last night to ensure her safety in case the two attackers who'd escaped from the mangrove swamp knew which boat was Jack's. She'd been exhausted to the point of passing out last night and feared she'd enter the wrong codes and accidentally initiate the lockdown program, so she slept a few hours, then had trouble with the uplink this morning.

She finished with:

```
Someone needs to warn my seaplane
pilot, Ulai Umetaro, that PH's cronies
```

```
could target him. I didn't think to
warn him last night and am worried.
```

Through the wonders of technology in the new millennium, Mara's reply came from halfway around the world mere minutes later:

```
We received word this morning that Ulai
Umetaro's hangar and his living quar-
ters were broken into, but neither Ulai
nor his seaplane were there. He took
off for Kayangel an hour before dawn.
He phoned in to say Jack Keaton woke
him last night before you departed and
told Ulai that he was taking you out to
sea for your protection. Once we had
that information, the SEAL team in Guam
was told to stand down, but we've been
monitoring your location, just in case.
Surprised Keaton didn't tell you.
```

Ivy felt the blood drain from her face, making her dizzy. He'd known Ulai was safe all along, and even that Mara was likely to presume Ivy was safe as well. There'd been little chance of a team of SEALs swooping in to save her.

"You manipulative bastard," she said through a clenched jaw.

"You said I couldn't threaten you. So I made you worry about Ulai."

With shaking fingers, she typed yet another lie to her boss, the woman who'd given her a chance when so many believed she was complicit with her ex-husband.

```
I   was   in   bad   shape   last   night   and
didn't   think   to   ask   him   this   morning—
too   busy   trying   to   get   the   uplink   to
work.   It's   been…stressful.
```

Mara's reply was swift.

```
Believe   me,   I   understand.   You've   been
through   an   ordeal.   Take   a   few   days   off.
Right   now,   I'm   hearing   from   the   brass
that   they   want   you   to   stay   and   complete
the   project.   Would   Keaton   be   willing   to
provide   your   security?   He's   being
lauded   as   a   hero   after   last   night.
```

She rubbed her temples. Was Dimitri working with the men who'd attacked the party? Was it all an elaborate ruse to ingratiate himself to her and NHHC?

"If I were part of the group, I never would have told you my real name. Plus I had *everything*, including your complete trust. Why would I fuck with that by bringing you out to sea, if I were one of them?"

His words were proof he was good at reading her, or at least knew which avenues her thoughts would take. But wasn't that what a good spy did? Weren't they excellent at reading people and anticipating their actions and choices? Or rather, according to a coworker's boyfriend, that was what a covert case officer—someone who ran spies—did. And Ian Boyd would know, as he'd been a case officer for the CIA when he helped take down Patrick.

Was Dimitri the equivalent of a case officer in the GRU? That would mean he recruited spies—convincing people to betray their country and provide intelligence to the enemy. The only person here he could be recruiting was Ivy, and the minute she gave him access to the mapping database, she would be committing treason. Ian had told her the spies he'd recruited had been willing. Several were volunteers. Ivy was neither.

She sighed. Her every response to Mara was just buying time. Time to figure out what Dimitri's game was. Time to find an escape, because she had no intention of betraying her country. She began typing.

```
Dimitri is eager to provide security
and has already offered his services.
```

"Change the name to Jack."

"Sorry. That was unconscious on my part." She corrected—or rather, edited—the name. He'd seemed affected by her tears earlier, and it wasn't hard to produce another one as she told her boss she'd accepted "Jack's" offer.

Before she hit send, she flicked the keys so the computer's camera snapped a picture of her and Dimitri. The sound was off, so there was no telltale snick, and his gaze had shifted to her wet cheek.

A few more keystrokes and the photo attached. The no-frills program didn't have a mouse interface, and attachments didn't appear as icons. Unless he was familiar with the system, he wouldn't know to look at the bottom of the screen for the attachment log. Her heart pounded at the risk she was taking. She made it look like she struggled with the last line of the email and typed, deleted, then finally signed off and hit send.

Her heart pulsed erratically, and her face flushed. She wasn't cut out for spy work, but she managed to show him a defiant gaze, passing off her wild heartbeat as anger at being forced to lie to her boss.

He reached out to wipe the tear from her cheek, but she flinched backward and gave him a stern look.

He dropped his hand. "Give me two days, Ivy. Just two days, and either you can tell your boss everything, or you'll realize I mean you and the US government no harm. I love America, probably as much as you do. It's the home I wish I could have."

"Yet you're making me betray my country."

"No. I'm just going to look over your shoulder as you do your job. You aren't doing anything wrong."

She tapped the screen, pointing to a key line from Mara's email as she read the words aloud: *"Right now, I'm hearing from the brass that they want you to stay and complete the project."*

Those words had sent a prickle up her spine and were part of the reason she could produce that distracting tear.

"Mara has been requesting funding for this mapping project for years with zero results. Then all of a sudden, four months ago, the Pentagon made it a big priority and said they wanted me to field-test CAM—in Palau—ASAP. I told them I was at least six months out from being able to field-test, but they insisted. I worked night and day to get CAM ready right up until I boarded my flight. Now the Pentagon wants me to stay, even after I was assaulted and threatened by terrorists associated with my ex? That doesn't add up. Even if they don't give a crap about my safety, they care about CAM. Why do you think my government wants me to stay?"

He shrugged.

"*Who* are you working for?" she asked.

"I can't answer that."

A tiny bubble of hope popped. Of course, if he'd been working for the US government, he'd have told her in an attempt to gain her trust. But still.

"Thor had a Russian accent. Is he with you?"

"No. I told you that already. I had nothing to do with the men who attacked the party."

"Forgive me for not believing you. You have a history of lying."

He shrugged again. "Lying is in my job description."

She cleared her throat. "My job description includes mapping wreckage from the Battle of Peleliu for Naval History and Heritage Command—but ultimately, my boss on this is the Pentagon. What are the odds the Pentagon funded this project in such a hurry because they're *also* hoping I'll locate something specific in the Rock Islands?"

He let out a reluctant sigh. "I'd say the odds are high. You see Ivy, you're the perfect spy. Because you didn't even know you were one."

Chapter Nine

*M*ara Garrett stared at the computer screen. Ivy's emails didn't sound like Ivy. Everything about this was off. Of course, she'd been assaulted and had taken off in the middle of the night without seeing a doctor or talking to the police beyond a phone call. The trauma of it all was likely catching up to her.

But still, it had taken her hours to get in touch, and Mara found it hard to believe Ivy had that much trouble with the uplink. Ivy could make a toaster talk to a coffeemaker, networking them through the microwave. Hard to imagine anything less than a catastrophic crash could take her hours to fix, and when she did run into glitches, she was the type to go into detail over what the problem was, not realizing that Mara's brain blanked out the moment the explanation got technical.

It just wasn't *Ivy*. Which meant there was something wrong.

She reread the last email for the third time. Formal to the point of being stiff. They'd passed that stage of their email communications when CAM had crashed and Ivy worked sixty-eight hours straight to fix it. Or rather *him*. Ivy had made it clear in her hilarious, ranty emails sent during the coding marathon that CAM was male in her mind. He was a bad, obnoxious, boastful boy who made all sorts of promises but failed to deliver. And then, when her bad boy started working again, even exceeding her expectations, he was all muscles and abs and bytes and bits.

Ivy on a rant was one of Mara's new favorite things.

She'd wonder if the emails really came from Ivy, except the biometric coding would make it hard for anyone to pretend to be her, and there was just enough Ivy in the word choices.

She scrolled down the last message, and her eye landed on the attachment list. Ivy had sent a jpg file?

She opened the attachment and studied the photo. There went her doubts about the email coming from Ivy. Her brown eyes looked haunted, and a tear ran down one cheek. The photo wasn't posed. It was a quick snapshot of Ivy with a man by her side, neither one of them looking at the camera. It was almost as if neither of them knew the computer camera was even activated. Yet clearly Ivy had known. She'd attached the photo.

Mara had never seen the man by Ivy's side before. The photo backdrop was nothing but blue sky. She opened the photo's metadata file, and it had been taken just minutes before and included the UTM location where CAM showed up as a red dot on the digital map.

Why had Ivy sent the photo? To prove she was the person at the keyboard?

That there was no mention of the photo could mean Ivy was under duress.

It was just after nine in the morning in Palau, but it was after eight p.m. in DC. An hour ago, Mara had sent Cressida and Trina home. It could be a long night waiting for Ivy to report in, and Mara's husband had insisted on being the person to keep her company in her anxious vigil.

After all, as the US attorney general, Curt could get answers from the Pentagon as to why the Navy hadn't demanded that Ivy be brought home. Nothing added up, but if anyone could get answers, it was Curt.

Sometimes it was incredibly convenient being married to the head of the Justice Department. She'd miss that aspect of his job when he stepped down in a few months, but she was eager to have more of his attention, eager to start their family.

But right now, she was damn grateful he was a cabinet member and even the highest brass at the Pentagon had no choice but to take his calls.

Curt paced the length of her office, deep in phone conversation with a general who'd ignored Mara's repeated calls. She caught his eye and pointed to the computer. "I need you to look at something."

He nodded and wrapped up his conversation. A minute later, he stepped behind her at her desk. His hands fell to her shoulders, and his thumbs dug into her shoulders in a quick, casual massage. She leaned back. The top of her head brushed against his stomach, and she smiled up at him.

He leaned down and brushed his lips over hers. "What's up?"

She nodded toward the computer. "Ivy attached a picture but didn't mention it in her email. I'm wondering why."

"That's Jack Keaton?" Curt asked.

"I presume."

He pulled his computer glasses from his breast pocket and slipped them on, then leaned toward the screen. There was something about when he put on his glasses. Like he was Clark Kent. Sweet. Nerdy. And hot as hell. She never got tired of it.

He stared at the image. "Holy crap. That's Parker Reeves."

She sat upright, her infatuation with her husband brushed aside. "Parker Reeves? The Coast Guard lieutenant who turned out to be a Russian spy? You're sure?"

"Not a hundred percent. I never met him in person, but I saw enough photos when we investigated him after the fact. We need to get Luke Sevick or Undine Gray on the phone. Luke can confirm if it's Reeves."

*D*imitri had hoped it would take Ivy longer to figure out how the Pentagon was using her, but those were the breaks when working with a woman with a high-genius IQ. Then again, her brain had also created CAM, which just might find Sophia and Yulian's salvation, so he couldn't complain.

"I'm *not* a spy," she insisted.

"No. Not intentionally, yet there's no doubt you're collecting data. The same kind of data spy technology would gather."

"Data you intend to steal." She frowned. "Have I mentioned it's illegal to collect artifacts or debris from the Peleliu wreckage or from any archaeological or historic site? Artifact trafficking is closely tied to drug trafficking. If you're looking for something to be used in the drug trade, you can bet your ass I'll make sure you fry for it."

He huffed out a sigh. "The object I'm looking for isn't part of the Peleliu battle, and it isn't an artifact." His gaze flattened. "I'm also not a low-life drug smuggler." Ridiculous that the accusation should rankle so much, considering she had no reason to believe he was even a remotely decent human being, but still it did.

"So it's some sort of spy thing, and you're going to take it and leave me holding the bag." Her vocal cords sounded dry. "I'll be sent to prison for aiding and abetting a spy."

"Not if they never know you found it. Right now, no one has given you any orders regarding anything except mapping Peleliu. It's not your fault the Pentagon is scouring your uploads to the database for the object. And not your fault they haven't told you what to look for."

"They'll see it, and you're going to take it. I am so fucked."

There was nothing he could say to that. Would it have been better if he'd stayed Jack? He could have spent the next week screwing her brains out and she'd have trusted him completely. However, she still wouldn't have given Jack access to the GIS mapping database, and it would have come down to this anyway. After a life of lying, it was refreshing to choose the truth. And at least going this route, he'd given her a modicum of power. If she was half the hacker he believed her to be, she'd follow the trail that would lead straight to Luke Sevick, and then maybe she'd find a reason to trust him.

Luke probably received his card today. He would vouch for Parker. At least, he hoped the former SEAL would. Sending Luke the card had been the ultimate gamble—and he'd wagered his life. Ivy's too, if he couldn't protect her from others who were after CAM.

No further messages arrived from her boss, and she logged out of the system, then fixed him with a hard gaze. "Take me to Peleliu. I need to pick up where I left off on the survey."

"No. We're going to the Rock Islands. Your boss will understand why you've switched to the more remote survey areas. It's safer to hide there when boys from ISIS will be coming after you."

She glared at him. "Patrick's terrorist group wasn't affiliated with ISIS."

He laughed. She was quibbling over *that*? "Sweetheart, a terrorist is a terrorist—you can try to console yourself thinking at least your ex was in deep with *better* terrorists than ISIS, but really, it's a bullshit argument. Better how? Al Qaeda better? Taliban better? Al Shabaab? Boko Haram? Does that ease the sting for you? They're all killers who believe in raping little girls. They're the kind of people who board school buses and shoot fifteen-year-old girls in the head. That's who your ex aligned with. And you can bet your ass that once Dr. Patrick Hill was out of the equation, his followers turned to ISIS. They've got the money and recruiting, and now they could get CAM. *Your CAM*. Handed over to ISIS thanks to your husband's promises. You picked an evil sonofabitch to marry."

She flinched, and he suspected she wanted to lash out. But she couldn't, because he was right. She scanned him from head to toe. "Apparently, my taste in men hasn't improved since the divorce."

"There's one major difference: I'm *protecting* you and CAM from ISIS."

"You haven't given me a single reason to believe that." She crossed the deck.

"Put together the drone," he said before she disappeared down the hatch. "So you're ready to work when we reach the Rock Islands."

He turned back to the helm. He'd known she'd lump him in with the likes of her ex, but the words grated anyway. Dr. Patrick Hill *chose* his path. He actively sought to become a player in the Middle East and was nothing better than a slimy arms dealer, buying weapons from lowlifes who'd managed to stockpile them when the Soviet Union dissolved. Hill had sold arms to all sides of the conflict in Syria and Iraq, because conflict meant more access, more customers, more power.

Dimitri's life had been proscribed from the moment he was plucked from the orphan home. He'd been part of a new wave of fully embedded spies, like the Soviet sleeper agents dispatched during the Cold War, but he was from the new Russia. A post-Yeltsin-era spy.

He'd done his duty for his country on one condition: his sister, Sophia, had to be removed from the training program. Of course, that was his fatal mistake. He'd let the spymasters in the GRU know he cared about his little sister.

When he found the man who'd hurt his sister this time, he'd break every bone in his body with a ball-peen hammer.

His breaking point as Parker Reeves had come when he received orders to take out Luke Sevick if needed to maintain his cover.

He could have done it. There'd been a moment when they were pulled into the Osprey, when Luke was removing his harness. One little push, and Dimitri would still be in the US Coast Guard, stationed in Neah Bay, no one the wiser that he was a Russian agent. He'd have been the surviving hero of the night, and Luke would have been mourned for his tragic, heroic, accidental death.

But Dimitri had reached out and pulled Luke into the Osprey without regret.

Luke had calmly met his gaze, said thanks, and handed Dimitri a parachute. *"Better get going,"* he'd said. *"Because it won't go well for you if you stay."*

Dimitri jumped moments later, thus killing his alter ego, Parker Reeves.

In Ivy's eyes, Dimitri was every bit the lowlife her ex was. She wouldn't give a damn that he was protecting the only family he had.

He ran his hand over his face, trying to erase his thoughts

so he could focus on the job at hand. It would take a few hours to reach the Rock Islands. He could get there faster thanks to the souped-up engines, but there was no point in tipping off the Navy as to what *Liberty* could do. Plus, Ivy needed time to hack.

He started the engines, setting a course for the islands where Russia's prototype Air/Underwater Unmanned Vehicle went missing, hoping to hell he'd be able to find it before other hostile nations got their hands on it.

Chapter Ten

Not a day had gone by since that cold November night when Luke Sevick had taken flight in a boat with Parker Reeves that he didn't think about the Russian spy and wonder if he'd survived the jump from the Osprey. Jump conditions had been less than ideal. The aircraft had been low, and Parker had been rushed. No time even to inspect or secure the chute.

It had bothered him that, in all likelihood, he'd never know if Parker survived, not unless the Russian's body turned up on the Canadian coastline.

Every day that no body was found was another day he breathed a small sigh of relief, even though it didn't mean anything, really. Parker's body was just as likely to have been washed out to sea. But still. Luke couldn't help but root for the guy.

Yesterday, at last, his question had been answered in the form of a card. Parker was alive, and he'd reached out to Luke.

He'd spent the night trying to figure out why, then early this afternoon, he'd heard the news from Palau. He'd bet everything he had that Parker Reeves and Jack Keaton were the same man.

Parker was wanted in the US for espionage. Luke had had no choice but to tell Curt Dominick and the other investiga-tors the truth of what happened on the Interceptor, and the Justice Department had quietly issued a warrant they knew they were unlikely to ever serve.

Undine was the only person who knew Luke had let Parker go. Now, thanks to Parker's note, he faced a difficult choice. Rat out the man who'd helped save everything Luke held dear? Or quietly catch a flight to Palau and track down the spy himself?

As appealing as a trip to Palau was—given that the scuba diving was among the best in the world, he and Undine had discussed it as a potential honeymoon destination—their wedding wasn't until August, and the sudden trip could raise questions.

He and Undine had been living in a damn fishbowl for most of the winter. There'd been no hiding what had happened in November, and to his horror, he'd been made the face of the news story. It was only in the last two months that life had begun to settle down—after they'd moved yet again and this time managed to keep their home address secret. But had things settled enough for him to go after Parker anonymously?

News reports from Palau were scant on details. Palau was hardly on the international radar, and there hadn't even been guns involved. So far, reports indicated the only people hurt were the terrorists—who'd suffered broken bones thanks to Jack Keaton. Only Palauan government officials had been identified as guests at the event.

It was unclear if any terrorists had escaped arrest or not.

Unable to concentrate, Luke left work early. At home, he could make discreet phone calls to find out more about the guest list. He frowned as he passed the gym on the drive home. He and Undine had made plans to meet there in an hour. Maybe they'd have time for a run later in the evening.

Undine yanked the door open before he had a chance to pull out his key. "Oh, thank God you're home. I've been trying to reach you. I was just about to call the gym to ask if you were there." She flung herself at him, and his arms closed around her. He would never get enough of this, the moment of holding her at the end of the day. Even when she was upset as she was today—or maybe especially when she was upset—it was a gift to have this woman in his arms, to be able to comfort her.

Last November, he'd been within ten minutes of not having this life.

He tilted her head up to meet his gaze. "What happened?"

"I just got a call from Mara. Ivy MacLeod was at the party in Palau that was attacked by terrorists."

The name was vaguely familiar. "Ivy. The new hire at NHHC? The woman who replaced you?"

"She's a new hire, yes, but she didn't replace me. She's not an underwater archaeologist. She's the GIS person. The mapping and remote sensing expert. Patrick Hill's ex-wife."

Patrick Hill. The traitor who was about to go on trial for espionage and arms dealing. He frowned. "Is she okay?"

"I'm not sure. Mara and Curt want to talk to us both. Something strange is going on, and I'm worried about Ivy."

"You're sure Ivy doesn't have ties to Hill's terrorist group?" What did this mean for Parker? Could Luke have been wrong about him?

"I'm sure. Mara's sure. Curt's sure. She went through massive vetting considering who she'd been married to and the technical work she does. Ivy's crazy smart. I hear her mapping drone dabbles in artificial intelligence."

Well, that could explain Parker's involvement. What spy organization wouldn't want an AI drone in their arsenal?

Damn. He'd hoped the card meant Parker wasn't in the trade anymore. Letting him go might have been a massive mistake.

He kicked off his shoes and peeled off his jacket, then crossed the living room to the couch. He wanted to call Curt, but first he needed to get up to speed on the situation. "How well do you know Ivy MacLeod?"

Undine canted her head to the side, thinking. Finally, she said, "I met her at least a half-dozen times when the Underwater Archaeology Branch was doing that joint project with MacLeod-Hill. She's Alec Ravissant's cousin, which is why Hill did so much campaigning for Alec. Apparently her marriage fell apart during the election, but she didn't tell Alec at the time because it was messy and Alec had bigger issues on his plate. I was diving in the Great Lakes that summer, so I missed most of the drama.

"Trina told me a while ago that Cressida and Ivy have grown close. They both started working at NHHC around the same time and have a shared dislike of Ivy's ex. According to everyone, Ivy fits right in at the office. She works hard and knows GIS better than anyone. She's got a freaky awesome brain. She does trigonometry for fun." Worry clouded Undine's green-brown eyes. "She's one of the smartest people I've ever met. Possibly even *the* smartest."

Luke rubbed a hand over his jaw. Parker had mailed the card before the party. Had he known the attack was coming? Had he suspected Ivy was in danger?

"Time to call Curt," he said and reached for a phone. He set the volume to speaker before he dialed. The attorney general answered right away and didn't waste time with pleasantries before turning on the speaker on his end as well, including Mara in the conversation.

"Before we get started, I've emailed you a photo," Curt said. "I need you to take a look."

Luke pulled his laptop from his satchel and opened the top, positioning it so Undine could see the screen. It took a moment for his email to load. He knew in his gut what he would see when he clicked on the attachment from Curt, but still, his breath left him in a rush. "Parker Reeves, you sonofabitch."

"That's him in the photo?" Curt asked.

"Yes. I take it the woman is Ivy." She looked vaguely familiar, and he realized he'd seen her photo in various news stories about Hill. It was widely reported Ivy would testify against her ex in his upcoming trial. He frowned. "Could this be about the trial? Is Hill trying to keep her off the stand?"

"Unlikely," Curt said. "The prosecution doesn't need Ivy's testimony to convict. She'll be testifying on lesser charges, not treason or espionage."

Relief rippled through him. The idea that Parker had sunk to kidnapping women to keep terrorists from conviction was...beyond distasteful. In his gut he believed Parker was one of the good guys, or he wouldn't have handed him that parachute.

"What's going on with Ivy MacLeod?" he asked.

"We aren't certain yet," Mara answered. "But there's a chance Parker has her because he wants her mapping equipment, which is biometrically coded to her, not to mention that no one else would begin to know how to use it."

"What would Parker want with it?" The technology was hardly useful as a spy tool if Ivy had to be part of the package.

Curt cleared his throat. "I finally received an honest briefing from the Defense Intelligence Agency and the Pentagon. You both were cleared to receive this level of information last fall, so I'm not violating the law in bringing you into the loop, and right now, Luke, you're my best source for insight into Reeves—or Keaton—we honestly have no clue what his real name is." He paused. "Is your phone secure?"

"Yes." Luke had hired Lee Scott to secure all their phones when he found himself at the center of a media circus last fall. He had no idea if anyone had tried to hack his phone, but he wasn't about to take that chance, especially given the number of calls like this one that had gone back and forth as the feds investigated everything that had led up to that cold November night.

"Good. You aren't to repeat this to anyone or to discuss it in any public place where you might be overheard."

"Yes, sir."

"Agreed," Undine said.

"According to intelligence sources, five months ago, a prototype Air/Underwater Unmanned Vehicle—AUUV—a drone that can seamlessly transform from flight to swim, which was in beta testing by Russian engineers was quote, *lost*, unquote, during a field test."

Luke let out a snort of disbelief. "Right."

"Exactly. Someone took it and headed for Hong Kong. The guy who'd nabbed the device was tracked. He disabled the tracking chip and continued south. GRU knows this because they managed to re-enable the tracker, and it pinged near Palau before tracking was destroyed. GRU—or someone —caught up with the man who stole the drone. He was tortured, but all he would say was he'd hidden it in the Rock Islands. One of the GRU guys was overzealous in his meth-ods, and the guy slipped into a coma and died before he divulged the coordinates.

"Russians attempted a search, but given the Compact between Palau and the US...it got sticky. They disappeared, but periodically, Palauan patrol boats have caught unregis-tered boats in the islands. They only have eighteen marine officers to patrol over two hundred thousand square miles, and suddenly they're seeing a rise in piracy and other nasty business. The Palauan government has been keeping it quiet because the Rock Islands are their primary tourist destination, and they've no idea why there's been a sudden crime surge. No clue that there's something important hidden in their territory. No one even knows if it's on land or in the sea. Rumor has it the AUUV can last in salt water for up to six months."

"Which means they're running out of time to find it," Luke said.

"Yes."

"And you think Parker is looking for the AUUV," Undine added.

"Yes."

Mara let out a curse. "That's why the Pentagon finally funded the survey? Why they pressured Ivy to finish CAM early? The Defense Intelligence Agency learned about the stolen technology and saw an opportunity." She made a sound that was something like a low growl. "Those assholes sent Ivy there *alone* and didn't even bother to warn her about what she was walking into?"

There was a short pause before Curt said, "That appears to be the case. It seems they felt that Ivy's cover story of mapping Peleliu was foolproof—especially because it was the truth. She herself didn't know. And the US military could get full Palauan government approval for the project, because the Republic of Palau has been asking for the survey for a long time."

"Jesus. They could at least have sent her in with a team," Undine said.

"I was told they figured that would only draw attention," Curt said. "She was to work with locals—a local pilot for the aerial survey, and charter a boat and scuba partner for the underwater spot-checking of her mapping data."

"Parker Reeves was more than qualified to be her boat captain and scuba partner," Luke said.

"Yes," Curt said. "We figure that might've been his original plan. Jack Keaton has a charter service. How long did you know Reeves?"

They'd covered this last fall, but reiterating the past could always spark a new, relevant, memory. "About a year. I'm based in Port Angeles but spend a fair amount of time in Neah Bay with a few of my ongoing research projects. Parker volunteered to help with a project early on; that's when we first met."

"You said in November you got the impression he wanted to leave the spy trade."

"He said he wouldn't go back to Russia right before he jumped from the Osprey. I had no reason to think he was lying."

"Do you think he returned to GRU?"

Luke had always hoped Parker had made his escape. But he told Curt, "Maybe. I really don't know."

"Is it possible he's working for Russia now?"

"Yes."

"Wait," Undine said. "If Parker is working *for* Russia, and he abducted Ivy to force her to use her technology to work for Russia, isn't that…an act of war?"

Her question was met with silence. Finally, Curt said, "It's on the continuum. We need to determine exactly who Reeves is working for. For now, the State Department is monitoring the situation. We're doing everything we can to keep this from escalating."

"And to protect Ivy," Mara added.

"Yes. And protect Ivy." Curt paused. "The GRU fed Reeves

information about the sub last fall." It was a statement—Luke and Curt had gone over all this in great detail months before—but he had a feeling he knew where Curt was going with this line of thought. Mara and Undine weren't going to like it.

"Yes. He knew almost as much about the sub and what she carried as Yuri did." Yuri was the man who'd set events in motion last fall that could have resulted in massive destruction in the Pacific Northwest—if not for Parker's assistance that cold night in the Osprey.

"So if he's working for Russia right now, he probably has a strong lead on where the missing drone is. Perhaps better than anyone else on the hunt."

Mara gasped. "Curt Dominick, you can't be thinking of using Ivy to—"

The sound cut off. Probably a mute button had been hit. The woman had just last-named her husband. That didn't bode well.

Curt came back on the line. "Luke, I need your honest gut evaluation. Is Ivy MacLeod in danger from the man you knew as Parker Reeves?"

Undine grabbed Luke's hand. He knew the answer she wanted him to give: the one that would get Ivy away from Parker. Away from Palau.

But that answer would be a lie.

He sighed and released Undine's hand, fully expecting she'd last-name *him* before this conversation ended. "I gave Parker a chance to take me out on the Osprey," he admitted.

Undine gasped.

He met her gaze. "I was never in real danger. I know not to take off a harness on the open ramp of a tilt-rotor aircraft. If he'd tried to push me, he'd have been the one to take flight. But the important thing is, Parker *thought* he had an opportunity to get rid of me while the airmen were busy hauling in the boat. At that point, I was the only person who knew he was working for the GRU. In his mind, one shove and he would've been able to return to Neah Bay, and no one would have known. But instead, he pulled me into the Osprey."

"You let him go, didn't you?" Curt asked. "You tested him, and he passed. So you let him go."

Luke decided to exercise his right to remain silent. The man was the US attorney general, after all, and Luke was fairly certain handing Parker that parachute had broken several laws. He'd chosen not to read up on which ones, but he'd bet aiding and abetting were among the key verbs.

"Thank you for the information. It's been invaluable," Curt said.

"You're welcome, sir."

The line clicked dead. Undine stood, crossed her arms, and glared at him. "He's going to order Ivy to work with Parker."

He stood and wrapped his arms around her. "With good reason. If Ivy helps him find the AUUV, and a team of SEALs manages to rescue her, her technology, *and* the AUUV, we'd dodge escalation with Russia over the fact that their spy abducted her. This could easily turn into Cold War brinksmanship all over again."

"And Ivy's at the center of it."

She was stiff against him, so he ran his hand up her back. "I had to tell the truth." She relaxed into him by slow degrees. "Ivy's in danger, from the men who attacked the party, and others searching for the AUUV. There's no one better to have by her side. Did you read the news reports of what he did to the party crashers?"

"I hope you're right," she said as she pressed her face into his chest. "Because it sounds like Curt is planning to gamble with Ivy's life."

Chapter Eleven

The problem with being at sea in the open ocean was the roar of the engine would cover the sound of Dimitri sneaking up on Ivy, should he decide to put the boat in cruise control and step away from the bridge.

No good captain would leave the helm while a boat was underway, but she had no way of knowing if Dimitri Veselov was a good captain or not.

She had no choice. This could well be her only opportunity to have unfettered communication with Mara. She settled on Dimitri's bed, facing the stateroom door with her cell phone in her hands. He hadn't confiscated her cell—why bother when there were no cell towers for at least fifty nautical miles?

Her satellite uplink had safeguards to prevent cell phones from connecting to the signal, but Ivy knew the hack for that. Linking an unsecure phone to the military's ultra-encoded system would get her fired, but committing treason would send her to prison.

Sometimes in life, you have to make hard choices, but this wasn't one of them.

In less than ten minutes, she was in. Her cell phone was live. She sent a text to Mara, as that would be least likely to be detected and trigger a shutdown of her hacked link.

IVY

Did you get the photo?

A reply came a minute later.

MARA

Curt here. Photo received. Do you know who he is?

She didn't know why she hesitated for a moment before responding. She owed Dimitri no loyalty. He was a good lay. Nothing more.

Yes. Dimitri Veselov, Russian. Says he's former GRU.

Has he hurt you?

Nothing but my pride. Didn't suspect. Feel like a fool.

You aren't the first to be fooled by him.

You know of him?

I knew him under another name. Will pass Veselov identity to CIA and DIA. Has he told you what he wants?

He's looking for something in the Rock Islands.

> Confirmed. Has he told you who he's
> working for?

> No. He said he's freelancing now. Wouldn't
> name his employer. He's forcing me to help
> him. Said he'd drop CAM in the sea and
> abandon me on an island if I don't
> cooperate.

There was a long break between messages. Was Curt disappointed in her for not fighting back? Should she have chosen that fate and hoped she'd be found? Should she feel bad for cooperating? For not wanting to see the first CAM prototype destroyed?

Finally, her phone chimed again.

> Do you believe you're in physical danger?
> Beyond his threat to leave you stranded?

She paused and considered the question for a long moment. Curt needed an honest assessment of her situation.

> I don't think he would hurt me.

Two minutes passed before she received a response.

> I want you to help him find what he's looking
> for.

She stared at her phone in shock. It took her a full minute to come up with a reply.

> This is a direct order from US Attorney
> General Curt Dominick? You want me to
> cooperate with a Russian spy? To give
> Dimitri Veselov access to CAM and the
> database?

Would this communication stand up in court? She doubted it. Especially because she'd have to delete it from her phone the moment they were done. But still.

> Yes, yes. And yes. Don't endanger yourself.
> Your safety comes first. But yes, we want
> you to cooperate. Confirmed with the
> Pentagon and DIA. State Department is
> monitoring your situation.

She couldn't believe this wouldn't somehow bite her in the ass when this was all over. She decided to come clean now, because it would only get uglier later.

> For the record, I had sex with him. Last night.
> Before I knew who and what he was.

Another pause in the conversation. She hoped to hell it was because the satellite signal was interrupted, not because he was planning to file a federal case against her.

> Did you in any way compromise CAM and
> the security surrounding the system because
> you had sexual relations?

> No.

> I can't promise it won't be a problem. But Ivy, you're human. You'd been through an ordeal. He'd helped you and offered refuge. I ran a preliminary background check when you gave Mara the name Jack Keaton last night. He checked out. These factors will be taken into consideration. You might lose your security clearance, but I doubt you'd face charges.

She swiped at the tear that rolled down her cheek before it could land on her phone. Was she really going to survive this? She might not face legal consequences, but the press was a different matter. They would flay her. Again.

> Are you saying this as attorney general or as a friend?

It was presumptuous to call him a friend. She didn't know him well, but he was in her cousin's inner circle and they'd met socially several times over the years, long before she began working for his wife. And right now, she wanted to believe Curt saw her as something other than a pawn.

> Both.

> I should go. Dimitri could come looking for me.

> Protect yourself first and at all costs. Text again when it's safe.

> Will do.

She cleared the message history and unlinked the phone from the satellite feed, then tucked it back into her purse.

Task completed, she returned to the head of the bed and pulled her knees to her chest. Part of her wanted to sob—and she didn't know if it was from relief or fear. She'd been given orders to cooperate with Dimitri by no less than the man who was seventh in line for the presidency.

Dimitri had presented himself as a reluctant spy, and she wanted to believe him. She even felt sorry for him but didn't know if her feelings were influenced by the fact that she'd slept with him.

She didn't have to fight Dimitri—not unless he threatened her. She couldn't be obvious in her reversal. It had to happen slowly, or he'd wonder at her sudden about-face.

His claims he wouldn't hurt her had been convincing. And then there was his erection when she straddled him on the deck. She had pathetic little power here, but she'd use every tool in her arsenal, including her body if she had to. But that interrogation method had backfired, and she'd been shamefully aroused when she had him pinned. There had to be a way she could use his attraction to her without risking herself.

She glanced at the ladder to the front deck, and an idea took form. While they were underway, he expected her to assemble the drone for this afternoon's survey. She hadn't responded to his command because she wanted to try to contact Mara.

Now it was time to show some rebellion.

*D*imitri nearly swallowed his tongue when Ivy emerged through the front hatch onto the sunbathing deck above the galley and dropped the beach towel that covered the tiniest of bikinis.

Tall with lush curves, she had a beautiful body he could

stare at all day. And given that she set her towel on the padded bench directly in his line of sight, it appeared she was inviting him to enjoy the view for a while.

He smiled. This battle of wills with Ivy was going to be fun.

The sunbathing deck was a rectangular inset in the fore-deck, tucked down to provide protection from the wind, should a group wish to relax in the sun while the boat was underway. A low, tilted windscreen ensured the inset didn't mar the sleek lines and therefore slow down the high-speed yacht.

The well boasted four benches and a low wet bar, but the noise and wind would be too much for conversation, so there were four noise-cancelling headsets that connected to each other and the bridge.

Ivy might think she'd escaped talking to him by choosing the foredeck, but no such luck on her part. He donned a pair of headphones and flipped the switch for the intercom system, triggering a green light on the bar to flash. She paused in mixing her drink and stared at the light, then looked up toward the bridge.

Between the tinted windshield and the glare of the sun, she wouldn't be able to see him. She was probably just realizing her mistake. He chuckled when she flipped him off. Maybe it was weird, but her spirit turned him on, plain and simple.

As did her brain and body.

There was a speaker, but it had to be irritatingly loud to be heard over the whirr of the engine and rush of wind. He turned the volume to maximum and said, "Put on the head-phones, Ivy. Or I'll play death metal over the speakers."

When she didn't immediately comply, he pulled up the death metal playlist on his iPod and hit Play. He'd done the same thing to charter clients when they were dickheads and ignored him and every rule of boat safety. He might be using the charter boat captain thing as a cover, but he was once a lieutenant in the US Coast Guard, and he'd been damn good at it. He took boating safety seriously.

Ivy's chin jutted out as she glared up at him, but she put on the headphones, then grabbed a bottle of vodka from the bar. "What do you want?"

He turned off the music. "There's passion fruit juice in the galley. It goes well with the peach vodka."

"*That's* why you wanted me to put on headphones? Bartending instructions?"

"No. I wanted to tell you that you are rocking the bikini."

She tugged at the tie around her neck. Her breasts were full, the weight straining against the scant triangles that tried to contain them. There was a softness in her body that twenty-somethings didn't have. A maturity he found irresistible.

"Thank you."

"I'd have guessed you were more the one-piece type."

She looked up at the glass that wrapped around the helm as she ran her hand down her side, a nervous gesture, adjusting to the feel of the suit. "Trina made me buy it."

"Trina?"

"A coworker. The only clothes hound at NHHC. She has the shopping gene the rest of us lack."

Trina. Dr. Trina Sorenson, Navy historian. He remembered her from one of the conference calls last November. Trina was a close friend of Undine's.

Should he tell her about his alter ego, Parker Reeves? Would it make a difference? Probably not, considering she thought Parker was a Ukrainian terrorist. She needed time to get to know him, not be fed stories she probably wouldn't believe anyway.

"Trina has good taste."

"She also made me buy the stilettos I wore last night. I'd never have been able to fight off Spiderman without those shoes."

"That makes her my new favorite person I've never met." He meant it. If Ivy hadn't been wearing stilettos, they could be in a very different situation right now.

"Her fiancé is a badass former SEAL who runs a mercenary organization. The kind of guy who's protective of Trina's friends and has a small private army—which happens to be owned by my cousin—to back him up."

He chuckled. "Point taken."

She settled on one of the padded seats and set her drink to the side. She relaxed into the cushion, and the sun caressed her peach orchid skin. Thoughts of the flower reminded him of last night, and that fast, he was hard. "If we capsize, it's your fault for wearing that bikini on the front deck while we're underway."

She poked her head up and scanned the horizon. "I see nothing but water. No boats. No land. No reefs to snag us until we're closer to the islands. Waves are low, no threatening storms. You mess up, it's on you." Her smile turned sly and a little bit wicked. "What the hell, it's not like you haven't see it all anyway." She untied the strings around her neck and unhooked the back of the suit, then dropped the scrap of fabric on the deck.

Oh Jesus. She did have torture in mind.

Her heavy breasts spread and relaxed. Soft to the touch. A feast for eyes and mouth. He could close his eyes and remember her taste, the feel of her puckered nipple against his tongue, but he had a boat to drive.

"Fuck but you have beautiful breasts." The words slipped out. But then...she was practically inviting him to comment, given that they'd slept together and now she put herself on display for him.

She covered her nipples with her hands in what appeared to be a moment of self-consciousness, then gave up and took another sip from her drink and settled back on the cushion.

The sun beat down on the deck, and lying on the bench as she was, sheltered by the well, he could imagine the breeze skipping across her skin, a soft, warm caress.

He wanted to be that breeze. To forget Jack and Dimitri and lost technologies and spies. And just be a man with a beguiling woman. The bench was the perfect height for him to kneel between her legs, to lick open her flower petals, and feel her thighs curl around him as he brought her to orgasm.

"What are you thinking right now?" he asked.

"Honestly?" She let out a hard laugh. "I'm thinking sitting here topless in front of you was a stupid idea. I'm bored and tense at the same time. I'm scared the guys from the swamp will find me. That I'm going to prison. That I'll be abducted from my abductor. And that I'll get a sunburn and my nipples will peel."

"That's a lot on your mind."

"That was just the last five seconds. Before that, I was worried CAM will malfunction, and we'll never find what you're looking for. I'll rub up against a poison tree during the survey and get a rash, and then mosquitos will bite me and I'll get dengue fever. I'll die lost and alone in a mangrove swamp, and the world will believe I betrayed my country."

"Now I think *I* need a drink." He couldn't promise her the world wouldn't believe she'd betrayed her country. Many already thought exactly that.

"Tell me who you're working for, Dimitri. Make me understand why you're doing this."

He'd been expecting that question again and remained sorry he'd disappoint her. "I can't tell you for your own protection."

"But I can't trust you unless I know what's going on."

"Trust is irrelevant. Just know that I'll protect you from the others. No one will be able to come at you while you're with me."

She rolled to her stomach and hugged the bench pillow to her chest. "Maybe…maybe I can help you. I know people. I can talk to the attorney general. Maybe you can cut a deal. Maybe it doesn't have to be this way."

He could practically smell her, wanted to touch her sun-warmed skin. "Here's one more truth for you: I'm going to die before this game ends. There is no future for me. No deal could ever save my ass."

She tucked her head down. Her breathing was ragged through the microphone. "If you have nothing left to lose, then maybe a deal *would*—"

"Oh, sweetheart, therein lies the problem. I have something left to lose. People I hold more precious than my own life."

Her gaze zinged in his direction, seeking him behind the glass, but all she would see was a dark, reflective surface. "Are you married? Do you have kids?" she asked.

"No children, and I'm not married. No girlfriend. Not even a friend with benefits in the wings. You're the closest thing I have to being involved with someone."

Her body stiffened. "We are *not* involved."

He would argue that her decision to sunbathe topless before him belied that point, but she gathered the towel to her chest in a way that said she didn't need the reminder.

She let out a deep breath; the puff of air hit the microphone and blasted his ears. "Who is it, then? Your parents?"

"I won't tell you, Ivy. Don't think I don't know that you'll hang me out to dry at the first opportunity. There will be no deal, and I'm not about to hand the FBI the weapon that will hang me and endanger all that I hold dear."

Sophia and Yulian had been used against him enough.

Ivy grabbed her bikini top from the floor and hooked it behind her back. Good. Hopefully she'd go inside.

He grimaced, realizing her interrogation technique might not have gained her the answers she'd wanted, but he'd revealed more than he'd intended.

She was trying to figure out how to get the upper hand. If she only knew, she already had it. He'd given it to her when he admitted he'd never hurt her. Hell, he'd had to take her a hundred nautical miles out to sea because it was the only way he knew to scare her without actually touching her.

He was supposed to be a badass spy, but he'd frozen at the idea of physically intimidating her.

He wanted to tell her. Everything. He wanted to make love to her on the sundeck. He wanted to turn the boat around and head to Malaysia, to flee this life and start a new one.

Dammit. She needed to get inside before he did something stupid, like tell her about Sophia. "Go below. Build your drone. We're going to start searching once we reach the Rock Islands."

She glared at the reflective glass. "You don't get to boss me around."

"Fine. Then stay on the deck and I'll whisper in your ears how much I want to fuck you. How amazing your body felt wrapped around mine. How much my cock wants to be deep inside your wet heat right this minute. How hard I am for you. How it felt to hold you against the shower wall and slide home. You were so slick—"

She yanked off the headphones and tossed them in the corner. She finished tying the bikini bra around her neck and refilled her drink. She went light on the vodka, heavy on the juice. Telling him she wanted him to believe she was getting wasted, but proving she was too smart for that.

Too smart for him.

Ivy MacLeod was the type of woman he'd always been fascinated by. Brave. Forthright. Quick. And that amazing brain. Relationships had never been in the cards for him, but if it had been possible, she was the type he'd have gone for.

She lay back on the bench and closed her eyes. Her body was stiff. She was probably cursing herself. Cursing him.

Much as he wanted to deny it, he *had* abducted her. He just hadn't used physical force or coercion. He was a regular fucking saint, just like Ivy had said.

He deserved her hate. Her revulsion.

Yet…he knew an irrational part of her was turned on by him, even now. He didn't deserve that, but he'd take it. As he'd take any other breadcrumb she tossed his way. But Ivy MacLeod was too good for a lowlife spy like him.

She deserved someone like Luke Sevick. Much as he liked Luke as a person, he also hated the golden boy. Or at least resented him. Watching Luke fall ass over teakettle for Undine Gray had been a sharp, painful reminder of everything Dimitri couldn't have.

Chapter Twelve

*T*he conversation on the deck had served its purpose, Ivy reminded herself. She'd needed a way to transition into a working relationship with Dimitri, something that would bridge their morning argument and her orders from the US attorney general to cooperate.

She hadn't expected to be turned on knowing he could see her but not touch her. Hadn't expected to be aroused by having his voice in her head when she couldn't see him.

Well.

But what surprised her most about the whole conversation was…she felt empowered.

There was a raw honesty he gave her. She could hear it in his voice, but it was something he managed to hide when they spoke face-to-face. He was desperate to find hope in his hopeless situation. She'd bet even he didn't know that about himself.

More important, she'd learned he wasn't doing this for himself. There were people—presumably family—who he cared about. If Curt could locate them…maybe they could be used to put pressure on Dimitri to cooperate with the FBI.

Of course, that was exactly *why* Dimitri hadn't revealed who they were. But dammit, she hadn't asked for this situation, and she would damn well do whatever necessary to escape, even if it meant finding Dimitri's weakness and exploiting it.

Knowing he was vulnerable had shifted the balance of power. She no longer felt helpless.

Plus, she believed now more than ever he wouldn't hurt her. Again, it was the tone of his words when she couldn't see his face. She could swear the tiniest hint of Russian accent slipped through, meaning his emotions were getting the better of his control.

She'd been watching his amazing body for a week as he swabbed the deck and otherwise put himself on display for her. As he'd intended, she'd viewed him through a lust-filled lens from the start. But he'd been studying her—reading her articles in scientific journals. Memorizing her IQ and accomplishments.

In the course of that, she suspected he'd developed a respect for her. And that respect was getting in his way.

She suspected he wanted a human connection beyond what he'd been allowed as a covert operative. A connection beyond sex. Sex was merely a placeholder for what he craved.

She imagined his life had been quite lonely, and now he faced what he believed to be his final days. He might be viewing Ivy as his last chance to make that connection.

Or it was all bullshit and she was seeing what she wanted to see. She wasn't a psychologist—although she'd read enough books on the subject. She was a tech geek, because at least there she could find concrete answers. Except, she'd gone deep enough into mathematics to know even numbers could betray her with outliers or unknown variables. There were problems that far exceeded her ken.

Dimitri Veselov was the ultimate equation, and her future hinged on being able to solve him.

Who was he before he showed up in Palau and became Jack Keaton?

Curt had said the name Veselov was news to him, but clearly he'd identified the photo as *someone*.

Dimitri glanced over his shoulder, his blue eyes questioning. Concerned. And holding a trace of lust he couldn't hide. He turned back, returning his attention to the water as he guided them through the Rock Islands.

Her fingers paused on the keyboard. How could she feel attracted to him, even now?

But she did. She'd felt the caress of his gaze in the same part of her body that he'd lavished with attention late last night. Thank goodness she'd instilled the no-touching rule, when just a look could turn her on.

She was messed up in a way that belied her vaunted IQ. She'd married a traitor. And now a spy had aroused her with a glance.

She finished setting up CAM's control console. Dimitri had insisted she work at the aft end of the uppermost deck so he could keep an eye on her and the equipment as he navigated the channels between islands.

She'd come to the conclusion Curt told her to cooperate with Dimitri because the CIA, DIA, and FBI wanted whatever it was Dimitri was looking for. Curt must know what Dimitri was after. She understood why he hadn't shared the information. She could easily slip and let Dimitri know *she* knew what they were looking for.

Best for her to remain ignorant and keep her acting to a minimum. After all, she'd ruined the fourth grade play with her rendition of sunflower number three. But was it her fault the director didn't understand that fully mature sunflowers don't follow the sun across the sky? Their heads are too heavy and their growth cycle is complete. If you ask a girl to play a sunflower, at least understand the science before you tell her it's October and her petals are turning brown.

She flashed on the memory of her parents laughing in the front row as she dramatically drooped under the weight of her seeds, stealing the spotlight from students singing songs about Halloween and candy corn.

Her heart squeezed. She hoped to hell she'd see her parents again. She wanted to thank them for embracing her kooky literal side and going to bat for her with teachers who were irritated by being corrected by a know-it-all student.

She'd been a handful for her parents and teachers. Socialization came naturally to some, but to Ivy, it was a skill that had to be learned and ten times harder than advanced trigonometry. Triangles made absolute sense, but the boy in seventh grade English who thought she was a freak because she was tall, busty, pimply, and obsessed with astrophysics had been a complete—and painful—mystery to her.

But then, triangles were the best shape, the key to time and distance. Triangles were poetry and magic and explained the entire universe.

She puffed out a deep breath and shook her head. She was losing it if she was mentally escaping to her excruciating adolescent years and fawning over triangles. Why would she want to return to that time?

Again her mind flashed on her parents, giving her the answer. At twelve, no matter how awkward she'd been, she'd always felt safe at home, grounded. Loved. But right this minute, she felt vulnerable on twenty-seven different levels. No wonder she wanted to find triangles in the wood grain lines on the deck.

Coping mechanism. Pure and simple.

She flicked the power switch for the drone, which gave a soft whirr as the system booted up.

"I've been meaning to ask," Dimitri said from the helm, "what does CAM stand for?"

"Officially, it stands for Computer-Aided Mapping, but it's a bullshit name. I named the system after my grandpa, Cameron MacLeod. Grandpa Cam." Her Scottish grandfather with the heavy brogue who loved triangles too. She nodded to the drone as it lifted from the deck. "The drone is named RON."

"Does RON stand for anything?"

"Not yet. There's a pool at NHHC. The person who comes up with the best name that fits the acronym gets the kitty. Costs ten bucks to enter a name. I pick the winner."

"Any good entries?"

"Nothing yet."

"Recording Orientation…and Navigation?"

"See. It's not easy. But you have to give me ten bucks if you want me to consider your entry."

He laughed. "I'll wait until I have something better." He used reverse to bring the boat to a stop, then powered down the engine. She heard the metal clank of the anchor descending into the water. "If you want to get closer to the island, we'll have to use the trolling motor to stay in place. I won't drop anchor on the reef."

She smiled, glad that he was considerate of the fragile live corals that were both beautiful and the habitat of thousands of species. She felt the same protectiveness for the Peleliu wreckage, where dropped anchors could damage historic debris and human remains.

RON checked out, all systems running, so she returned her focus to the computer. This was a test run in which she would use the drone to map the seafloor where there were known Peleliu wrecks. RON was equipped with regular and enhanced Lidar and infrared mapping technology. It was the enhanced Lidar she was testing here. To create the enhanced system, she'd bundled radio signals into the light beam so the laser could penetrate to the bottom without the radio signal being attenuated by water. Above-water mapping of the seafloor without distortion. A cartographer's dream.

A Japanese Zero had crashed in the vicinity. RON would capture a three-dimensional image of it.

Her job at the keyboard was to integrate the data collected by RON using CAM, which could interpret the enhanced Lidar signal and break out the radar data. With calibration, CAM's brain could learn the terrain, and then her baby would do the heavy lifting of separating the data into different map layers—seafloor, corals, metal wreckage, natural and artificial voids that represented tunnels. CAM and RON together were an X-ray machine for land and sea, with the ability to generate three-dimensional images.

Last week she'd done aerial survey with a seaplane instead of RON, using both types of Lidar and the infrared. She crunched the data through CAM, but in broader swaths, to get the overall landscape, nothing to a scale that allowed for 3D. RON was meant for slower, small-scale, meticulous survey, which she hadn't been scheduled to start for another week.

Dimitri had altered her timeline.

She tested the regular Lidar system on RON, data she would gather for comparison and calibration. Regular Lidar checked out. Enhanced and infrared were also online. She was ready to begin the field test.

This was the part of the job that got her adrenaline pumping, where the magic happened. In the seaplane with Ulai, she'd barely even looked out the window at the spectacular views of Palau, because on the monitor, she saw a different kind of beauty. Patterns. Heat signatures. Markers of the past.

So many lovely triangles.

She could forget everything as her computer translated the data into terrain that was invisible to the human eye.

The Battle of Peleliu was fought between September fifteenth and November twenty-seventh, 1944. In the battle, over two thousand three hundred US soldiers and marines and nearly ten thousand seven hundred Japanese soldiers had been killed. Long and brutal, the battle left scars above and below the earth.

Her job was to record them all. She was creating more than a map; each layer added to the known history of the battle. Data points were a tribute to the men who'd fought and died on both sides.

Maps told a story. Maps showed power, sacrifice, tragedy, even love.

With GIS, she could choose which layers to show, which story to tell. The natural landform. The vegetation. The scars of war. In a sense, she was the author of the map—and therefore of the history—but she believed it was her job to get out of the way and give each layer their say.

Did the terrain influence the battle, or did the battle reshape the terrain?

Usually the answer was both.

For the next two hours, she lost herself in the beauty and simplicity. She forgot about Dimitri and lies and treason and sex. She forgot about terrorists and betrayal and heartbreak as CAM and RON did their thing and collected data, just as she'd designed him—*it*—to do.

She should probably stop anthropomorphizing CAM. People were going to think she was nuts. Well, if they didn't already.

She tapped a few buttons, and the three-dimensional image transformed into flat contour lines. She traced the zig and zag of an underwater ridge. Crystal clear, better than if it had been mapped with side-scan sonar. And she'd done it all above water. "Is there anything more beautiful?" she murmured, not even really hearing herself.

"I can think of one thing," Dimitri said.

His voice pulled her from her mapping-induced intoxication. She shook her head, to break away from the haze. "What?"

"You."

"Me, what?"

He laughed. "You have no idea what I'm talking about?"

"No. Did you say something?"

"You're freaking amazing. That's all."

She felt a little flutter at the way he said that. His voice was light. Warm. Jack's tone, when they were in bed together.

Except that had been Dimitri. There was no Jack.

He'd sat by her side these last hours and watched her work. He'd asked questions, even helped. But he hadn't interfered. Hadn't directed. She would never know he was looking for something except that he'd studied each image she created intently. Part of her wondered if today's work was just a test, to familiarize himself with the system, or if he believed the object he sought was nearby.

It didn't really matter, because she'd been able to do her job unfettered.

She used the remote control to land RON on the deck. "That's it for the day. It's going to take another hour or two for the system to process the data and upload to the satellite." She glanced around the deck. They were close to the island, and another boat was anchored in the distance. "I need to leave everything on the deck while it uploads. I'm concerned about security."

He tapped the portable console. "I'll take us out farther. It'll be shallow enough to anchor but far enough out radar will pick up anyone approaching." He cleared his throat. "In fact, we'll stay out overnight. I haven't slept since yesterday morning. I need to rest tonight. We'll be safest if we're in open water, with no islands to hide an approaching vessel."

She furrowed her brow. "You didn't sleep...at all? I could swear I remember..."

A corner of his mouth curled up. "I crawled into bed for about an hour, right before dawn, but didn't sleep."

That was what she remembered, the way he'd held her. She'd been comforted by his body pressed to hers. Together they were a study in soft and hard. He was all muscle, triangles galore, while she was round, circles and spheres.

The last months of long hours meant twelve- to sixteen-hour days on her ass in front of the computer and not in the gym. She'd gained weight because all she ate was junk food at her desk. The result was bigger breasts—which she didn't mind—but also a bigger butt and belly—which she did.

Given her height and extra pounds, she felt like a giant. But next to Dimitri, she felt normal. Petite, even. He was taller and broader.

His shoulder muscles alone were a turn-on. He had abs she could have—and had—stared at all day. His body narrowed perfectly at the hips, and his thighs were a thing of beauty. She'd enjoyed the feel of those thighs tucked behind hers, his hand resting on her round, soft belly.

She cocked her head, her thoughts had taken an alarming path. "What are the sleeping arrangements tonight?"

He frowned, and she could guess his thoughts. There was a decent-size inflatable motorboat mounted to the stern. The tender was for use at ports that were too shallow for *Liberty*'s large draft. Ivy could take the inflatable and escape.

If not for her orders from Curt, she'd do it without hesitation.

"As I mentioned when you first came aboard, the alarm system will let me know if anyone enters or exits. But of course, an alarm won't prevent you from leaving any more than it can stop someone from breaking and entering."

"I won't try to leave," she said.

"I want to believe you, Ivy. But I can't."

"Don't—don't lock me in. I—it—the idea freaks me out. Please don't make me a prisoner."

He sighed. "You have a choice: share my stateroom, or sleep in a locked room alone."

"That's not much of a choice."

"But still, it's a choice. And it's yours."

"I'll sleep with you. But no touching."

He grinned. "You, however, can touch me all you want."

If he only knew how tempted she was. Proof she was a bigger fool than anyone ever imagined.

*D*imitri wasn't sure who would be more tortured by the sleeping arrangements. In spite of everything, Ivy was attracted to him, and understandably, she found that desire unsettling.

He had no such qualms. He wanted her, period. But he'd take nothing less than the uninhibited woman who'd begged him to take her in the shower, and that... Well, that was never going to happen.

At least after nearly forty hours without sleep, he was too exhausted to care. He moved the boat farther out to sea, then they shared a light meal on the upper deck so Ivy could keep an eye on the upload progress.

Once the data finished uploading, Ivy broke down the equipment and carried it down the ladder into the salon.

He slid the walls that enclosed the helm into position, then followed her below. From the security panel, he locked the helm, hatches, and side doors, then set every alarm on the boat. *Liberty* was a fortress at anchor in remote, open sea.

Chores complete, they retreated into the captain's stateroom. After a moment's hesitation, he pulled back the rug at the foot of the bed and removed the drawer.

He glanced over his shoulder at her. "Find the opening."

She knelt beside him and looked into the dark space under the bed, her brow furrowed. "Flashlight?" she asked.

He grabbed one from the utility drawer and passed it to her. She ran the beam over the exposed wood that lined the cubbyhole. She laid it flat, allowing the wash of light to spread across the surface. She pressed at the corners and tried to move the flooring. "I don't see it."

"Good. It's big enough to hold CAM with room left over. Do you want to store CAM there while we sleep?"

The compartment was below the bed, under the obvious storage one expected to find on a boat. To the searching eye, it was invisible, perfect for a smuggler—or in the case of the previous owner of the boat, human trafficker.

"Probably a good idea." Then she frowned. "Is it lined with something that will block the tracking signal?"

"Nope. Just a wood box." He ran his finger along the front lip that housed the drawer and flicked the hidden latch. The panel dropped down and slid soundlessly to the side on tracks that ran under the bed and stateroom floor. It was invisible because the panel was one large polished piece of wood—larger than the bed itself, leaving no seams visible.

She let out a gasp of shock as she took in the assortment of guns and ammunition tucked within the hidden compartment.

He'd have to lock the stateroom when he wasn't in it with her from here on out. This show of trust was either brilliant or stupid on his part, but then a spy's life was always about choices in the extreme.

He helped her load CAM and RON inside, then showed her how to close and conceal the panel.

Task complete, she stared at him with her head cocked. "What does it mean that you let me see where you keep your guns?"

He shrugged. "Probably that I'm a fool." He stepped toward her but didn't touch her. "If anything happens to me, you know where they are. Use them. Protect yourself." He paused again. "Tomorrow, I'll show you how to shoot."

"I know how. A little."

He raised a brow in question.

"Cressida—one of my coworkers—invited me to go to the Raptor compound in Virginia to learn how to shoot. She's been taking lessons from her boyfriend since they returned from Turkey. Given that I received threatening hate mail thanks to Patrick, I accepted."

"Raptor. That's your cousin's mercenary company."

"They do more military trainings than mercenary work, but yes, Raptor is Alec's company. He doesn't run it, though. Conflict of interest now that he's in the senate."

"And Trina-of-the-good-fashion-advice's boyfriend runs the place now."

"Yes. You have a good memory for names."

He did, but that wasn't why he remembered Dr. Trina Sorenson or Keith Hatcher. Again he wondered if he should tell her about Parker Reeves. But she'd never met Luke and didn't know Undine well. Plus, Undine likely hated him for everything he'd done last fall. "Some of the names are familiar from the news," he said, playing it safe.

"I would imagine there are stories you tracked down when you decided to use me."

"Yes." No use denying it. "But I also followed the story of Cressida Porter and Ian Boyd's exfiltration from Turkey closely. A covert operator always wants to know what the other side is doing."

She flinched at the reminder they were on opposing sides. But again, no point in denying it.

"And of course, your ex-husband became the focal point of that story, which made it more relevant to me." He stepped into the head and grabbed his toothbrush. "Is it weird, working with Cressida after what happened?"

She canted her head in a motion that was both yes and no. "At first, but only because I hated that I didn't warn her and others, even though I didn't know myself."

"You feel guilty."

"Of course I do. I never suspected… I feel stupid and responsible."

"The head of the CIA didn't know, and he was the guy who recruited Hill at one point. He's the one who should feel guilty." He lowered a brow. "Why did you divorce him?"

She brushed by him to grab her toothbrush, everything about her manner telegraphing her irritation at his question. "To answer your first question," she said as she applied paste, then handed the tube to him. "Cressida and I bonded over our mutual dislike of my ex. NHHC is a good fit for me—I knew most of my coworkers already thanks to joint projects with MacLeod-Hill. Patrick was the public face of the organization, but I ran things behind the scenes."

"Why did your father bring Hill onboard when he retired? You were more than capable of being both the face of the organization and the actual director."

"At the time, I was only twenty-five and didn't feel ready to step into my dad's shoes." She glared at her toothbrush. "Plus, it's long been known there's a gender gap in funding scientific research—and we relied on research grants a great deal. We felt more funding was likely to be approved with a male at the helm."

Dimitri frowned. "And you went along with that?" he asked, unable to hide his incredulity.

"It's a shitty world. I had to set aside my personal feelings on that topic for the good of the organization." She sighed. "There's also the fact that Patrick had great charisma—which I lack. I told myself his magnetism was the key to bringing in more funding. It wasn't solely because he had a penis."

"You don't lack charisma." *Hell no.* He'd been drawn to her from the moment they met.

She gave a hard laugh. "Well, I don't stroke male egos and have an intolerance of idiocy, which is two-thirds of the game." She shrugged. "There was also the fact that Patrick was bringing money to the deal. On paper, he was wealthy and pledged much of his money to the institute's scientific endeavors. The initial endowment set up by my grandmother —she was a Ravissant—had long since run out. We were hoping with Patrick's money we could fund the studies that were passed over by NIH grants." She frowned. "And projects like CAM, which we wanted to keep in-house."

"But then you found out sea exploration and mapping was his method for moving arms and gave him legitimacy to travel in the Middle East."

"Bingo. And when the true source of his wealth was revealed, all that seed money he gave the institute was seized. I had to fight to hold on to CAM and made a deal with the Navy to avoid losing him—it—altogether."

"And here we are," Dimitri said.

"Yeah. Here we are." Bitterness tinged her voice. "I thought I'd made the deal on *my* terms, figuring I'd learned something about negotiating in the divorce."

Her jaw tightened. "The Defense Intelligence Agency tried to recruit me to claim CAM, but I refused. I went to NHHC because it was the type of organization I believe in, the type of work I *want* to do. I have an MA in GIS and remote sensing." She stared at her toothbrush, as if it held wisdom. "I knew the Pentagon and DIA would eventually duplicate the technology for intelligence-gathering purposes. I could live with that, as long as *I* wasn't going to be the one spying on the countries I was graciously permitted to work in. But the DIA is using me. They forced me to become a spy without even a whispered heads-up."

"Because they knew you'd refuse."

She met his gaze and jutted out her chin. "Damn right. Spies are soulless traitors."

His nostrils flared. But what the hell did he expect? Her blessing? Still, he couldn't let the barb slide. "Easy for you to cast judgment when you have no clue what brought me here." He backed her into the counter. "Let's just say your little betrayal by your ex? The way the DIA is using you? It's a fucking cakewalk in comparison."

He stalked out of the head and stateroom, crossing the salon to the galley. He'd brush his teeth at that sink.

He kicked the cabinet and cursed when he remembered he'd left Ivy alone with enough weapons to mow down an army.

Chapter Thirteen

*S*he should grab one of the guns right now. End this
nightmare and move on. But Curt had said to
cooperate.

Dammit!

Did that mean she shouldn't try to escape if given a
chance? Probably, considering he'd said as long as she didn't
feel endangered by Dimitri, he wanted her to work with him.

And, in spite of everything, she did feel weirdly safe with
him. Like the fact that he'd let her know where the guns were
hidden. She'd never have found them on her own, and
there'd been no need to show her. He'd protected CAM and
given her a deeper sense of security by showing her how to
access the weapons.

But that didn't change the fact that he was a spy. One
she'd pissed off, no less.

She heard him stomping around in the stateroom. Even
hardened spies stomped around like little boys when grumpy,
apparently.

It wasn't lost on her that her opinion seemed to matter to
him. Exactly how much power did she wield here?

She washed her face and combed her hair, going through her normal bedtime ritual on an evening that was the definition of abnormal. Ready for sleep, she abandoned the bathroom and came face to face with Dimitri. Without a word, he brushed past her to use the head.

She changed into a T-shirt and shorts, then climbed into the bed, taking the far side against the wall. She was utterly exhausted, but wound up. Tonight would be fun.

Not.

A few minutes later, he joined her in the stateroom and stripped naked before pulling back the bedcovers.

"You're not sleeping naked," she said. *Why does his body have to be so damn beautiful?*

"Yes. I am."

"I'd prefer you didn't."

"Does the sight of my body offend you? It's just a penis. Half the world's population has them. And you've already been intimate with mine."

She rolled her eyes. Then, Lord help her, she flushed at the memory his words brought forth. Yes, she'd been intimate with that part of him. She'd done no less than beg for it.

In unison with her thoughts, his penis thickened.

He laughed. "I figured I was too exhausted for sex, but apparently, there is no such thing as too tired to want Ivy MacLeod."

She glared at him, even as her thoughts ran along the same lines. How could she feel aroused...by *him*? She tucked herself closer to the wall.

He sighed. "I won't touch you, Ivy. No matter how much I want to. But again, you can touch me all you want."

"It's just physical," she said, her tone defensive. She forced her shoulders to relax. She was supposed to play along, and they needed to return to their earlier cease-fire and general accord. She raked his body with her eyes and allowed a slight smile. "It's unfair that your body is so frigging gorgeous."

"Unfair? I work hard for this body. It's not about fairness, it's about dedication." He climbed into the bed and pulled up the covers, which tented over his ever-growing cock.

"Admit it, you're only sleeping nude to rattle me."

"I always sleep nude. But yeah. That too."

The mattress had to be small to fit in the stateroom. It was a double bed, nothing more. Dimitri wasn't a small man, and he took up more than half the space. She wasn't a small woman. She pressed her back to the wall, giving him as much room as possible.

Exhaustion won, and sleep came surprisingly fast. Hours later, she woke to find she'd migrated to his side of the bed and curled up against him.

She'd dreamed of men chasing her and had sought his protection in her nightmare. She placed a hand on his chest and breathed in his scent. Ocean, sun, and testosterone all wrapped in a ripped body. His thick-muscled arm closed around her. She felt his strength across her back and found it a comfort, not a threat.

"Sleep, Ivy," he murmured, more asleep than awake himself. "I've got you."

If anyone wanted to hurt her, they'd have to get past Dimitri. She pressed closer to his side and dropped into a deeper, thankfully dreamless, sleep.

The night was dark and deep when Dimitri surfaced from sleep to find Ivy still curled at his side. Her T-shirt had ridden up, and his hand rested on her bare back. His arm was numb, but still, he didn't move, not wanting to wake her and have her retreat to the far side of the bed again.

Had she managed to contact Dominick yesterday? He hoped she had. He'd gambled on the assumption the attorney general would seize the opportunity to exploit Dimitri's inside information. For his part, Dimitri was more than willing to use Curt Dominick to gain Ivy's reluctant cooperation.

It would play out in a vicious circle. Once they found it, Ivy would attempt to take the AUUV from Dimitri, but there was no way he could let her walk with it. No one was double-crossing anyone, because they weren't really aligned, but it would feel that way to her once she realized the depth of his manipulation.

They were two people doing what they had to do. Plain and simple as that. In the end, Dimitri would win; Ivy would lose. And she'd spend the rest of her life hating him.

For him, the rest of his life would be short, and he'd probably spend it with a hard-on, aching for her.

He'd wonder why God hated him, but he'd stopped believing in any benign deity when the fifty-year-old sadist who controlled his life raped his little sister—again—as a means to control Dimitri. A dozen years later and he could still hear Sophia's screams.

Ivy's hair tickled his nose. She'd showered in the interval between finishing her work and their dinner on deck, and the scent of shampoo pulled him back to the present, away from the fetid apartment where he'd sold his soul a second time, too late to protect his sister.

He breathed Ivy in. Salt air, tea tree shampoo, and sweat mixed to create essence of her. Curled against him as she was, he could almost pretend that in a different world, she might belong by his side. Her aroma and warm body were a silent lullaby. Tactile poetry. He drifted toward sleep, numb arm and all.

Sometime later, a soft noise outside jolted him awake. The sound wasn't right, not the usual water lapping against the hull. A footstep, or a small craft bumped against the stern. Someone was here. He could feel it. A glance at the clock indicated it was less than an hour before dawn.

He inched his arm from beneath Ivy's shoulder and whispered in her ear, "We've got company."

She snuggled tighter for a moment, then woke fully and stiffened at his side.

"There are men on the aft deck," he whispered again. He nodded toward the window above the head of the bed. "They're climbing onto the deck above us."

Her eyes rounded with alarm. Her reaction appeared genuine, so it wasn't SEALs or her cousin's mercenary army, unless she was a better actress than she'd let on so far. He was sure that if she'd managed to call in for reinforcements, triumph would have flashed in her eyes.

"Do you suffer from claustrophobia?" he whispered.

She pushed against his chest. "You can't stuff me in the cupboard—"

"Shh. Okay." He pressed his mouth to hers, then slid from the bed and pulled on skintight black pants and top, and tucked his gun into the built-in holster at the small of his back. He tossed matching clothes to her. "Hurry and put these on. It was supposed to cloud over in the night. It'll be dark on deck."

The ankle-to-wrist-to-neck clothing would be warm in the tropical climate, which was why he didn't sleep in it, but the camouflage on the dark deck was a fair trade.

She changed quickly, and they left the stateroom. Lights on the security panel in the salon indicated the men had moved to the upper deck. Thank goodness the helm could be enclosed and locked. Dimitri turned on the monitor for the night-vision camera mounted outside the helm. Three men, all dressed in snug-fitting assault wear.

Dimitri gave thanks once again that paranoid mafiosi believed in sparing no expense on their security systems. *Liberty* had plenty of secrets that gave him and Ivy the advantage.

"Will they get in?" Ivy asked.

"Not without setting off the alarm. They're trying to avoid that, to keep the element of surprise. My guess is they want to take the helm and control the boat, then come after us."

"So we just wait for them?"

"No. First we listen, find out who we're dealing with, then I attack."

Liberty's cameras all had microphones. He handed her a wireless headset, then slipped a second pair over his own ears.

"We don't need the boat. We need the whore," a man with a heavy Syrian accent said.

"That's Spiderman," Ivy whispered. "I have a good memory for voices and accents."

A glance at the monitor showed a dark blotch over one man's eye. He was half-blind thanks to her stilettos.

"Underestimate the Hammer, and you're dead," a man with a Russian accent said.

Shit. How had he been identified? "Thor?" Dimitri asked, before Ivy could ask what the man meant.

She nodded.

At least the common language among the men appeared to be English. Dimitri could translate Russian, but he only knew a few Arabic words, and nothing in Ivy's bio indicated she knew any Middle Eastern languages. But then, he hadn't known she spoke Japanese.

Was the third man a sign reinforcements had arrived? Dimitri wondered what his accent would tell them. Each man had at least one gun visible. No more messing around with machetes and adzes.

The attack on the party must've been an impulse. They'd figured on a quick grab. Ivy was there, and CAM was in her hotel room. Easy job, given that no one expected violence to break out in Palau. Security, even at large political events like that one had been, was always lax. And they'd dressed in traditional Palauan clothing, making it appear they were a local faction making a political statement. There was a vocal group of Palauans who took issue with the US being allowed to operate nuclear-powered vessels within Palau territory thanks to the Compact of Free Association, and the party was to celebrate another Compact-agreement success—solid cover for the Syrians to pose as political dissenters.

They hadn't expected Dimitri at the party, but this time they were prepared.

"We don't need Keaton. We don't need this fucking boat. We need the bitch and her computers, and our homing signal indicates the equipment is down there." On the screen, the one-eyed pirate pointed aft, toward the captain's stateroom.

Ivy stiffened at his side. "How the hell—?" She paused and a moment later sucked in a sharp breath. "Fucking Patrick." Her words were soft but angry. "The fail-safe in CAM was part of the design from the start. He must've told them about it and given them a receiver to follow the signal."

"You didn't change the design when you moved to the Navy?"

"It didn't occur to me. Patrick had little to do with CAM beyond the initial concept. He must've been following my progress far more closely than I thought."

"How accurate is the signal? Targeting accurate?"

He suspected her face had paled but couldn't be certain in the dim cabin. "It's accurate within three meters."

Dimitri swore. "The secret compartment will never hold up."

No time for cat-and-mouse, then. He needed to take these assholes down and then get Ivy to turn off the signal while *Liberty* hauled ass for open sea.

Through the headphones, they heard the third man side with the Syrian—not surprising given his accent was also Syrian. The two men returned to the aft deck, while the Russian stayed to search for ways to take over the helm.

"They're separating." He met her gaze. He'd wanted her to hide with CAM, but now that they knew these guys had a homing device, he was glad she'd refused. "Will you hide in the bow? There's another secret compartment.

She shook her head. "No way."

Now wasn't the time to delve into her phobias. He pressed his Sig into her hands. "Fine. Take this. No safety. Long pull on the first shot, then a hair trigger. Wait for me in the guest stateroom. Hide as much as you are able."

"Where will you be?"

He fixed his gaze on his stateroom. "I'm going hunting."

She nodded.

After a moment's hesitation, he cupped a hand behind her neck and pulled her face to his, giving her a deep, thorough kiss. If he failed, he'd damn well live his last moments without regrets, rules or no rules.

That she kissed him back didn't surprise him. Adrenaline and fear were powerful factors.

"You're amazing, Ivy," he whispered against her lips as he cradled the back of her head. "You make me wish I really were Jack." He released her and kept talking to prevent a reply. "If anyone approaches your hiding place without saying"—he smiled as the code came to him—"four-two-five, shoot first. Even if that person is me. Four-two-five is the all clear. If I say anything else, it means I've got a gun to my head and they're using me to draw you out. Save yourself at all costs. Can you do that?"

Her nostrils flared, but she nodded, which didn't surprise him either. Ivy was a steel orchid.

But then she did surprise him by pulling his head down for another kiss. Her tongue stroked his, quick and deep. She released him and said, "Please don't make me shoot you."

Chapter Fourteen

*I*vy tucked herself in the point of the bow on the bed. Not exactly a hiding place, but she had a straight shot at the door and a hatch above her head, should the men get past Dimitri.

Or use him as a shield.

Could she shoot him?

She hoped to hell she'd never find out.

Air-conditioning was off in this part of the boat, and the stateroom was stiflingly hot. Sweat beaded on her brow and trickled between her breasts, and she wanted to peel off the clothes Dimitri had given her. The pants were too long even for her height. They bunched at the ankles, while the top was loose on her shoulders.

The man kept a spare ninja suit on hand. Dimitri Veselov was so very different from the computer geeks she usually hung out with. They had ninja suits too, but only wore them to gaming cons, while for Dimitri, it appeared to be his work uniform.

She tried to imagine Dimitri at a con. The badass real deal, card-carrying Russian spy.

Jesus, being scared shitless must make her punchy. The man was hunting invaders, and she was fantasizing about taking him to a gamer con.

She stared at the closed hatch above her head. When the alarm went off, she could open it and slip onto the upper deck. There were a series of short ladders on the side of the boat that led to each deck. All attention would be focused aft, and it was dark. She was dressed in her ninja best.

She could climb to the top deck and shoot the Russian.

Could she shoot a man?

Through the headphones, she heard the Syrian's plans for her.

Yes. Yes, she could.

She tucked the gun in the holster and positioned herself below the hatch, hands at the ready to open it. The moment the alarm sounded, she'd join the fray. No one would expect her; the element of surprise was all hers.

*D*imitri crept into his stateroom. Two men were at the back window. They couldn't see him through the dark tint of the one-way film that covered the glass, but he could see their legs and hear their chatter through the cordless headphones.

He grabbed another gun from a hidden compartment in the nightstand. Too bad the windows were bulletproof, or he'd take them out with two shots. But he could use the thick glass to his advantage.

The paranoid mafioso who'd commissioned the custom-built luxury yacht had feared being trapped, and interior releases had been installed on all stateroom windows.

Dimitri stood on the bed in front of the window. Two

terrorists were less than two feet away on the other side of the thick pane.

Timing was everything. One window release was on the lower sill to the left and the other at the top on the right. Flick the release, shove outward, bottom first. The alarm would sound, alerting the Russian on the upper deck.

He'd need both hands on the frame. He tucked his gun into the holster at the small of his back. He'd be armed with nothing but a thick three-by-five bulletproof pane as he engaged two terrorists with guns in their hands.

"First, I'm going to blind the whore. Then I'm going to fuck her like the dog bitch she is." The words were a soft whisper, carried through the headphones. Dimitri hated that Ivy could hear him.

He'd take out Spiderman first.

"We need the woman alive," the second Syrian said.

"We might need her eye for a retinal scan," the Russian added. "No blinding."

Dimitri held one hand over each window release, like a gunfighter waiting for the signal to draw. He'd know the signal when he heard it.

"I will fuck her while she screams for mercy."

That was it. Dimitri released the window and pushed out. The alarm blared as the pane dropped into his hands. He rammed the upper edge into the legs of both men standing above.

They tripped backward against the rail and Dimitri launched himself onto the shelf at the head of the bed and through the opening, gripping the window. He let out a bloodcurdling yell as he passed through. He shoved the edge of the thick pane into one man's face, then the other man's neck.

One man squeezed off a shot. The glass bucked but held. Dimitri rammed him in the face a second time. The man's head snapped back, and he tumbled over the rail into the water.

Dimitri was out on the deck now, exposed from behind. He kicked the remaining man in the chest as he spun on instinct and used the glass as a shield.

Three bullets hit the pane in rapid succession, fired by the Russian.

Behind him, the second Syrian splashed into the water. Now it was just him and the Russian.

It was just light enough in the predawn to see the glass held, but was opaque in the middle, where it had fractured. Through the top of his shield, he could see the Russian had moved to the aft end of the upper deck.

He couldn't hesitate, or the Russian would have the upper hand. He charged, leaping onto the deck that was the roof of the stateroom he'd just been inside.

The Russian kept firing, and Dimitri kept coming, leaping to the next deck in one bound. He lunged at the Russian, shoving the man's gun upward with the crazed shield. The gun hit the Russian's chin. Dimitri leaned on the shield, applying hard, fast pressure on the fingers wrapped around the hair trigger. The bullet entered the Russian's brain through his palate and took out the top of his head.

With one last shove, Dimitri pushed him over the rail, dropping the man into the ocean before his blood could stain the deck.

He dropped the shield and leaned his head on the railing as he caught his breath. Adrenaline coursed through him. Fight-or-flight had kicked in, but the fight was over, and he never chose flight.

He should return to the stern and make sure the two Syrians weren't coming back. He thought he'd snapped one's neck but needed to be certain.

"Dimitri?"

He lifted his head and turned. Ivy stood several feet behind him, holding his Sig, pointed right at his chest.

He felt the blood drain from his brain as he gazed into her eyes in the dim predawn light.

He should have seen this coming. He'd known the risks when he handed her the gun. But he hadn't believed she'd do it.

Steel orchid with brass balls, that was Ivy MacLeod. She could teach some former KGB agents he knew a thing or two about tenacity.

He raised his hands. Full surrender. It was probably better this way. He was a killer. He couldn't get away from it no matter how hard he tried. Proof was floating in the water below him.

And if he were dead—for real with proof this time— Sophia and Yulian would be freed. He'd struck a deal, his life for Sophia and Yulian's freedom. Did it matter who took his life in the end? Plus, while his handlers were far from honorable, there was no need to keep his sister prisoner without Dimitri to control.

Fight-or-flight again. But he would never fight Ivy.

"Do it," he said, his voice just above a whisper.

Her hands shook. She held the gun for another second or hour—time stretched like it did in the heat of battle, so it was hard to tell—then she lowered the weapon and rolled her shoulders. "We need to make sure the others are dead or gone."

He didn't know if he was relieved or disappointed, but he took the stay of execution and jumped through the opening in the rail to the next deck down, landing on the roof of his stateroom. Before he'd gone two steps toward the lower walkway where he'd shoved the men overboard, something thumped against the stern.

Ivy was right behind him and he held out an arm to halt her.

"What is it?"

"Shhh," he said. There it was again, another thump… and a sound that turned his stomach.

"Stay here," he said and pulled his gun as he crossed to the stern, looking down to the water.

He lowered his gun. The Syrians weren't a threat anymore. A small mercy, they were either unconscious or already dead. Otherwise, they would be screaming.

"What is it?" Ivy repeated.

"Sharks," he said.

*H*orror spread through Ivy even as she acknowledged a feeling of relief. She'd heard what the one terrorist wanted to do to her.

She stared at Dimitri's back. She'd shocked herself when she pointed the gun at him.

The fight had been fast and furious, and she'd only just made it to the upper deck and pulled the gun when she'd witnessed Dimitri's efficient and brutal disposal of the Russian.

She'd been prepared to shoot the Russian, but he was gone and Dimitri was in her sights, and for a moment, she saw a way out of this mess.

If she shot him, she could take *Liberty* back to Koror. She could hand CAM over to whatever US military official wanted it and hightail it home. Without CAM, no one would be after her. She wouldn't be guilty of aiding and abetting a Russian spy.

But there stood Dimitri, the man who'd just risked his life to protect her. The man who'd just killed on her behalf.

He'd...not even flinched at the idea of her shooting him. He'd just accepted it.

Proof he wanted out of this tangle too. Proof he wasn't doing this for some anti-American ideological purpose. He wasn't serving his government in the belief some greater good would come of abducting her. He wasn't doing it for money or power.

To want money or power meant wanting to live to spend or wield. Working to achieve an ideological goal meant passion and drive, and when staring into the face of failure, frustration, and devastation floated to the top of the emotional cesspool.

Dimitri showed her in that moment he had no desire to live. No devastation. No anger. No passion. No drive.

He was well and truly hopeless.

She finally had the variables she needed to triangulate Dimitri Veselov's position. He wasn't doing this for himself. Someone was forcing him to play pawn. Alpha Dimitri would chafe at being someone else's tool.

So she'd lowered the gun.

Now she stood on the deck with him, at a loss for what to say. She wanted to cover her ears and close her eyes against the sound of breakfasting sharks, but hiding from the situation wouldn't help anyone. "What do we do now?"

"Their Zodiac is tied to the stern. They probably have a bigger boat nearby, with more of them." Dimitri ran a hand over his face. "I need to get us out of here, before they come searching."

She nodded and met his gaze without flinching. "And I need to turn off the locational beacon on CAM."

Chapter Fifteen

*T*urning off the beacon was easy, but she had to call Mara or her boss would freak out. She needed to update Curt on what happened anyway. Emails and texts wouldn't do. She had to speak with them both.

She could set up the satellite uplink and hook up her phone, but it would be faster and easier if Dimitri let her use his satellite phone—because she didn't doubt for a second that he had one. The boat had to be riddled with hiding places. She'd never find it on her own.

She climbed the ladder, bracing herself for the confrontation. At least this way, her backdoor communication with Mara and Curt would remain secret. She stepped behind him, making noise that would carry over the loud engine. She didn't want to startle him. Not now, when they were both coming down from adrenaline and knowing the man had lethal reflexes.

"If you're here for the sat phone, it's in the storage compartment under the captain's chair."

He stood at the helm, the deck-mounted chair pushed back on its track so it wasn't in his way.

"You're giving it up that easy?" She lifted the cushion and found the compartment.

He shrugged. "Saves time."

Not surprisingly, she found three more handguns in the compartment along with the phone. She frowned. The phone was locked. "Pass code?" she asked.

He was silent for a moment, then said, "Tell me why you didn't shoot me."

She couldn't begin to name the emotion that flooded her in that moment. All she knew was she wasn't ready to tell him why. She studied the phone in her hands instead of meeting his gaze. She could probably get past the security feature if she hooked it to her computer.

"You had the perfect opportunity, and you let it go," he continued. "Why?"

Only a lunatic would admit to believing him. Only the delusional would believe there was a way out of this that would save them both. And only a fool would want him to have hope and a reason to live.

She was none of those things.

She met his intense gaze. His jaw was tight. There wasn't a laugh or smile line to be seen. It made her sad that in his thirty-four years, he had no creases on his face put there by joy.

She offered only a slight shake of her head.

His eyes lit with a different kind of shine. Calculating but not cold. "Fine, then. Kiss me, and I'll tell you the code."

She debated for a moment, then decided to give him a win. She'd bet he expected her to cheap out and give him a simple peck, but she enjoyed surprising Death Valley. Plus, even in giving him this small victory, she'd have him off-balance. Yet another test of her power.

She set the phone on the seat and stepped closer to him, then reached up slowly with both hands and cupped his cheeks. It had been a day and a half since he'd shaved. She stroked his cheeks, enjoying the feel of stubble against her palms as she held his gaze. Then she gave him a soft smile and pulled his head down. She started slow, brushing her lips across his, then settled in and deepened the kiss, opening her mouth and slipping her tongue between his lips.

His hands found her hips. He pulled her body flush with his, his arms crossed her back and hugged her to him as his mouth slanted, taking the kiss to the next level as his tongue delved deep.

The kiss was intense, hot, a slice of pleasure in a world gone haywire. She threaded her fingers in his hair and lost herself in the hot bliss of his mouth.

She wanted to push him into the captain's chair, crawl onto his lap, and just kiss like this for hours.

He raised his head but then returned for quick nips at her lips, as reluctant to end the moment as she was. She pulled his mouth back to hers one last time, sucking on his tongue, savoring the flavor, texture, and heat of him. With regret, she dropped to her heels and released her grip on his hair. She held his gaze for a long moment and felt a flutter at the heat and intensity she saw there.

With a mental shake, she came back into herself and extracted her hips from his arms, then picked up the phone. She found her most businesslike voice, raised a brow, and said, "Code?"

And there was his smile. A thing of beauty that turned the hard lines of his face into something special.

"Steel orchid, that's my Ivy," he said. "The code is four-two-five-zero."

"Four-two-five. You have an affinity for those numbers."

"Yes."

"Birth date?"

"No."

"I suppose you could tell me, but then you'd have to kill me?" The irony was, with Dimitri, the ridiculous phrase could actually be true.

He returned his attention to the helm and pushed the throttle forward. "Kill myself," he said, eyes facing forward to open sea. "Because I'd never hurt you."

Foolish though it sounded, she believed him.

*T*hat kiss…was something else. If Dimitri didn't know better, he'd think Ivy was trying to give him something to live for. And if he believed there was any way they could have a future, she might've had a chance at succeeding.

"Stay where I can hear you," he said before she could disappear with his phone.

"Power down, then, or I'll never be able to hear Mara."

He eased back on the throttle, then powered down. It had been thirty minutes since they'd pulled anchor. They'd put at least twenty nautical miles between themselves and where the sharks were having breakfast, safe enough to stop here, but they couldn't stay long. *Liberty* was too recognizable.

He had a backup plan for the boat. He hadn't expected to need it this soon, but he was prepared. He'd set it in motion after Ivy spoke with her boss.

"She's going to insist I talk to Curt."

He nodded. "He'll want to report the attack to the local police. I'm sure FBI agents are en route, if not already in Koror."

"What do I tell him about you?"

"Just say I saved your life and I'm protecting you and CAM." His heart pounded as he considered the possibility of speaking with Dominick directly. No. It was too soon. He had too much to lose if he misread the attorney general.

*M*ara sat on the carpet next to Erica. They both leaned against the sofa in Erica's living room, Erica with her nine-week-old daughter sleeping on her chest.

"As much as I wish she'd sleep more at night, I really love this part," Erica said. "When she falls asleep just like this after nursing."

Mara smiled. "Motherhood looks good on you."

Erica buried her nose in Grace's soft, dark hair. "Thanks. That's…one of the reasons we asked you to dinner this evening. I—I hate doing this to you when the listing for Undine's position hasn't even been posted yet, but I won't be going back to UAB when my leave is up." She took a deep breath and continued. "Lee and I have been talking. We can afford for me to stay home, and I've decided that instead of feeling guilty, like I need to turn in my feminist card, I'm going to embrace it and be thankful we can afford to make the choice I want the most."

"Oh, honey, being a feminist doesn't mean you *must* be a career woman in addition to being a mom. It's about being allowed to choose your own path instead of it being proscribed." She reached out and squeezed Erica's fingers.

They'd been close friends for a long time, but the fact that she was Erica's ultimate boss meant at times Erica didn't open up to Mara as much as she did with others in the office. "I wish I'd known you were struggling with that, sweetie. Work be damned, I'd have encouraged you to do what's right for you, Grace, and Lee."

"Thanks. I just… It was hard for me to articulate my

thoughts and fears to anyone but Lee, and I realize now I couldn't possibly have made the decision before Gracie was born. I...well...you know how much I worried I lacked maternal instincts."

Mara did know, but she'd never doubted Erica's ability to mother for a second.

"But then I pretty much fell in love the moment she was placed on my chest." Erica squeezed Mara's fingers back.

Mara scooted closer to Erica and rested her head on her shoulder. From this close, she could smell Grace. Newborn baby smell—slightly sour milk, baby soap, and love.

Grace's fine lashes rested on her cheeks as her head tilted up toward her mother. Perfect contentment on the infant's sleeping face.

"I'm pregnant." She whispered, partly to avoid waking Grace, but also because this was the first time she'd told anyone outside immediate family.

Erica let out a soft squeal, causing the baby to stir.

"It's early yet—only nine weeks—so we're keeping it quiet for now. But Curt's going to announce he's stepping down in a few months."

"Curt is quitting?"

"He feels it's time. And I am so ready to have him for more than a few hours a week." Mara reached out and stroked Grace's soft hair. "Especially if we're going to have one of these."

Erica sniffled. "Gah. It must be the new-mom hormones that are making me cry. Everything makes me cry. But I'm really happy for you. That you'll get more Curt time. That Grace will have a little buddy." She laughed. "I guess that means basically, I'm happy for *me*."

Grace woke up and let out her own cry.

"Now that she's awake, do you want to hold her?"

"Sure, offer her to me when she's *crying*." But she reached out and lifted the disgruntled bundle from Erica's chest. She hadn't held Grace in a week and had been suffering baby Gracie withdrawal.

She climbed to her feet and gently bounced the baby as she paced Erica and Lee's house. They'd moved in to the old house in Alexandria right before Christmas. They had a yard and room for Lee to move his business to a home office so he could be there for the baby twenty-four seven.

Grace quieted in Mara's arms. "She's put on weight."

"She outgrew most of the newborn clothes before she even wore them." Erica stood and stretched. "Oh! I can give them to you. Are you and Curt going to stay in the city after he leaves the Justice Department?"

"We haven't decided. We might move closer to a Metro line for my commute." She flashed a grin. "I saw a For Sale sign up the street on our way here."

The back door opened, and Lee and Curt stepped inside. Curt approached Mara and dropped a kiss on Grace's head before kissing her. He was as eager to be a dad as she was to be a mom, which was unexpected because when they'd first married, they'd agreed to forgo parenting altogether. Her biological clock had slammed into her with a vengeance about two years ago, but they'd agreed to wait until Curt was ready to quit. His job was all-consuming, and they both wanted him to be present for their family.

"The grill is ready for the fish," Lee announced.

Grace lifted her head at the sound of her father's voice and smiled.

"She's only been smiling for a few days," Erica said. "And Lee always gets the best ones. She already knows how to wrap her daddy around her tiny finger."

Lee cooed to her. At six-five, he towered over Mara.

There was something adorable about watching the giant of a man melt over his baby girl.

"That's because my Gracie is as smart as her mother," Lee said in a singsong voice directed at the baby.

Mara passed Grace to Lee and gave Curt a sheepish look. "Remember how we promised not to tell anyone yet? I sort of slipped."

Lee laughed. "So did Curt. I was playing it cool." He leaned down and kissed Mara's cheek. "I'm so happy for you both."

Mara's cell phone vibrated. She'd usually ignore her phone, but with Ivy's situation, that wasn't possible. She frowned at the work number on the display. With an apology to Erica and Lee, she took the call and stepped into the kitchen. Curt followed.

She answered using the speaker feature. "Mara, this is tech security. Fifteen minutes ago, CAM stopped transmitting."

Adrenaline shot through her system so hard and fast, it made her nauseated. "Do you know if it was turned off, or destroyed?"

"No clue. One second the signal was solid. The next it was gone. We spent ten minutes rebooting. I've made a call to see if we can get real-time satellite images, but by the time they come online, the boat could be long gone."

"If Ivy did it willingly, she'll get in touch with me—if she can. I should get off this line." She met Curt's gaze.

"Mara and I will be there as soon as we can," Curt said. "If you need to reach us, call my cell." He gave the number, then hit the End button.

They gave hurried apologies for bolting before dinner to Erica and Lee. The couple knew about Ivy's situation and understood. Before Mara had her coat on, her cell phone rang again.

The number on the screen was unfamiliar. Her heart pounded as she answered the call—again on speaker for Curt's benefit, to hell with the fact that Erica and Lee could hear too.

Hope and fear had Mara in a tight, warring grip. She hoped to hell it was Ivy but was terrified it would be bad news.

Chapter Sixteen

*J*vy gripped the phone as if she was afraid Dimitri would take it from her. She was so confused by him and even more confused by her feelings toward him.

She should hate him. Yet she didn't. Couldn't.

She wanted, more than anything, to know why he was doing this. To know what made him tick. If she had that piece, maybe she could find a way out for him.

Mara answered, and the call was brief. Curt was with her, and she gave them the rundown of events, why the transmitter had been disabled, and why there were no bodies to bring to Koror for the police to examine.

Curt launched into a series of questions, but Dimitri gave a hand signal indicating she needed to end the call. "Sorry, Curt, but we need to keep the boat moving," she said, offering the prearranged excuse—which also happened to be true. "We need to put distance between us and the last point where CAM was transmitting, in case they have a boat and are searching for us. We're going to spend the next thirty-six hours at sea to give the police a chance to catch up with the

Syrians, if there are more, before we return to the Rock Islands. I'll call again when I can."

Dimitri hit the End button, and it was done. He returned the phone to the storage compartment under his seat and throttled up the engine. They headed out to deep, open sea—but not, Ivy soon learned, for a thirty-six-hour jaunt. Thirty minutes later, they turned, heading toward Palau's southern edge.

Twenty minutes after that, Dimitri cut the engine, full stop.

"Why are we stopping?" she asked.

"Load CAM and RON in the tender. We're abandoning *Liberty*. We're sending her out to sea."

"What? We can't—"

"There's a lot of ocean *Liberty* can cover before she runs out of gas. If she's spotted, she might draw off the Syrians. Plus, *Liberty* is too big to maneuver in the waters where we need to search for the AUUV," he said.

"AUUV?"

"Air/Underwater Unmanned Vehicle. The Russians lost their prototype. We're going to find it."

"I thought you weren't going to tell me what it is?"

He shrugged. "We need to work together if we're going to find it quickly—before everyone has a chance to regroup."

"And you know where it is?"

"I've narrowed down the search to ten islands and their surrounding waters. CAM will do the rest."

"You lied when you said we were going to spend a day and a half at sea."

"I lie about a lot of things. Say good-bye to *Liberty*. We're going camping."

*C*urt glanced at the clock before answering the phone. Ten p.m. Caller ID sent dread up his spine: Rudy Fredrickson, from the Defense Intelligence Agency.

He didn't waste a moment with pleasantries. "Dominick, I just got a call from the office. We got a hit on the Veselov name. As soon as my wife gets home to stay with our son, I'm heading into the office for a full debriefing and figured you'd want to be there too."

Curt tightened his grip on the phone. Finally, a lead. "Thanks for the tip. You going to catch shit for keeping me in the loop?"

"No more than the usual."

Like Curt, Rudy had been bothered by the way his bosses had set up Ivy. Curt wasn't surprised he wasn't toeing the DIA line and locking Curt out as others had been intent on doing.

"When do you think you'll get there?"

"The embassy event Alyssa is coordinating is supposed to end in forty-five minutes. She said she'd try to slip out, but it's hard to say. They'll start without me, though, even though in theory I was the lead on this one. I'm thinking my days with DIA are numbered."

Curt was tempted to tell the man to submit his résumé to the Justice Department, but in a few short months—long before a transfer would ever come about—he planned to be out of there himself. No point in inviting the man to further screw up relations with his current bosses when Curt couldn't make promises.

"Thanks, Rudy. I'll see you when you get there."

Traffic was heavy—as usual—through Georgetown, but it cleared as soon as Curt left the city. He wished he could bring Mara along for this, but if he wasn't officially invited, sure as hell the DIA didn't want Ivy's boss present. Mara had been livid at the way they'd manipulated and used Ivy. She was only marginally less angry at Curt for telling Ivy to cooperate with Veselov.

But really, what choice did they have at this point? Attempting to flee from the spy would have left her vulnerable to the Syrians. If she hadn't been with Dimitri, she might have been taken.

He finally reached the Northern Virginia offices of the Defense Intelligence Agency and was admitted through the layers of security, his ID subjected to thorough scrutiny even though the guards greeted him by name before he even pulled out his government credentials.

The meeting was well underway by the time Curt entered the room. No one dared question how he'd known about the meeting, considering he should have been the first one notified and everyone from the general at the head of the table to the lowest-ranked officer in the room knew it.

In a firm voice, Curt asked to be brought up to speed on what he'd missed.

General Ellis cleared his throat and offered a tight smile. "Of course, Mr. Dominick." He nodded to the analyst working the digital projector.

The analyst tapped his keyboard, and the images projected onto the screen at the front of the room changed in rapid procession. Curt recognized Parker Reeves from various points in his Coast Guard career, along with some candid snapshots Curt's team had gathered when they investigated Reeves last fall. His office had given the DIA all the data they'd gathered.

Not everybody, it seemed, was in the mood to share.

"Have you had any luck determining if Veselov is working for the GRU?" Curt asked while the analyst found his starting point.

"That remains unclear," General Ellis said. "But then, the

man we knew as Parker Reeves was never confirmed to be from GRU."

A fact that kept this investigation in intelligence circles and out of the State Department. For now. But the situation grew more volatile each day.

At last the images stopped on a shot of *Liberty*, Veselov's boat. Curt recognized the image from Keaton's charter tours website. The analyst cleared his throat. "The boat is legally registered to Jack Keaton, with a license filed in December, but tracing the history of the vessel prior to that was a stumbling block. We started by working backward with known vessels that fit the basic description—of which there are hundreds in that part of the world. But we caught a lucky break when we cross-referenced with Russian owners."

He clicked a button, and the image changed to a blurred photo of an older man with a hard look about him.

"This man was the head of a Bratva group. What's known as the Pakhan. Word has it he was getting too powerful and not paying the kickbacks that usually flowed up government channels. Last September, he disappeared. Not long after he went missing, Russia made it known to the new Pakhan—and the other Bratva groups—that the problem had been taken care of by the Hammer, a known Russian enforcer."

"An assassin," Curt said as his belly rolled. He did not like where this was heading. This could explain why they'd been unable to confirm Reeves was GRU.

"Yes, a government assassin. The Hammer has at least a dozen suspected kills, all Bratva who wouldn't play nice with official channels and were seen as getting too big or greedy to contain."

"Is there meaning behind the Hammer name, besides the obvious, I mean?" another man asked.

"At first we thought it was because he was old-school—

from the hammer-and-sickle days of the Soviet Union—but another story has come our way. It seems that the Hammer's first kill didn't go smoothly. He and his target fought. The victim was finally taken out by several blows from a ball-peen hammer to the skull. Word is the crime scene was…brutal."

Curt winced.

"The hit took place in Japan, and it's the only incident in which investigators believe DNA from the killer was collected," the analyst continued. "We've requested they provide the data for comparison to blood on the clothing of the men who attacked the president of Palau in the ballroom, in case some of the blood belongs to Keaton."

"How long until we'll have the results?" Curt asked.

"Unknown. The request was submitted less than two hours ago." The man hit the button, and more faces appeared. "These are other kills attributed to the Hammer. We're cross-checking with dates for when Parker Reeves was on leave from the Coast Guard, although it's difficult, because like the first victim I showed, most simply disappeared. No precise date, just a range in which they went missing.

"*Liberty*—as she is now called—was in the Philippines at the time of the Pakan's disappearance. The boat disappeared in December, which, as you all know, was after Parker Reeves also disappeared. We believe he had it repainted, numbered, and named. He then sailed for Palau and set himself up as charter captain Jack Keaton. His paperwork for entering the country was pitch-perfect. The guy knows boats and port protocol, and acquired every special permit he could get his hands on for his charter business—which gave him the perfect cover to search Palauan waters and islands for the missing Russian AUUV."

It went without saying that having served with the US Coast Guard for five years, Parker Reeves likely knew boats better than he knew cars.

"There are various descriptions of the Hammer that have surfaced." Next came the series of slides of Parker through the years. "But there was never anything specific—at least, outside Bratva circles—we believe a handful of Bratva know what the Hammer looks like, but they aren't sharing that information. Our search on the name Veselov, however, produced one interesting result. The name was associated with a hit in Moscow. But the first name wasn't Dimitri, it was Sophia."

"Sorry I'm late, what did I miss?"

Curt turned to the door to see Rudy Fredrickson looking anxious and irritated. The man must've broken speed records to get here so soon. Curt didn't meet his gaze, not wanting to offer a hint of who had informed him of the meeting.

"Nice of you to join us, Fredrickson," someone snickered.

"Fuck you, Pfeiffer, I have a four-year-old at home who I couldn't leave alone." He took a seat at the table. "Some of us give a crap about our kids."

As much as Curt had thrived on his job, he looked forward to leaving the late-night emergency meetings behind as he and Mara started their family. Rudy's situation was a prime example. This life was hard on families, hard on relationships.

The analyst continued as if there'd been no interruption, making it clear Fredrickson didn't rank high enough to warrant starting over. "Our source believes Sophia Veselov is Dimitri Veselov's sister."

"Sophia Veselov is an assassin too?" Curt asked.

"No. Sophia Veselov had accused the victim of raping her. A few weeks later, the guy was found in a river, bullet through the brain." The man cleared his throat. "But this time, there were other wounds. Notably, a hockey puck in the man's mouth, held in place with duct tape. The victim's teeth were cracked from biting down. But most notably, a ball peen hammer was lodged in the victim's anus."

Several men at the table shifted uncomfortably, and the man Rudy had called Pfeiffer cursed.

"Sophia Veselov had an airtight alibi for the time of death. Our source said rumor had it ballistics on the bullet matched a hit made by the Hammer. Worth noting, the government *didn't* put forth a statement that the Hammer did it. But then, this guy wasn't Bratva, like the others. He worked for the government—and some suspect he was affiliated with GRU."

At last, there was that GRU connection. But not in the way they'd expected.

"So either it was a copycat, or it wasn't a sanctioned hit," Rudy said.

"Exactly."

"If it was, indeed, the Hammer," General Ellis said, "we can conclude Veselov cares about his sister."

"Agreed," the analyst said.

"How long ago was this?" Curt asked.

"About five years."

"So where is the sister now?" Pfeiffer asked.

The analyst shrugged. "We're looking into it."

With each fact that had been laid out, Curt swallowed bile. It appeared he'd told Ivy to cooperate with a Russian assassin.

Chapter Seventeen

Water splashed over the bow of the inflatable boat, soaking Ivy and her backpack of clothes. The cases that housed CAM and RON were airtight and waterproof, a necessity for this type of job, or she'd be thoroughly freaked out as they navigated between islands.

At last they reached Dimitri's destination, an S-shaped island, steep on the opposite curves with a saddle in the middle connecting the bowed rises.

They unloaded the boat, then Dimitri pulled it up onto the beach and into the woods, while Ivy hauled the cases two at a time up the narrow, steep path. By the time she had all six cases, her wet backpack, and another backpack full of assorted guns, Dimitri had the boat well hidden in the vegetation.

He donned the gun-filled backpack, picked up four of the cases—two in each of his large hands—and nodded toward the steep, vine-covered slope. "Follow me."

She settled the wet pack on her back and grabbed the two remaining cases and followed. He had no trouble navigating the thick foliage and steep slope of the mushroom-shaped mound. Ivy wasn't quite so agile and cursed as vines caught on her ankles and branches whipped her cheeks.

It was humid, and her shirt, already damp from the boat ride, quickly soaked through with sweat. She didn't pause to complain. She found she was strangely grateful to be off the water and enclosed in the canopy. No longer exposed. She'd feared coming across a yacht full of terrorists intent on taking her and CAM while they were on the inflatable.

They'd crossed paths with scant few other boats in the two hours they navigated the narrow waterways between islands, and those were either dive boats or kayakers enjoying an afternoon in paradise. It was hard to believe there were people living normal lives, on vacation, enjoying the beauty of the Rock Islands, when her life was in utter disarray.

She'd seen happy couples kayaking, and she'd envied that they didn't know about terrorists and spies and missing AUUVs and how long it took for grey reef sharks to smell blood in the water.

Sweat dripped into her eyes, and she brushed it away. *Focus on something more pleasant.* Like Dimitri's ass, which she was dutifully following up the steep slope.

His army-green, quick-dry hiking pants hugged his butt, reminding her how his glutes had felt under her fingers. She was about to spend an unspecified amount of time on a deserted tropical island with a man who had awoken her libido and more than delivered on the sexy promise of his body and words.

But he also was a spy and had abducted her.

Since then, he'd saved her a second time, and she was starting to believe she would be sympathetic toward his reason for abducting her.

Jesus. She was mentally making excuses for him. Was that libido or honest assessment?

Dimitri came to a halt in front of her. She was so preoccupied with her thoughts, she bumped into him. This caused her to stumble on the slope, and, quick as a flash, he dropped the cases and slipped his arm around her waist, preventing her from pitching backward.

A smile played about his lips as he continued to hold her close. "You don't have to play games, Ivy. You want me to hold you, just say so."

She rolled her eyes and pushed on his chest. He released her, and she couldn't help but regret not taking another moment to savor being pressed against him first. "Why did you stop?"

"We're here." He brushed aside a curtain of vegetation, revealing a low opening in rock.

She took a step back. "No way. I'm not going in a small, dark cave."

"It's just small at the opening. It widens out."

"It's not small spaces I don't like, it's the lack of windows. No light. No way to see out. Nothing to triangulate from." It was hard to articulate this concern, not without sounding crazy. But then, maybe she was crazy.

Dimitri just smiled and took a step closer to her. He cupped her cheek with one broad palm, then leaned down and brushed his lips across hers. The kiss was sweet, yet savory.

Like a fool, she opened her lips and deepened it, sliding her tongue over his.

This was forbidden, this kiss, which she allowed for no reason other than she wanted it. Which was probably why it felt so damn good.

His hand moved from her cheek to the back of her head, and he groaned against her lips as he pressed his erection against her belly. She let out her own groan. She wanted him. In spite of everything, she wanted him inside her body. Her memory of the other night was so crisp, it was almost eidetic, and she wanted every hard inch of him again.

He ended the kiss, his breathing uneven. "Damn. You're going to be the death of me, Poison."

If only they could return to that surreal night when he'd been a stranger she'd dubbed Death Valley and they'd shared the empowerment of recreational, healing sex.

His hand returned to her cheek again, where the kiss had started. "Do you trust me, Ivy?"

"No."

His eyes lit. "Not even a little bit?"

She frowned and considered his question. "Okay, maybe a little."

He brushed his lips over hers, soft and light, one more time before releasing her. "This cave has windows. If you can squeeze through the opening, you'll be fine."

She wanted to argue, but in the end, she agreed to follow him in, and if she didn't like it, she could leave.

He slid the cases inside in front of him, a train of them, each one nudging the one before it forward. She'd freak at the potential for them to be lost in an unknown abyss, but at this point, it was clear CAM was as important to him as it was to her, and he knew this place.

At last, she'd crawled through the two-foot-high hole, through a slightly larger tunnel until the opening expanded into a chamber. She gasped at the light shining through two openings in the cave ceiling.

"Skylights?" she asked in awe.

"Four of them. Two here, two over the lower chamber. Carved though the limestone by Japanese soldiers during the war."

He handed her a flashlight, which she cast on the walls and ceiling. "The cave looks natural."

"It is, but the entrance we came through was cut, as were the skylights. And the stairs."

She frowned, then her light landed on what appeared to be steps cut into the natural downward slope of the limestone floor that extended into darkness. "What's down there?" The ceiling also sloped downward, mirroring the floor.

"A chamber with a pool that leads to the sea."

She ran the light over the walls. "This is amazing. I knew caves like this existed in the Rock Islands, but this is more extensive…" Her words trailed off as the light landed on writing on the wall. Japanese and Palauan writing.

She studied the characters, which were kanji. Her ability to read Japanese was limited, and she couldn't read Palauan at all—but the symbols were familiar. "Names, maybe," she murmured. "I wonder if this was created by the Palauans who were pressed into duty by the Japanese during the war? There are stories that eighty young men were trained to participate in suicide guerrilla raids against American forces. The *Kirikomi-tai*. Some said they set up outposts on other islands, refuge from the Americans."

"I believe that's exactly what this was. Ulai said there are rumors of a handful of caves like this one in the Rock Islands. I found this one thanks to the tunnel through the pool. The tunnel we crawled through was filled with dirt and well hidden."

She shuddered. "You swam through an underwater tunnel to find this?"

"With scuba," he said. "It's a hard without scuba, but possible."

She didn't want to know how he knew that. The idea of swimming through a tunnel of rock gave her shivers. She was a decent swimmer and had learned scuba due to the need to ground-truth CAM's results, but she was far from experienced enough to try underwater caving. That would be every nightmare come true.

"When I first found this place," he continued, "I was sure this would be it, where the Chechen had hidden the AUUV. It wasn't, but I realized this would be a good base camp for you." He turned toward the steps. "Follow me."

She reached for two of the cases.

"Leave them up here. This is your office. Below are the living quarters."

Bemused and strangely enchanted, she followed. She'd known these caves existed and expected to find more like it with CAM, but she and Ulai hadn't done an aerial survey of these islands yet. As far as she knew, this particular cave wasn't on any map or mentioned in any historical account.

The flight of stairs took her into a lower second chamber. Larger than the one above, it had an irregular kidney shape, the whole space being about four hundred square feet, with a ceiling that ranged from four feet high at the edges to ten feet in the middle above a pool of still water.

Light shone through a skylight in the ceiling above the pool, while dim illumination filtered through a hole in the east wall. "Is that a window cut by soldiers?"

"Yes. It's hidden by vegetation and too small for anyone to climb through." His voice echoed off the walls as sound did in caves. "I could clear it for more light, but instead I installed these." He flicked a switch, and a floodlight came on, illuminating even the dark corners.

Supplies were stacked in an alcove she hadn't seen in the dark. Food. Water. A camping stove. Propane. Sleeping pads and blankets.

Relief flooded her. She'd feared they'd be fishing for every meal and sleeping on rocks, and she'd wondered where they'd find drinking water.

She snapped open the lid of a bottle of water and took a

long drink before passing the bottle to Dimitri. The water was cool and refreshing after being stored in the dark, damp cave.

He took a drink, then nodded toward the stairs. "We have everything we need. The latrine is in the jungle to the south of the cave entrance. We can bathe in the pool. Salt water, but better than nothing." He handed the bottle back to her. "There are chairs if you want to rest while I go up and cover the entrance again."

She nodded toward meter-tall rolls of paper tucked in with the supplies. "What are those?"

"Charts. Places I've searched. All the information I have. We'll go over them together."

She gripped his shirt and pulled him to her for a quick, soft kiss. "Yes. Yes, we will. Go hide the entrance while I get started."

*L*uke set down the phone, shaken to his core.

Parker was an assassin, an enforcer for the hardest criminal edges of the Russian government, and Luke had let him go.

Luke had told Curt he didn't believe Parker would hurt Ivy. Did he still believe that, knowing the man was a killer?

Jesus, that night on the ferry, Parker had claimed he'd never fired his gun in the line of duty before. That may well have been true as far as the Coast Guard was concerned, but...the way he said it, he'd been so utterly convincing that only now did Luke accept that likely *everything* Parker had told him was a lie.

Even the part about not returning to Russia. Or that he hadn't killed the kind tribal member who worked at the museum.

God. What if Parker had killed Annie?

Dimitri, he corrected himself. Easygoing Parker Reeves didn't exist. He was Dimitri Veselov and an assassin.

"It's not your fault, Luke," Undine said softly.

He met her gaze. His Undine. She'd been livid with him after he'd told Curt that Parker wouldn't hurt Ivy, and now she offered comfort when she could be saying *I told you so*.

She wrapped her arms around his waist. "It's. Not. Your. Fault. Parker—Dimitri—fooled everyone. You had reason to trust him."

He closed his eyes as she tucked her head under his chin and held him. "What if…what if he killed Annie?" There. He'd said it aloud. The question that turned his gut and sent cold chills up his spine.

"Parker had an alibi for Annie's time of death. The tourist boat on the Pacific that got in trouble when the storm rolled in. Parker was in the helicopter that rescued the tourists."

His eyes burned with relief at the reminder, and he squeezed her tighter. He'd forgotten. Parker Reeves' last months in Neah Bay had been reconstructed with meticulous detail, to make sure he'd had no connection to Yuri and his crew. Part of that had included clearing him of Annie's murder.

Knowing Parker—*Dimitri*—didn't kill Annie made it possible to breathe again. But the man was still an assassin.

"Why did he send you a card? What does he want from you?" Undine asked.

He'd been asking himself the same thing. He could think of only two possibilities. "Either he's luring me to Palau because I'm his next assignment, or he wants my help."

"There's no reason for Russia to want you dead at this point."

She had no idea about some of the ops he'd been on when he was a SEAL, but those had been years ago.

"I think…" Undine's chest rose as she took a long, deep breath. "I think he wants your help. He knows Curt would bring you in the loop. He knows my connection to Ivy. He knows you trusted him."

"He sent the card *before* the party. Does that mean he was behind the attack?"

"I don't know," she said. "But one thing we know about Parker is he can read people, and he knows how to plan. Maybe he saw the storm brewing and sent that card simply because he wanted you alert when the typhoon hit."

"Ivy's in the eye of the storm now."

"She is." Undine pulled back and gripped his shirt. "I think—God, I hate saying this because it's the *last* thing I want you to do—but I think you should go to Palau."

Relief flooded him as she suggested the thing he'd feared they'd fight over. He'd known he was going to Palau from the moment Curt had said the word *assassin*.

Chapter Eighteen

$\mathcal{D}$imitri should have known the way to seduce Ivy would be with maps. He wished he'd forgone the solar-powered lights, because candlelight would only make the scene more beautiful. She'd draped herself over the plastic table as she studied the notes he'd written on the chart. A long tress had slipped from her hairclip and fell over her cheek, draping down to sweep the chart spread across the table.

He could swear he heard her coo when she saw the underwater cave he'd located to the southeast. The soft noise made him wonder about the sounds she'd make if he took her from behind as she bent over the table.

He turned to the supplies he'd placed here over the last several weeks, and found a bottle of red wine and two stemless metal wine cups, purchased on a whim after reading an article she'd written on the infrared signatures of grapevines in drought conditions, and the possibility of using aerial mapping to ensure water was distributed in the right amount to the neediest crops. An offhand remark had given her favorite vintage.

She might find the purchase stalkerish, and yet she already knew he'd studied her like she was the final exam that would decide his fate.

Because, in truth, she was.

He pulled the cork and poured the wine. She smiled when he offered her the cup, then purred after her first sip. "I've always loved this wine, and right now, I think it's the best thing I've ever tasted."

He couldn't help but smile. "Second best for me."

She returned her gaze to the map, still caught in its thrall. "What was the best?" she asked, distracted as she traced a triangle he'd drawn where he'd noted Peleliu wreckage on the seafloor.

"You."

Her finger paused on the shape, but her body didn't stiffen. She straightened, lifted her cup, and took a slow sip. "Tell me more."

He stepped up behind her but didn't touch her, much as he wanted to. "I could describe you like a fine wine, smooth and tangy with an erotic bouquet, the way your flavor bursts on the tongue. But none of it would capture how sensual you are, how you intoxicate me, or explain my addiction to you."

She leaned against him, pressing her ass to his erection. He groaned at the contact. He wanted to cup her breasts and grind against her, but he set his fists on the tabletop, trapping her. He wanted to lick the dried salt on her neck; instead, he breathed in the fresh ocean scent that infused her skin.

"I want to bury myself inside you, but not for a hot, fast fuck. I want slow, sensual, and intense. Methodical. Fucking you was glorious, but I'm thirsty for more than that. I *need* more." He couldn't stop the flow of words, his mouth having been hijacked by an organ far more powerful than his brain. These were his last days on this earth, and if he could have one thing, it would be something real with Ivy to take to the grave. "The next time I'm inside you, I want it to be making love."

He pressed his lips to the side of her neck and trailed downward. "Believe in me, Ivy. Know that I'm protecting you. First, last, and always."

She let out a small whimper at the back of her throat, and his erection strained to escape his boxer briefs. Home was so close. The place he wanted to be more than any other.

"Do you trust me, Ivy?"

She lifted her cup and drained it in one long swallow.

"Do you trust me, Ivy?"

"No," she whispered.

*I*vy was so aroused, she wanted to bite his neck. Instead, he stepped back and let her go. She wanted to halt his retreat. To take him deep in her throat and change his mind.

But his words had both seduced and stopped her.

Make love?

That would never happen.

His retreat was logical. He wanted her, she wanted him, but she could never trust him. That equation couldn't be balanced using any type of known math.

And she had to ask herself, how could she have sex with a man she didn't trust? This wasn't stranger sex, like the first time. Now he was a man she *knew* she couldn't trust.

And what would it mean for her later? It was one thing to have had sex with him before she'd known what he was, but would Curt Dominick offer her absolution and exoneration if she made the same mistake again, fully aware of his crimes against the US?

She paused at that. How did she know he'd committed

crimes against the US? They were in Palau. She knew nothing about his actions as a spy. Maybe he'd done his spying elsewhere.

But there was that perfect American accent. Hardly necessary if he did his spying in other countries. She stepped away from the table, crossed her arms, and turned to face him. "Tell me about your life as a spy. Give me a reason to trust you."

"What do you want to know?"

"Where were you? What did you do? Have you killed people?"

"Spy and assassin aren't the same thing."

"But if your cover were to be blown, did you—or would you have—killed someone to protect yourself? And I'm not talking about self-defense, like today."

He held her gaze for a long moment, then reached for the bottle of wine. "Let's get comfortable. I'm going to tell you about Parker Reeves."

It was strange—and yet felt so right—to be tucked against Dimitri's side as they sat on thick inflatable sleeping pads and leaned against the cave wall and he told her the outrageous story of everything that happened on a cold night less than a week before Thanksgiving.

Parker Reeves. Dimitri had been the second man on the Osprey, the man she'd believed was a Ukrainian neo-Nazi terrorist who the government had allowed to escape.

First she needed to wrap her head around the fact that he'd been in the US Coast Guard for nearly five years. Then that he knew Undine. She could confirm his story. As could Luke Sevick. One phone call, and she'd know if he told the truth.

But the point that made her heart pick up speed and which had her pulling away from his side to pace the cave as she processed the data was that in the course of events last fall, he'd participated in several phone conference calls with Curt Dominick.

Curt had known *exactly* who Dimitri was. He said as much in his text. And he'd ordered her to cooperate with him, knowing that. Surely that meant he trusted Parker/Jack/Dimitri at least a little?

But could *she* trust Dimitri? She felt better knowing this, but still, it raised more questions. Like who was he working for now?

But he would only tell her so much, and his story ended in November.

She frowned at her wineglass. He'd refilled it at the start of the story, but after nearly thirty minutes, it remained half-full. She abandoned it because she needed a clear head.

She turned back to the table with the chart laid across the surface. "I've been thinking. I could fly RON out through the large skylight and have him collect data at night. People are less likely to spot it in the dark, especially out here. It will be safer that way."

"You don't need daylight?"

"No. The lasers provide their own light."

"I'll help you set up the workstation." He stood and crossed the rock floor to her side. "You won't be able to upload the data to the military database with the satellite uplink."

She nodded. "I know. The beacon transmits with every upload. Patrick's men could find us." She ran her hand across the surface of the chart on the table. So many beautiful contours and, added to the printed data, markings in Dimitri's own hand. He'd been at this for months, and he'd been systematic. She could see the pattern in his notation. Insight into his beautiful mind.

"CAM collects a massive amount of data. At some point, I'll run out of storage on the hard disk."

"You'll have to dump it."

The thought of erasing her baby's memory caused her to shudder, but she nodded.

"I'm sorry, Ivy."

And she knew he was apologizing for so much more than the idea of deleting precious data. Because he *got* her. Probably better than any man she'd ever known. He'd researched her to the nth degree—hell, he even knew her favorite wine and had stashed it in the cave. Her gaze flew to his. "The wine. Did you put it here hoping to seduce me?"

"Not seduce. Just a comfort. I figured you'd be hostile. Afraid. The wine is as much an apology as anything."

She nodded. His words rang true.

"If I could find the AUUV without involving you, I would."

She grabbed his shirt with both hands. "And if I could finish what you've started without *you*, I would."

"If you were to do that, then two people who matter to me very much would die."

She'd suspected as much. What would happen, in the end, if she had a chance to take the AUUV from Dimitri? Could she make that decision?

She had no answers, only more questions and the uneasy feeling that before this was over, she'd be asked to make more impossible choices.

She rose on her toes and pressed her lips to his. Brief. Chaste. "Thank you, for the apology. And the wine."

"Do you trust me, Ivy?" His voice held the same pained edge that had infused the question when he'd asked it before, as they stood in this exact same spot, right after he'd seduced her with words.

"No." She gave him a wry smile. "But I'm willing to consider a heartless screw."

"No, thanks. Not with you."

She released him and stepped back. "Well then, time to set up CAM and RON. Bring the maps. I want you to tell me everything you remember about the corals and wreckage and geology you observed on your dives as you searched for the AUUV. I can calibrate CAM using your charts and first-hand knowledge."

☠

*J*an Boyd opened the door of his small house in Maryland and faced his boss, Keith Hatcher, and the ultimate owner of the company he worked for, Alec Ravissant. He didn't bother to hide his surprise at the unannounced early morning visit.

He'd met Rav many times in the months since he started working for Raptor, but it had always been in a social capacity, outside of Raptor business. Rav, the junior senator from Maryland, had to stay out of Raptor business, which was why he had Keith.

They most frequently crossed paths at JT Talon's private gym in the heart of DC, where Ian and his small group of new friends sparred on a regular basis. Cressida had been his ticket into the unofficial club, and he'd been surprised at how much he enjoyed being a member.

That the two men had showed up at his house at eight a.m. without calling first didn't bode well. Official Raptor business happened at the office. But then, Rav couldn't be there. So this couldn't be official.

"Sorry to drop in like this," Keith said.

Cressida peeked into the entryway, and her mouth formed a surprised O at seeing their guests. "This is about Ivy, isn't it?" she asked.

Alec gave a sharp nod. Ian had to wonder how the man was holding up, knowing his cousin was in trouble. It had been a tense time all around. Cressida and Ivy had become close, but for Alec, Ivy was family.

To Ian, Keith said, "Alec needs your take on the situation, as a former CIA operative."

"Can I stay?" Cressida asked. "I don't have the security clearance…"

"Sorry, Cress," Keith said. "This is off the books, but still, there are rules we can't break."

She nodded. "I understand. There's a fresh pot of coffee in the kitchen. I'll grab a mug, then get out of your way."

She led everyone into the kitchen and poured herself a cup of coffee.

Ian caught her waist before she left the room. He held her gaze for a long moment, then kissed her forehead. He'd tell her what he could, but she knew he had to respect the limits of the job. He might not work for the CIA anymore, but he still held to the rules, and there were oaths he'd never break.

She smiled and nodded. She understood.

He watched her walk down the hall to their bedroom, enjoying the sway of her ass. Eight months they'd been together, and he still wondered how he'd ever hesitated, why he'd even considered walking away from her. She was the family he'd never known he needed and everything he couldn't live without.

He turned to his boss and his ultimate employer and shifted to covert operative mode. He had a mortgage and a reason to live now. These men were important to the goal of meeting the first obligation and enjoying the second.

Cressida had coached him on how to greet guests. In his old life, he'd never had guests—at least, not in his real home. "Cream or sugar?" he asked.

"No coffee for me," Alec said.

Keith took his coffee black. Ian poured himself a mug

and settled at the kitchen table with his boss and his employer.

They each sat on the edge of their chairs, bodies pitched forward. Ready to spring into action and easier to converse in low voices.

"What's going on with Ivy?" Ian asked.

"This is a side job I'm offering you," Alec said. "Not a Raptor mission. Paid for from my personal bank account."

To the best of Ian's knowledge, Rav was a straight arrow. He'd backed out of Raptor as the law required and left management in Keith's hands without batting an eye. Legal and ethical to a T. Ian couldn't help but cock his head toward the man who funded his newfound homeownership and happiness and ask the direct question. "Why?"

"Because it *is* personal. And this has nothing to do with government contracts. I ran it by Curt. He thinks I'm legally clear, and even if I'm not, I'm finding it hard to give a fuck. An assassin abducted my cousin. I want Ivy home."

Years of training to control body language couldn't compete with Rav's revelation. Ian's spine shot to the upright position. "Parker Reeves is an *assassin?*"

"Russian enforcer. Known as the Hammer. Heard of him?"

Acid flooded Ian's stomach. "Shit. The ball-peen guy?"

Keith shot him a look.

Ian ran a hand over his face, stopping himself from sharing gruesome details he'd learned when he'd been working a Russian informant years ago. He cleared his throat and grunted. "Yeah. I know of him."

Rav's nostrils flared, giving Ian the impression his employer had already heard the rumors and more. "This is a private job," he repeated. "You can say no. But if you say yes, you'll be well paid. I'm renting a jet from Raptor." He smiled at the notion of renting a jet from himself. "It'll be ready to roll in two hours. First stop is Washington State to pick up Luke Sevick."

"Why me?" Ian couldn't help but ask. Sevick was the one who knew Reeves. Ian was primarily acting as an analyst and interpreter these days, giving Keith his informed opinion on how to run ops in the Middle East, in addition to providing tradecraft training at the Virginia compound.

"First, because we need someone who speaks Russian and Arabic—Hill's people are involved," Keith said. "And second because we figure the best way to catch a spy is with a spy."

Ian agreed. But Parker Reeves wasn't just a spy, he was the Hammer, which changed everything. As an ally, he'd be an ace in the hole. But as an enemy? To the best of his knowledge, no one had ever faced the Hammer and lived to tell the tale.

When it came to bringing the assassin in, all bets were off.

"Sevick's on board with this?" he asked.

Keith nodded. "Luke is the one who called me with a plan to bring Reeves in."

Chapter Nineteen

"When I isolate this layer"—Ivy keyed in the command, and the other map layers disappeared from the display—"you can see the mangrove swamp that edges the island, but nothing else. Perfect for calculating the disappearing habitat and monitoring the effects of global warming, but there are other applications as well."

Dimitri smiled. She was lit from within after hours at the computer, completely engrossed in her work. It was clear that for her, the images on the screen were as alive as if she were astral projecting herself into the swamp that edged an island two miles away.

He was utterly fascinated with how she brought such passion to what was for most a cold, data-derived universe.

How bizarre to be so utterly captivated by a person just days before what was sure to be his end. Was this love? He couldn't rule it out, and could only assume that if it was, maybe he was open to the emotion now, knowing his time was limited, where he'd been closed off before.

"Have you killed people?" Her question had left him cold, but it was his cop-out answer that filled him with shame.

"Spy and assassin aren't the same thing."

No. They weren't. Yet he was both.

Would Ivy take comfort knowing all his victims had been Bratva? Mafiosi who trafficked in guns, drugs, and people? He was an old-school enforcer. The Hammer. His boss just happened to be his government.

He'd cry no tears over the men he'd killed—the world was better off without them. But still, without the benefit of judge or jury, he'd acted as executioner, and he had enough of a moral code to know that was wrong.

Would it matter to Ivy that he'd become an assassin to stop his sister from being raped and tortured again? Or was it more worrisome that he'd been so damn good at it? After the first three, a cold mantle had settled over him, and he no longer felt remorse for the act. That should raise Ivy's alarm bells if she wasn't already repulsed by his second career.

He'd selected only one victim himself. He'd taken out the man who'd made him into an assassin to begin with. It wasn't wise to force a man to be a killer, because once stripped of that part of his humanity, it had been so easy to set his sights on his puppet master.

He'd had to wait years for the opportunity. Sophia had contacted him in the usual manner and told him of the rape. But this time, the man was out of favor in the shadow organization. Unprotected. And so Dimitri had taken him out.

It was the only kill he'd...*enjoyed* wasn't the right word, but it was on the continuum. There'd been satisfaction.

And now he'd killed for Ivy. There hadn't been enjoyment in that either. Just necessity. No regrets.

But the underlying fact was, he was a killer who operated outside the conventions of war or rule of law. He didn't even have a 00 license to make it palatable to American and European audiences.

Ivy MacLeod would be repulsed when she learned the

truth, which meant he needed to keep her from that knowledge for as long as possible. They had to work together to find the AUUV so she could get her life back and he could save his family.

And he was wasting time lusting after her and acknowledging that just once in his short life, he wanted something real, to have a soul-deep connection before he left this earth.

"Have you killed people?"

And all he could do was give a chicken-shit answer. *"Spy and assassin aren't the same thing."*

In deflecting her question, he'd made it impossible. There could be no soul-deep connection without her knowing exactly what he was. But she could never give herself over to an assassin.

So instead, he sat next to her as she worked her magic, flying the drone in the dead of night, collecting data. Her cheeks flushed with the thrill of seeing her life's work performing optimally. His hard-on a perpetual, dull ache as everything she did turned him on.

"Can you isolate other plants?" he asked.

"Yes, as long as I can extract the infrared signature of the flora, as I did with mangroves in this climate and the different grapes in the drought study. The infrared camera captures the temperature and emissivity—the thermal radiation—and other data points that make up the signature. Once I have the infrared signature for a plant in a certain climate and setting, it's just a matter of training CAM on what to recognize, which is part of the calibration process."

She clicked a few buttons, and a different layer appeared. He recognized it as the first data she'd collected after launching RON hours before. The screen showed a scale 3D map of the chamber they were in. The lower chamber, with the pool and underwater tunnel, were also shown, but in less detail. "It's easy to strip off the trees to find the rock," she said, "and the void, where this chamber is, was easy for the Lidar to spot. It gets harder with the lower chamber, because the limestone is thicker. But this cave can be used calibrate CAM to recognize others like this one—where the rock is thick and the cave drops deep and flows under the water. Once CAM learns this, just like he can learn the thermal radiation of mangroves or grapevines, then when CAM comes across another area that reads like this one, he can extrapolate that he's identified a cave."

"*He.* You slip between 'it' and 'he' with CAM."

Her flush deepened. "I can't help but anthropomorphize him. It. Whatever."

"To me, CAM would be a woman. Because CAM is you."

"No. Not me." She gave a hard laugh. "But maybe, sometimes, who I'd like to be." She frowned. "I suppose that sounds nutty."

He shrugged. "Who wouldn't want to fly and see through walls?"

"Put that way, it sounds like CAM is Superman. I should have named it Kal-El."

He laughed.

She tapped the power meter for the drone on the computer screen. "Time to bring RON back."

"In the morning, I'll set up the solar panels. There's a place at the top of the island where they'll catch the sun, but there's enough cover to disguise them if there's a flyover searching for us."

She nodded even as she yawned. "I collected enough tonight to be able to calibrate for our search. Tomorrow, we'll grid out the areas that are the most promising and start there."

Our search. He was such a fucking sap to find pleasure in hearing her say that.

*I*f Ivy could forget the events leading up to her current situation, she'd feel like she was living a fantasy. She was stranded on a deserted island in the tropics with a hot man, and the project she'd poured her heart into over the last five years was working better than she'd ever imagined.

CAM and RON *worked*. Together, her software program and her hardware drone collected and processed data seamlessly. What would have once taken months—or even years—now took only a few hours to produce maps that should be impossible.

If only she had a printer. Then she could hold the end result in her hands and lick it. She cast a glance sideways at Dimitri and considered licking him instead.

Yeah, he was more fun to lick than paper. Well, most things were more fun to lick than paper. But it wouldn't be just any paper, it would be a seamless land/sea map created by CAM.

But on the Dimitri side of the equation, licking him would be simple fun. Maybe it was wrong, but at this point, she knew at his core, he was protecting her. Without him, she'd either be dead or hostage to a terrorist group.

Maybe she should feel ashamed of the attraction, but she was tired of the world telling her how she should feel. She'd had enough judgment from total strangers when Patrick was arrested.

It didn't help that all she had to do was close her eyes and she remembered how Dimitri had felt inside her. He'd awoken her libido, and now she craved him like a drug.

She'd start with his neck and work her way down. His

pecs and abs would garner special attention, but they would just be stopovers on the way to his cock.

She wondered if he'd submit to scan by RON. Dimitri's body would be her pièce de résistance. The ultimate merge of art and chart.

And oh, how she would study his contours. The peaks and valleys of muscles and their attachment points, the rise of his broad nose, the cleft in his chin, the hollows under his cheekbones. The scar that bisected his brow. Each slope and mark told a story, just like her beloved maps.

Most noticeable was what wasn't there, that sad lack of lines around his eyes and mouth. She loved making him laugh, because she wanted to believe he had enough time left to put humor lines on his face.

He fascinated her as much as the images on her computer screen.

Maybe even more so.

Which made her wonder who she'd become that this man who'd abducted her felt more an ally than the fine folks at the DIA who'd set her up for a nightmare without so much as a heads-up. A simple *"Hey, you might run into some terrorists who are after the same thing we haven't told you we're sending you to find"* would have sufficed.

Getting to hear a terrorist describe how he planned to rape and torture her had been a special treat.

Really, it was no wonder Dimitri felt like her only safe option. He'd at least set up a secure place for her to work and had seen to her comfort in his thoughtful provisioning of the cave.

She rolled her shoulders. She'd been sitting at the screen for too long, tweaking the data layers as only a human could. CAM was good, but she still needed to teach him how to zero in on the different plant species.

"I need to go out. Walk around a bit. Get some sunlight," she said. "I may as well check the solar panels."

"I'll go with you."

"I'd like to go alone." Here was his chance to prove she wasn't a prisoner.

He frowned at her, then gave a sharp nod. "Take a gun, then. Just in case."

Yeah, if only the DIA had said *that*, she might trust the bastards to get her out of this mess. As it was, she had no intention of letting Dimitri keep the AUUV once they found it, but she at least trusted him to protect her until that moment.

Then of course, all bets were off.

She donned a holster to carry the gun at the small of her back and grabbed a water bottle before setting out. She crawled through the tunnel and stepped into the dappled sunlight. The salt breeze just reached her through the canopy.

She took a deep breath and turned her face toward the sun. She'd been on this island for over twenty-four hours now. If she could just forget the circumstances that brought her here, this would feel like paradise. But watching a man's brains get blown out before he became shark food had a way of sticking with her.

Would she ever know that man's name or how he was aligned with the other factions? Was he with Patrick's cell, or had he represented Russian interests?

Was Dimitri—even unknowingly—working for the same man the dead man had been working for?

She'd known spies and assassins weren't the same thing, having become well versed in spy terminology over the last several months as she tried to understand what Patrick had done and why. Most spies were informants, people who were recruited by agencies like the CIA to collect and pass on information about their governments. Dimitri had described his role as Parker Reeves, which had been more in the vein of the sleeper spies deployed by the old Soviet Union, but with modern technology keeping him in touch with his Russian handlers.

He'd made his life sound tame until all hell broke loose last fall.

But somehow she found it hard to believe Dimitri could settle for tame.

Ivy brushed aside branches and vines and made her way to the small clearing where the solar panels for CAM and RON were set up. After checking the power meter, she flopped on the ground and closed her eyes. If Dimitri was right about the size of the search grid, it would take three to five days—or rather nights—for RON to fly over and collect data.

Their schedule was simple: gather data until one or two in the morning. Sleep six to eight hours, crunch data for four to five, then send out RON again two hours after sunset.

It was possible this would all be over in five days. Sooner if they got lucky.

She didn't want to think about what would happen then. Much as she wanted out of this situation, the actual ending of it scared the hell out of her.

Dimitri believed he would die. He was certainly facing prison in the US. But what would Russia do to him if he went back there?

He'd killed a Russian to protect Ivy. Sure, the man had been actively shooting at him at the time, but still. What if they were ostensibly on the same side?

She glanced around the clearing. Covered by trees on all sides, only aircraft could find her here, and it would be impossible for Dimitri to approach without her hearing.

She pulled out the satellite phone she'd managed to grab

and tuck in the holster with the gun. Her fingers hovered over the keypad. Should she call Curt and give him a full update?

Dimitri had told her everything he knew about finding the AUUV. She no longer needed him. Except for protection.

They'd be here for a few days at least. All she had to do was call Curt, give him their GPS coordinates, and a team of SEALs would come to her rescue.

But what would happen to Dimitri?

She knew in her gut he'd never survive the confrontation. Not that the SEALs would gun for him, but because he might have a death wish.

She needed to know more about his situation, more about who he was protecting and why. Without that information, it was too soon to call Curt.

Later, maybe she could call Alec. He could send a team of Raptor operatives who could help her bring Dimitri in alive.

*H*e'd known she'd take the phone. Hell, it was what any sane person would do. He could have stopped her, but she wasn't his prisoner anymore, and he wanted her to know that.

So here he was, stuck in the cave, giving Ivy the freedom to destroy him and trying to decide if he should be packing up CAM to flee to another island.

He should have asked her to track down Luke's phone number. It was time for a direct conversation.

He paced in the lower part of the cave, antsy. He was usually so good at reading people, but he was at a loss for what to expect from Ivy. But then, she'd surprised him at every turn.

He'd expected her to be smart but also cold. Calculating.

Potentially in league with her ex. But she'd been charming and engaging and innocent.

Then he'd expected her to collapse in the mangrove swamp in hysterics. Instead, she'd gone after CAM with a coolheaded understanding of her dangerous situation.

Then she blew his mind by begging him to take her in the shower.

The twists of the funhouse ride kept coming at her, but each time, Ivy MacLeod met it and demonstrated a different kind of strength than he expected from her in that moment, whether she was pulling a gun on him or taking charge and shutting down the transmitter.

She was resilient. Smart. Strong. He wanted to support her strength with his own, be her reinforcement as new challenges were tossed her way.

He was falling hard for her. How fucked up was it that she was the only woman he'd ever abducted? That he was all in on his final mission, and he'd finally met someone who made him want to defy his rules of detachment?

She was probably calling in a SEAL team right now to come and fry his ass. Because he was a dumbshit and refused to follow abductor/abductee conventions.

She had all the power. All he had was muscle he'd never use against her.

He stared at the pool of water and, without thinking, began to strip. He was hot, wound up. A swim would do him good. Nude, he dove in. At its deepest point, the pool was fifteen feet deep. He swam down, clearing his ears, the water a cool brine on his hot skin.

He groped in the darkness until he found the lip of the rock that edged the tunnel. Did he have enough breath to swim out? Yes. It was the return trip that would be the problem. He could swim around the island and climb the hillside, but there was risk there. Kayakers could be paddling in the channels between islands. They might not bat an eye at seeing a nude man circling the beach, but if they were questioned later, they'd almost certainly remember him.

As tempting as the vigorous swim was, he needed to keep a cool head. Like Ivy. Logic dictated he stay in the cave. No unnecessary risks.

If he screwed up, he'd be putting Ivy at risk as well. He had to be fair to her and live up to his promise to protect her.

He kicked for the surface and took a gasping breath when he reached it.

"Jesus! You scared the shit out of me!"

He smiled. Ivy was back. "Join me?"

She pursed her lips and canted her head. "I suppose I could put on a suit."

"No." His cock thickened in the cool water just thinking about getting a naked Ivy in the pool. "No suits," he said.

As was her custom, she surprised him by stripping down right there in full view. She never did what he expected.

He couldn't read this woman. Not at all. Which left him at a loss half the time, missing his greatest skill at a time when he needed it most.

She slipped into the water and swam directly toward him. Surprise again. He'd be better off if he considered the opposite of what he imagined she'd do, and work from there.

She slipped her arms round his neck as he treaded water. Her body was soft and slick against his, and his hands found places to grab to support her. He'd be lying if he claimed he hadn't fantasized about making love to Ivy in this pool. The thought only occurred to him every thirty seconds or so.

"Did you call Curt Dominick?" he asked.

She stiffened in his arms. She'd been kicking and bobbing before, but now she was a weight in his hands, and he kicked to bring them both to the rocky edge, shallow enough for her to sit, with the globes of her breasts breaking the surface, glistening. Beautiful. He wanted to cup them with his hands as he sucked on her nipples and rolled them against his tongue.

But first things first. "Did you call the AG? Do we need to abandon this cave?"

She cradled his face. "No. I was going to…but I couldn't. I'm afraid for you, Dimitri. If SEALs come at the wrong time, I'm scared they'll kill you."

"Any time will be the wrong time, sweetheart. If a team comes to your rescue, I'm a dead man."

She pressed her mouth to his and slipped her tongue inside. Trying to give him a reason to live again?

He kissed her back. *Damn. She might win with this.* Right now, he very much wanted to live. To explore. To have. To bury himself deep inside and stay there. To watch her face as he made her come again and again.

He ended the kiss before he could be pulled in too deep by the promise of it.

He pushed back so a few feet of water separated them. "Why didn't you shoot me when you had the chance?"

She held his gaze. Finally, she said, "Because I want to help you find a way out of this. Because I believe you care about my safety more than the DIA, who sent me here blind to the danger. And maybe even more than Curt Dominick, who told me to cooperate with you so you'll help me find the AUUV."

So she had reached Dominick. And he'd done his job, pushing her to cooperate with Dimitri. And now, that very order had her trusting Dimitri more than the US attorney general.

Irony.

He swam back to her side and climbed up on the rocks, his body sliding over hers. She opened her legs, and his hips settled between her thighs, his erection pressed to her clit.

She let out a soft groan as he rocked his hips, sliding over her as she thrust her pelvis into his. His mouth hovered above her lips. "There will be no happy ending for me, Ivy. You understand that, right?"

She nodded.

"There is only now. This moment. This is all the happiness I get." He rocked his hips again.

She whimpered.

"I want to fuck you. To bury myself deep inside you and grab every inch of happiness from this moment that I can have."

"Yes."

His penis was at her opening. One thrust of his hips and he'd be home, but the condoms were over with the supplies. Control. He was a master of control. Time to exercise some.

He kissed her deeply, all while rocking his hips against hers. The rock had to be hard and jagged in places, hurting her back. Control. He'd do this right.

He lifted her up and set her on the gradual ledge of the pool. Her ass remained in an inch of water, her thighs in two inches. Her knees were submerged.

He nudged her thighs wide and kissed along her soft skin, moving toward her center. This he could do without putting his weight on her and hurting her. Without a condom. He licked her clit, then slid his tongue inside her vagina. She groaned and sighed and might've even purred. He planted his hands under her ass, lifting her from the salt water so he could better taste her.

Salty, tangy, Ivy.

She wrapped her legs around his head and gasped and panted as he devoured her, alternating between slow and fast strokes, working her into a frenzy without bringing her to the edge of orgasm.

God, he loved this. He stroked her with his thumb as he paused to gaze up at her face. So beautiful, the way she gave herself over to him. She was all in the moment. Taking the pleasure he gave her, eager for more.

His tongue alternated between vagina and clit while his cock throbbed with arousal. When he reached his final moment, he hoped this would be the memory that ran through his mind. Ivy giving herself up to him. The sounds she made as he learned her body and gave her exactly what she wanted.

On the edge of coming apart, she pulled back from his mouth. He followed with his hand.

"No, Dimitri, we're moving to the sleeping pads, where you can fuck me properly."

He laughed and followed her from the pool. She went to the supplies first and grabbed a box of condoms he'd stashed with his toiletries.

She turned to face him. "Did you bring these here when you stocked the cave before we met?"

He shook his head. "No. I grabbed them when we abandoned *Liberty*. I didn't really think we'd need them."

She wrapped a hand around his erection and stroked the length of him. She smiled wickedly and dropped to her knees. "We could get by without them," she said, then took him deep into her mouth.

He groaned and braced a hand on the cave wall, off-balance from the intensity.

She released him and looked up at him. The tip of his penis on her lips. Such a beautiful sight. "But I'm glad you brought them. Because I want this. I want you. I want to be thoroughly fucked." And then she took him in again, a long, slow slide as deep as he could go.

She sucked down and back, and he couldn't remember the last time he'd felt anything this good. But then, he couldn't remember anything beyond this moment, anything other than Ivy's mouth on his cock.

"You're my first uncircumcised penis," she said. She played with his foreskin, pulling it back and licking the exposed head, swirling her tongue around it. Then she took him deep, as much of him as she could take, all the way back.

His hips bucked. "You don't"—he let out a low groan—"seem put off by it."

She sucked on him as she slid up the shaft, then released him from her lips and stroked some more. "Hell, no. It's fun." She gave him another lick. "I never really thought about it before, but it's just more skin. It's you. It's beautiful. Hot. And I can't get enough."

This wasn't the slow lovemaking he'd claimed to want, but to hell with it. If all he could have was this, he'd take it.

Ivy was giving herself to him, freely. She was going down on him and enjoying it as much as he'd enjoyed going down on her.

"Time for me"—he firmed his stance and moved his hands from the cave wall to cup her face—"to fuck you properly." He pulled back from her mouth.

She whimpered. "I'm not done."

He put his thumb in his cock's place, and she sucked on it.

He squeezed a breast with his free hand. "Get on the air mattress. On your belly, ass in the air so I can see you."

Her eyes widened at his commanding tone, and she released his thumb and obeyed.

He paused to stare at what had to be the most beautiful thing he'd ever seen. Ivy MacLeod presenting her beautiful, wet body.

He grabbed a condom from the box and planted himself behind her. He licked her clit, then dipped his tongue inside. She turned her face to the mattress and groaned.

"Make as much noise as you want, sweetheart. We've got this whole island to ourselves."

"That's part of what makes this so hot. I feel like I'm living my darkest fantasy—one I didn't know I even had."

"Being fucked by a spy in a cave on a deserted island?" He wouldn't call himself her captor, because she wasn't a prisoner. He could only hope that wasn't the fantasy she was referring to.

"Exactly." She reached between her thighs and stroked her clit. "Touch me, Dimitri." She slipped two fingers inside her vagina.

"God, that's hot."

"And it's yours."

He licked her again, then he slipped the condom on. He positioned himself on his knees behind her and reached around her thigh to stroke her clit as he pressed the tip of his penis against her wet slit. In one thrust, he was in deep, and she let out a groan of satisfaction that bounced off the cave walls.

He stroked her clit as he thrust, all thoughts of going slow long gone in the wake of the heat. She was slick and tight and hot and his.

All his.

She rose up on her hands, lifting her breasts from the mattress. He cupped one breast while he stroked her clit with his other hand. She let out a guttural sound as her vagina clenched around him. "Harder," she said. "Don't be gentle. Squeeze. Pinch. And fuck."

He squeezed her breast and pinched her clit as he thrust into her with the force she demanded. The sounds she made morphed into a drawn-out moan that was as hot to his ears as her vagina felt on his cock. Her elbows gave out as she came, and she dropped to the mattress, her ass still high as he pounded into her and stroked her clit. She grabbed the blankets in her fists and groaned. "Yes. Oh. God. Yes." A litany of pleasure he was making her sing.

Fucking beautiful. She was beautiful. The arch of her back, the roundness of her ass. The way his penis disappeared inside her body. Everything about the moment was glorious.

He came. Hard. Fast, and so very hot. He groaned as his body spasmed and pulsed with ejaculation, the pleasure of it as intense and consuming as he'd ever felt.

He collapsed on top of her, then shifted his weight to the side, rolling with her so he stayed inside her in a spooning position.

He was torn between wanting to nibble on her neck and wanting to pass out. He settled for cupping her breast. "You're an amazing woman, Ivy."

She rolled to her back, causing him to slip from her body. She turned her head and met his gaze. "I don't want you to give up, Dimitri. Promise me you'll try to find a way to live. To get out of this—whatever the situation is you're in. I *know* people. Curt can help you cut a deal—"

His body went from hot to cold in the blink of an eye. That fast, his contentment vanished. That was what this had been about for her?

Once again, she'd surprised him. Jesus. Maybe she *had* called Curt from the hilltop. He wouldn't be surprised to learn the attorney general had ordered her to fuck him into surrendering.

Chapter Twenty

"Well, aren't you the patriotic soldier?" Dimitri said with a sneer in his voice. "I didn't take you for someone who'd use her body for a mission."

Cold shot through Ivy as he launched himself from the bed. She scooted backward and hit her head on the cave wall, momentarily stunning her from speaking. She rubbed the back of her head and tried to get her bearings. Finally, she managed a weak-sounding "What?"

"Give it up. You aren't the best actress. Jesus. Did Dominick order you to fuck me? Or was that all improv?"

If he'd been next to her, she would have slapped him. As it was, she was rendered speechless by a mix of hurt and rage. She'd just surrendered her body to him as completely as she could, and his first response was to accuse her of being a whore and then say she was lousy at it?

Anger broke the mute barrier, which was good, because if hurt won, it would be with tears. And she'd be damned before she'd cry in front of him over his insults. "You complete and utter ass. I don't fuck for my country—between the two of us, *I'm* not the one who's a spy. How many women have you fucked for the job? I hope you had the decency to do a better job with them."

She grabbed her clothes and yanked them on. She wanted to dive into the pool to wash his sweat from her skin, but she'd feel less vulnerable clothed.

"A better job? You didn't seem like you were having a terrible time."

"Yeah, well, maybe I'm a better actress than you think." God, how was it that they were even having this argument? What had she done?

But she knew what she'd done. She'd fucked a spy. Again.

She was too stupid to live.

Clothed, she headed for the stairs to the upper chamber.

"Where the hell are you going?" Dimitri asked.

"As far away from you as I can get."

"Don't try to leave the island, Ivy."

"I'm not stupid." But she was. So very, very stupid. Part of her had wondered if she was falling in love with the spy. She couldn't get much dumber than that.

She reached the bottom step before he caught her arm and swung her around to face him. "Why did you fuck me?" he asked. "Were you trying to get me to surrender?"

The pain in his eyes caused her own heartache to find its voice. "No," she whispered.

"Why, then?" he asked again.

"Because I wanted you. I'm sorry you found me lacking, but I wasn't acting and had no agenda." She yanked her arm from his grip.

"I found you lacking?" He shook his head. "When did I say that?"

"You accused me of being a whore, then said I'm not the best actress." Her hands shook as humiliation engulfed her. She curled them into fists to fight the emotion from seizing control. "I said what I did because I'm a dumbass and what we just did meant something to me. But not anymore. Go ahead and give up, but don't expect me to give a damn when you're gone."

She turned and ran up the steps and crawled through the tunnel, determined to get away from him before tears fell.

She reached the top of the island where the solar panels were set up, and curled up at the base of a tree.

This was why she'd given up sex. She'd forgotten it was the heartache that accompanied emotional attachment that had killed her libido.

It was debilitating to have opened herself up to someone so completely—whether it was the man she'd married or a spy she'd picked up at a party—and have him turn so ugly, so insulting, right at the moment when she was most vulnerable.

She'd wanted to give Dimitri a reason to live—a reason to fight. Such a fool to think *she* could be that reason.

Apparently, Patrick was right. She was lousy at sex. She had the social skills of a robot and only another computer could ever love her.

She swiped at her tears with the heels of her palms. On one level, she knew Dimitri had lied when he claimed the sex wasn't good, and Patrick was just plain full of shit. But it was hard not to internalize when she'd had so much invested in her marriage, and Dimitri was the first man she'd been with since then. She was rusty, and, well, they hadn't exactly had a normal relationship progression.

That thought made her laugh as well as cry. The last three words didn't belong in the same sentence when it came to Dimitri.

She blotted her face with the hem of her shirt. She needed to get her emotions under control and get back to work, or she'd never escape this nightmare.

She stared at the wet blotches on her shirt. Proof Patrick was wrong. She wasn't a damn robot. She felt as deeply as the next person. Patrick had been the coldhearted prick. He'd just covered it better with his veneer of charm.

"Why did you divorce Patrick Hill?"

She jolted at the question and bumped her head again—this time on the tree trunk. She hadn't heard Dimitri's approach.

"Go away," she said.

"You misunderstood me. Before. When I said you aren't that good an actress, I wasn't talking about the sex."

"I. Don't. Give. A. Fuck. Go away."

"Sex, being with you, was amazing. *You're* amazing."

"Great. You can post that on Yelp if they have a whore page."

"I was out of line."

She finally lifted her head and met his gaze. The mouth she'd devoured—and which had devoured her. Those lips had felt so good on her…everywhere. "Ya think?"

"It's just, I can't turn back. Not for you. Not for me. It's impossible. And when you asked me to cut a deal… Well, you don't know what you're asking."

"Then *tell* me. Why are you doing this?"

"Why did you divorce Patrick?" he asked again.

She was too raw to go there, to share that pain with this man who'd cut her nearly as deep after she'd surrendered so completely. She pushed up from the ground. The landscape had shifted. Or maybe she had. Either way, she needed a new map to navigate what she'd just discovered was landmine-laden terrain. "I'm going for a hike. Don't follow me."

"Ivy, it's not safe—"

"Just leave me alone. Please." She pushed aside branches and headed for the saddle of the island. She'd give herself an hour to get her head together, then it was back to the cave to get ready for another night of data collection. She would find the AUUV, hand it over to a team of SEALs, and go the hell home.

*D*imitri watched Ivy escape through the thick vegetation. He had no choice but to follow her, for her safety. She was unarmed, and he had no doubt more men from Hill's former organization were on the hunt for her and CAM.

But he'd give her space, as she requested, and follow at a distance.

Shit. Could he be a bigger asshole? She'd misinterpreted his words in the worst, most painful way, which told him something about her relationship with her ex.

He'd witnessed so much of her strength, he'd failed to see how much pain she hid. So maybe she was a good actress—in one area, at least.

But then, hiding pain from one's enemies was a basic survival skill, and this was a reminder that even though they'd made love, even though he'd come to care about her far more than he should, they were still and would always be enemies.

And he'd unintentionally used sex to break through her strongest defense shield.

Ahead of him, she skirted around one of the skylights, a small opening that looked down on the lower chamber of the cave. Where he'd just made love to her, then gutted her because she dared to ask him to find a reason to live.

He covered her trail as he followed. He'd have to do the same on the return. At least the soft canopy bounced back quickly, and evening rain would likely erase any vestiges of their passing.

At last, Ivy settled in a patch of sunlight, but instead of staring upward, she faced the soft ground and drew shapes in the dirt. Thirty minutes passed as he watched her, hidden from her view by a leafy plant, but he had no doubt she was aware he guarded her.

She jumped up all at once and turned back for the cave. He tucked himself deeper in the shadows as she passed, then visited her seat in the sunlight. He paused before erasing her markings, his heart feeling tight at the necessity for wiping away this glimpse into her psyche.

A series of triangles were drawn in the dirt, followed by symbols and complex equations he couldn't begin to understand.

Chapter Twenty-One

*L*uke held Undine on the tarmac and kissed her one more time. The Raptor jet was refueled and ready for the long flight to Palau.

She dropped back to her heels with her hands behind his neck. "Don't underestimate him. He's Dimitri Veselov, not Parker Reeves, and he's not your friend."

He nodded. "Don't worry. I won't make that mistake again." He released Undine and nodded to Ian Boyd. "Let's roll."

Undine hugged Ian. "Watch his back," she said. "Or I'll kick your ass."

Ian laughed. "Yes, ma'am."

Luke took a step toward the jet, then stopped and faced her. Her long dark hair whipped up in the wind, and, as it always did, his heart flipped just looking at her. His fiancée. His past. His future. "I love you," he said with feeling, not the rote words of their daily good-bye before he headed to work.

Her eyes lit, and she smiled. "Cool."

He laughed. Her reply only pulled him in deeper. Leaving

Undine for a job would never be easy; they had too much lost time to make up for.

She grabbed his shirt and kissed him one more time. "I love you too. Stay safe, both of you. And bring Ivy back."

"Will do, Undine," Ian said, then climbed the steps to the private jet.

With one last look at the woman who'd become his world, Luke followed Ian up the steps, then gave a low whistle as he took in the plush corporate jet. "This is quite the step up from the military flights we used when heading to a deployment."

"Working for Raptor has its perks."

"Did Keith give you a spiel to pass on to try to recruit me?" Luke asked as he stowed his suitcase in a storage compartment.

"Pretty much. But he also knows it's futile."

"Yeah. I'm out of the game. If this weren't personal, I wouldn't be here."

They settled into their seats. One of the pilots sealed the door, and they were airborne just moments later—a perk of being able to use the small Port Angeles airport—no waiting as they would have at SeaTac or Boeing Field.

Definite perk. But still, Luke wasn't interested. His life was in Washington with Undine, and he was happy working for NOAA—and thankful his bosses had approved open-ended leave at the last minute so he could embark on this mission.

It didn't hurt that Curt Dominick personally made the request, but still, after last fall, his employers were more than happy to give him whatever he wanted, as long as he continued to wear the NOAA uniform. They wanted to move him into public relations, but he'd flat-out refused. He didn't want to be the poster boy for the organization. He wanted to be an anonymous marine biologist. He wanted to continue his study of the effects of sonar on marine mammal navigation.

But today, the whales would have to wait.

"Here's everything we know about Veselov," Ian said, setting a thin stack of files on the table between them. "And here's what we know about Jack Keaton." He set another, even thinner stack on top. "There is a real Jack Keaton. He was in the Air Force. Right age, height, and build for Veselov to pass as him. Eighteen months ago, the real Keaton took off, crewing on sailboats to travel the world. His last known stop was Australia about six months ago. Someone fed Veselov the ID, which has the DIA worried about the real Keaton. They're trying to trace his steps and track him down.

"Veselov showed up in Palau about five weeks after Reeves bailed from the Osprey," Ian added.

Luke flinched. Dimitri Veselov wouldn't have escaped if Luke hadn't let him.

"He set up shop as a charter captain," Ian continued. "And generally ingratiated himself with the locals and American expats very quickly. Took several officials out on multiday trips for free—to get a feel for the ports, he said. Likely he was laying the groundwork for his search. Had a reputation for being congenial. Good drinking buddy, and he knows boats and the water like no one's business." Ian paused. "A good spy is always everyone's best friend. The friendship is usually genuine, or his cover might crack—it's hard to fake it for extended periods of time. As a case officer, I always zeroed in on one trait I liked in the spies I ran and used that to work my way in."

Luke grimaced again. He'd met congenial Parker. He hated that he'd still believed the persona, even after learning he was a spy. "Who invited him to the party?"

"The governor of Melekeok—who he'd taken on several cruises through the Rock Islands. It's possible Veselov chose to target the party, knowing Ivy would be there and he could swoop in and save her."

"I thought it was assumed he got lucky there? He wasn't connected to the men who attacked the party?"

"The DIA believes there is a link between Veselov and the assault."

"According to Ivy, he killed three men on the boat—two of whom were the same men who attempted to abduct her in the mangrove swamp."

"Yes. The DIA believes he betrayed his partners. Probably to further win Ivy's trust."

"Motherfucker," Luke said.

"It gets worse. She told Dominick that she slept with him after the assault—before he abducted her."

"So…if he's had any luck winning back her trust, we can assume Ivy's drinking his Kool-Aid. She may even try to protect him."

"Yes. Given that she willingly turned off the signal for CAM and she hasn't reported in since the initial call when she explained why, it's possible she's protecting him already."

"Everyone seems pretty certain she wasn't involved in Hill's treason," Luke said. "What's your take?" He figured no one else would have as honest an assessment, given that Ian had been the one to take down Hill in the end.

"I wondered when I first met her, but after getting to know her, no way. She doesn't fit the profile. She's not like the women who ally themselves with terrorist groups and arms dealers. Believe me, I know the type. She and Cressida have grown close. She feels guilty in the way that only the innocent feel, like she's responsible for what happened because she didn't see through Hill's lies and couldn't warn anyone."

"Why did she divorce Hill?"

"She told Cressida he was banging an intern."

Luke picked up the file that outlined Veselov's life as

Jack Keaton. He read the statements gathered by the DIA and FBI, surprised that both organizations were willing to pass on the information, but then, Ivy was a senator's cousin and once again, the attorney general was personally involved because one of his wife's subordinates was in danger—and it appeared the DIA had set her up for the bullshit assignment.

DIA was in full damage-control mode and were probably more than happy to have Alec Ravissant privately fund her exfiltration—as long as they did it nice and quiet like and left the DIA out of it.

After he reviewed everything twice, he tapped a name that had popped up in both Ivy's and Veselov's dossiers. "Ulai Umetaro lives in an apartment above his floatplane hangar in the same marina where Veselov lived aboard *Liberty*. They are drinking buddies, and Umetaro was Ivy's pilot for that first week in Palau. We start with Umetaro."

"Agreed," Ian said. "He's the most likely to know where Veselov has been searching for the AUUV over the last few months."

*J*vy rubbed her eyes again as she slouched in front of the computer. It was two a.m. and clear that she was fried, yet she resisted going to bed. Of course, Dimitri understood. The wall between them was impenetrable, but their sleeping arrangements remained the same. "Time to bring RON home and get some sleep," he said firmly.

She tapped the power meter on the display. "There's enough juice to finish the flyover of that island."

"You're so fried, you're liable to crash him into a hillside."

"I suppose you're right." She sighed. "Tomorrow, we need to visit the island. I need to ground-truth the data.

CAM is having trouble identifying a few features and needs calibration."

"Can we go at dusk?"

"I'd rather go earlier. I don't have the same night vision that RON has, and the vegetation there is really thick. My luck, I'd rub up against a dozen poison trees in the dark."

"Fine."

She brought RON back to the cave and closed down the system, then retreated to the lower level. "You coming?" she asked when he didn't follow.

"No," he said. He'd give her the space she needed. "I'm going to sleep on the hilltop. Too hot in the cave." Too hot sleeping next to Ivy, wanting her but knowing it wasn't fair to her. The deeper they got involved, the more she'd want him to fight. The harder it would be for her to face the final outcome.

So he'd leave her alone. Done and out.

She stopped on the staircase and met his gaze, then gave a sharp nod.

He grabbed a sleeping pad and thin blanket from the supplies and climbed the hill. He set up his bed near one of the skylights. He could hear her, guard her, from here.

He stripped down to boxer briefs and lay down. Without light pollution, clouds, or moon, the stars were crystal clear. A vast universe unfolding above him.

It put him in his place, seeing the cosmos. He was but one man, insignificant amid the vastness of time and space. He'd done something good and important once, that night with Luke on the Interceptor. He'd helped save thousands of lives. But even that wouldn't register against the hundred billion planets in the Milky Way galaxy, let alone the multiverse and all the infinite possible universes.

In an infinite number of those universes, he'd never been a spy. In at least one of those, his parents didn't die in that car wreck, and after the Iron Curtain came down, they moved to the US, where he met Ivy in college. In that universe, he probably was a science major of some sort. Marine biology, or astrophysics if that Dimitri could handle the math. They married after graduation and had three kids. Patrick Hill was a goat who was killed in a farming accident, and the man who raped Sophia was never born.

In that universe, he wasn't a killer.

A satellite drifted across the sky, hard to spot among the multitude of stars. It could be a US spy satellite, searching for him, here, in this universe, where he was a spy and an assassin for Team Russia with no future.

They'd better get a lead on the AUUV tomorrow. He didn't know how much longer they'd be able to work together before he did something stupid, like start to hope for a future with Ivy in this world.

Chapter Twenty-Two

"*I*'ve done all I can without visiting the island to calibrate," Ivy said as she stood from the workstation. She checked RON's resting place, the narrow area where floor met ceiling in the dome-shaped space. Ninety percent charged, he'd be ready to fly by darkfall.

"We'll go out an hour before dusk. Tourists kayaking through the channels will be heading back to port then, and we'll be less likely to be spotted."

She nodded. That gave them a few hours to kill. "May as well eat something. What can of food should we open tonight?"

"We could fish. There's a decent beach on the lower inward curve of the island."

"You aren't worried we'll be seen?"

"I'll set out the inflatable kayak. You'll put on your bikini. It'll look like we're day trippers."

She crossed her arms and fixed him with a stern look. "If I'm going to wear the bikini, you're going shirtless."

He laughed. "Of course."

It would be good to spend time out of the cave, to

pretend, even if only for an hour, that she was just a simple tourist enjoying paradise.

It wasn't until she dropped her towel on the beach and reached for the sunblock that she realized her miscalculation. They didn't have any spray, so Dimitri would have to apply it. It was too early in the day and she burned too easily to forgo the lotion.

She held up the bottle. "When you're done messing with the fishing pole, could you...?"

He dropped the rod and reached for the bottle. She lifted her hair and presented her back, bracing herself for his touch.

Which didn't come.

"Dimitri?"

Featherlight touches came, high on her back, but there was no scent of lotion. No rubbing. The fleeting caress of fingers. Like the first night in the shower. He must be tracing the bruise she'd forgotten about.

"Does it hurt?" he asked, his voice hoarse.

"Not since the day...after." The day he'd abducted her, and the pain in her back had become the last thing on her mind.

It must've been too dark in the cave for him to notice it when he'd made love to her, or he'd simply been distracted.

As he had that first night, he kissed the mark on her back, the physical reminder of all the ways in which a man who'd promised to love, honor, and cherish her had betrayed her in the worst possible way.

"I'm so sorry, Ivy. I tell myself I'm better than your ex, but I'm not. I'm worse."

She turned to face him, but then couldn't meet his gaze. She rested her forehead on his chest. "You can't possibly be worse than Patrick." At least, she didn't want to believe it. "If

I tell you why I divorced him, will you tell me who is so important to you, you're willing to abduct me?"

It was unfair, really, this trade. Her story was minor compared, she suspected, to his. But he wanted to know why she left Patrick. Telling what happened was always humiliating, but she'd do it if it meant understanding Dimitri's actions.

He released her and picked up the fishing pole again. After a long silence in which he tied on a hook and baited it with grubs he'd collected from the jungle, he cast the line into the sea, then planted the pole in the sand.

He dropped down on the towel next to her, then plucked the forgotten bottle of sunscreen from the sand and applied the sun-warmed lotion to her back. He ran his hands over her shoulders—more caress than application at that point—and kissed the back of her neck above the bikini tie.

"I'll tell you," he said at last. He leaned his forehead on her back. "I'm no longer certain who is captive here and who is captee."

"I'm no one's prisoner," she said. "From the moment I had the opportunity to shoot you and didn't take it, I've stayed with you of my own free will. Don't for a moment think it's been otherwise, or I'll prove you wrong and leave right now."

He nodded and took her hand in his. "I don't want you to leave. And not because of CAM."

His low-voiced words were exactly what she needed to hear. Patrick had only wanted her for the institute. The Navy only wanted CAM. And the DIA hadn't wanted her to leave Palau even after she'd been assaulted because of what they'd hoped CAM could find for them.

Even if it wasn't true, it was nice to think Dimitri was interested in her for something other than what her high-tech little buddy could do.

"You first," he said. "Tell me what happened with Patrick."

"The simple version is he was banging one of the interns at the institute."

"How very cliché of him."

"I said the same thing when I caught them."

"There's more to it than that, or you wouldn't have remained mum when accusations were flying hard and fast your way. Every reporter covering the story wanted to know why you left him a year before the world learned he was a traitor."

And here was the hard, embarrassing part. She raked her fingers through the warm sand. She drew a triangle, then another, before wiping them away and looking out toward the gently lapping waves. "After we'd been married for three years, Patrick and I began trying to conceive. The timing was right—I was thirty-three and ready to be a mom." She stroked her belly. "I didn't even know how much until we started trying.

"He was in his early forties and had said he wanted to start a family almost from the moment we got married, but it took a little time for my biological clock to catch up with his. For about six months, we were actively trying to get pregnant. The day the test showed two lines, I was so excited, I couldn't wait to tell him."

She closed her eyes. The shock of going from ultimate joy to ultimate pain hit her, even now.

"I went to the office to surprise him, and like every bad cliché you've ever heard, I stepped into his outer office—it was after hours, and Perry, his right-hand man who was indicted along with him, had left for the day. I heard voices in his office. One shrill, young. I recognized the voice. The intern. Twenty-two. She'd been with us for three months, and I'd thought she had a thing for Perry—who, like Patrick, was too old for her. But she was an adult, and it was none of my business as long as it didn't interfere with her work."

She dug her fingers in the sand again. It was grounding, the warmth and texture. She was here. With Dimitri. She just had to accept the pain that accompanied the memory would never fade. "I don't blame her. She was young. Foolish. Starstruck. Don't misunderstand—I was and remain pissed as hell at her—but I can cut a small amount of slack for her immaturity. Patrick did have that charisma. He was hard to resist."

Dimitri's knuckles turned white. Was it wrong that she liked the outward sign of jealousy?

Probably.

"The news articles always made it sound like yours was a marriage of convenience. The logical choice—a merger of MacLeod and Hill."

"If only it were that simple." She closed her eyes. It would have hurt so much less if that were the case. She opened her eyes again and stared out at the turquoise water. "And that right there is one of the reasons I never bothered to set the record straight. They had their own narrative. The truth was irrelevant. The media wanted to paint me as a villain right along with Patrick. They implied repeatedly that anyone cold enough to marry him for his money must be in league with him. If I denied their accusations, they would have said, 'the lady doth protest too much.' I couldn't win. So I said nothing." She raised her chin defiantly. "Sorry to disappoint you, but I married Patrick for love."

She traced another triangle in the sand, swallowing to fight the heartburn that came with admitting her shameful secret aloud. She'd loved Patrick and he'd…he'd sold CAM to terrorists while she was still in the research and development stage.

"Perhaps the only thing more insulting than the press's

treatment of me was being called a whore by the man I'd just had sex with."

"I'm sorry. I was so far out of line."

"Yes. You were." She wiped away the shape. "No one in the press seemed to care there was no *reason* to marry Patrick for a business alliance," she continued. "MacLeod-Hill had already merged. Jessica—the girl. And yeah, I'm going to call her girl, not woman, because she might have been twenty-two, but she was still such a child." She shrugged. "The feminist in me has to justify my word choice, even in private."

"No objections."

"Jessica was upset. Crying. I'm human, so I eavesdropped. After all, a girl was crying to my husband after hours in a closed office." She glanced out toward the sea. Her hand curled into a fist. "Patrick told her she needed to be patient because he couldn't leave me until after I was pregnant. He needed the baby to hold on to the institute, because of the contract he'd signed when we added him to the name. A MacLeod or MacLeod descendant would always be on the board and would have an equal part in all financial decisions regarding the institute. If no MacLeod wanted the task, they could appoint a representative. Patrick was trying to lock up the institute. He intended to steal it from me and use our child to retain control."

She cleared her throat again. "It's humiliating to discover your entire marriage was a lie from the start. I mean, I know I'm awkward. Geeky. As a woman, everything I do will be based on my looks and not my accomplishments. I know I need to lose fifteen pounds and my laugh is too nasal. And I utterly hate it that in that moment, I went into that awkward, insecure place where I felt ugly and undesirable. I have a fricking genius IQ, and I still went to the same low common denominator where I judged myself on my looks and desirability.

"Jessica was young, beautiful, skinny. Probably better in bed. I mean, he actually *wanted* to be with Jessica, otherwise he'd just have sent her on her whiney way. But he laid out his timeline so he could keep fucking her, me, and keep the institute."

She wanted to jump up and pace, but if she did, she might make a break for the jungle, to escape before hearing Dimitri's story. This was the price she'd agreed to, and she would pay it.

"When I confronted Patrick, he went there too. Blamed me for his affair. Don't forget, I still didn't know what he was. I didn't know he was an arms dealer. A traitor. At the time, he was the center of my collapsing world. And he said I was too cold. Too obsessed with my work. It was my fault he turned to a twenty-two-year-old twit for entertainment. And yeah, I knew he was full of shit, but at the same time, it's hard not to hear it, when the man you're in love with says that to you. Hard not to believe it."

Dimitri ran a hand over his face. "And when I said…what you thought I meant, you went right there again."

"Well, yeah. You're the first man I've had sex with since Patrick."

"I'm sorry."

She shrugged. "So in the end, I blamed myself for my sham of a marriage and not the asshole who was a lowlife con man. I felt so utterly stupid. Inadequate. And less than a woman."

"And you were pregnant."

She swiped away a tear. Dammit, she'd thought she was done crying over Patrick's betrayal. "Yes."

He sucked in a breath and held it there. Finally, he let it out in a rush and said, "Did you…?"

"No." She let out a deep sigh. "No matter who the father

was and no matter how mercenary his reasons for providing sperm, I *wanted* my baby."

"So what happened?"

"It was what's known as a chemical pregnancy. I took the test early—more than a week before my period was due—and there was just enough hCG in my urine for a positive, meaning the egg was fertilized and implanted, but for whatever reason, it didn't take. Research indicates up to seventy percent of all conceptions end in miscarriages, which sounds really high, but most women never knew they were ever pregnant. With a chemical pregnancy, usually the period arrives on schedule, as mine did. If we hadn't been trying to conceive, I'd never have taken that early test, never would have known about the chemical pregnancy."

"And you wouldn't have surprised Patrick at the office."

She stroked her belly. Sometimes she felt as if that phantom pregnancy was still a part of her. But then, it had shaped everything that had come later, so maybe it was.

"At first when I confronted him and Jessica, Patrick pulled the classic 'she means nothing to me' right in front of her. My stupid ego… For half a second, there was that gratifying surge, that feeling of being desirable. Being wanted. But I didn't believe the lie for more than a moment, and then he launched into how it was my fault. I didn't tell him I believed I was pregnant. I went to a hotel and tried to figure out how I could get him out of my house, life, and the institute all while carrying his child.

"A week later, he was hosting a big political party for my cousin Alec. I'd been crying nonstop. Was utterly humiliated. Later, I wondered if the crying, if the heartbreak made my uterus inhospitable. You know, so the chemical pregnancy was also my fault." She swiped at another annoying tear.

"I told Alec I had the flu and skipped the party. Late that afternoon, I got my period. That was a shock. I spent the night laughing and crying. Grieving and feeling relieved and then feeling guilty. Basically I was an utter wreck and completely alone. My sister Hazel and I are really close, but she never liked Patrick, and I…I just didn't need that kind of support. I was too raw. Humiliated at work. Homeless. Baby-less." She glanced around the beach. "I could've used an island escape like this one."

She pushed to her feet. She was through the worst of it and could pace without fleeing now. "The divorce was ugly. I wanted him out of the institute, but there'd been a prenup separating the business from the marriage, so that wasn't going to happen. He fired Jessica, then she sued for sexual harassment and named me as one of the defendants. Possibly because I'm so unappealing, my husband had to go hunting among the interns. He paid her to make the suit go away— there was a nondisclosure, so I don't know the details. All I know is he didn't use a dime of MacLeod-Hill money to pay off his mistress. I think he must've used blood money from Syria." Her breath caught. "I suppose it's possible he got the money for selling CAM."

"You could have told the press all this when they hounded you."

"They already hated me. Why would I want to share my humiliation with them?"

"They might've had sympathy for you."

"Right. Have you noticed how kind the media has been to Hillary Clinton for her husband's affair? They attacked her sexuality, her brains, her decision to stay with him. If she'd left him, they'd have attacked her for that. I *had* left my husband. The reason was no one's business but my own."

"You still blame yourself," Dimitri said. "Even knowing your ex is a sociopath and terrorist, you still internalize it."

She grunted an acknowledgment. "I'm a human and insecure in some areas. What he did tapped into it."

"For the record, I think you're the sexiest woman I've ever known. And being with you has been by far the best sex I've ever had."

He said it with such sincerity, she couldn't help but smile. Her ego was easily fed. "I'm supposed to be above these things. To want to be judged by something other than my value as sexual plaything."

"It's not wrong to want to be desirable. That's basic evolution right there."

"My libido died that day, in Patrick's office. I didn't want or even think about sex until you started flaunting your body at the marina."

He grimaced. "I suppose I should admit they taught us to use all our assets in spy school."

She winced. To be taught to use sex as a tool from a young age—if she remembered correctly, he'd been barely more than a child when he started spy school—horrified her. "*All?*"

"If I'd wanted sex training, it would have been provided. But the idea of that left me cold."

"How old were you? When you started?"

"Sex or spy school?"

"Well, I meant spy school, but now I'm curious about sex too."

He stood and crossed the small stretch of beach between them. He slipped an arm around her waist and kissed her. Deep, but not a precursor to anything more. Just a kiss. Sweet and soft. "I was seventeen the first time I had sex—on my own terms, consensual on both sides." He released her and stepped back. "And I was fourteen when I was selected for the embed program. My sister was eleven."

"Your sister?"

"Yes. She's the reason I need to find the AUUV. If I don't, she and her son will both be killed."

Chapter Twenty-Three

*I*t was Dimitri's turn to share, but before he launched into his story, he checked the fishing line—coming up empty. "Would you believe I caught a fish this"—he held his hands three feet apart—"big just last week?"

Ivy laughed. "Never."

He tightened his lips as if in deep introspection, moving his hands an inch closer together. "Well, maybe this big?"

There was something so...north-northeast of normal about the moment. Stranded on a tropical island with a Russian spy. His earnest, silly joke.

For a moment, she felt...light. Like everything would be okay. Or at least not like Spontaneous Combustion Man lurked around every corner, holding lighter fluid in one hand and a blowtorch in the other.

Worst. Superhero. Ever.

And then there was Dimitri. Who, come to think of it, also resembled the actor Ryan Reynolds, just a tiny bit. More Green Lantern in looks than Deadpool. But if she had to choose, she'd go for the darker hero. More Dimitri-ish.

Deadpool with Captain Kirk's eyes. Now there was a superhero she could root for.

She noted that his fishhook was clean of bait. "I suppose it's my turn to collect grubs."

"Not today," he said. "We should head inside and not push our luck being exposed like this." His voice had turned serious. Break time was over.

"Canned tuna for dinner again, then," she said with an exaggerated sigh.

"We can dress it up with ramen noodles."

"What, you're not willing to splurge on macaroni and cheese?"

He smiled and kissed her. "Do I know how to wine and dine a woman or what?"

"Well, at least we have wine."

Dimitri hid the kayak in the jungle, leaving it inflated and ready so they could use it later to row to the other island, then he grabbed his fishing gear and followed her up the path, wiping away their footprints in the sand as he went. The coming evening rain would take care of the rest.

Inside the cave, she witnessed a subtle shift in Dimitri's demeanor and recognized it as the return of his darker self as he braced himself for the coming tale.

"I think this calls for something stronger than wine," he said, making a beeline for the provisions. He grabbed the lone bottle of scotch. "Drink?"

She shook her head and settled in a camping chair in front of the folding table. He sat across from her. "So. Your sister and nephew," she prompted.

"As I said, Sophia was eleven when we were recruited. We'd been orphaned—drunk driver in the other car—and had no extended family. Wards of the state. We were sent to an orphanage. If you know anything about Russian orphanages, I can promise, they're even worse." He cleared his throat. "Officials came looking for kids with high aptitude who could speak English and found us." He paused, then added, "Our mother was American."

Ivy startled at that. It had never occurred to her that he was part American—even legally so. If his mother was born in the US, he had a claim to citizenship.

"Montana," Dimitri said in answer to her unasked question. "She ran away from home at sixteen. Ended up in West Berlin when she was nineteen. She was there for the music scene at first. Travel was allowed from West Berlin into the East with a visa. My mom had friends with family on the East side and made several visits. She met my father, who was from Grozny but serving in the Soviet military, in East Berlin."

"So you're Chechen and American."

He shrugged. "The name Veselov is more Russian than Chechen, and to the best of my knowledge, I have no family in Chechnya. I was born in West Berlin. Raised in Moscow and trained to be an American. I've lived in the US since I was twenty-two. I really don't know what I am."

She shook her head. "Born in West Berlin. You could claim German citizenship too."

"It would take some work to find my birth certificate, and I doubt the surname on the document is Veselov. You see, my mother never told me her last name or why she ran away. She promised she would, when I was older." He shrugged. "Any paperwork that included her maiden name was lost when we became wards of the state—if not sooner."

"You mean you don't know if you still have family in Montana?"

"I probably do. When my parents died, I fantasized about grandparents or aunts and uncles who would claim us. But I gave up those dreams. Dreams are dangerous. Plus, when I was older, I started to suspect what she might've been running from, and that maybe her family wouldn't be any better."

She slid a hand across the table and gripped his fingers. His story was going to be a hell of a lot more painful to share than hers had been.

So her husband cheated on her with someone younger and prettier. *Boo-fucking-hoo*. Sometimes, all one needed was a bit of perspective.

"I was six months old," Dimitri continued, "when my mother was granted a visa to bring me into East Berlin. At that point, she just…stayed. My parents married, and when my dad was discharged from the military, we all moved to Moscow. I don't remember Berlin or anything about living in the former GDR. My first memories are in Moscow, around the time my sister was born."

His grip on her fingers tightened. "When Sophia was six, bullies at school began harassing her because our mother was American, and my mother sat me down and told me it was my job to protect her. I was the boy and was tough like my dad. Bullies never messed with me. I vowed to my mother that no one would hurt Sophia under my watch.

"We were a typical happy family, with the slight oddity of having an American mother in the Soviet Union, until our parents died when I was eleven. After that, we were sent to the orphanage, and there were more bullies to contend with. But I kept my promise. After three years, when we were recruited into the embed program, it was…a huge relief. It wasn't a *home* per se, but it wasn't the hellhole we'd been in. In the program, we were safe. There were no more threats of separating Sophia and me. Food was plentiful and hearty. Our English was an asset, not a reason to pick a fight. We were proud, patriotic Russians." He paused and held her gaze. "It's important to remember, I do love the Russia of my childhood. Hell, I love Russia—the place and people

—*now*. What I don't love is what I was forced to do for the government, and that the country has returned to a dictatorship."

He picked up the shot glass and stared at it without drinking. He set it back on the table. "By that time, the Soviet Union had fallen and the GRU was scrambling to figure out its role in a post-Cold War world. We were part of an offshoot shadow organization, a group eager to retry embedding Russians who could pass as Americans—a program that had largely ended in the seventies—but now was being revamped with extensive training and planning.

"My accent was cleaner than Sophia's, but then, I'd had our mother longer. When I was seventeen, how-to-be-an-American school took backstage to the more exciting stuff—how to fight. How to shoot. Tradecraft in all forms. I was good at it—better than Sophia—but at that point, I was less enchanted with the eventual goal. The training was fun, but the idea of living amongst Americans—my mother's people—and spying on them didn't sound great.

"When I was nineteen, after a six-week test trip to the US where I was able to pass flawlessly, I asked to be released from the program. The powers that be weren't happy. After all, they'd invested years and money on both Sophia and me, and we were the strongest contenders in the program. I was supposed to be just over a year out from my permanent assignment. Initially, they wanted me to establish my identity, then after a few years, join the US Navy. They wanted me to try to get on a SEAL team."

He picked up the shot glass again and this time drank half. He held the glass up to the light. "If I were a good Russian, I'd drink vodka." His mouth pinched as he glared at the glass. "But here I am with scotch." He met Ivy's gaze. "Because I balked, Sophia was beaten with a hockey stick. *My* hockey stick. I'd promised my mom that no one would hurt

Sophia under my watch, and then a sadistic bastard beat her, because of me."

"It's not your fault. Your situation was impossible—"

He cut her off. "Why do you blame yourself for your husband's cheating?"

"Touché."

He finished his shot and set the glass in the center of the table. "The bastard who hurt her miscalculated. He'd just spent five years training me to fight with whatever was at hand. And to pick locks. Climb walls. Track data. Hack computers. You name it. I was a fucking *master* of tradecraft. So I used what I'd learned to find out where he lived. Late one night, I escaped our compound and paid him a visit. I brought my hockey stick and gave him a lesson in the sport. Then I told him I'd finish my training and do my job, but Sophia was out. She was to be removed from the program. Move her to a nice apartment and maybe she could go to regular school, like other sixteen-year-old girls. I also told him that if he ever hurt Sophia again, I'd be back, but next time, I'd bring a puck."

Dimitri cleared his throat. "Sophia was moved out of the facility. They didn't give her an apartment like I wanted. She went into foster care. The family was decent. I was permitted to see her once a month—I needed to make sure the GRU wasn't punishing her for my actions. When my training was complete, I became Parker Reeves. I didn't see Sophia again for three years."

His eyes darkened, and she wondered what he was leaving out. He cleared his throat. "That visit, when I was twenty-five, was the last time I saw her."

How awful to have only one family member in the world and be cut off from that person for a decade.

He grabbed the bottle of scotch and poured himself another shot. "During my visit, Sophia was raped by the same man who'd beaten her when she was sixteen. He made me listen to her screams. He was higher up in the organization then. No way could I retaliate and expect Sophia to live."

Ivy wanted to cover her ears, to hide from the horror of his story. To hide from the pain in his voice, the pain Sophia must have suffered. Instead, she poured herself a shot, knocked it back, and grimaced at the burn.

She lifted her gaze from the empty glass. His blue eyes were unguarded, showing all the pain he must've had to cloak when he lived as Parker Reeves.

"Am I the first person you've ever shared this with?"

"Yes."

"Thank you. For telling me."

He studied his full shot glass, saying nothing.

She could feel him withdrawing, but he wasn't done yet. She braced herself to bear witness to more of his pain even as she nudged him to continue. "Have you been able to stay in touch with Sophia?"

He nodded. "She'd learned all the codes in the training, and we'd spent our evenings developing our own system. We'd known we'd be separated in the US and wanted to be able to keep track of each other without our handlers knowing."

"How did you communicate?"

"The Internet is a spy's best friend. Millions of blogs, news reports, op-eds, published weekly. Embedded within articles were coded messages. All I needed was to search for keywords to find the story and use my decoder ring to decipher the message."

She gave him a skeptical look. "I'm calling bullshit on the decoder ring."

He smiled in halfhearted amusement. "Close enough. The key depended on the date the story was posted among other factors. And on rare occasions, we used the dark web for more direct communication." He sat up straight in his chair and rolled his wide shoulders. "About five years ago, during a dark web chat, she told me she'd been raped again by the same man. This time, she was pregnant."

His gaze was far away. She imagined he saw the computer terminal where his sister's words appeared on the screen and was flooded with the same emotions now as he'd felt then.

His eyes focused once again. "She was ecstatic when Yulian was born. She finally had family. A life. Someone to *live* for. Not just exist. Since she was sixteen, she'd been used as a tool to control me. Yulian gave her joy and purpose." He shrugged. "Of course, Yulian gave them yet another weapon against me. His father and his conception don't factor into my feelings for the boy. I love the little guy with all the love I have for my sister. For my parents."

His eyes teared, and Ivy's followed suit. He cleared his throat. "The ability to love, that's basic humanity, but it's also a human *need*. I'm not a sociopath. I need that connection as much as the next person, but forming friendships and relationships as Parker Reeves was impossible. Every person I met, I was betraying in one way or another. There's only one person in my world who's always known exactly what I am and who I've never betrayed. My sister. She and her son are the only people I can love, so I've poured everything I've got into them. My family."

He bolted from the chair and paced away. He ground the palm of his hand into his cheek. "But the mere fact that I care about them has always been a threat to their very existence."

He paced back to the table and reached for the bottle of scotch but then withdrew his hand and shook his head.

Finally, he puffed out a breath. "This is harder than I thought it would be. Putting it all into words."

"I'm sorry." The phrase was paltry consolation. He wanted to stop spilling his heart, and she wanted nothing more than for him to continue. She rose from her seat, circled the table, and slipped her arms around his waist. She pulled him to her and pressed her cheek to his chest, holding him. She offered nothing more than comfort, something she suspected he hadn't received since his parents were alive.

He was stiff against her for a moment, then his arms wrapped around her back and he tucked his face into her neck. A low sob escaped.

Her heart opened to his grief, and she cried with him, her tears an extension of his. They stood in the dim cave for a long time, her arms around his waist, holding him more than he held her.

Gratitude that he could accept her comfort surged inside her. That she could be his emotional conduit. Everything flowed through her, including strong emotions of her own for Dimitri. He needed to receive love as much as he needed to give it.

He lifted his head and met her gaze, unabashed by his tears. His strength in his willingness to show what some fools called weakness triggered a rush of awe.

He was the strongest man she'd ever met.

But then, it was safe to say she'd never met anyone like Dimitri Veselov. In the short time she'd known him, in spite of everything, she'd come to respect him. And now, she was shocked to realize, she trusted him too. With her life, but also —and this was where things got scary—with her heart.

She searched his gaze, taking in the pain in his eyes, and beneath it, a new calm. "Thank you," he said. "I needed that more than you can possibly know."

But she suspected she *did* know. He had a lifetime accumulation of needing that. Her crying jag in the wake of her marriage falling apart was nothing compared to the emotions he'd bottled up for the more than twenty years since his parents' deaths.

He gave her a wry smile. "I've never even met Yulian. I've just seen a few photos over the years. I suppose that sounds crazy."

"Not at all. I didn't have to meet my sister Laurel's daughter to love her. I loved that baby from the moment Laurel told me she was pregnant."

He pulled her tight against him—this time, he was the one doing the primary holding—for a long squeeze. Then he pressed his lips to her neck and released her.

He stepped back and dropped his gaze to the table, but the unseeing stare was back. She could tell he wasn't thinking about the bottle of scotch or the table. She suspected in his mind, he wasn't in the cave at all.

"When presented with the opportunity to kill off Parker Reeves last fall, I took it. I figured Sophia and Yulian would be safe if everyone believed I was dead." His gaze focused again, meeting hers. "Except they didn't believe it. I told Luke Sevick I wouldn't return to Russia. I knew he'd have to tell investigators. What I didn't expect was someone at the GRU would get wind of it. An informant had to be privy to the investigation because there's no way the US would share that information with Russia. I don't know where the mole is —they could be in the FBI, CIA, DIA. Hell, it could be someone in the Coast Guard, but I'm guessing the list of those who knew the details of my conversation with Luke was damn short."

"But someone in Russia found out, and Sophia and Yulian were back in danger," Ivy said.

"Even worse than before. Because now I was a spy who

didn't return to the fold once his cover was blown. I was—am —a traitor on both sides. A man without a country."

He swallowed hard. His Adam's apple bobbed with the effort. "They were both beaten. Yulian's arm was broken. Sophia had broken ribs and clavicle. They knew…"—he took a slow breath—"they knew she could communicate with me. Knew I wouldn't be able to resist checking for a message from her. So she sent one, passing on clear instructions: report in to receive new orders, or Yulian would lose a finger. One per day. On the eleventh day, they'd start on hers. And on the twenty-first day, they'd both be shot."

She wanted to hold him again but could tell he wanted physical space, so she stepped away, to fight the urge.

"I followed instructions and received orders to find the AUUV."

"But the job—following orders—isn't that simple anymore," Ivy said.

"No. Not simple at all. They don't trust me to deliver, and I'm useless as an embed now. The only thing I'm good for is —" He stopped short, took another breath, then continued. "The only thing I'm good for is one last mission. I have no incentive if they're just going to repeat the cycle of threats and harm to keep me in line. Knowing Sophia and Yulian face ongoing torture is worse than giving up. So we struck a deal. I'll deliver the AUUV, and Sophia and Yulian will be freed."

"Where will they go?"

"I've set aside money for them, and a place to hide. Enough that they can start over with new identities." He glanced around the cave, his gaze landing on the stockpile of supplies. "When you spend your entire adult life biding your time looking for an escape, you have time to plan."

"But you won't join them."

"No. They agreed to give up their leverage against me if I

surrender myself for trial. And by trial, I mean immediate execution. No way would the people I'm dealing with waste time with legal proceedings. These men aren't part of the visible—official—GRU. They're in the shadows of the shadows. I honestly don't know who's pulling my strings at this point."

"What about Yulian's biological father? Is he involved?"

"No. He's dead." His flat tone didn't invite follow up questions. "So there you have it. That's why I abducted you. When Ulai told me two months ago that you were coming to Palau to map Peleliu, I knew you were my only hope.

"I'm going to accomplish one thing before I die. I will get my sister away from the bastards who've been running us since we were kids. To do that, I need CAM, which means I needed you."

He took a step toward her. "I know you intend to steal the AUUV away from me once we find it."

Another step planted him firmly in front of her. All the emotions he'd shared were now cloaked. His eyes were cold in a way she'd never glimpsed before. Here was the hardened spy he'd kept hidden from her. "Don't forget, I have *nothing* left to live for, so simply threatening me with a gun won't work. I can't let you have the AUUV, not when Sophia and Yulian's freedom hangs in the balance. So if you plan to take it, you'd better be prepared to shoot me. My unequivocal death is the only thing that will save them at this point."

Chapter Twenty-Four

The nose of the kayak ran up on the sand, and Ivy climbed out onto the narrow strip of beach. The early evening sun baked the sand. Heat emanated in waves. This was the hottest day she'd experienced in Palau so far, the temperature over ninety degrees and the humidity at ninety-five percent. She wanted to go back to their cave and swim in the cool waters of their hidden pool.

But she had data to field-check, and after an afternoon full of revelations, she needed to focus on work as she processed her reaction. The readings on this island had been promising. There might be another cave here. That was what mattered right this moment.

Dimitri tucked the kayak in the trees, then together they used branches to erase their trail. It wouldn't pass close inspection but would do for the cursory glance of a passing kayaker. Thank goodness they could count on the evening rain as they moved closer to Palau's rainy season.

They slipped into the canopy of the small mushroom-shaped island. Conversation had been strained since Dimitri explained his situation.

He planned to surrender, and she could see no way out for him.

She wanted to build an emotional wall that would make the inevitable somehow acceptable. If only she were a computer, she could build that firewall with code. She knew exactly which commands she'd use. Once it was written, she'd type the final command: RUN. And her heart and mind would be safe.

But no such code existed, because Patrick was a dickhead and she was all too human.

And now here she was, helping Dimitri march toward his death, and she wasn't entirely sure why. She could take the boat now and head to Koror, and he wouldn't stop her. She knew that right down to her soul.

Which meant she was committing treason in helping him.

No. The US attorney general ordered me to help him.

Yeah, but helping didn't include sex. She'd crossed the line when they'd had sex after she knew exactly what he was.

No turning back. The problem was, she didn't have a map for the road forward either.

Everything was a vicious dead end.

"Thinking about it doesn't help," Dimitri said quietly.

She hated the way he seemed to read her mind. "Maybe Raptor could send a team into Russia and extract your sister and nephew?"

He grunted. "You think I haven't thought of that?"

She sighed. "I suppose you've considered everything."

"Repeatedly. I'm locked in but good. For the record, my sister doesn't even know where she and Yulian are being held."

"I might be able to extract that information. If you were able to get online with her again."

"The dark web—which is how we were able to chat—really doesn't work that way."

"I'm familiar with the dark web. There is always a way to force computers to give up secrets. All you need is time."

"Time is one thing we don't have. It's a moot point anyway—Sophia was given access to a computer so she could tell me what happened, but she hasn't been in touch with me since. I have no way of contacting her. This time, I have to play by my puppet master's rules."

She frowned. "Is he here? In Palau? Keeping tabs?"

He shrugged. "I assume so. I wouldn't know, though. As I said, I don't know who is running things now."

"Because the man who raped your sister is dead. You don't know who took his place."

"That man was killed years ago. I knew his replacement and was in direct—albeit coded—communication with him until last November. It appears he paid a steep price for my apparent defection. What I don't know is who replaced him."

"So it could be anyone."

"Yes."

"I don't suppose he could have been on *Liberty* the other night?"

"No way. I'm already doing his dirty work. He wouldn't risk himself that way."

"Who do you think the Russian was, then?"

He shrugged. "Probably one of the mafiosi who sold old Soviet weapons to your ex."

"He said 'underestimate the Hammer, and you're dead.' Who—or what—is the Hammer? Could that be your new boss?"

"It's possible. It also could be a reference to the old Soviet Union, or a code name for someone in his organization. The Russian wanted to take *Liberty*. Maybe he had orders from someone higher up—the Hammer—to take the boat."

"I suppose we'll never know."

It was a good reminder that Patrick's former allies were

still searching for her and CAM, and she was exposed away from their safe haven. She cleared her throat. "Let's go. I need botanical samples for teaching CAM the signatures, and I want to see if there's a cave in the northwest quadrant."

*N*ow he'd out-and-out lied when he could have told her the truth, but he'd long since passed the point of no return. They had to work together to find the magic elixir so she could click her heels and go back to DC. The truth about his other work for the GRU would only turn her against him.

Jesus, why couldn't the Russians have held on to their damn high-tech toy? He suspected his mysterious new boss was the dumbass who let the AUUV slip from his fingers, hence the high pressure on Dimitri to recover it at all costs.

He followed Ivy through the thick vegetation that covered the limestone island, watching the sway of her ass as she climbed the steep hillside.

"Careful," she said, pointing to a nearby tree. "That's poison tree, and the trunk is coated with sap."

He paused and studied the tree. He'd heard of poison tree but hadn't come across one until now—at least not knowingly. He'd never suffered a rash and so assumed he'd been lucky, but now he realized he had come into contact with a few—but they hadn't been weeping sap like this tree.

"The problem is the sap?" he asked.

She nodded. "The leaves can trigger a rash—like poison oak or ivy—I hear you don't want to stand under one in the rain. But the sap is much worse. Contact with the sap can lead to blisters. Bad ones. Often like a second-degree burn."

All at once, his body flooded with adrenaline. "The sap causes *burns*? Real, actual, second-degree burns?"

"So I hear."

"*Sonofabitch*," he muttered.

"What's wrong?"

"The guy who stole the AUUV—he had what looked like first- and second-degree burns over seventy percent of his body. It's believed the burns killed him."

"Well, he was tortured, right?"

"He was, but burns like that…that's not a way to get information. Waterboarding. Starvation. Sleep deprivation. Tried and true methods that cause suffering but don't tip the scale toward actually *dying*. The guy was burned—and my source said his interrogators claimed they didn't do it."

"They could just as easily be lying to cover their asses."

"That was the consensus. When he was taken, there were no blisters. So it was assumed his interrogators were overzealous and burned him to get him to talk."

"How do you know all this?"

"Photos. Video. Reports. I was given everything I'd need to find the AUUV—except money, a boat, and actual mapping equipment. I was expected to come up with those on my own."

"And so you did."

"Nothing prepared me for you, for embroiling an innocent in my shitstorm."

She held his gaze before returning to the key point. "Poison tree doesn't kill. It's a rash that blisters, like poison oak."

"A severe reaction combined with torture? The stress alone could overload a heart. Best speculation, the poor guy went into cardiac arrest, and his interrogators didn't know what to do. No medics, no one who would recognize the signs that the stress was too much for him. This wasn't a sanctioned operation. The front office of GRU wasn't running the show.

We're talking third-string hacks doing damage control. And the poor bastard died."

"And you think he was exposed to poison tree?"

"It's possible. If so, the exposure was severe."

"But the blisters didn't develop until *after* he'd been taken into custody." She frowned. "A severe rash like that means he either brushed up against a sappy tree or was standing under one in the rain."

"Or he buried the AUUV in the roots. Either he didn't know what it was, or he knew poison trees would be avoided at all costs, making it a damn good hiding place."

Chapter Twenty-Five

*U*lai Umetaro had departed for Kayangel Island and wasn't expected to return until evening—if then. Luke and Ian moved to plan B and went to the hotel where the party had been held. They walked the edge of the mangrove swamp, assessed the layout of the property, examined the ballroom, and spoke with hotel employees about the party and aftermath of the attack.

Task complete, they returned to the rental car. Luke started the engine and stared out the window toward the turquoise sea.

"I'm no investigator," Ian said, "but I know how cells work. It's my guess they knew Ivy was in the garden. The assault on the party was a distraction. From what the hotel manager said, these guys weren't prepared to dig in and use the hostages to their advantage. They had no long game, or even a short one, which would fit the suicide operator. The fact that the three men in the ballroom were taken alive is unusual."

"If they knew she was in the garden, why not just take her there? Why reveal themselves by attacking?"

"She wasn't alone in the garden," Ian said. "She was with Dimitri Veselov."

"That would indicate that they weren't allied with Dimitri —unless the whole attack was to win her trust." Using Parker's real first name still felt strange on Luke's tongue, but it was a form of conditioning for facing the man. He would adapt and use every tool at his disposal. Speaking to Dimitri as a friend was perhaps his greatest weapon—presuming Dimitri had a conscience.

"It's either-or. Yes," Ian said.

"If Dimitri *isn't* allied with them"—Luke's most fervent hope at this point—"then how did they know where she was and it was time to attack? They wouldn't have spent hours waiting on the off chance she'd step outside on her own. You heard what the manager said, the garden was all but abandoned during the party."

Ian's answer was quick. "They'd have needed an inside man at the party—one whose job it was to get her outside, but then Dimitri did it for them."

"Think we can convince the local cops to show us the security video from that night?" Luke asked.

"I think we have better odds of that than of getting to interview the men in the holding cells."

Luke put the rental car in gear. "Let's give it a shot, then."

It ended up being easier than they'd hoped. Upon arriving at the station, they were introduced to Assistant Special Agent in Charge Kaha'i Palea, who'd been dispatched to Palau from the FBI's Honolulu Field Office. The Palauan police had invited the FBI into the investigation, because it involved both US interests and terrorism. More importantly, Luke learned, Agent Palea knew Curt personally. One phone call to the attorney general was all it took to authorize the agent to consult with Ian and Luke, who were acting as private investigators, hired by Alec Ravissant to track down his cousin Ivy MacLeod.

Nice and legal, and they wouldn't have to be skirting local and federal authorities in their search.

The men who'd been arrested at the party, they learned, weren't in holding cells in Palau. They'd been sent to the US military base in Guam, where military investigators could question them in Arabic. A disappointment, because Ian's Arabic was fluent, but odds were they couldn't—or wouldn't —offer clues as to where Ivy was at this point anyway.

Credentials established, they settled down in front of a monitor with Agent Palea and a local police officer to watch the security camera footage from the party. First, the party unfolded at high speed, but they slowed the playback speed once Ivy arrived. "We're looking for anyone who pays undue attention to her," Luke said to the local officer pointing to Ivy on the screen.

For thirty minutes, Ivy was in full meet-and-greet mode. The local officer identified the men she spoke with: the Palauan president, governors, other local officials. Several paused to chat, but, reading Ivy's expression, none of the exchanges were of note.

"We're coming up on when she meets Keaton," Palea said as they watched Ivy break away from a small group and head toward the bar in the corner. She received a drink and turned to face the crowded ballroom. Her profile was to the camera. After a moment's hesitation, she stepped into the fray. It appeared she was heading toward the president when a man bumped her from the side in a move that could only be intentional. Her drink splashed on the man's shirt.

"Who is he?" Ian asked.

"And where did he come from?" Luke added. "I didn't see him earlier."

"He's there," Palea said, "But his back was to the

camera." Palea instructed the officer to back up the recording. They watched again, but instead of following Ivy, they followed the unknown subject, or UNSUB, as Palea called him.

There were scant few seconds of footage, and as Palea had indicated, he kept his back to the camera.

"Not only was he aware of the cameras, he's afraid of them," Ian said. "Which means someone might recognize him."

"I don't think I've ever seen him," the local officer said. "But it's hard to know without at least a profile."

"There's a glimpse of him at the end, but not much," Palea said.

Luke stared at the image on the screen. The man's clothes and hair were perfectly nondescript. "Go back to where he intercepts Ivy."

They moved forward again in time and watched Ivy's drink slosh in slow motion. The film quality was good enough on zoom to see Ivy's mouth move—likely apologizing—and she tried to step away, but the man grabbed her arm.

Ivy's body language hinted at her irritation, but she stayed and nodded when he asked her a question. Several minutes later, two men joined them, forcing the UNSUB to adjust his angle toward the camera. They now had one ear and a hint of jawline.

Luke recognized the first man as the governor of Melekeok, who'd chatted with Ivy earlier. "Who's the guy with the governor?" he asked the cop.

"Shiro Kimura from the Japanese embassy."

"He upset Ivy," Ian observed.

Luke didn't know Ivy at all, but he had to agree from the look on her face.

"He can be a dick. But he helped bring down one of the terrorists," the officer said. "He needed stitches afterward."

He stopped the video. "That's Jack Keaton." The officer's voice was more buoyant.

It made sense that the FBI hadn't informed the locals about Veselov. On the surface, Ivy's disappearance had nothing to do with the party—the locals only knew she'd been assaulted in the garden—the search for Ivy and the Russian assassin was classified as need to know. The locals were cooperating of their own accord, so they had no need to know.

Dimitri Veselov joined the four people clustered in the corner near the bar. Ivy's face lit up at something Dimitri said.

"He's a good guy," the officer said. "Beat the crap out of the terrorists, as you'll see in a moment."

Luke couldn't judge the officer based on his attitude toward the hero of the night. Once upon a time, Luke had shared his opinion of Parker Reeves.

He studied Dimitri's face. He'd seen other photos lifted from the video—ones Palea must've supplied to the FBI and DIA. This was nothing new. But still, it felt personal. Seeing Parker like this after all these months.

He helped me save thousands of lives. Including Undine's. Maybe my mother's. Major cities could have been destroyed along with long swaths of coastlines.

Was Dimitri Veselov a hero then and now? Or was he playing a different role here?

He cleared his throat. "Keep going," he said to the officer. He wouldn't get any answers to that vital question from this video.

It only took a moment for Dimitri to talk Ivy into leaving with him. Or maybe it was the other way around. Hard to say without sound.

The moment Ivy and Dimitri disappeared from the frame, Shiro Kimura turned to leave, brushing against the mystery man, who was too busy watching Ivy leave to see the bump coming. For a brief moment, his face turned toward the camera.

Next to Luke, Ian sat bolt upright. "Back up. Pause on the bastard's face."

The officer did as instructed, zooming in until the image pixelated, then backing up until it was clear again. They only had one eye, a line of cheek. But apparently, that was enough for Ian.

"Motherfucker," Ian said.

Luke studied the image. "I take it you recognize him."

"Yeah." He glanced sideways at the officer. "The details are classified. Sorry."

Luke took that to mean it was CIA business and he and Palea would get the full story later when they didn't have company.

"We're going to need a printout of that image," Ian said. His hand curled into a fist. "And you'll want to post it in the squad room." He glanced at Palea. "He's wanted by the FBI for treason and a host of other crimes."

Awww, shit. Suddenly it made sense. This was one of Dr. Patrick Hill's men, and Ian knew him—well enough to recognize him with only part of his face visible.

"He's changed his appearance, but not enough for someone who knows him." Ian met Luke's gaze. "Good news for you, Sevick. No way was your boy in league with the men who attacked the party."

"How can you be certain?"

Long-banked anger burned behind Ian's eyes. "No chance in hell would a chickenshit like Zack Barrow run the risk of being caught in the ballroom just so someone else could win Ivy's trust. Barrow was the inside man—probably because he could pass for an American party guest. I'll bet anything that when he watched his prize walk out the door with another man, he called in the others." Ian slammed the side of his fist on the desk. "And, I'm the dumbshit mother-fucker who drilled it into him that he always needs a backup plan. He called me his mentor."

Luke wasn't the only one here who nursed guilt over misjudging a former ally. Luke, at least, had the hope that Dimitri was still playing for the right team, while there was no doubt Zack Barrow—whoever the hell he was—was aligned with the kind of scum he and Ian had spent years trying to isolate and eradicate.

It was time for Luke to show Ian the card he'd received days ago. Maybe, if Dimitri really wasn't a threat, there was a chance he'd left a trail of crumbs for them to follow.

He hoped so, anyway, because they sure as hell needed to find Ivy before Zack Barrow did.

Chapter Twenty-Six

$\mathcal{I}$vy marked the location of the sap-covered trunk on the computer tablet that acted as her field map. When she got back to the cave, she'd find the tree in the database and use the data to teach CAM the infrared signature for sap-covered poison trees. With that data, she could isolate every weeping poison tree within the target area and it would simply be a matter of a second flyover with the drone and an intensive scan of the landform and tree-root system.

"This will take a few days," she said. "To get the data isolated and extracted. If we're wrong, and the AUUV is underwater after all, we're screwed."

"It's the best lead we've got," Dimitri said. "I say we focus on it instead of the broad survey."

They finished exploring the island. If there was a tunnel in the rock, it was a natural void—she could find no entrance that led to the anomalous reading taken by RON the night before.

It was strange, the feeling of homecoming she felt when they returned to their island haven. Shelter, food, water, and Dimitri. This would be quite a life if it were sustainable.

But she had family in DC: her parents, two sisters, a niece, her cousin, and his fiancée, Isabel.

The wedding was next month at Alec's estate. It would break her heart if she missed it.

She had a life, and a damn good one at that, even if the last two years had been difficult.

Plus, she'd promised herself she'd pursue artificial insemination once CAM was complete. Her marriage had fallen apart, but that didn't mean she'd stopped wanting a child.

While Dimitri provided an emotional connection she hadn't realized she'd been missing, he couldn't replace everyone she cared about. Not that he was offering to run away with her. He'd made it more than clear that he'd never endanger his sister and nephew that way.

Best for her to focus on CAM and the search and forget about Dimitri altogether. She immersed herself in the work, her lifeline, sleeping only when RON's batteries recharged, eating when Dimitri insisted. She'd probably forget to breathe if it weren't an involuntary reflex.

When she wasn't working or sleeping, she mentally mapped Dimitri's contours, taking in his ridges and lines. Committing his body to immutable storage so he would remain unchanged and she could access the memories when he was long gone.

She dreamed about coding and crawled out of bed at four a.m. on the eighth day since she'd met Dimitri, the fifth day since they'd retreated to their own private island. An idea had come to her that required troubleshooting. Two hours later, having isolated a variable that would make it easier to separate vegetation layers, she crawled back into bed beside him.

He woke as the air mattress shifted. His reaction was startling considering he'd been deeply asleep a moment before. He pinned her to their air mattress. "You're supposed to wake me if you get up. For your safety. Even if you're only visiting the latrine."

"I didn't leave the cave." They'd agreed she wouldn't leave the safety of their hiding place without letting him know. Not even to relieve her bladder. Not because he needed to control her, but because she could be taken.

Others were on the hunt for the AUUV. The danger was very real. The longer they were in the cave, the easier it was for her to forget, become lax. Dimitri battled that with increased vigilance.

"Were you working?"

"Yes."

"Tell me next time. Even if you don't leave the cave. You were close to the entrance. Even if you screamed, I wouldn't be able to get to you in time."

She couldn't see his face in the dark cave, but she heard in his voice something that reminded her of when she'd been wearing the headphones on the sunbathing deck on *Liberty*. His voice held more emotion when she couldn't see him. Probably because without an expression to read, she listened better.

"I'm sorry. I'll tell you next time."

His hands cupped her face. She wished she could see his eyes. "I'm falling in love with you, Ivy, which means you're in more danger than ever. More danger than my sister and nephew, because you're here, while they're in Russia and out of reach."

All drowsiness left her.

"You're falling in love with me? You've barely talked to me for three days. And we're stranded on an island together."

His lips were on her throat and trailed along her neck to the sensitive spot just below her ear. "Because I thought it would be easier for us both if I stayed away. But it didn't make it any easier. And now I feel stupid because I'm on short time as it is, and I'm wasting it."

He nibbled on her earlobe, then nipped at her jawline, moving toward her lips. Then his mouth was on hers, and she let him in.

He kissed her deeply. She reveled in it and kissed him back, taking over when he would retreat. She opened her thighs, and his body settled against hers, pushing her deep into the air mattress that needed more air.

He finally lifted his mouth from hers. "This isn't fair to you. I'm endangering you."

She ran her hands over the stubble on his cheeks and chin. Texture to add to her mental map. "I'm needed to run CAM. There is no interface. I'm the only person who knows the commands. And frankly, I keep changing them as CAM learns the terrain."

"But once we have the AUUV, all bets are off." He kissed her neck again. "I'll kill anyone before I let them hurt you. Anyone."

"I know." After all, she'd seen him do it. Maybe it hadn't been intentional, but all three men had died just the same. "What happens when we find it?" she asked softly.

"I contact my handler and arrange for the exchange. You'll call whoever Dominick has sent for your exfiltration— my guess is Luke and maybe the former CIA operator, Ian Boyd. They'll take you back to DC, and I'll hand over the AUUV."

"Nothing is ever that simple."

"No. But close enough."

He would be killed, likely executed on the spot. The thought made her want to vomit. Instead, she stroked his chest and tried to wipe away the vision of a Dimitri-less future. "Make love to me."

"I shouldn't. It's not fair to you," he repeated. "All I can give you is right now."

"There's something else you can give me." The words were a low dry whisper, spoken before she even knew if she could follow through and state the wild, dangerous idea that had tickled at her thoughts for days.

It was a future, of a sort, for him, and also what she'd wanted desperately for years.

"What do you mean?" Dimitri asked.

"You could give me a child."

Dimitri stiffened against her, then pushed back as if to rise, but she grabbed his shoulders. "Please, Dimitri. I want a baby—I'd planned to attempt in vitro when I get back to DC. I'd already started reading through the sperm catalogue. And it's not like there are any guarantees. I'm two weeks out from my period, so I'm probably ovulating, but that doesn't mean it will take. Believe me, I know that better than anyone. But I'd like a chance. I'd like to think maybe, when all this is over, a piece of you will live on."

"No." His voice was hard. Cold. "Absolutely not."

She cupped his face. "I would love your baby with every ounce of my soul."

"But don't you see? A baby is another weapon. My God, I can't imagine what the GRU would do to my own child."

The reverence in his voice on the words "my own child" told her he wanted what she offered, even though he feared it. "But they'll never know it's yours. And if you…if you really don't survive this, they'll have no reason to hurt the baby or me."

"And if they take me prisoner instead of killing me on the spot, it would be torture knowing you were unprotected."

She pressed her mouth to his. "Then we won't let them take you prisoner."

He buried his face in her neck. "It's not that simple. My love is poison, and that's all it can ever be."

"Please, Dimitri. I want a baby. I want *your* baby. I want someone to love when all this is over. I want a piece of you to live on, for you to be a father."

*D*imitri could barely breathe. She was offering him the one thing he'd never dreamed he'd have. Which he still wouldn't have. He'd be gone, and his child—if she conceived—would grow up fatherless.

And ah, fuck, if he gave her this, he'd have to try to live. He couldn't give up when he had a son or daughter who needed him.

He closed his eyes and imagined Ivy pregnant with his baby, and a wave of possessiveness unlike anything he'd ever felt washed through him.

His baby. His Ivy. *His.*

All at once, he loved this child who didn't exist. It wasn't even an embryo, yet his body lit at the prospect. His primal core, his hard wiring, drove him to touch her, to slide his hand beneath her panties and stroke her clit. Biology told him to take her offering, fulfill a natural predisposition to reproduce. But his heart…that was where he lost the battle. His heart wanted to stake his claim by planting a child within her.

It was primal. Raw. Fierce. A perfect mirror for how he felt about her. He wasn't lying when he said he was falling in love with her. He'd slipped over that edge days ago.

Now she was offering him the only form of immortality available to humans. And, oh God, it was embarrassing how he wanted it. Proof he was human after all.

"Make love to me, Dimitri," she whispered. "Give me a piece of you."

His voice was hoarse as he said, "No one can know the baby is mine. If you get pregnant, that's the one thing you can't tell *anyone*, not unless you're certain I'm dead. As in you've seen my body with your own eyes, *dead*."

"No one will know."

He thrust his pelvis against hers. "If we do this, it won't be sweet. It won't be tender. It will be hot and animal. A fuck to end all fucks. I've never had sex without a condom before, and honey, I'm going to enjoy this in all its primal glory."

He kissed her then, holding nothing back. As promised, his kiss was hard and primal. He owned her mouth as he would own her body. "You're mine, Ivy. You'll always be mine."

She nodded. "Yours. Always yours."

He explored her body methodically with his mouth. Enjoying every shape and texture. "Just so you know, when I was in the Coast Guard, we were tested regularly for STDs. I haven't been with anyone but you since my last test. I'm clean."

"You're perfect," she said in a husky voice as she slid her hand across his abs, under his briefs, and stroked his erection. "I was tested multiple times, months apart after I learned about the cheating. I'm clean too."

He pulled her T-shirt over her head and licked her breasts. "These tits are mine."

She laughed. "Yours."

He reached to the side and found the power strip for the lights and flicked it on. "Dark won't do. I'm going to see all of you."

She was gorgeous, splayed beneath him. He sat up and moved to her side so she could spread her thighs and he could play. He stroked her clit, then slipped two fingers inside her vagina. "God, but you are beautiful. Don't ever listen to anyone who tells you otherwise. They're either blind or they have an agenda. You're strong and tall, and you have these gorgeous curves." He stroked her hip, his hand trailing upward to cup her breast.

He leaned down and whispered in her ear, "And when I'm done with you, you're going to need to buy some serious hardware, because you won't be able to *imagine* ever fucking another man."

She panted out a laugh as he stroked her clit.

He nibbled at her lips, then slipped his tongue in her mouth, a tease, not letting her suck on his tongue. "Your mouth is *mine*."

"Yours," she repeated. "And I want to taste you."

He scooted up on the bed and slipped his dick into her mouth. She took him, and he groaned with the sensation. He pulled out, but she sucked him back in.

Why had he wasted days when he could have been making love with her? Stranded on a deserted island in the tropics with the most amazing, sexiest woman he'd ever met, and he'd spent his days and nights *working*?

He pulled out of her mouth, then settled between her thighs. "Let's do this, then."

She gripped his shoulders and pressed up against his cock. He positioned the tip at her vagina. Unsheathed. What a glorious thing. He paused to look, to watch so he could enjoy the moment with all his senses.

He slipped the head in and groaned. He pulled out, just to savor the moment. He thumped his cock on her clit, dampening her with precum, then rubbed with his thumb, causing her to pant and groan.

He dipped his cock back into her opening. Again just the tip, watching her face as he stroked her clit and ever so slowly filled her, one thick inch at a time.

The sensation was exquisite. Just like Ivy. He paused when he was in as deep as he could go and leaned down and kissed her. Her thighs were wrapped tightly around his hips. He was home at last.

He lifted his mouth and held her gaze. He pulled out just as slowly as he'd entered her. She was slick and hot and everything he ever wanted.

"I love you," he said, then thrust hard and fast. She met his thrusts with her own, and they rocked together in a rhythm as old as time.

Right now, this was the only multiverse he wanted to be in.

Chapter Twenty-Seven

"It's done," Ivy said as she leaned back in her chair and stretched her neck. "I've isolated every poison tree on the ten islands within the circle of highest probability of being the AUUV's hiding place, along with the closest five islands outside the circle."

Dimitri stood behind her and planted his hands on her shoulders. He dug his thumbs into the muscles, and she groaned with pleasure. "Your shoulders are a mess," he said.

"All this computer time is killing my back." She tilted her head back and batted her eyes at him. "Maybe before we go find the AUUV, we can spend the day at a spa where I can get a ninety-minute, four-hand massage?"

He dropped a kiss on her lips. "I'm afraid you'll have to make do with my lousy two hands." He leaned down and whispered in her ear, "But you'll get more than ninety minutes of pleasure."

She laughed. "I'm going to hold you to that promise. And your hands aren't lousy." She tapped the mouse and directed his attention to the monitor. "Based on your specs for the AUUV, I think our best shot of finding the little beastie is in one of these seven locations." She toggled the display, and the seven areas changed from green to red. "They're large enough, and three of them have the potential for caves under the tree's root system. I want to send RON to do another flyover of each location before we attempt a physical search. We might be able to find it without leaving this cave, and we don't want to get up close and personal with poison tree sap unless we have to."

"As soon as it gets dark, you can send RON."

"I could do the closest island now. We haven't seen any boats in the channels in two days."

"Too risky. We'll stick to the night flying."

She flicked the sleep button on the computer. "Well then. For the first time in days, we've got hours to kill with no work to do. Did you happen to include a deck of cards in the stash of goodies down below?"

"I don't think so. Why?"

She stood from the chair and grabbed his T-shirt. "I was going to challenge you to strip poker."

He grinned and cupped her ass. "How about we just strip instead?"

"You promised me a ninety-minute massage just a few moments ago."

"Keep in mind, I never promised to massage your *back*."

"If Jack Keaton doesn't want company, then it's not my place to help you find him," Ulai Umetaro repeated.

"But he does, Mr. Umetaro. He sent me this card to bring me here." Luke tapped the card he'd set on the workbench that lined the wall just inside the pilot's floatplane hangar.

Umetaro flicked the card away. "Rubbish. Anyone could have posted that."

Luke wasn't buying his act. He'd seen the man's eyes widen when he saw the card. Ulai Umetaro knew something.

Ian returned after walking the U-shaped hangar well to admire Umetaro's de Havilland Beaver seaplane. "She's a beauty, Captain. Any chance you'd take us for a flight?"

"Charter's booked for the rest of the week, mate. Sorry."

"I thought Ivy MacLeod booked you for the whole month?" Luke asked. He was bad cop in this scenario. Palea had opted out of this interview. He'd questioned Umetaro twice already to no avail and believed Ian and Luke would have better luck in their unofficial capacity with the card from Dimitri as their ace in the hole.

Umetaro spit into the water. "Nah. Just two weeks. When she didn't show for the second week, I had to take what jobs I could to make up for the lost income."

Ivy had been off the grid for five days. Her friends and family back in DC had passed frantic in their worry.

Luke and Ian had spent the last two days running down leads in Koror with Palea, as they waited for Umetaro to return from a second trip to Kayangel. The only new information that had come their way was forwarded to Palea by the DIA. The real Jack Keaton had been tracked down in Madagascar. The man was happy and healthy, but a dead end as far as information on Dimitri was concerned.

As they waited for the seaplane pilot to return to Koror, Ian and Luke had outfitted a boat for cruising the Rock Islands. If Umetaro hadn't returned this morning, they'd have set out already.

"We'll pay you twice the going rate," Ian said.

Alec Ravissant had given them carte blanche over the budget for this job, and Luke knew that for Ian, the search was more urgent knowing that Zack Barrow was here and on the hunt for Ivy.

"Where do you boys want to go?" Umetaro asked. His thick accent thinned the longer they talked. Umetaro was an interesting man. He seemed like he'd been playing an exaggerated version of himself until Luke presented him with Dimitri's card.

"Rock Islands," Ian said.

"That's a little broad. Have a fancy for a particular island?"

"Wherever it is that Keaton has spent the most time in the last few months," Luke said.

Umetaro stood. "Tell you wot, if Keaton calls me and says he wants to talk to you, I'll pass on your number."

Luke rolled his eyes, while Ian gave the man his Raptor business card and, Luke suspected, at least two hundred dollars. "There's a sat phone number written on the back, for when we're out of cell phone range."

"I'll let you know if I hear from him."

They thanked the man and left the enclosed hangar and proceeded down the dock to the yacht they'd rented. Once they were aboard, Luke asked, "Did you plant the tracking device on the plane?"

"Yep. He knows something. Bet he flies out of here in ten minutes."

"Nice of you to give him gas money," Luke said.

"If he's going to lead us to Veselov, I figured it was the least I could do."

For the third time, they heard a plane pass over their refuge. Ivy glared at the cave ceiling. The solar panels on the hilltop might be missed on a first or even second pass, but a third flyover was a bad sign. "What do we do?"

"I'm going to swim out through the tunnel and see who it is." Dimitri rolled from their mattress and reached for his Under Armour briefs and shirt.

"With scuba?" Ivy asked as she grabbed her own discarded clothes from the cave floor.

"No time."

"Dammit, Dimitri, it's too dangerous!"

"I've done it many times."

"I don't care. It scares the hell out of me."

"Scarier than being snuck up upon by one of your ex's cronies?" He wrapped a hand around her neck and pulled her to him and kissed her, hard and fast. "Do you remember the PIN for the satellite phone?"

"Yes."

"Good." He grabbed the neoprene holster with his Sig sealed inside and strapped it on. "If I'm not back in thirty minutes, or if you hear gunfire, use the phone. Call Curt Dominick and give him your coordinates. Then shoot anyone who tries to enter the cave, unless you know it's someone Dominick sent. It'll take a team of SEALs at least an hour to mobilize from Guam."

He turned to the water, then glanced over his shoulder, giving her a meaningful look. "I love you," he said, then took a deep breath and dove into the pool.

He disappeared in the dark depths, his bubbles lost to the rippling surface.

She hadn't had a chance to say the words back. She didn't know if she could, so maybe it was for the best. But now she held her breath in unconscious sympathy, wondering how long it would take him to traverse the tunnel and surface again.

Given the pounding of her heart and panic in her soul, she suspected she did love him.

She should have insisted on exploring the tunnel herself. They had scuba equipment. She might feel better if she knew what he was facing.

Or that might make her feel even worse.

He could drown here. Now. And she wouldn't know he was in trouble until it was too late to help him.

She ran a hand over her belly and wondered how she'd cope if she never saw Dimitri again.

*R*elief washed through Dimitri when he recognized the floatplane. Ulai Umetaro's Beaver. It could only mean one thing: Luke Sevick had arrived and had shown Ulai the card.

Dimitri had stashed a radio in the vegetation for just such an occasion, and made a beeline for it. Ulai knew what frequency Dimitri would use. He hailed the pilot, and a moment later, Ulai responded.

Dimitri told the pilot where to land, then returned the radio to its hiding place and made his way up the hillside to the cave entrance. "It's safe, Ivy," he shouted before entering the tunnel. "Ulai is here." He dropped down to all fours and crawled through the entrance. "Which means we're going to have more company in a few hours."

He emerged into the upper chamber, blinded momentarily by sunlight that angled through the skylight. He blinked as he stood upright and realized it wasn't the sun at all. One of the floodlights had been angled to shine on the tunnel entrance. In the darkness behind the light, he could just make out the face of a man who'd spoken with Ivy at the party in

Koror. The man had one hand over Ivy's mouth, the other hand held a gun to her temple.

Chapter Twenty-Eight

"It seems your company is already here," the man said.

"Who are you?" Dimitri asked. He didn't look at Ivy. He couldn't. He had to stay focused on the intruder and figure out how the hell they'd been found, and what the man intended now that he had Ivy.

"No one you know." He ran the gun across Ivy's temple. "I gotta admit, I was pretty pissed when you took Ivy away that night, but damn, then I did a little digging and decided I'm grateful. I was just there for the mapping equipment and the girl, and then my little Russian Bratva friend identified the Hammer.

"Well, knowing the Hammer was involved, I got curious about what Mother Russia was after. Now I get CAM and a brand-new prototype AUUV. Plus, you got rid of the Russian for me. Fucking jackpot."

He kissed Ivy's other temple, all while watching for Dimitri's reaction.

Only a lifetime of training allowed him to pull off an indifferent shrug.

"You're good, Veselov," the man said. "One might even think you don't care. But I was listening to you fuck like rabbits through those convenient skylights." He released Ivy's mouth to squeeze her breast. "So tell me, was your last 'I love you' a ploy? Or did you really fall for a honey trap?"

He ran his hand down her side. Ivy remained stiff and mute.

"Ivy was up to her eyeballs in her ex-husband's business. I should know, I was Hill's case officer. She's playing you, man. Imagine that. The Hammer played by an Amazonian computer geek with great tits, but not much else to speak of."

"Who. The fuck. Are you?" Dimitri asked.

The man shrugged. "You won't be around to tell my old mentor, Ian, so no harm in introductions. Zack Barrow. Formerly CIA. Now I freelance."

It brought bile to his throat to hear the scumbag use words so similar to what he'd said to Ivy when he revealed himself.

"I was never in Patrick's business," Ivy said, her voice shaking with anger.

Good, she was more angry than scared. That would help her. And Dimitri. "I know," he said.

"Touching, but we really should get the AUUV," Barrow said. "So I can take CAM and split before Ian gets here."

He pushed Ivy forward, toward the computer console. "Show me where the bad man hid it, babe, and I'll make sure the boys in Syria are sweet to you when you teach them how to use CAM."

Ivy inched toward the sleeping console.

Dimitri felt the weight of his gun at the small of his back. He knew exactly why Barrow hadn't taken it from him. He'd listened long enough at the skylight to know seeing a gun to Ivy's temple would incapacitate Dimitri. Plus, he knew getting close enough to disarm him would be lethal. The Hammer's reputation in spy and mafia circles was well-earned.

The gun at Ivy's head was effective. He wouldn't go for his weapon as long as there was a bullet that close to her brain.

He needed to keep the prick talking so he could find an opening. "How did you find us?"

"You tell him, love. I get tired of repeating myself." His smug tone told Dimitri all he needed to know about the man's ego. Barrow was so proud of himself, he wanted to hear his exploits from Ivy. But he also wouldn't do the talking, like Dimitri wanted.

Zack Barrow wasn't dumb, but he was narcissistic. Which could make him blind to his mistakes and faults. Dimitri could use that.

"It was RON," Ivy said. "He guessed we were flying RON at night, and patrolled the islands from sunset to dawn, looking for it."

"It took a few nights to spot it," Barrow interrupted. "And then I had the general area. The next night, I had my own drone ready. It followed RON back here." He tsked. "You broke the number two rule of spying." His gaze flicked to Ivy. "And the number one rule. One: don't fuck the girl who might be a honey trap. Two: don't stay in one place too long. Plus your drone didn't utilize a surveillance detection route. Sloppy."

He flashed a grin. "Look at me, giving advice to the Hammer. My mentor will be so proud."

The sound of a plane landing in the narrow channel between this island and the next drowned out the rest of Barrow's boasts. Once the noise faded, he continued. "Hurry your ass up, Ivy. If your pal Ulai is coming, Ian is sure to follow, and I really don't want to see my mentor until *after* I have the AUUV in hand. Then I can give him the attention he deserves."

She stood before the computer. "It's shut down. Startup is biometrically coded to me."

Barrow stood behind her, his gun at one temple, his mouth at the other. One hand on her belly. He ground his hips into her ass. "So do it."

Dimitri would rip the motherfucker's head off.

"It's a three-part biometric code."

Ivy was lying. First, the computer was only sleeping, not shut down, which meant no need for biometric login. But also, the biometric security required only one step. The weight of his gun was heavy at his back. He doubted he'd have time to grab it.

"First it must scan my left retina, then my fingerprint, and then my ear."

Fucking brilliant. Ears were as unique as fingerprints, and this would force him to lower the gun.

"It all has to be done quickly too. Delay too long and I have to start over. Three mistakes and it's game over."

Barrow pressed tightly to her back. "Do it."

She elbowed him in the chest. "Give me room! I have to do this right."

Barrow gave her a scant inch of breathing space, and Ivy leaned her eye toward the apple-sized infrared scanner built in to the console. Barrow followed her motion with the gun. She reached toward the scanner with her left thumb in the same moment she turned her head slightly to expose her ear. The barrel no longer pointed at her head, and she punched the gun upward with her left hand.

The gun went off as Dimitri lunged and took Barrow in a chokehold, shoving him into the limestone floor. The gun fired again, and Ivy yelped.

Dimitri smashed a fist into the man's face and kicked the

gun from his now slack hand. Barrow slumped. Dimitri checked his eyes. Unconscious. Bleeding from the nose. Possible skull fractures. Breathing. All that mattered was making sure he was out so Dimitri could tend to Ivy.

He turned to see she had blood on her arm and face. Her eyes were wide with shock as she held her forearm.

She gazed up at Dimitri, fear in her eyes. "I think my arm is broken."

"We've got to stop the bleeding." He lifted her arm above her head. "You okay with this?"

She nodded.

"Are you going to pass out? I have a first aid kit below. I need to get it."

"Go. Hurry."

He bolted down the steps and grabbed the kit along with a radio. He called to Ulai as he took the stairs two at a time. "Ivy needs to go to the hospital. Now. Bring the plane as close to the shore as you can and I'll carry her to you."

"What happened?" Ulai asked.

"Gunshot wound. I'll explain later."

Ivy had slipped to the floor and leaned against the cave wall with her arm raised and resting across her head. Blood seeped between her fingers, dripping over her face. Her pupils were dilated and her breathing uneven.

"You're going to be okay, sweetheart." He pulled out a bandage, the kind medics used in war zones because they were packed with clotting powder, and wrapped it around her forearm. "Once the bleeding is stopped, we'll get you on Ulai's plane. He'll radio the hospital. They'll be ready for you. You're going to be fine."

"Good thing I'm right-handed."

He smiled. "They'll set the bone, and you'll be good as new."

"Volleyball is probably out, though."

"For a while."

"That's okay. I hate volleyball." Sweat covered her brow and trickled down her neck. She sucked a breath between her teeth. "Getting shot…h-hurts. Even when it's just in th-the arm." Her skin had paled. "I feel…dizzy."

He touched her forehead. Cool. Clammy even. He glanced at the unconscious man slumped on the floor. He needed to tie him up but feared Ivy was going into shock. Her breathing was rapid in addition to the clammy skin and dizziness. He needed to get her out of the cave and to the floatplane, fast. "We've got to get you out of here, Ivy."

"Pack up…pack up CAM," Ivy said. "And RON. I need to keep them with me."

Dimitri shook his head. "That'll take too long. You need to get to the hospital right away."

"You just want to use it…" She panted with pain. "To find the AUUV."

He took a deep breath and reminded himself she had good reason to make that accusation. He cupped her face between his hands, the blood on her cheek slick against his palm. "I love you, Ivy. Getting you to the hospital immediately is the only thing I give a damn about right now. You might be going into shock. I need you to try to breathe slower. You need more oxygen."

She nodded. "'Kay." She took a long, slow breath. "Not at my best right now." She winced, and he imagined pain had just pulsed up her arm. "Wonder if labor pains are anything like this?"

"I hope you get to find out in nine months."

Her smile was more of a grimace, but he'd take it. "Me too."

He grabbed a fresh bandage from the kit and removed the first one. A glance at the wound showed the clotting agent had begun to work. He wrapped the new bandage around her arm, then fitted a sling around her that held her arm in a snug V-shape against her chest, with her left hand at her right shoulder.

He scooped her up in his arms and headed for the entrance. "Now that the bleeding has slowed, I'm going to pull you through the tunnel."

"I can crawl."

He set her down by the opening. "No." He dropped beside her and lay on his back, then pulled her onto his chest. "Ready?" he asked.

She nodded, and he scooted headfirst on his back, hauling Ivy through the tight space. It took precious minutes to get through the tunnel, but she made it without passing out, and her breathing was steady by the time they emerged. Her pulse had slowed. With the bleeding under control, they might've avoided her going into full-blown shock.

Thank God.

He picked her up and slowly descended the steep slope.

By the time he reached the beach, Ulai had the plane close enough that Dimitri could wade out with Ivy in his arms. Ulai helped him position her in the rear seat of the floatplane.

"Stay awake," Dimitri said, "until you get to the hospital. Breathe slowly. You're going to be okay, but you need to be conscious so you can tell the doctors what happened."

"You aren't coming with me?" Her eyes widened.

He shook his head. "I need to deal with Barrow."

"You'll come to the hospital as soon as you can?"

He nodded but deep down suspected he was lying and already hated himself for it. To Ulai he said, "After you get her to the hospital, bring Luke here—if there's someone who can guard her. She's still in danger."

"Will do, Major."

"I was never an Air Force major, Ulai. I lied."

"I know. I always knew. You might know a lot about airplanes, but you're no pilot." He handed Dimitri a business card and said softly, "Keep in touch." With that, Ulai waved him away.

Dimitri retreated to the beach and watched the Beaver take off, wondering if he'd ever see Ivy again.

Chapter Twenty-Nine

*D*imitri returned to the tunnel entrance and pulled out his gun. This was every operator's worst nightmare—a blind tunnel with a known enemy on the other side.

He should have tied Barrow up, but Ivy had been in bad shape and she was his number one priority. Now Dimitri had to crawl through the tunnel and hope Barrow was still unconscious. And he wouldn't mind if the asshole was bleeding out.

He inched through the opening, moving as silently as possible. He paused before emerging and listened. Silence.

Gun at the ready, he exited the tunnel. A quick scan of the chamber showed...nothing.

Fuck.

A blood trail led down the steps. He followed it, scanning carefully, prepared for Barrow to pounce.

Nothing.

The former CIA agent was gone. The blood trail stopped at the pool. He must've swum out through the tunnel—knowing it was possible thanks to listening at the skylight.

It would be too much to hope the bastard got stuck in the narrow tunnel.

Once he was certain the cave was empty, Dimitri set to work, moving quickly in case Barrow decided to return. He woke the computer and pulled up the final map Ivy had created, the one with red areas marking seven potential hiding places for the AUUV. He copied the data onto a chart he'd grabbed from the chamber below. He had no intention of being here when Luke or Ian arrived, but he wouldn't take CAM with him. He couldn't betray Ivy in that way.

If the AUUV was in one of the other locations that Ivy hadn't flagged as high probability, he was fucked. He deleted the last map layer and turned off CAM—now it would need Ivy's fingerprint at startup—and descended the stairs to grab his escape kit.

He donned a wetsuit, then grabbed a dry bag filled with three days' worth of supplies. There was another cave on a nearby island with supplies and a kayak at the ready. He was moving on to Plan C.

And once again, he was alone.

*I*an found the tunnel entrance without much trouble. Veselov hadn't bothered to erase his passage the last time. The opening was practically neon lit and just as Ivy had described.

He considered calling out to give Veselov warning that he was about to enter, but there was no way in hell the sonofabitch would be there. There might be someone in that cave, but it sure as hell wouldn't be the Russian spy.

He hoped it would be the American one, and he had no intention of tipping Zack off that he was here. He crawled through the tunnel silently, gun at the ready.

Ivy would be waking from surgery soon, and would want to talk to Veselov. He didn't envy Luke's job of telling her that her new boyfriend had taken CAM and fled. Of the two of them, Ian knew her. She'd had dinner at his house and was friends with Cressida.

She was friends with *him*.

He should have drawn that straw, but Zack Barrow was his first priority. Ivy would understand.

He emerged into the upper chamber—again, just as Ivy had described—and his eyes adjusted to the afternoon sun that beamed down from openings in the rock. First his gaze landed on the spatters of blood on the walls and limestone floor, then he took in CAM and the assembled drone in the corner.

Well. He'd been wrong on one count. Did that mean Veselov was still here?

"Hammer?" he said, his voice bouncing off the cavern walls.

No response.

No sign of Zack, but a blood trail led down the steps. He followed it to the lower chamber where it ended at the pool.

Shit.

He'd expected this, but his anger spiked nonetheless. Too bad Veselov hadn't used the ball-peen on Zack.

Zack must've left in a hurry, or he'd have taken CAM. He probably escaped while Veselov carried Ivy to the floatplane —or Ian would be seeing signs of struggle, including a more dramatic blood trail.

The boat Ivy had told them about was still hidden in the vegetation near the beach, which meant Veselov had swum to his next destination. He couldn't have gone very far.

Zack was a different story. He probably had a boat full of allies not far away. The question was, would he go after Ivy or Dimitri?

Ivy had said they'd zeroed in on possible locations for the AUUV. The assassin hadn't given up, he'd simply moved on.

Cold, when Ivy was in the hospital having surgery to repair a gunshot wound, and it was obvious she was infatuated with the Russian.

Which card would Zack play?

Ian returned to the upper chamber and studied the computer. It was shut down, which meant only Ivy could start it. He'd pack it up and bring it to her. They'd use it to find Veselov before he found the AUUV and made his escape.

Ivy was the key. To the AUUV. To Veselov. And to Zack.

He needed to call Luke, the CIA, FBI, and his boss to tell them all what he'd found in the cave. But he had one other call he needed to make first. He stood under the largest skylight in hopes of making a connection and dialed the number on his satellite phone.

Cressida answered on the first ring. "Well?" she asked, the single word as anxious as he felt.

"Sorry, honey. Zack got away."

"We knew that was likely." He could hear the disappointment in her voice.

"True." His gaze fixed on the trail of blood. "The good news is he bled. A lot. And Ivy said it was a head wound."

"Well now, there's a reason to celebrate."

Ian smiled. "He's still here. He's after CAM and the AUUV. We'll get him."

"You will. But protect Ivy. She comes first." Cressida paused. "Is Veselov—?"

"Gone."

"If what you suspect about their relationship is true, that's going to crush her," Cressida said.

Ian fixed his gaze on CAM and the drone. "I just hope she's right about him. Because Dimitri Veselov would make a dangerous enemy."

☠

*I*vy woke in stages, logic being the last thought process to come online. Disoriented, it took her a moment to grasp the concept of hospital room. Well, really more medical clinic, and a small one at that considering Palau's population was lower than that of her outer-beltway hometown in Maryland.

Her arm was numb, as though it didn't exist. Surgery, she remembered. To remove the bullet, clean the wound, and set the bone. They'd used a general anesthetic in case they needed to use metal pins to connect the bone.

She looked toward the man sitting in her visitor's chair. Luke Sevick. She'd told him and Ian as much as she could before the surgery.

"The break was relatively clean," Luke said. "But they did have to rebuild the break with metal reinforcement."

She offered up a weak smile. "Please tell me they gave me bionic parts."

He smiled back. "Sadly, no. Your arm is splinted for now. The doctor said they won't cast it until after the swelling goes down in a day or two."

"Thank you. For staying with me. I know you wanted to go with Ian."

He tilted his head to acknowledge her thanks. "Zack Barrow escaped."

She'd feared that, but she had another concern. "And Dimitri?"

"He wasn't in the cave either."

If she wasn't drugged from the surgery, she might feel more pain—or even relief—at that statement, but as it was, there was a veil that separated her from really feeling. "And CAM?" she asked. She doubted any drug could mask the pain she'd feel if Dimitri had taken CAM.

"Ian found both CAM and the drone in the cave."

A tear spilled down her cheek, but her brain was too fuzzy to quite understand why. Happy or sad, she didn't know.

"If you have any idea where he's gone, Ivy, you need to tell us. There are things about Dimitri you don't know."

"He told me you were friends. That he trusts you."

Luke's lips flattened. "I no longer trust him."

"Is it true he was the other man on the Osprey? He helped you that night?"

He gave a sharp nod.

"If you'd failed, he would have died right along with you and everyone in the Osprey. He risked himself just as much as you did, with one difference. He knew exactly what he was facing when he stepped on the ferry that night. You and Undine were clueless. For you, it was just a PR event. But he knew, and still he got on the boat."

Luke's nostrils flared, and she knew she'd hit a nerve. She rubbed her eyes with her one good hand. The world was becoming clearer by the second.

"He's a spy. For Russia. And in case you haven't noticed, our relationship isn't as sweet as it was in the early post-Cold War era. Don't fool yourself into thinking they're our allies."

"I'm not. But Dimitri Veselov is—our ally, I mean." She closed her eyes and asked herself if she could betray Dimitri's secret to Luke. Would Luke use Sophia and Yulian in the same way Russia had? Dimitri had feared the US government would use them, but Luke wasn't government—well, he was in the uniformed service for NOAA, but that wasn't armed forces. Luke was here as a private citizen. Seeking an old friend, or settling a score?

His attitude suggested the latter, but something in his expression suggested the former. Luke wanted to believe in and maybe even help Dimitri. She believed it in her gut.

A knock on the door was followed by a man poking his

head inside her small clinic room. When the man saw she was awake, he stepped into the room. "I'm sorry to disturb you so soon after surgery, Ms. MacLeod. I'm Assistant Special Agent in Charge Kaha'i Palea, from the Honolulu FBI Field Office. Curt Dominick asked me personally to handle this investigation, and I have a few questions for you."

There went the idea of telling Luke about Sophia. This man *was* government.

She pressed the button to raise the head of her hospital bed so she was almost sitting up. "Of course, Agent Palea. I'll do anything I can to help you track down and arrest the man who shot me—Zack Barrow."

"We're just as interested in the man who abducted you, Dimitri Veselov."

"Dimitri didn't abduct me."

The agent's brow furrowed. "I was under the impression that you told Attorney General Curt Dominick in a text message conversation that you'd been abducted by Veselov."

She frowned. The anesthesia must still be clouding her brain. She should have seen that coming and tried a different tactic. She cleared her throat. "I thought he had, but not long after that conversation, it became clear that not only was I not his prisoner, but that he was protecting me. I'd be in Syria right now if not for Dimitri Veselov."

"You are aware, Ms. MacLeod, we don't need your testimony to convict him on the theft of top secret military technology."

She shrugged. "I hear the Navy is getting it back. And he never actually touched the cases or equipment without my permission. CAM was always under my control."

"We're on the same side, Ms. MacLeod."

"I'm not entirely sure of that, Agent Palea. You see, my country—the government I work for—sent me to Palau with top-secret equipment, intending to use me as a spy, without warning or assistance. That's not feeling like the same side to me. So if you're here hoping I'll help you go after Dimitri, when he's the one person who *did* protect me when my government failed, you're going to be disappointed."

He sighed. "Regardless, I need to question you." The agent—whose name, features, and accent indicated he was hapa, if not full Hawaiian—cast a sideways glance at Luke. "I'm afraid my questions will get personal."

This man was sent by Curt, which meant she could trust him, but in the back of her mind was the memory of FBI interrogations she'd suffered right after Patrick's arrest. They hadn't always played fair, and a few agents had twisted her words to make her sound like she'd confessed to something she'd known nothing about. Up until the night in the mangrove swamp, it had been one of the scariest experiences of her life.

"Lt. Sevick stays," she said firmly.

Agent Palea cleared his throat. "Fine, then. I understand you had sexual relations with Veselov on the night you were attacked in the mangrove swamp. Did that relationship continue after you were made aware Veselov was a Russian spy?"

*C*urt stroked Mara's back as she leaned against him on the sofa. He had at least a half-dozen calls to make, but right now he needed to be a husband, and holding Mara was his number one priority.

She'd been battling severe nausea from the moment Ivy disabled CAM's tracking beacon, likely a combination of stress and morning sickness, but the result had been difficulty keeping food down and he'd been worried for her and their unborn child.

She'd managed to eat and hold down a decent-sized meal after Luke called to say Ivy was back in Koror, but the news that she'd been shot had tempered their relief.

"I can't help but feel like it's my fault, Curt. I was so excited we finally got the funding for the survey, I didn't question why."

He kissed her temple. She'd been beating herself up for days, and no amount of talking could convince her she was blameless. It didn't help that she was more than a little angry with him for telling Ivy to cooperate with the assassin.

He blamed himself too.

He'd fucked up, but from what Luke had told him, Veselov *had* protected Ivy. Zack Barrow had been the one who fired the shot.

Without Veselov, Ivy could well be en route to Syria right now.

His cell phone rang, vibrating against his chest where Mara pressed against him. She leaned back and pulled the phone from his breast pocket.

"It can wait," Curt said.

She frowned at the screen. "It's Fredrickson from the DIA. You'd better take it."

"I'll call him back."

"What if they've called another damn meeting and left you out of the loop?"

Mara was right. Fredrickson was the only person within the DIA who kept Curt informed in a timely manner. He took the phone and swiped the screen to answer. "Rudy. What's up?"

"The briefing I just received on the situation in Palau is pretty ugly for Ivy MacLeod. The boys here know they fucked up, and now it sounds like they're going to hang MacLeod out to dry. There's even speculation she and Veselov were colluding from the start."

Curt's head throbbed, and the look on Mara's face as she took in his reaction to words she couldn't hear made him worry for her health.

"That's bullshit, and everyone knows it."

"I wish it were that simple, but there is evidence she called Veselov twice prior to her departure for Palau."

*D*imitri held the satellite phone in one hand and Ian Boyd's business card in the other. He needed to know how Ivy was doing. One call. He might even get to speak with her.

But every contact was a risk. Raptor might have technology to track his location through the phone.

It was easier this way. It would hurt Ivy, but she was going to hurt no matter what.

He shoved Boyd's card back in his pocket and dialed the number he'd memorized months ago and which he'd been reporting in to on a weekly basis, a requirement of their bargain. The phone was answered on the first ring.

The Russian on the other end of the line used a voice distorter as before. Dimitri didn't know if the person was male or female, young or old. "You have acquired the AUUV?"

"Not yet," he said in Russian. "But I expect to find it soon."

"You are taking too long, Veselov. Your sister suffers while you waste time fucking the cartographer."

He tightened his jaw against issuing a denial. Nothing he could say would protect Ivy. The person was fishing for a response. He wouldn't fall into that trap. "Send your man to collect the AUUV. Have him wait at the new resort in Koror. I will have it in two days."

"We wish to amend our arrangement."

"No fucking way. You will release Sophia and Yulian, or you won't get the AUUV."

"We will still release your sister and nephew. That hasn't changed."

"There is nothing else you can offer me that I want."

"Not even your own life? A chance to be with the cartographer?"

Were they fishing, or did they know something? If they had an inside man in the FBI, CIA, or DIA, then everything Ivy said would reach his handler's ears.

"We'll release you from your commitments to Mother Russia," the person on the line continued, "if you kill Luke Sevick as you were ordered to do last fall."

"No. I won't kill for you again."

"You don't understand, Veselov, this isn't up for negotiation. If you don't kill Luke Sevick, Ivy MacLeod will die."

Chapter Thirty

"You push too hard. He'll never kill Sevick."

"I don't want him to kill the SEAL."

"Then why issue the order?"

"Because we can't have him balking because of love at this point. Now he'll be too afraid for MacLeod to step out of line. Make him choose between Sevick and MacLeod—his honor or his love—and he'll be off his game during the handoff."

"He might not love the woman."

"This is the Hammer. He kills without remorse, but he has never used a woman for a mission in this way."

"Because he never needed to."

"He could have used Undine Gray. She was vulnerable when she had the panic attack, and he could have cemented his role as her dive partner—which is what he should have done. He didn't. Be grateful I know how to push his buttons, because you could never take on the Hammer by yourself. If he realizes who you are, you don't stand a chance. If I'm right, then he's just fallen in love for the first time. He's finally got a reason to live and won't be taken easily. But with

MacLeod's life hanging in the balance, he'll fall in line to save her."

*H*e had to stay one step ahead of everyone and come up with a new plan for handing over the AUUV. A warning to Luke was in order, to protect both him and Ivy.

Scenarios ran through his head as he paced the tiny cave. He followed each one to the logical conclusion, and no matter how he played it, someone died. Sometimes it was Luke. Sometimes Ivy. Usually it was Sophia and Yulian.

He'd planned carefully. Sophia would video chat with him from a specific hotel in Taiwan. From there, she and Yulian would travel to the Philippines and then on to Jakarta, where he had stashed enough money for them to start a new life wherever they chose. Sophia knew her way around the dark web and had the language skills and tradecraft to obtain passports and whatever else they needed.

But now he needed to control the whereabouts of Ivy and Luke while Sophia and Yulian were en route to safety—without revealing his own location. He'd enlist their help, except he was fairly certain Luke was honor bound to take Dimitri in custody, and he had Ian Boyd with him to make sure he followed through.

If Dimitri were taken, Sophia and Yulian were dead. And Ivy was vulnerable.

This was his every nightmare come true, why he didn't get attached, refused to make friends. Refused to fall in love.

"*I*t took me days to make the poison tree map," Ivy repeated. "We didn't back up to the Navy database because Zack Barrow and his terrorist buddies knew how to track the signal. The information is gone, and it would take me the same amount of time to recreate it." Not entirely true, but close enough.

"Gone because Dimitri deleted it," Ian said.

She nodded. What could she say? The Raptor operative was pissed at Dimitri, and frankly, so was she. But she also understood why Dimitri had done it. Explaining to Ian and Luke served no purpose except to further alienate the two men who'd traveled halfway around the world to rescue her.

Luke had sat right there in the room when she admitted to the FBI agent she'd had sex with Dimitri after she knew the truth about him.

Luke and Ian didn't trust her judgment when it came to Dimitri, and she couldn't really blame them either. In their eyes, she was a pathetic fool who'd fallen for her captor.

She needed their respect if she was going to be able to use them to help Dimitri.

"Surely you remember something," Luke said.

She did, but she kept her face blank. Her acting skills were improving. She hoped. "The area was huge. There are lots of poison trees. I didn't memorize it because we had the database."

She paced the hotel room. She'd been released from the hospital after twenty-four hours, and now here she was, back in the hotel where her ordeal began. Her arm throbbed and was in a sling. She'd get a hard cast tomorrow, but for now it was splinted and bandaged, and she was taking strong painkillers that couldn't mask the fear and hurt she felt both for and because of Dimitri.

"He's searching for the AUUV right now. You can help us

narrow down the area and find him," Luke said. "We want to *help* him, Ivy."

So maybe her acting skills weren't improving. "You want to detain him. That's why you came to Palau, isn't it?"

"No," Ian said. "Alec sent us to Palau to rescue you, but you refuse to leave."

She shrugged. No way was she leaving before the AUUV was found.

"We're going to take a boat out and search near the cave island with or without your information," Ian said. "But that involves risk to us. Don't send us in blind."

The guilt she'd been battling over lying settled in her belly. Ian was a good guy. He'd taken down Patrick. Cressida was a friend, and she'd be pissed that Ivy wasn't doing all she could to help her boyfriend, who'd come all this way to rescue her. Then there was Luke Sevick. He'd been nothing but kind. This was a shitty situation all around.

In keeping her silence, she was betraying her friends and her country. But to lead them to Dimitri...that was another betrayal.

It was Russia's lost AUUV, and Dimitri was returning it to them. His actions weren't actively against the US. Not here.

But she doubted anyone else would see it that way.

She cleared her throat. "Take me with you."

"No fucking way," both men said in unison.

She crossed her good arm over her bad and tried to hide her wince at the motion. "Way. Bring me and CAM, and I'll use RON to find him. I'll recreate the poison tree map."

"You're injured," Ian argued. "And it's dangerous. Zack and his men are still out there. They want CAM—and you."

"I thought you were in the personal protection business," she said to Ian. "And my cousin is paying you to protect me." She glanced down at her sling. "And I'm right-handed. I can still work the computer."

And fire a gun. Maybe.

"Fine," Luke said. She turned to face him, and from the set of his jaw and light in his eyes, she suspected she'd walked right into his plan. Ian was here to protect Ivy, but Luke... He was here for Dimitri, and the jury was out on whether or not he considered Dimitri a friend or foe.

Ivy was to be his bait.

She turned and marched into her private room in the large hotel suite. Her cousin was sparing no expense for her lodging. Alec had been so mad when Ivy explained to him why she refused to leave Palau. But he was family, and he trusted her. So he grudgingly agreed.

She stopped dead in her tracks when she saw the orchid on the pillow. Her gaze flew around the room. She lifted the bedcovers, but no one hid beneath. The closet and attached bath were also empty. She checked the lanai, surprised to find the French doors were unlocked. The lanai was empty too. Search complete, she finally collected the flower and note from the pillow.

The orchid was the same peach color as the one he'd given her that first morning, and the note was in the same crisp handwriting.

Ivy —

My handlers know about us. About you. About how I feel. You're in danger. Luke Sevick too, because anyone I have affection for will always be used against me. You and Luke must leave Palau, now. Also, the security on your lanai sucks. Surely the CIA trains their agents better than this?

— DV

She gripped the flower in her fist. How did his Russian handlers find out about their relationship so quickly? Zack Barrow knew, but he'd wanted to steal the AUUV for himself, so he wasn't on Team Russia.

She had no doubt the FBI agent had shared the information up the hierarchy. Likewise, Luke and Ian had likely made it known to Alec and Curt in their debriefings. Thanks to the FBI agent's questioning, and Ivy's lack of acting ability, she had few secrets.

But everyone who knew about Ivy's relationship with Dimitri was on Team USA.

Unless there was a mole hidden in the system.

"$\mathcal{W}$e should have told her what the Hammer is," Ian said after Ivy returned to her room in the suite.

"And risk alienating her from Veselov when she's our best chance for bringing him in?" Luke said in a quiet voice. "No way."

"She might be even more anxious to bring him in if she knew the truth. She regrets not warning anyone about Hill. This could be her chance to make up for that."

"Maybe, but we can't take the risk. Dimitri will come to her if he believes she cares. But if he caught wind of the fact that she hates him? He'd know it was a trap and stay far away. She's not good at hiding her feelings. You saw her in there. She all but broadcast she knows exactly where Dimitri is searching."

"I hope you're right, Sevick, because taking Ivy and CAM out to play bait when she's injured is damned dangerous." Ian ran his hands through his hair. "You're sure the Hammer isn't a threat?"

"I'm not sure of anything when it comes to Parker Reeves or Dimitri Veselov anymore. But I think Ivy is in love with him. If any of that emotion goes both ways, we have an opportunity to take him in, get the AUUV, and save Ivy. Isn't that what we came here to do?"

Chapter Thirty-One

*D*imitri stared at the tree. The trunk was coated in sap, and according to CAM, there might be a void under the roots. He'd have come here first, but two other islands had been closer. Better to check them on the way and be methodical.

But standing here, facing the tree, his gut said this was it.

Thunder boomed in the distance. The evening rain was coming soon. Great timing. Poison tree and rain was a bad combination, according to Ivy.

He scanned the roots of the tree and the surrounding area. If the AUUV had been hidden here, it was five months ago, and nature had long since covered up the intrusion.

No help for it except to dig—which he'd done at the base of four other poison trees on two islands already, yielding nothing but sore muscles and the potential to break out in a blistering rash sometime soon.

Good times.

He broke the dirt with the spade, probing to see if there were voids he could exploit. When he found none, he chose what seemed like the most likely spot and began to dig in earnest. This was where RON would've come in handy. Ivy had explained her specialty in remote sensing—more than Lidar, she'd also equipped RON with ground-penetrating radar to glimpse below the surface without touching a shovel.

Digging in an archaeological site, she'd explained, was a destructive process. Documenting a site destroyed it. So archaeologists had turned to remote sensing, ways to gather data without ruining the site. It was why her process of mapping the Peleliu battle site was preferred—thousands had died and destruction was also desecration. But remote sensing could find the remains without disturbing them. The best of all worlds.

But he didn't have Ivy anymore nor her technology. The truth was he missed the woman a hell of a lot more than the machines he'd abducted her for to begin with.

CAM might make this easier, but Ivy would make it fun.

It killed him not to know how she was doing. He'd wanted to wait for her in her hotel room, to surprise her and hold her and make love to her one more time.

But only a fool would take that risk when Luke and Ian would be right outside the door.

He doubted she would follow his instructions and leave, but he'd had to try. His next step was to contact Luke and convince him. Luke would never leave on his own account, but protecting Ivy was a different story.

At least they had Ian Boyd for backup.

The shovel hit limestone, and he grimaced. So much for his gut feeling. He adjusted, moving a meter south, and tried again.

He was on his fifth probe—following the technique Ivy had described for attempting to find or explore the boundaries of archaeological sites—when the shovel slipped through the soil and disappeared nearly to the end of the handle.

He'd found a void.

He dug with renewed energy. Thirty minutes later, he had an opening. A tunnel under the roots of the tree, just as CAM had predicted.

Rain was starting to fall as he crawled into the void. Maybe his wetsuit would protect him from the toxins. All he could do was hope. And strip as soon as he was done here.

Did the Chechen cling to the same feeble plan? Was Dimitri repeating his mistakes?

Would Dimitri too be found, taken, and tortured?

He had to dig as he crawled and wondered if the tunnel would collapse behind him. Days from now, Ivy and CAM might find him, delirious with thirst and hunger, desperate and pained from the blisters caused by tree sap.

It was a shame there was no Occupational Safety and Health Administration for spies. The hazard pay would be out of this world.

He'd never officially received a paycheck from Russia. Every dime had gone into a numbered account, which Sophia would find out how to access when she reached Jakarta.

He held on to that thought. Sophia and Yulian would be free.

Ivy… She might carry his child.

It was crazy the emotions that thought brought with it. He'd never realized how much he was ruled by biology. How much he'd had a need to fulfill that genetic imperative.

But dammit. He wanted to *be* there. To see Ivy's belly grow. To witness sonograms and listen to heartbeats. To hold his daughter or son. To cheer for first steps. To hear his baby call him Daddy.

Ahh, fuck, and wasn't this a shitty time to want the impossible?

He pushed through soil and vines. Crawled through musty earth and poisonous roots.

Fuck it.

He couldn't have any of the things he wanted, but he could save his sister and nephew. He could save Ivy and Luke. He could do one damn thing right before he died. But to do that, he had to find the AUUV to draw out the sonofabitch who was calling the shots in his life.

He would die before this was all over, but he wasn't going alone. This handoff would happen in person, or it wouldn't happen at all.

He felt something hard in front of him. Limestone, probably, but he probed it with gloved fingers.

Smooth surface. He pulled off the dive glove that protected his fingers—getting a rash hardly mattered at this point—and palpated the surface. Cold, but not stone cold.

Plastic cold.

He wiped dirt from the surface as more rained down from above. He pulled out a flashlight and shone it on the object with one hand while he wiped the dirt away with the other.

He brushed away more soil, his light exposing a wide, curved panel that could be a wing, tucked up against the fuselage, like a bird's wing tucked against its body.

Sonofabitch. He'd found it.

Or CAM had found it.

Either way, he had the AUUV, and the endgame had begun.

Chapter Thirty-Two

The house on Peleliu was untouched since Dimitri's last visit, and had everything he needed to wait for the exchange. It even contained the tools he needed to open up the AUUV and see what secrets she held.

The AUUV was the length and width of a surfboard, but with wings that tucked in, like an eagle that could transform into a seal. The organic design felt more Asian than Russian to him. But he wasn't an engineer, so what did he know?

He carefully opened the panels to access the data ports and power pack. He didn't really give a damn if he returned the AUUV intact—the deal was he'd hand it over, not that it would be functional—but he didn't want to advertise that he'd cracked it open, if he could avoid it.

The design was impressive. Lightweight, durable, and sleek housing. Watertight, yet it could transform shapes and launch from the water to take flight, or dive from the air and swim.

But the feature he found most worrisome was when he powered up the AUUV after it had rested under a poison tree for five months, it *worked*.

It had a hibernation mode that lasted for months, meaning it could be planted in a strategic place and be called into action much later. The ultimate sleeper spy.

He quickly powered it off, in case it could somehow contact its home base, although that had been Russia's problem to begin with—the person who hijacked it had disabled the two-way communication with Russia. They could no longer control it by remote, and couldn't locate it to recover it themselves.

Whoever had stolen the AUUV must've been able to hack the code to hijack it in mid-flight or swim. Was it possible the AUUV had been on a mission and not just on a test run when it was taken?

Could there be data here that would be valuable to the US—or damaging to Russia?

The technology the AUUV represented was one thing—a tool for the new Cold War, and highly advanced at that. The sleeper-spy ability was worrisome in an age where both Russia and the US were trying to gain advantage with tools instead of weapons.

This tool all by itself could be very, very dangerous. But if it contained actual intelligence, if it had been spying on China, Taiwan, or a US military base in Japan when it was hijacked... That was different.

Intelligence was the real commodity. Intel could change the balance of power as tensions between the US and Russia grew ever more precarious.

Dimitri wasn't a fan of the president of Russia and the way the man had returned the country to a dictatorship. Acting as the Kremlin's enforcer had been an ugly, horrific pill.

His final act as the Kremlin's puppet was to return their lost technology, but what if the cost of that was too great? His life, his sister's life, and even his nephew's life weren't worth more than the thousands—even millions—of lives that could hang in the balance if the Russian president's quest for power was bolstered by this technology or the data it contained.

Before he blithely handed over the AUUV, he needed to know if it held any actionable intel. He needed someone who understood computers and coding, and intelligence gathering via drone.

He needed Ivy.

He pulled out Ian Boyd's business card again. No. Less risky to contact her through Ulai.

*I*vy paced the deck of the cabin cruiser. It seemed all she could do these days was pace. At least now she had a hard cast protecting her arm. She'd opted for a vivid aqua-colored cast, because it matched the tropical sea, but now she wished she'd gone for bright pink, because she was getting tired of blue as they fruitlessly trolled the islands for signs of Dimitri.

She'd shown Dimitri's note to Luke and Ian the evening she found it. Not surprisingly, they'd made sure her spy wouldn't be able to access her via the lanai again, which was a bummer. Although she doubted Dimitri would have taken such a risk a second time.

Ian was more irked at the breach than angry. He admitted he'd left the lanai vulnerable in hopes Dimitri would do exactly what he'd done—thus triggering an alarm Ian had set up. But Dimitri had disabled the alarm, remaining one step ahead.

They were now heading back to Koror after a second day on the water. They would spend the night in the hotel again and plan their strategy for tomorrow.

Her cell phone buzzed, telling her she was within tower

range as they neared the marina. She headed below so she could hear the call over the loud boat engine, noting as she went that the call came from an NHHC number.

"Ivy, it's Mara."

"Hey, Mara, I heard you've been ill, so why are you at the office?"

"I'm not ill, I'm pregnant, but I have been sick as a dog."

"You're pregnant? Congratulations! I'm so—"

"Thank you, we'll celebrate when you get home," Mara said, cutting her off. "Listen, you need to know something important. The DIA is doing their damndest to pin this on you. Curt didn't want to tell me, but I overheard everything —my ear was practically right next to the cell phone—and I had an idea this morning, so I came to the office to check."

"How can they pin this on me? I mean, I slept with Dimitri, but that was *after* they set me up for this nightmare of a job. They were the ones who sent me here."

"Your phone logs indicate you called Dimitri twice before you even left for Palau."

"That's bullshit!"

"I know. But once Curt told me the calls came from your work phone, I decided to see for myself. You did call the number, twice, just like the DIA claims."

"I didn't call him, Mara. I didn't know Dimitri Veselov existed."

"I figured that. So I cross-referenced it with that list of contractors I'd passed on to you—people you were approved to work with on the Palau project. Because of CAM, we needed to do a background check on anyone who would have access to the equipment. Dimitri's number was on that list as a scuba dive charter."

"Liberty Charters was *not* on that list. I would've remembered when I saw the boat. It was clearly out of my price range."

"On the list, it's called DV Scuba Tours."

Ivy closed her eyes, trying to picture the list of contractors. Trying to remember if she'd spoken with Dimitri in March. She had a good memory for accents—and that included voices. She came up blank. "I kept a copy of that list in my desk, with notes on who I talked to, pricing, et cetera. Did I have a note next to DV Scuba Tours? I don't have the copy I brought with me anymore." It had gone out to sea with *Liberty* when they abandoned her.

"You did. You wrote 'automated voice mail, left message' and the date and time you called. Which match the call log. As far as that goes—you're in the clear. This can't be used against you."

"Good."

"But, Ivy, I think—and Curt, who is here with me now, agrees—the more important point is this list was provided by the DIA. They supposedly vetted every contractor on the list to protect you and CAM. But I can't find any record that DV Scuba Tours exists. If you can talk to Dimitri, ask him how his nonexistent business ended up on a DIA list of approved contractors."

The conversation ended, leaving Ivy wondering how the hell she could get in touch with Dimitri. Talking to him had been the one thing she'd wanted since she woke up after surgery three days ago.

She returned to the deck to see the boat was pulling into their slip at the marina. Luke was at the helm as Ian was perched to secure the bow line. Five slips away was the enclosed hangar that housed Ulai and his seaplane.

The door to the hangar was open, a sure sign Ulai was there.

She glanced at the men who'd been guarding her for the last three days. If anyone knew how to get in touch with

Dimitri, it was Ulai, but the seaplane pilot would likely clam up in their presence.

She took a deep breath and touched the holster at her back. It was completely illegal for her to be carrying concealed in Palau, but that was the least of the rules she was willing to break to protect herself.

Luke and Ian were focused on the boat. She slipped under the railing and onto the dock as silently as possible—not easy with one hand, but the engine noise covered the thump of her feet. She ducked down and darted around the boat in the next slip, using it for cover. She was halfway down the long main dock before she stood to her full height and hurried toward Ulai's hangar.

When she reached it, she knocked once on the open door before stepping inside. "Ulai?"

A grunt sounded behind her.

She reached for her gun as she turned toward the sound. A leg—at the end of which she recognized Ulai's broad bare foot—rested, toes up, on the dock just behind the open door.

"Run, Ivy!" Dimitri shouted.

The door slammed closed, revealing Ulai, stretched out on the aluminum floor. His head was bleeding. A bloody hammer rested on the dock next to his body.

Chapter Thirty-Three

The shock of seeing Ulai froze Ivy. She wanted to drop to her knees and check his pulse, but standing above him was Dimitri, his shirt and face covered in blood. Behind him was another man, who held a gun to Dimitri's ribs.

The man shoved Dimitri forward and brought them both into the spill of light from the window. Ivy's paralysis broke. "Rudy Fredrickson?" He didn't look like the stiff bureaucrat she'd taken him for when they first met last fall. "What are you doing in Palau?"

Rudy continued to nudge Dimitri forward until he reached the bolt on the door and slid it home. "Tracking down a Russian spy. I found him over the body," Rudy said. "He killed Umetaro."

"I was helping Ulai. He's not breathing," Dimitri said.

That explained the blood around his mouth.

"That's because he's dead. You killed him." Rudy pushed Dimitri to the side, and while the gun in the DIA man's hand remained on Dimitri, the barrel tipped her way in a subtle threat. To keep Dimitri in line? Or her?

"Who is this guy, Ivy?" Dimitri asked, his eyes bright with a fierce anger.

"He tried to recruit me and CAM for the DIA last fall."

"Ivy!" The shout came from outside. Luke's voice.

"Don't even think about letting Sevick in, Ms. MacLeod. He's here to help the spy escape. *Again*. But I caught him —*literally* red-handed." He smirked at his joke. "He's not getting away this time. He'll face charges in the US. Now help me tie him up."

She glanced down to make sure her gun pointed at Rudy, not Dimitri. Not that she could aim worth a damn one-handed. She frowned at the DIA analyst. "I don't understand. You aren't a field agent."

"Oh, but I was. Before I had a kid and settled down into office life."

"Did you kill Ulai?" she asked.

Is Ulai really dead?

Grief and horror threatened to take her down. It took effort to remain focused on the man holding a gun to Dimitri's side.

Rudy's gaze dropped to the pilot. Her friend. "Judging from the calling card, it was your boyfriend here."

"Calling card?"

"He didn't tell you about his other profession? I've been hunting the Hammer for most of my DIA career. First in the field, later in the office."

"Was it your idea to have NHHC send me to Palau?"

He shrugged. "It's hard to know who suggested it. There were so many in the room. So many eager to take credit." He smiled, and she knew without a doubt this man had set her up, and he'd done it in such a way that no one in the DIA could exactly point to him and put his fingerprints on the arrangement.

He'd set her up to go to Palau and find the AUUV. Did he set her up to meet Dimitri too? And Ulai, who was also on the approved contractor list?

Who was he really working for?

"You could have warned me what I was facing here."

Rudy shrugged. "We thought ignorance would be a protection. We didn't know you'd be in danger. Didn't know your husband sold CAM to his terrorist buddies."

Now wasn't the time to correct him by adding ex to his statement. "You're the Defense *Intelligence* Agency. What *do* you know?"

Rudy flashed a grin. "That this asshole is the Hammer, and he killed your pilot."

Dimitri had denied knowing who the Hammer was when she'd asked what the Russian had meant that morning on *Liberty*. Later, Zack Barrow had made it clear *Dimitri* was the Hammer. But she'd assumed it was his spy code name. Now it was clear the Hammer was something far worse, and Dimitri's initial denial made more sense.

"I didn't hurt Ulai," Dimitri said. "He was my friend." She heard the stress on the word. A reminder anyone who Dimitri befriended was at risk. "I found him like that. He had a pulse but wasn't breathing. I was breathing for him when this asshole jumped me." He held Ivy's gaze. "I would never hurt a friend."

"He's the Hammer, Ivy," Rudy said. "Enforcer for the Kremlin. Over a dozen kills to his credit."

The words were a blow, a statement of the thing she realized now she'd suspected but hadn't consciously acknowledged for some time. She remembered his evasion when she'd asked if he'd killed.

Dimitri didn't deny it now. He couldn't, not with the haunted look in his eyes. The tightness of his jaw.

He hadn't told her everything, and that left a hollow feeling in her stomach. Luke's hostility toward a man who'd helped him on the most dangerous operation of his life now made sense.

"Ivy!" Ian said from outside the door. "Let us in! We know Dimitri's in there."

Ian and Luke had probably let her escape down the dock, hoping she'd lead them to Dimitri.

Every person here had claimed to be protecting her at one point or another. And every person here—Rudy, Luke, Ian, and Dimitri—had manipulated and lied to her at some point.

Everyone here had used her.

But only one of them had attacked Ulai.

She fixed the gun on Dimitri. "Let him go," she said to Rudy. "My aim isn't great, and I might shoot you."

"You can't—" Rudy said.

"Oh, but I can. I can save the expense of a trial, and no jury would convict me. He abducted me. He used me. He killed Ulai. I can take him out right now and no one will hold me accountable. So move the fuck away, Rudy, or risk getting shot." She fixed the gun on him. "I could take you out too and call it an accident. Don't think I'm not tempted after you set me up for this."

Rudy's eyes widened, but he released Dimitri and stepped to the side, his gun still pointed at the Russian assassin.

She took a step toward Dimitri, and he stepped back, closer to the edge of the well that housed the floatplane.

She shifted her stance, facing Dimitri head-on, with Rudy in her peripheral vision. "I had a chance to do this once before, but like a fool, I didn't. I'm not a fool anymore."

"You'll never find the AUUV if you do this," Dimitri said. "I hid it again."

"I don't give a damn about the AUUV. I never have. I came here to map Peleliu."

"Yeah, but he"—Dimitri nodded toward Rudy—"wants it badly enough to kill Ulai."

"I'm so done with your lies," Ivy said aloud, then mouthed, *I love you,* and pulled the trigger.

Chapter Thirty-Four

The report of the bullet sent fear jolting through Luke's system. He paused at the side of the building. Ian's job was to make noise by the door on the dockside of the hangar, while Luke circled around, heading to the large bay door that opened onto the water.

Behind him, he heard a shout from Ivy, while in front of him, a man swam under the hangar wall. Luke dove into the water, cutting off Dimitri's escape.

Dimitri fought against his hold, but froze when his gaze met Luke's underwater. All at once, he flung his arms out. No fight. Absolute surrender.

Blood swirled in the water between them as Luke weighed what he knew and what he believed about Dimitri Veselov.

He gripped Dimitri's shirt and kicked off the sandy seafloor, lifting them both to the surface.

He didn't know what he was going to ask until the words came out of his mouth. "Why am I here, Dimitri? Why did you send me the card?"

"To protect Ivy. The DIA is here—with her in the hangar. Ulai is dead or dying. The DIA's involved somehow.

But you'll need proof. Ivy faked shooting me so I could escape."

Luke dropped his gaze to the water that had taken a purplish hue. "From the blood, I'm guessing she shot you for real."

He glanced down. "Her aim was off, she didn't mean to hit me. Bullet grazed my hip."

"Can you swim?"

"Yeah."

"Swim to our boat. You know which one?"

Dimitri gave a sharp nod.

"Hide in the cabin. We'll get help for Ulai and deal with the DIA. Hurry. Before the sharks smell the blood."

In a flash, Dimitri was gone and Luke had to ask himself if he was the biggest dumbshit on the planet.

Sometimes all you could rely on was gut feeling. Dimitri might be the Hammer, but he was also the man who'd been ready to sacrifice his life to save thousands of others.

Luke believed Ivy and trusted Dimitri.

He swam to the ladder and prepared to lie to the DIA.

*J*an kicked at the door as the shot echoed. Inside, Ivy let out a low yell; the dock shook. He kicked again. On the fifth kick, the lock snapped. He entered, gun drawn, to see Ivy throw a wrench she must've grabbed from the workbench at a man he'd never seen before.

The man ducked. "Chill out, Ivy! We're on the same side!"

"Bullshit!" She grabbed another wrench and threw it. "You set me up for this!" The man stepped backward, his eyes darting to the edge of the dock, where a Sig hovered on the brink of falling into the water.

He dove for the weapon, and Ian dove for him.

He didn't know what was going on, but he'd been hired to protect Ivy. They fought for the gun, rolling on the dock. The gun landed in the water, and the stranger landed a blow to Ian's jaw.

He grunted and clipped the man on the chin just as a wrench hit the man's temple.

The man slumped backward, out cold. Ivy stood above them both, breathing heavily, holding a wrench in her good hand. "God, I hope I didn't kill him. We need to know who Rudy's working for, and for him to tell his boss that Dimitri is dead."

Ivy stood to her full height. She nodded toward the unconscious man. "Rudy Fredrickson killed Ulai—" She dropped the wrench and turned to the pilot. "Dimitri was helping him breathe. He said he still had a pulse. Maybe there's still time."

From the look of the wound, Ian suspected it was too late.

Ivy dropped to her knees at Ulai's side and placed her fingers on his neck, while Ian did the same for the man she'd called Rudy Fredrickson. Fredrickson's pulse was steady, as was his breathing.

"No pulse, not breathing," she said of Ulai. Her gaze dropped to her cast. "I can't do CPR." She turned her desperate eyes on Ian.

"It's too late, Ivy." But he dropped to his knees just the same and started chest compressions.

Ivy plucked his phone from his pocket as Luke entered the hangar.

"We need an ambulance," she said into the phone. "A man is down. No pulse and unresponsive. CPR is being administered." She gave the location, described the injury, then hung up. To Luke and Ian, she said, "Agent Palea needs to investigate. Rudy did this, not Dimitri."

Her gaze fixed on the dead man Ian was trying to revive. "He'll get away with everything because Dimitri is the Hammer. But Dimitri isn't who you think he is."

"You know about the Hammer?" Luke asked as he positioned himself at Ulai's head.

She nodded. "But that's not *who* he is."

"I'll do the breaths at the next interval," Luke said.

Ian nodded, counting compressions as sweat dripped down his brow. "Where is Veselov?" he managed to ask, then said, "Twenty-nine, thirty," to signal Luke to breathe for Ulai.

Luke gave Ulai two breaths. His chest rose with the infusion of air into the lungs. No blockage.

Ian resumed chest compressions.

Luke looked toward the unconscious man several feet away. "He's out?"

"Yes," Ian said. "Ivy hit him with a wrench."

"When he comes to, we can convince him it was a mistake and give Agent Palea time to investigate," Ivy said. "Ian thought he was a threat to me. Rudy is involved. He attacked Ulai. We can't let Dimitri take the fall."

"Twenty-eight, twenty-nine, thirty," Ian said.

Luke breathed for Ulai again.

When Luke was done, Ivy asked, "Is Dimitri okay?"

"Your bullet skimmed his hip."

"Shit." She took a deep breath. "Where is he?"

"Our boat."

Sirens sounded in the distance. Thank God, the ambulance was almost to the marina.

Ian continued chest compressions as silence passed between Ivy and Luke. He caught Luke's nod with his peripheral vision.

She leaned down and kissed Ulai's bloody cheek and whispered, "Pull through. Please stay with us." She rose to her feet. "I'll check in as soon as I can." Her footfalls pounded on the aluminum dock as she darted out the door.

*E*very part of Dimitri hurt.

He'd been shot once before. He'd been beaten before. But he had to acknowledge he wasn't as young as he once was. And the bullet might've gone deeper than a graze.

Climbing onto the boat deck was a special slice of hell, but he made it, fighting through the agony. The burn.

He would survive this. It was what he did.

He checked his wound. The shot had torn his flesh, a deep furrow, but the bullet wasn't embedded.

It was nothing compared to what others suffered. His sister. Ivy.

Ulai.

Motherfucker. Ulai.

A good man.

Why had Rudy Fredrickson gone after the pilot? Ulai didn't know anything.

Aw fuck. Ulai.

His only sin was becoming Dimitri's friend. And he'd paid for it with his life.

Dimitri slammed his fist into the deck even as he crawled toward the hatch to the interior.

He could grieve Ulai once he was inside and got his hands on a first aid kit.

Focus on not passing out. Two days without sleep combined with blood loss had caught up with him, because next thing he knew, he was at the bottom of the steps, with only a vague memory of tumbling into the galley.

The world spun like he'd had too much booze, but he hadn't had alcohol since the scotch in the cave with Ivy.

Footsteps sounded above him, and he curled into a tight, defensive ball, tucking himself into a dark corner. Ready to fight. Training. Years of training came through for him when he should have passed out.

He had muscle memory. Practice. Blows from the hockey stick when he failed.

It was effective training to ensure he used only English when in pain, when dreaming, when delirious. Only English. Or the blows would make the pain much, much worse.

"Water?" a woman asked at one point.

"*Da*," he said, cringing the moment he realized his mistake. But the blow didn't come. Just a straw between his lips and a cold liquid filled his throat.

He drank until the cup was empty, and then it was refilled.

The next time he opened his eyes, it was dark all around. He discovered he slept on the floor of the galley, a pillow under his head, a bandage on his hip, and a woman's body curled next to his.

He pulled Ivy close and breathed her in, then dropped back into oblivion.

He woke again with the dawn, feeling a thousand times better. His hip ached, but sleep and liquids had replenished his energy. He felt the gentle rocking motion of the boat and tried to get his bearings.

He had only the vaguest memories of the intervening hours. Water and electrolyte drinks for hydration. A cool cloth to clean his wound. Ivy's attempts to get him to the bunk, then giving up and making a bed for them both on the floor.

He was alone on the floor now, an indentation on the pillow next to him telling him he hadn't dreamed Ivy by his side.

He sat up, wondering where they were. Safe from the DIA man?

Or was he a prisoner?

He stood slowly, then climbed the short ladder, his head emerging through the hatch to the deck.

Sunlight hit his eyes, and he squinted against it. A glance to the port side showed nothing but sea. Fore and aft, just water. Finally, he gazed starboard and took in beautiful Ivy at the helm, nothing but water stretched in that direction as well.

"Where are we?" he asked.

Her mouth curved in a slow, sexy grin. "Somewhere between Palau and the Celebes Sea."

He shook his head, then a smile stretched across his own face. "Really?"

"Yes. Really. I've abducted you, Dimitri. And there is nothing you can do about it."

Chapter Thirty-Five

"Well then, if I'm your prisoner, I guess that means I get to set the rules," Dimitri said in a low, sexy voice.

Ivy smiled as she took a step toward him. "That sounds fair."

"You can touch me all you want."

She placed her good hand over his heart, feeling the strong, even beat. "Good. Because I want."

"And I get to touch you as much as you want."

She took his hand and placed it on her breast. Then rose on her toes, locking her fingers behind his neck. Resting the hard cast on his collarbone, she paused with her lips a scant inch from his. "I want. I want. I want."

He leaned down, closing the gap between their mouths and kissed her as his hand cupped her breast and his other arm circled her waist. His tongue slid into her mouth and she groaned as she gripped his shoulder with her right hand.

She was in love with a Russian spy and assassin. Crazy, wild love. And this might be all they'd ever have.

His mouth explored hers slowly. Russian words spilled

from him in a low, sexy whisper as he kissed her. She could only guess at what he was saying, and loved that he was lost enough in the moment to slip into his other language.

She pulled his bottom lip between her teeth and sucked on it, then nibbled along his jaw, working her way to his ear. Once there she took the lobe into her mouth. "I love you, Dimitri," she whispered.

The Russian words ceased. His lips pressed against her brow, then he lifted his head and gripped her shoulders with both hands, one thumb pulling down the spaghetti strap of her tank top as he stared into her eyes. "I was hoping I didn't imagine that yesterday."

"You didn't."

"I love you too." He closed his eyes and took a deep breath, then met her gaze. "Dammit—I want to live. I want a future. With you. I'm willing to cut a deal. I'll tell the CIA and Justice Department everything I know about the GRU's covert operations—which is a lot—if they can protect Sophia and Yulian."

Her eyes teared. She'd given up hope that he'd choose to fight. "Curt is amenable." She paused, afraid of how he'd react to what she was about to say. She might have given up hope, but that didn't mean she hadn't spoken to Curt to explore the possibility. And that had meant telling him everything. Even about Sophia and Yulian. "The first step—as a show of good faith—will be to hand over the AUUV."

He gave a sharp nod. "There's another way we can do it, to draw out my handlers and get Sophia and Yulian out of Russia and into protective custody. We can stage the handoff here, and I can demand Sophia and Yulian be present."

She gripped his shoulder, weak with relief, dizzy with joy. "Ian and Luke have already agreed to be your backup."

☠

*E*motion swamped Dimitri at Ivy's words. "Luke... He believes I didn't kill Ulai?"

She nodded. "Ulai—" Her voice broke, and she cleared her throat. "He's alive. Barely. He was airlifted to Guam so he could receive the best medical care. They're probably going to have to send him to Okinawa once he's more stable—there's a Navy neurosurgeon there. But there's hope he'll pull through."

The idea that Ulai might live nearly overwhelmed him. "I didn't hurt him. I would never—"

"I know. Local authorities invited the FBI to consult. I spoke with Agent Palea this morning. He knows my suspicions about Rudy Fredrickson, but he's going to need to interview you."

Dimitri nodded. "Even if Curt won't cut a deal with me, I'll talk to the agent. I want the person who assaulted Ulai to pay."

He pulled Ivy against his chest and simply held her. The coming days were uncertain. He would risk everyone he cared about and couldn't decide if that was the ultimate in selfish, except that his goal was to free all of them—Luke, Ivy, Sophia, and Yulian—before they were in the same position as Ulai.

He never should have befriended the man. He should have realized that even being a casual acquaintance was a risk.

And Ivy. What had he done to Ivy?

He cupped her face. "I don't deserve you."

"Yes. You do. What you haven't deserved is how you've been used your whole life. We're going to change that. Together. You won't be alone anymore." Her smile warmed him as much as her words.

She kissed him, a deep, hungry kiss that did more than simply warm him.

He pulled back before the kiss got out of control. "What's our plan? Do I call the FBI agent now?"

"We'll rendezvous with Luke and Ian at dusk on Angaur," she said, naming the southernmost of Palau's two hundred and fifty-plus islands.

"You were that confident I'd change my mind?"

"No, but I suggested the rendezvous just in case. I need to call and tell them you're in. You'll need to call Curt too."

"And if I hadn't agreed?"

"Then I had no plan beyond going back to Koror without you." She cupped his cheek with her right hand, the hard cast on her left arm pressed against his side—a painful reminder of how he'd failed her already. "We can do this, Dimitri. We can save your family and cut your ties with the GRU."

He furrowed his brow. No more lies or omissions going forward. "I've killed for them, Ivy. I am—was—the Hammer. I had to be, but still, I did it."

Her fingers stroked the stubble on his chin. "You killed Bratva. Child traffickers, arms dealers, and rapists. And I understand you had no choice."

"My orders were always men I could dispose of without guilt—except at the end, when I had orders to kill Luke." He gripped Ivy tighter against him. "Days ago, I was told if I didn't kill Luke, you would die."

Her eyes widened, but she didn't pull back. That she didn't fear him with that admission meant everything to him.

"You didn't kill Luke, and you'd never hurt me."

"Never. For either of you."

"It sounds like the GRU knew your limits and chose not to push you too far lest you'd balk. Until now."

He thought of the one time he'd balked, and the results— when he'd beaten the hell out of his handler with the same hockey stick used to beat Sophia, and later, how he'd exacted his revenge after the man raped his sister a second time. Yeah, the GRU knew not to test his limits. He'd made it clear he could be pushed only so far.

He pressed his lips to Ivy's forehead. "So. We call the others, then we have hours before the rendezvous?"

"It's middle of the night in DC. You can probably wait a few hours to call Curt."

"And Luke?"

Ivy picked up a satellite phone, which rested on the helm. She dialed a number and a moment later said, "Luke? Dimitri's in. See you at dusk." Then she hit the End button and dropped the phone on the padded captain's chair.

She smiled at Dimitri and pushed him toward the open hatch with both hands, unimpeded by the cast. "And now," she said, "I have plans for you."

He crossed his arms, blocking her path. "You expect me to make love to you inside when we have the whole ocean to ourselves?" He took a step toward her, nudging her back toward the padded bench seat. "Since that first morning when you sunbathed topless in front of me, I've fantasized about making love to you in the sun."

She bit her bottom lip and smiled. "I had the same fantasy—and felt so guilty for wanting you."

"So we're going to live that fantasy—guilt free." He slipped an arm around her waist and backed her toward the bench. "You've given me hope and a reason to live, Ivy. Starting now, I'm never going to let you go again."

Jan watched Rudy Fredrickson's face as the DIA analyst spoke with ASAC Palea on the other side of the conference room they'd taken over as their base of operations in the new hotel where all the trouble had begun.

Yesterday, Fredrickson had roused and recovered quickly after the blow to his temple. Ivy, thankfully, had used a light touch that got the job done with no apparent lasting damage, which would go a long way toward saving all their asses if it turned out Fredrickson was innocent.

Ian's vote was still out on that; however, an eyewitness on the dock had seen a kayak glide into Ulai's hanger—likely Dimitri—*before* Fredrickson entered Ulai's attached apartment, followed a minute later by Ivy, who entered the hangar directly from the dock. It didn't look good for the Russian spy.

Ivy had been adamant that Dimitri wouldn't have harmed Ulai Umetaro, and Luke, surprisingly, had backed her up.

Ian didn't know what to think.

Palea made no effort to lower his voice as he questioned Fredrickson, which gave a hint as to how the FBI agent leaned. "I'm just saying I find it hard to understand why you didn't tip off Curt about your trip, or check in with me upon arrival, knowing I'm heading this investigation thanks to the DIA's screwup."

"I didn't tip off Dominick for the same reason I went straight from the airport to the marina. Because I wanted to question Umetaro before Veselov—or one of you—stopped him from talking to me."

The DIA agent glanced at Luke then Ian. "I have reason to believe the private contractors here are in league with the assassin. In fact, I believe they let him escape along with Ms. MacLeod." He touched the bruise on his temple. "Which brings us to MacLeod. Everything the woman has said is suspect. She was in league with the assassin before she ever arrived in Palau. Phone records prove it."

Mara had adequately rebutted that argument, which

Palea knew. The fact that he didn't answer the charge and merely nodded to Fredrickson said a lot about the Fed's take on the DIA analyst.

The DIA had sent Fredrickson to Palau to aid in the hunt for Veselov, meaning the FBI agent couldn't shut him out of the investigation—not without tipping off the DIA that they might have a mole in their midst. Such a warning would only make it harder to flush out the guilty party. For that reason, Palea, Luke, and Ian had to keep Fredrickson in the loop. But he was a suspect, not an ally.

Back in DC, Curt had FBI agents digging into the DIA analyst's background, looking for clues to his loyalties. But Ian knew those kinds of investigations took months, while the handoff would happen in just a few days. It would make the exchange that much trickier, given that they'd have to keep an eye on the analyst, another on the Russians, all while protecting Sophia and Yulian Veselov—if mother and son were actually delivered for the handoff.

In two short hours, they would rendezvous—Luke, Palea, Ivy, Dimitri, and Ian—and formulate a plan. Then Dimitri would make his demands to his handlers.

It would take at least a day for Sophia and Yulian Veselov to travel to Palau. This would be all over in two days—three maximum—and he could go home to Cressida.

The one loose end was Zack Barrow. Ian didn't know if he could leave while Zack remained free.

Chapter Thirty-Six

*A*t last, Ivy had the AUUV wired to her computer. She'd ensured the tracking system was disabled, and a scan had confirmed it emitted no radio or satellite signals. Now it was time to get the hardware to reveal its secrets. The interface built into the AUUV was in Russian, which Dimitri translated for her until she had it connected to her computer, and then she was in the code, a language she could speak.

In the middle of the night, they'd retrieved the device from a house on Peleliu. Ivy had marveled at the number of fallback positions Dimitri had outfitted; even Ian was impressed. AUUV acquired, they'd returned, just the two of them, to open sea for safety. Zack Barrow and his allies were still in the islands and hunting for both the AUUV and Ivy. The vast open ocean was the safest hiding place.

Ivy had initiated lockdown on CAM, and it and RON had been sent to the US military base on Guam, giving them one less item to guard, which was a relief. Luke, Dimitri, and Ian had all wanted to send Ivy to Guam as well, but she refused because she was the only person with the technical expertise to hack into the AUUV. If they were going to turn the device over to the Russians, they would damn well have a copy of the data and programing for the US to sift through. To that end, Luke had given Ivy her laptop when they rendezvoused the night before.

Another advantage of having her computer; she'd exported copies of the detailed map layers created from the flyovers of Peleliu she'd done with Ulai during her first week in Palau. She and Dimitri would pore over that data and pick the site for the handoff. Once they settled on a location, they'd rendezvous with Luke, Ian, and Palea again and plant the AUUV in the jungle of Peleliu and prepare for the handoff.

The time for the exchange had yet to be set—but they expected it to be the following day. Everything was coming together. Now she just needed the AUUV to spill its guts and give them yet another advantage in this proxy war of spies.

She found the data files, hidden and encrypted, but she dispatched with the layers of security easily enough. A little easy, but what she'd expected for the first-tier security. The real data would be much harder to breach. The AUUV had several cameras. Most of the data would be either photos or videos. She'd bet anything that embedded within massive video files was the real data.

She'd have to break apart the videos—she'd be a miner, smashing through rock to find hidden gemstones. Like gems in their natural state, the data would be rough, flawed, and need precision cutting to bring the true value to light. She didn't have time for that, but she could look for the markers that told her the gems were there. She'd make copies of everything, and CIA hackers could play to their hearts' content.

Behind her, Dimitri leaned down and kissed her neck. "I love watching you at the computer. How absorbed you get. You could be anywhere in the world—a palace or a closet—

and you'd never know it because your focus is razor-sharp on one thing."

She arced her neck back to look up at him and made a face—surprised and amused. "Most people find my absorption irritating."

"Not me. I get off on it. It's like you're fully being you without filters or lenses that we all present to the world on a regular basis. And I see the same intensity in your eyes when you touch me, when we make love. It's potent to be the recipient of that kind of attention."

His mouth dropped to hers for a deep, intense kiss. She gripped her seat as she leaned back, enjoying the slide of his tongue against hers.

This heat and intensity could be an everyday thing if they succeeded. Curt had warned her witness protection would be necessary if the GRU didn't believe Dimitri was dead.

Could she—would she—give up her family to be with Dimitri?

The idea made her ill. She touched her belly with her left hand, the cast hard and abrasive even through her cotton tank top. It was still too soon to know if she'd conceived, but the idea of being able to raise their baby together—then choosing not to because she didn't want to go into hiding—also made her ill.

He had to be successful tomorrow. It was a simple imperative.

He lifted his head, ending the kiss. He touched her cheek, where a tear had spilled. "I'm scared too, Ivy."

She loved that she didn't have to explain her torn emotions to him. He understood her in ways no one ever had.

"I love you," she said, taking strength from the simple words. Love had given him a reason to fight, a reason to hope. It was a powerful force, and she would harness it for all the fuel it would give them. She pulled his head down for a last quick kiss, then she stroked the stubble along his jaw. "Now stop distracting me. I've got hacking to do."

He laughed. "I'll do something useful and make lunch."

She smiled and faced the computer screen again, slipping back into the cyber world, forgetting for the moment all the reasons she was afraid.

*J*an supplied night vision goggles to everyone, and Dimitri was grateful Raptor had seen fit to fully stock the private jet before it left DC for Palau. They had enough gadgets to make Q in a James Bond movie giddy.

All Dimitri cared about was that they were armed and he wouldn't be alone in protecting Sophia and Yulian as he faced down his handlers.

Ivy, at least, would not be anywhere near the site during the exchange. She'd used her expertise to find the perfect hiding spot for the AUUV, and she'd managed to copy the entire hard disk and started parsing data, but after tonight, she'd be safely tucked away. She was injured and was not and had never been trained for this sort of op, unlike Luke, a former Navy SEAL, Ian, who'd been Delta Force before he was CIA, FBI Agent Palea, and Dimitri.

Even Rudy Fredrickson had been a field agent for the DIA prior to taking on the analyst position. Fredrickson knew nothing about the current plans, just in case he was indeed the DIA mole.

Tomorrow, an hour before the handoff, the DIA would be informed of the deal Dimitri had struck with the head of the Justice Department. The DIA would insist on their man being present for the exchange, and frankly, they all wanted him where they could keep an eye on him. If he was a traitor, they might be able to use him against his Russian allies.

Fredrickson would witness the exchange, but Luke and Ian would make certain he didn't have the opportunity to warn accomplices that Dimitri wasn't alone in the jungle.

"Another twenty meters north-northwest, and you'll be on top of the semi-subterranean Japanese bomb shelter," Ivy said.

"Isn't inside the shelter too obvious?" Palea asked.

"Exactly. But near it is an aluminum Japanese seaplane float. It's large enough to tuck the AUUV underneath. The shelter is a red herring. The meet point will be a concrete Japanese gun emplacement. It's a bowl shape—twelve meters in diameter, two meters deep. Dimitri and I chose the south-ernmost of three emplacements due to the proximity to the bomb shelter, and there's a good vantage point above the shelter, north of the seaplane float, west of the emplacement, for Agent Palea to watch over the exchange with a sniper rifle." She cocked her head. "I understand you've had sniper training?"

He nodded. "In the Army."

She gave a sharp nod. "The data on the suitability for this as the location for the exchange was drawn from my survey with CAM, but I never had a chance to ground-truth Peleliu as I did the Rock Island survey. CAM was calibrated but not refined." She met each man's gaze. "The data combined with Dimitri's tactical training led us to choose this area, but it's up to you to decide if it works on the ground."

For the next hour, they explored the jungle. A slow process given that they needed to leave no mark of their passage, no hint they'd been here to scout the location and hide the prize.

"I don't like the way the ground slopes south of the float," Palea said from his position above the bomb shelter. "I'll have a blind spot. But otherwise I've got good coverage from here."

"I'll conceal myself southwest of the emplacement and cover the slope," Ian said. "We'll put Fredrickson to my right, so I can cover him as well."

"Good plan," Luke said. "I'll take northeast of the emplacement, keeping Fredrickson to my left."

With the location selected, Ivy oversaw the hiding of the AUUV under the aluminum seaplane float. "This is violating so many rules of historic preservation," she griped. "Messing with wreckage as we are."

"It's garbage," Luke said. "Abandoned by troops when they abandoned Peleliu."

"Historic garbage, nonetheless."

"You and Cressida can start a support group," Ian said with a snicker, "for archaeologists who have to disturb sites for the greater good."

"Are you rolling your eyes behind those NVGs, Boyd?" Ivy asked, humor in her voice.

Luke laughed. "Badass covert operators don't roll their eyes. But then, Ian doesn't even share a zip code with badass."

Ian chuckled. "Luke is bitter because he knew he'd never get into Delta and had to settle for the Navy."

Dimitri's alter ego, Lt. Parker Reeves, and Lt. Luke Sevick had been somewhere between acquaintances and friends—as much of a friendship as Parker had allowed. Now Dimitri found himself embarrassingly jealous watching the easy banter between Luke and Ian. Palea had also developed a rapport with the others, and his Army background meant he'd taken Ian's side.

"Hey, big tough guys," Ivy said, interrupting both the teasing and Dimitri's thoughts. "One-armed woman here trying to lift an airplane. Little help maybe?"

Luke and Ian lifted one side of the large float, and Ivy peered underneath. "Sonofabitch. That's fricking TNT."

As one, they all tilted their heads to look under the raised corroded metal. Sure enough, there was a pile of World War II explosives pressed into the earth. The molded bricks looked like square candles—three inches long, an inch thick, and an inch wide, with a hole in the middle—he'd seen photos of similar finds and this resembled a cache that had been found by archaeologists several years before.

Old TNT would explode on contact with open flame. After seventy years, a spark could still set it off.

"It's well-documented that there's a lot of unexploded ordnance in these woods," Ivy said. "We knew this was possible." She met Dimitri's gaze. "What do we do?"

"We use it. The AUUV is already packed with C-4. TNT will just make a bigger statement." He collected two dozen explosive bricks from the pile and carefully set them aside.

Together, he and Palea positioned the AUUV under the float, resting it on top of the remaining TNT. Then he took the bricks he'd set aside and placed them around and in front of the Russian device. He stepped back and nodded to Luke and Ian, who lowered the float, fully hiding the modern spy equipment and explosives under rusted aluminum.

Ivy replaced torn moss and draped vines over the top. In minutes, it looked one with the jungle again, as if it hadn't been disturbed in years.

They hiked back to the beach, single file, ever careful to leave no trace. When they reached the shore, they pulled out the inflatable boat they'd hidden in the jungle and rowed out to the south, away from their anchored boat, which was in a hidden cove in the Rock Islands. The inflatable was small, so Ivy tucked herself in Dimitri's arms, and he was content to let the others row while he held her.

Voices carried across the water, so the crossing was silent

until they were far enough from Peleliu to lower the engine and head toward the larger boat that had been Dimitri and Ivy's home the last few days.

In sixteen hours, one way or another, this would all be over.

When they reached the boat, Ian asked, "Who's up for a round of poker?" He tapped the supply box that was his seat. "I've got the beer."

Dimitri doubted Ian Boyd did anything without an agenda, but in that moment, he didn't give a damn. Beer and poker the night before his life started or ended sounded damn good. "I'm in."

Ivy, it turned out, was good at calculating the odds in Texas Hold'em but had zero poker face when she had a good hand and was terrible at bluffing when she didn't have the cards she wanted. The result was when she won, it was a small pot because everyone else folded, but she was always so damn pleased to win, her exuberance was infectious.

Boyd played like a spy. It wasn't about winning or losing, it was about understanding the player across the table, and Dimitri knew *he* was the one being studied. If Ian were playing to win, Dimitri suspected he'd take every hand.

Luke was the competitive player, in it for the win but not for the stakes. He took his losses in stride and enjoyed the game aspect. Once the hand was played out, he focused on the next hand, not the results of the previous one. He bet low, and true to form, he stopped drinking at one beer.

Kaha'i—and by the third hand, they were all using first names—was like Ivy and into the numbers aspect, calculating odds based on his hole cards and what came up on the flop, turn, and river, but unlike Ivy, he had a solid poker face. Between that and his dry wit, he won just as often bluffing as he did with the cards he was dealt. Watching Kaha'i go up against Ian in a true contest would be interesting.

Deep into the night, Ivy was cleaned out of chips. She sat across from him and leaned back against the cushioned bench at the galley table and finished the last of her beer, then held Dimitri's gaze. Her bare foot stretched out under the table and found his crotch. She grinned.

"Whoa, wrong man, Ivy," Luke, who sat next to Dimitri, said.

Her eyes widened, and she jolted back, but Dimitri grabbed her foot—elbowing Luke in the process—before she could retreat. "He's messing with you, Ive." He stroked the arch of her foot with his thumbs.

Ivy's face reddened, but then she relaxed when Dimitri began massaging her foot in earnest.

"Sorry. Couldn't resist," Luke said, then stood and stretched. "Time to pack it in. We need to be back at the hotel before Fredrickson wakes and notices we're missing."

"I told you we should've drugged him," Ian said.

Kaha'i shook his head. "And I told you Dominick will have my ass if we can't prosecute because the evidence against him was obtained illegally."

Ian grinned. "Raptor's always looking for good operatives. There's even a compound on Oahu."

The Hawaiian FBI agent rolled his eyes. "I happen to *like* my job."

"Even though you have to do everything the hard way, by the book? When I was CIA, I broke the law ten times before breakfast." He cleared his throat and flashed a grin. "Outside the US, of course."

"Of course," Kaha'i repeated.

The CIA wasn't allowed to conduct operations on US soil, so Ian Boyd's lawbreaking was all done in foreign lands and condoned by the US government. Dimitri, however, had been a spy for Russia, operating in the United States. There was an outstanding warrant for his arrest, and Kaha'i had the authority to serve it—even in Palau. Curt Dominick had stayed the warrant thanks to the deal they'd struck, but Dimitri's future was uncertain even if everything went off without a hitch in the coming hours.

Given all he'd done, he probably shouldn't trust these people not to turn on him in the end, yet he did. Perhaps team building had been Ian's goal with this poker game, even more than to gauge Dimitri's character.

Ian stood and slapped the fed on the shoulder. "Some-times you've gotta break a few laws for the greater good." He winked at Ivy. "Or damage historic garbage."

The others stood, and one by one, they climbed the short ladder to the deck. Poised to step onto the inflatable boat, Luke paused and turned to Dimitri. "This is going to work," Luke said softly. "Hell, we're ten times more prepared than we were last November, and this time, we've got a full team."

"If anything happens to me, Luke, watch out for my sister and Ivy. They're why I sent you the card. To give them backup if I fail."

Luke gave a sharp nod. "I figured that out." He gave a wry smile. "I've spent a lot of months trying to figure out what—if anything—you told me was true."

Dimitri shrugged. "Not much. Except when I said I wasn't going back to the GRU. And I didn't. I was forced."

Luke glanced over Dimitri's shoulder, and his expression softened. "Be good to Ivy, or Undine is going to kick your ass—and mine."

Dimitri nodded. That was Undine, fierce and protective of everyone, even when she didn't know the person well. He glanced over his shoulder to take in the woman who'd made him want to live. "She means everything to me," he said, holding her gaze. "She should be on the next flight out of here, going home where it's safe."

She crossed her arms, drawing his gaze to her cast. Guilt kicked him in the balls. "Not a chance," she said.

"I'll leave you two to your arguing." Luke jumped into the boat. "Rest up. Tomorrow is going to be a craptastic day."

Ian lowered the engine into the water and pulled the cord. He pointed the boat toward Koror, and they sped off into the night.

Ivy pressed up against Dimitri's side, and he wrapped an arm around her shoulders. "Luke trusts you."

He stared after the boat as it raced across the water. "I'm amazed he does. And humbled."

"You like him."

"I do. I was also jealous of him—his life, his friendships. Everybody likes Luke. Everyone respects him. Even Undine's father—who once hated him—became Luke's biggest fan. Parker had friends on the surface, and respect from the other Coasties, but it was all a lie."

She ran her fingers over his cheek. Sometime in the last day, his whiskers had crossed the line between stubble and beard. "I never knew Parker Reeves, but I do know Dimitri Veselov, and Dimitri is the man I want to have a future with."

He couldn't help but grin. "Dimitri is one damn lucky bastard."

"Let's go to bed so he can explore just how lucky."

Chapter Thirty-Seven

*I*t was showtime. Ivy glanced at her watch again. She'd had to duct-tape it to the cast because she hated wearing it on her right wrist and knew she'd be checking the time constantly.

After some debate, they'd agreed that Ivy would stay on the boat, anchored off the Angaur shoreline. All the men they trusted were involved in the operation. There was no one left to guard her. The hotel wasn't secure and was also the first place anyone would look for her.

The exchange in the jungle of Peleliu was a covert operation on foreign soil, so the local police as protectors for Ivy were out. They'd start asking questions if she suddenly showed up at the station to hang out—plus she wouldn't be able to carry a gun if she were with the police. And she wasn't about to give up her gun.

She was comfortable on the boat and had an unobstructed view of all three hundred and sixty degrees. It was the logical choice. No one had reason to search near Angaur, and here there weren't any small islands for approaching vessels to hide behind.

But waiting for word from Dimitri was excruciating. It would likely be hours before she knew if he'd been successful. If he was even alive.

She paced, but the boat was half the size of *Liberty*. Very unsatisfying when it took less than a minute to circle the entire vessel. Finally, she paused in front of her computer.

She had the files she'd copied from the AUUV yesterday. She had yet to see if there was valuable intel stored in the memory. Work would distract her like nothing else could. But then, she doubted even work could distract her today, not with Dimitri in the jungle, trying to save his family. Trying to save himself.

But still, it was worth a try. She plugged in the hard disk and scanned the list of files.

She sorted the videos from the images. She clicked on a short video that filtered to the top. It wouldn't play, so she broke it open and looked at the stills. It looked like video from the seventies. A man in front of a brownish-yellow background. She separated out the audio track and hit Play.

A deep baritone made wordless, musical vocalizations. Weird. But then the vocalizations were interrupted by a song that was familiar to her: Rick Astley's equally deep baritone singing, "Never Gonna Give You Up."

She laughed. She'd just been rickrolled, Russian-style.

She shook her head at this first layer of security, wishing she'd thought to put a rickroll in CAM.

The idea of someone stealing her baby, only to be confounded by Rick Astley on repeat made her smile. She would add a rickroll to CAM 2.0.

She closed the video and flicked her finger across the mouse surface to randomly select a different file from the directory. Wherever it stopped was where she'd begin.

The first file was nothing. Either wiped clean or blank to begin with. She pulled out a notepad and jotted down the name. There might be a pattern even in the dummy files, and she may as well be methodical.

On the eighth file, she had an image. Pixelated, but still, there was something. She kept going through the files, surprised to note ten minutes had passed. Her stomach still ached with fear, but at least she was *doing* something.

She realized she was humming "Never Gonna Give You Up" and cursed the Russian programmers who'd planted the earworm.

The next file was a video again. Except...the images when she cracked it open were, like the photo file, pixelated. Was it possible that when all the images were stitched together and reduced to one thousandth their current size, they'd make a recognizable image? The video would be good for that because it had so many stills in one file.

A puzzle.

She sat bolt upright.

She had code that could learn this puzzle. Read the pixels and match the edges. It was a type of encryption she'd exper-imented with for CAM but had set aside when the Pentagon gave her only three months to prepare for the field test.

She pulled up her original test code and ran the stream of images—over seven hundred—through. It was rough, but the program made a dozen matches. She zoomed out on the matched sections and stared at the result.

It was an aerial photograph, maybe?

She tweaked the variables on the program and ran the images through again. This time she had forty-one matches, including one section of eighteen stitched images.

Zoomed out, she could see...a truck. A military truck. US —maybe? Had the AUUV had been tracking US troop movement in Okinawa?

A sound behind her caught her attention. *Oh shit.* She'd been so absorbed in her work, she'd forgotten to watch the water, to make sure no one approached the vessel from any direction.

She closed the pieced-together images with her left hand and reached for the gun holstered in the small of her back as she turned toward the sound.

Zack Barrow peeked over the gunwale, holding a small tube to his mouth. She identified the object a half second before she felt a sting on her neck. Blow gun.

Tranquilizer dart?

All at once, the world spun and the boat rocked as Zack heaved himself over the side. Her vision tunneled narrowing to an ever-smaller dot of light.

Zack said something—sounding much like a slowed-down recording—and the pinprick of light disappeared.

*E*verything was in place. Ian, Kaha'i, and Luke were hidden in the jungle, ready to engage if there was trouble. As planned, Rudy Fredrickson was hidden as well, with Ian covering him should he prove to be playing for the wrong team.

Dimitri paced the circular gun emplacement, changing direction frequently, but not in a pattern. He was a sitting duck out here; predictable movements were not his friend.

Five minutes to the deadline to deliver Sophia and Yulian. His terms had been clear. If they didn't show, he would give the AUUV to the United States. After examining the AUUV at length, Ivy felt certain there was intel on the disk. Between the data and the technology itself, giving it to the US was the last outcome Russia would want.

If any attempt was made to take the AUUV without releasing Sophia and Yulian, Dimitri would detonate the C-4 packed inside.

The minutes ticked by with Dimitri exposed. His security was the gun in his holster and the C-4 remote in his hand. All Dimitri had to do was press the button and the AUUV would be just another piece of historic wreckage.

They all wore earpieces for communication among the team. Dimitri's was hidden, with the microphone at his collar so he would appear to be without allies. Raptor had provided this equipment along with the NVGs and assorted weaponry. The C-4 had been provided by the US military.

This was the first time Dimitri had ever run an op with a team. It was a relief, but also disconcerting, with Fredrickson as a wildcard.

"You're looking nervous, D," Luke said in his ear.

"Don't I want to look nervous? Unprepared?" he asked without moving his lips.

"Disagree," Ian said. "If I were your handler, and you looked rattled, I'd wonder what was wrong and pull back to assess. They expect the Hammer. That's who you need to be."

He straightened at that. These last weeks in Palau— months, really—had changed him. He'd forgotten who he'd been, and who he'd had to become to fulfill his assignments as the Hammer.

The Hammer was a cold-blooded killer who acted with surgical precision.

In the past, he'd thought of Sophia and Yulian, conjuring the need to protect them. That had brought out the darkness inside him, the fierce warrior. Today he added Ivy to his mental lineup. He would protect her at all costs. Do whatever he had to do. Kill whomever he had to kill.

No remorse. This asshole had it coming.

He'd threatened his sister. Threatened his nephew. This asshole would kill Ivy without a second thought if needed to control Dimitri.

This was his last time acting as anyone's weapon, but today, for only the third time in his life, he'd been the one to select his target. Today, he was a weapon for Ivy.

The satellite phone he'd placed in the center of the gun emplacement rang.

*L*uke watched Dimitri's transformation with a hint of awe. Without a word, all vestiges of Parker Reeves disappeared. Here he saw a glimpse of the man who'd been on the Interceptor that night in November.

Dimitri had been rattled by what was about to take place and had lost sight, for a moment, of his own readiness and training. BUD/S training for SEALs was notoriously hard, but Luke had a feeling it was nothing compared to the years Dimitri had spent as a student in the embed unit.

He never wanted to go up against Dimitri Veselov hand to hand or any other way. It was a marvel how much the man had contained himself in Neah Bay last year.

Luke *almost* felt sorry for whoever was about to enter the jungle with Dimitri's little sister.

He could only hear Dimitri's side of the conversation, and that was in Russian. Ian, thoughtfully, translated. "D is refusing to leave the gun emplacement. He's sticking to the plan."

Dimitri spoke into the phone again, then Ian said, "Cover your ears. D's about to blow the warning charge."

A moment later, an explosion rocked the jungle.

Luke grimaced. Cressida, Ivy, and Undine were all going to be pissed at the damage they were wreaking upon the National Historic Landmark that Ivy had repeatedly referred to as the largest and best preserved World War II battlefield in the Pacific. No one had informed Ivy about the charges they'd set today, knowing she'd freak.

"Shit. They're still holding back. D's about to blow number two," Ian said.

Another explosion, this one closer.

Crap. Two minutes in and they were already on plan B.

"Stop wasting my fucking time," Dimitri said into the phone. "If Sophia and Yulian don't step into the jungle in the next ten seconds, I'm going to shoot your stooge, Fredrickson."

"What the fuck?" Fredrickson shouted in his ear.

Dimitri dropped the phone. They could hear him without it, and he was done playing games. He pulled his gun, pointing toward the DIA agent concealed in the vegetation. "I'm going to count to five," he shouted. "Produce Sophia, or Rudy dies."

He was going off script, but he knew in his gut Rudy Fredrickson was complicit. He might not be the one who attacked Ulai, but he was involved. Fuck him. "One," he shouted then paused for a moment. "Two!"

He stepped to the side, keeping his gun where he knew Rudy was, his other hand gripped the remote for the C-4.

"Where do you think you're going, Rudy?" Ian said in his ear. "Move and *I'll* shoot you."

So this was what being on a team felt like. Dimitri would enjoy the warm fuzzies later. "Three."

A snap of branches to the right caught his attention. "Four." He turned, keeping his gun on Fredrickson. "I'm done fucking around." He tightened his grip on the trigger.

"Dimitri! Stop!"

He turned toward the voice. A woman's. One he hadn't

heard in years. Broad leaves parted as she stepped through the thick vegetation. She brushed aside vines with one hand, while the other supported a child, sleeping against her chest.

She had their mother's eyes and their father's hair. The last time he'd seen her was the day he'd become the Hammer, to protect her.

His baby sister.

Chapter Thirty-Eight

"Shoot Rudy and you'll be killing your nephew's father," Sophia said.

Dimitri swallowed, trying to take in the words. "Yulian's father is dead." He knew this because he'd killed him.

She kissed the sleeping boy's forehead, then took a step closer. "No."

He watched his sister approach, uneasy and not sure what was off. Wasn't this what he'd asked for? But where were the handlers who used his love for his sister to control him? "I don't understand."

"Rudy!" Sophia shouted. "Come out. It's time for a family meeting. At last."

Family. Rudy really was Yulian's father?

"Stop pointing your gun at him, Dimitri, you're scaring him," his sister admonished. "And it's time for you to be introduced to my husband."

"You can lower your gun, D," Ian said. "I've got mine on Fredrickson."

"Thanks," Dimitri said as he lowered his weapon.

"Rudy, get the fuck out here." Sophia spoke in a singsong

voice, stroking the sleeping child's head in a show of not wanting to disturb the boy.

Leaves scraped against leaves as Yulian's father left his hiding place and descended into the circle of the overgrown gun emplacement.

"What the hell are you doing, Alyssa? You weren't supposed to bring Julian here."

"Well, I could hardly *not* bring him when Dimitri made his presence mandatory to the exchange. *You* were supposed to stop that from happening, but you fucked up and made everyone suspicious of you. How this goes down is on you."

"Why isn't Julian moving? What did you do to him?" Rudy asked, his gaze on the boy.

Dimitri couldn't quite take it all in. His sister and the nephew he'd ached for years to meet. The traitorous DIA agent.

This was his family.

"I gave him a sedative. He's fine."

"You *drugged* our son?" Outrage filled Rudy's voice. "Jesus, Alyssa. What if it makes him sick?"

"Would you rather he witness the shit that could go down here?" she asked, her voice full of hostility.

"What. The fuck. Is going on?" Dimitri asked.

Sophia—or Alyssa—faced Dimitri. "You struck a deal. Yulian and me, free of Russia, in exchange for the AUUV. I have good news for you, big brother. You're getting your deal. I'm going to use the AUUV to buy our freedom."

"*You* are going to use it. Meaning you've been"—he nodded toward the satellite phone he'd tossed into the over-grown center of the gun emplacement—"the person on the other end of the call?"

His baby sister had been calling the shots? She'd set him up to abduct Ivy? His body flushed as he glanced at Rudy. The analyst had used his position in the DIA to send Ivy here to be abducted by Dimitri. He and Ivy both had been set up from the start—by the one person Dimitri had been trying to save.

The woman he'd been protecting from the moment she took her first steps shrugged. "Guilty." Then she fixed Dimitri with a glare. "But I had my reasons."

"Your reasons." His voice came out hoarse. "How long? How long have you been pulling my strings?"

"Depends on which strings you're talking about."

He glanced from Rudy to Sophia. If Rudy was Yulian's—or Julian's—father, then the story she'd told five years ago had been a lie. How many other lies had shaped his life? "Were you raped by Boris five years ago?"

"No." She glanced at her husband. "I wanted to go to the US with Rudy to have my baby and finally fulfill the role I'd been trained for since I was eleven, which *you* denied me when you had me kicked out of the program. But Boris felt I was more useful in Russia as the Hammer's handler. Always, always my role was subservient to yours. So I lied to you, and you got rid of Boris, which allowed me to assume the identity that had been set up for me years before. And I, for the record, have been a much more valuable spy than you ever were."

She adjusted her son's weight against her chest and stepped closer, absolutely unafraid. But then she hid behind a child, and no matter what she'd done, Dimitri could never hurt the sister he'd cherished his entire life.

She cupped his cheek with her free hand. "You can thank me for your assignment to join the Coast Guard. The powers that be still wanted you in the Navy so you could join the SEALs as their ultimate inside man. You'd have been so good at it, and I was sick of hearing your accolades. When I learned they needed someone to watch over Yuri Kravchenko, I suggested you. You got to cool your heels reporting on nuclear sub movements—which anyone with a decent spy satellite could see—in the Strait of Juan de Fuca, while I was in DC, working as a party planner for several embassies and married to a DIA agent who was oh so very pliable."

"Fuck you, Alyssa," Rudy said.

She smiled. "He's still pissed about being caught in a honey trap. He didn't know I was either Russian or a spy until he was in too deep. He's a good father but a lousy American—more concerned with covering his ass than the secrets he's helped me pass on to Cuba, China, and Russia."

"Cuba and China?" Dimitri asked.

"Oh yes. You see, the real money—the real power—is in the information exchange. Cuba is a great dealer in secrets, and China has deep pockets. Plus, why would I want to give everything to Russia when our motherland has been so very awful to me?" Her jaw hardened. "You see, dear brother, when you had me booted out of the embed program, you took everything from me. I was nobody in that foster home, and the food was shit. My foster father was even worse than the caretakers at the orphanage. Worse than Boris. You have no idea what you put me through."

Her son stirred, and she returned to the singsong voice, an eerie shift in the jungle, as his allies who had guns trained on Rudy remained hidden in the vegetation. "But you were the golden boy, the one the GRU was eager to appease, so I was the outcast while you completed your training. Once a month, you'd swoop in like a gift from the heavens, your mere presence a blessing on my blighted existence."

"You could have *told* me."

"I *did*! I said I wanted back in the program, but you wouldn't listen. Because you were a *man* and so certain you knew what was best for me."

"I was protecting you. Like I promised Mom. If you'd told me—"

"I'd have been sent to a new home. Or worse, back to the orphanage. They would have done what *you* wanted. Not what I wanted." Her eyes flattened. "So I figured out how to deal with my foster father on my own. Just like I figured out how to deal with *you*."

She stroked her son's hair. "You know, you never *asked* me if I wanted out of the program. You just assumed you knew what was best for me. For all of your Americanisms, you were yet another pigheaded, sexist Russian man." She glanced at her husband again. "But then, sexism isn't confined to Russia. Dear Rudy couldn't fathom a women being as cunning as I was. His myopia was my opening. And I took it."

"How long, Sophia? How *long* have you been dictating my assignments?"

She sighed. "Your regular assignments came from the GRU. I controlled the Hammer."

He could have accepted almost any other statement, but he physically recoiled at that. "I...I *became* the Hammer because of you. Because Boris raped you and made me listen to your screams."

"Boris didn't touch me. At least not then. Faking that rape was my idea."

The day he'd listened to Sophia's screams, he'd crossed a threshold into a dark place that both haunted him and fueled the rage he needed to perform his duty. He'd given up a piece of his humanity in exchange for the hope—the belief—that he was doing the right thing to protect her.

She patted his cheek. "That day was my vengeance. For all the times you didn't hear me scream."

The embodiment of his nightmares stood before him, and he couldn't raise a hand to strike the demon down. She was the baby sister he loved, holding the nephew he treasured. No wonder she'd walked into the jungle unarmed and confident. She knew she had nothing to fear from Dimitri, no matter what she'd done.

"What do you want us to do?" Luke asked in his ear.

Dimitri stared at the remote in his hand. He could blow up the AUUV. But what would it gain him?

"What happens now?" he asked Sophia. Jesus, he'd lined up allies who would now be asked to protect a woman who might well be responsible for the biggest national security leaks of the last five years.

If she had sold DIA intel to Cuba, there was a good chance they'd sold it to Afghanistan, Syria, Yemen, Somalia, and Iran. Special forces operators had likely died because the enemy had advance notice of operations.

He couldn't ask Luke or Ian to protect her, not when men they'd fought beside might've died thanks to her.

But Yulian—*Julian*—was a different matter. The child deserved everyone's protection. And it was Dimitri's fault the boy was even here.

"Give me the AUUV," Sophia said. "You and your team walk out of the woods. You sail off with Ivy and live happily ever after."

His eyes narrowed. *Ivy.* She would be in danger now that Sophia couldn't be used against him. "How the fuck is that supposed to happen with GRU still jerking my chain?"

Sophia smiled. "Simple. They don't know you're alive. I told them months ago that you hadn't reported in, no matter how much I baited you on the dark web. You've been declared dead. There was quite the ceremony honoring your sacrifice."

"But what about you, Rudy, and Julian? You can't go back to DC after what you've done."

She shrugged. "I knew that was out the moment Rudy fucked up and suspicion turned to him. All you had to do was see a photo of his wife and my cover was blown. So I'm going to use the AUUV to cut a deal with Cuba. We'll be comfortable there."

"I'm not going to fucking Cuba," Rudy said.

"Don't be an ass, Rudy. Of course you will. Do you really think the DIA is going to overlook everything you've done?" She shifted Julian's sleeping weight to her other arm. "Right now, I bet Boyd is trying to decide if he should shoot you."

The crack of a bullet punctuated her sentence, and Rudy dropped to the ground. His forehead bloomed red.

Dimitri jerked toward Ian's position, hardly able to believe he'd done it. No. Ian was a professional. No way had he fired the shot.

Leaves rustled, drawing Dimitri's attention to the right. Ivy was thrust through the branches, Zack Barrow behind her, shoving her slack form forward. "What a perfect entrance line. There I was, wondering who I should shoot, and you gave me that little gem. Thank you—is it Alyssa or Sophia? I can't quite keep up with all the aliases." Zack pointed his gun at Dimitri. "Hammer, Jack, Parker, Dimitri. So fucking confusing. Pick one." The gun switched to Julian. "Even the boy has two names."

Dimitri held his breath. He'd blow the AUUV if he believed Zack would fire, but the moment he hit the button, any leverage he had was gone.

The gun returned to Ivy's side, under her arm, where a bullet would pass through a lung before reaching her heart. "And then there is poor, sweet, one-named Ivy."

Ivy's head lolled, and her body was limp. At five-nine, she wasn't light. Zack was expending a fair effort supporting her deadweight, something Dimitri could use to his advantage.

"What's wrong with her?" he asked. "What did you do to Ivy?"

"Sleeping beauty here was tagged by a tranq dart. I didn't

think it was fair you excluded her from the fun, and I knew my buddy Ian would take potshots at me if I didn't have a human shield. Where is Ian?" He glanced around the jungle. "Ollie ollie all come free." Zack's voice lost its playful edge. "Or I shoot the bitch where she'll slowly bleed out."

Branches parted, and Ian descended from his position in a tree. "It's 'oxen free,' asshole."

"Drop your gun."

Ian stooped down and set his gun at his feet.

"Where's your new SEAL buddy?" Zack asked. "The golden boy who doesn't take a crap without alerting the media. Surely he's up a tree somewhere?"

"He's in Koror holding a press conference," Ian said.

Zack forced a laugh. "Sevick better get his ass in the circle, or I'm going to start shooting." He glanced toward the dead DIA man and added, "Again."

Did Ivy's eyes flutter? Dimitri couldn't be certain. "Do as he says, Luke," he said.

Luke followed Ian's lead and emerged from his hiding place, setting his gun at his feet.

"Sophia/Alyssa, give the boy to Veselov," Zack instructed.

"No," Sophia said. Her arms tightened around her son.

"You don't understand, you aren't calling the shots anymore, sweetheart. I am. And while I'm sure you're a cunning spy and deserve all sorts of credit for how you've been playing everyone for years, I'm fairly certain you aren't the fighter Veselov is. Which is why I want *him* holding the goddamned child." Zack let out a low whistle, and four armed men emerged from the jungle behind him.

Shit. Their hidden ace—Palea perched with a sniper rifle above the bomb shelter—didn't seem adequate against Zack's small army.

Sophia stepped forward and offered her son to Dimitri.

He took the sleeping child. His nephew. He'd dreamed of meeting him. But not like this. Never like this.

"I'm sorry," Sophia whispered as Julian settled against his chest.

He couldn't even take in the weakness of her apology versus her actions over the years. "Do you hate all people, Soph, or just me?"

She shrugged. "I didn't *hate* you, exactly. I just…wanted something different. I found a way out, but it meant using you."

"Everything I did was to protect you."

"I never asked to be protected. Your protection was a curse."

"How is it you had a lead on where the AUUV was hidden?"

She flashed a proud smile. "Because it was one of my men who stole it and hid it before he was captured. His final message included the area, but not coordinates. Even he didn't know exactly where in the Rock Islands he was."

"You stole it from Russia with one hand—and then received information from the GRU about their interrogation of your own operative with the other. Information you then passed on to me so I could find it for you."

"You say that like it surprises you, brother, that I am a very, very good spy. And yet we went through the same training. You always underestimated me. Everyone underestimates me. That's why the GRU never guessed I was both their faithful spy and their biggest enemy. They never knew I cultivated China and Cuba as clients for my intel. I am loyal to no one but my son." She stroked Julian's head.

"The family reunion is touching but I'm ready to take my AUUV and go now," Zack said.

She glanced at her husband's body. "If anything happens

to me, you'll be Julian's only family. Protect him better than you did me."

Thirty-five pounds of boy rested against his chest. The woman he loved was unconscious in the clutches of a man who was using her as a human shield—a man who'd already shot her once. And he'd just learned his sister was the source of every evil act he'd committed in the name of protecting his family. He couldn't process the flood of emotions.

He needed to be the Hammer. He needed to be the monster his sister had created, so he could protect Ivy, Julian, the men who'd volunteered to back him up on this nightmare op, and yes, even his sister.

In spite of everything, he *would* protect her.

"Get the fuck over here, Sophia, or I'll shoot the boy and your brother."

Sophia backed away, then turned and walked purposefully toward the former CIA agent who'd allied himself with Ivy's ex-husband.

She stopped in front of Zack and lifted Ivy's chin, making a show of inspecting her face. "So. This is Ivy. Rudy always talked about how smart she was. When I saw her picture in the online tabloids, I wondered if he was attracted to her for more than just her brains. She's passably pretty, but there's also this innocence that would have appealed to him."

She glanced back toward Dimitri. "But I never would have taken her for *your* type. I would have guessed innocence would repulse you."

"Must be a case of opposites attract," Zack said. "C'mon. Show me where the AUUV is."

She looked up at Zack. At five-two, she was dwarfed by him and Ivy. "I have no idea where it is. Perhaps we should get Ivy's drone and have it scan the jungle?"

Zack pressed the barrel of his gun to Sophia's forehead.

"Or I can shoot you, then ask again nicely. He might not mind seeing you eat a bullet at this point, but he cares about Ivy."

Chapter Thirty-Nine

*I*vy had started to return to consciousness on the boat as they reached the island. It was a well-established fact that she couldn't act worth a damn—well, except for when she'd shot Dimitri, but then she'd taken all her anger at Rudy and projected it onto Dimitri. This time she was too terrified for that to work. But she could play unconscious. It was all about keeping the muscles slack and loose. She could do that. Her brain was damn fuzzy anyway.

With each passing minute, the world grew a degree clearer. But she didn't dare open her eyes. She pretended she was Raggedy Ann. Soft and lax. Her life—and Dimitri's— depended on her pulling this off.

When Sophia lifted her chin, she was certain it was to determine if Ivy was truly unconscious. She'd chattered on— her voice low and calculating. Ivy remained relaxed, blank faced, a burden to Zack.

Through slitted eyes, she saw the barrel against Sophia's forehead. She couldn't give warning by stiffening or taking a deep breath. She needed to go from rag doll to weapon in a single moment.

Her heels dragged in the soft earth. In one motion, she pushed up, slamming the back of her skull into Zack's chin. She swung out with her cast arm, smashing the hard case against the gun as Sophia ducked.

An explosion sounded in the same moment the gun fired. Ivy's vision was blurred thanks to the tranquilizer, but in the blur of movement, she could see Sophia coming at Zack. Ivy dove to the side. Her muscles were sluggish, and she stumbled and had to roll to get out of the way.

The jungle filled with the acrid scent of smoke. What had blown up? It wasn't the AUUV, because it was in the other direction.

Luke, Ian, and Dimitri fought hand to hand with Zack's men, who must've been disarmed in the confusion caused by the explosion.

Where was Julian?

She spotted the sleeping boy tucked in a nest of vines. His mother must've seriously drugged him for him to sleep through the explosion, but in this moment, Ivy wasn't judging. She crawled across the jungle floor toward the boy, trying not to put weight on her cast arm, which throbbed from smashing it into Zack's gun.

She'd grab Julian and take cover in the bomb shelter.

Feet from the boy, someone grabbed her ankle. She kicked backward, wishing for the first time in her life she were wearing stilettos. The grip only tightened, and she was pulled back, into the center of the fray. She twisted and saw Zack had her in his grasp.

Sophia launched herself at the man, kicking his forehead, snapping his head back. "Get Julian!" she shouted to Ivy. "Protect him."

Freed, Ivy scrambled to the sleeping child, scooped him against her chest, and ran for the bomb shelter.

a bullet pierced the air, and the man Dimitri had been fighting dropped. *Thank you, Kaha'i.*

He turned to go after Zack and saw Ivy and Julian were missing. "Where is Ivy?" he asked, using the ear radio.

"In the bomb shelter," Kaha'i responded. "I'm covering the entrance."

He ran toward Zack, whose head appeared momentarily on the other side of the float that hid the AUUV. Zack must've chased after Ivy, because the float was near the shelter.

"Good." If he blew up the AUUV, Zack would go with it. He patted down his pocket. "*Fuck.* I lost the remote for the detonator." His gaze scanned the ground. No time to search the jungle. "Where is Sophia?"

"She's on the slope below the float—I think." Meaning she'd disappeared in Palea's blind spot.

Zack's head had dropped below the float, but his hand appeared, holding a knife that arched downward.

Dimitri heard Sophia's grunt of pain, then glimpsed the top of her head as her body slammed into the rusted float, shaking it.

"Blow it up!" Sophia shouted.

It hit Dimitri that Sophia had known exactly where the AUUV was, because they'd had to tell Rudy in the thirty minutes before the handoff. He'd probably been wired and she heard every word as they went over the layout and plan, which meant she even knew about the TNT.

C-4 couldn't be ignited with a bullet, but TNT could.

"Get clear, D," Kaha'i said. "I've got a line on the TNT.

Dimitri rounded the float and pulled Zack away from

Sophia, taking a blow to the face and feeling the sting of a blade to the arm.

"Sophia's not clear!" he shouted to Kaha'i. He turned to see his sister slumped back against the aluminum hull.

She'd been stabbed in the gut. Blood trickled from her mouth. "Tell Palea to take the fucking shot." She kicked Dimitri in the chest, pushing him down the steep slope in the same moment she grabbed Zack by the hair, pulling him to her.

Dimitri tumbled down the hill. "Do it!"

A bullet sounded. Then came a small blast, followed by a second, roaring explosion. Dimitri's body pitched in the air.

He landed, bashing his cheek on a jagged rock and abrading his chin on the rough ground.

He slumped as the world spun around him. All he could see upslope was a haze of smoke.

One by one the team checked in on the radio. Luke, Ian, and Kaha'i were fine. The bomb shelter protecting Ivy and Julian was intact.

Slowly, the smoke cleared. Where Sophia, Zack, and the AUUV had been was a giant crater.

Chapter Forty

*D*imitri stared at the sleeping boy. Julian Fredrickson. He reached out to brush aside the soft blond hair on Julian's forehead, but stopped. This was normal, undrugged sleep; a touch might wake him, and Julian needed sleep.

Ivy had taken him to a doctor in Koror, who'd examined Julian both before and after he woke, and they'd determined the sedative he'd been given, while strong, hadn't harmed him. She'd waited until this afternoon, the day after the explosion in the jungle, when he was awake and alert, to break the news to him that his parents were gone.

She'd held him while he cried, and after hours of confusion and heartbreak and tears, he'd finally fallen into a fitful sleep just an hour before Dimitri was released from questioning. He'd been granted two hours to see Ivy one last time before being taken to Guam, where the process of dissecting Alyssa and Rudy Fredrickson's espionage, and assessing the damage they'd inflicted on US national security, would begin.

It was almost certain covert operatives abroad had been

compromised, and this work would be vital to getting those men and women to safety back in the US.

Dimitri would help in every way he could—which was likely extensive because he knew the keys to the codes Sophia had used. If it was determined the GRU really didn't know he was alive, or if they could be convinced of his death, the Justice Department would build a new identity for him. In all likelihood, it would be years before he could settle in the US. Years before he could see Ivy again.

He had a mere two hours with her and his nephew before the next phase of his non-life began.

Perhaps it was for the best that Julian was sleeping, considering Dimitri would disappear again. As he navigated his grief, Julian needed an adult who would stick around, which Ivy had said she wanted to do.

Dimitri draped an arm around her shoulder, and together they slipped out of the sleeping boy's room in the hotel suite. Ivy pulled the door shut without making a sound, then turned into Dimitri's arms.

"Thank you, for taking care of him," he whispered as he squeezed her against his chest.

"Of course." She pulled back from the embrace and took his hand, tugging him away from the closed door and toward the far side of the living room of the deluxe hotel suite, where she dropped onto the sofa and patted the seat next to her. Luke and Ian had gone down to the hotel bar, to give them time alone.

"According to the DIA, Rudy doesn't have living family members. You're Julian's only known living relative."

"But I can't claim him without tipping off the GRU."

"Exactly. If Rudy really has no family, Julian is likely to go into foster care until he can be adopted." She gripped his hand. "I'm going to request he be placed with me. As you're his only living family member, I'd like your permission to adopt him."

He couldn't meet her gaze, could barely breathe, so he studied the veins on the back of Ivy's hand as emotion swamped him. Finally, he managed a breath and a choked "You'd do that?"

"Of course," she repeated.

He met her gaze with his good eye. His face had been battered in the explosion, more than he'd realized at the time. His left cheek had fractured, and his eye was swollen due to lacerations above and below. He could still see, but vision in that eye was blurred. "There's no guarantee I'm ever coming back. If the GRU knows I'm alive, I won't risk you—or Julian —that way. I'll disappear forever. You'd be stuck raising a child who isn't yours."

"He's not mine—*yet*. But he will be. I can and will love him as my own. And I hope someday he'll come to love me, but even if he doesn't, I'll still be there for him and give him all the love you would, if you could." She gazed toward the closed bedroom door. "He's hurting even more than you are right now. If I can't be there for you as you wade through what your sister did, then at least I can be there to lavish love on him."

His heart ached for Julian, but at the forefront of his emotions was the pain of betrayal. "I still don't want to believe she could be so cruel."

His baby sister. He'd given up a part of his soul to protect her, only to learn that she was the person who'd orchestrated the forfeiture.

"I don't either. And I know it will be hard for you not to blame yourself."

"It *is* my fault. She said as much—"

"No, Dimitri. It's not your fault. Blame the GRU. Blame everyone who abused her. Blame the drunk driver who killed your parents and left you unprotected. Blame *her*. But don't blame yourself. You didn't make her into what she became."

He grimaced. "It's not that easy."

"I know." She snuggled close to him and pressed her lips to his neck. "I know."

He pulled back and studied her face. "It's going to be a long haul, Ivy. I can't ask you to wait for me when I might never be free."

"Well, it's not really so much about waiting. You see, my libido died a long time ago, and you revived it. I believe the resurrection is biometrically secured to you."

He tilted back his head and laughed. Only Ivy could make him laugh like this, now. "You're saying I'm the only man who can turn you on?"

She grinned. "Yes. That's exactly what I'm saying."

He placed a hand behind her neck and pulled her face to his. "I love you, Ivy. I'll do everything I can to come back to you and Julian, but it's not in my control." He kissed her then, pouring his emotion into a kiss that would have to sustain them for months, years, or even, possibly, forever.

When the kiss ended, she stroked his jaw, tracing scrapes along his chin, gingerly skipping over the bruises on his cheek. "I love you too." She tucked her head under his neck and snuggled against him. "Ulai's prognosis is better. They might bring him out of the medically induced coma tomorrow."

"I heard that from Kaha'i." He stroked her back. "He also said it looks like Zack is the one who attacked Ulai."

"I suspected as much. But why did he go after Ulai?"

"Kaha'i thinks Ulai caught him in the hangar, attaching a tracking device on the seaplane. They found similar tracking devices on the yacht and inflatable Luke rented—which is how Zack knew where to find you and where to find us. He didn't know where we hid the AUUV, but he knew where we'd tucked the boat away on shore."

With Ian acting as translator, Kaha'i had questioned Zack's men who'd been taken alive in the jungle. Ian had shared some details with Dimitri. Zack hadn't acted prior to the confrontation in the jungle because he didn't know where Dimitri had stashed the AUUV, plus he was well aware of the hazards of attacking the Hammer directly, as proven when he lost the three men who'd boarded *Liberty*.

Ivy frowned. "We led Zack right to the handoff."

Dimitri shrugged. "Given his history with Ian, he probably had been keeping tabs on him. He couldn't have known it would lead to me. He probably targeted Ulai so he could find me."

"What would have happened if Zack and I hadn't shown up? Would you have let Sophia have the AUUV?"

He'd thought about that a lot in the last twenty-four hours. "I honestly don't know. Sophia is probably responsible for the deaths of several special forces operators and for massive leaks that ravaged national security. I don't think Ian or Luke could have let her walk out of that jungle, and I couldn't blame them."

"She was counting on you to protect her," Ivy said, "once again."

He nodded. "I wouldn't have, though."

"So we'll hold on to her last act. She pushed you away and pulled Zack in. She sacrificed herself for you."

"She sacrificed herself for Julian."

Ivy nodded. "And in so doing, she saved you. We can give her credit for that."

Dimitri considered Ivy's words. Could one selfless act make up for the horror of what his sister had done?

No.

But it did help by giving him one moment to believe in. One morsel of the bright-eyed girl he'd played with as a child had survived and remained part of the complex and disturbing woman she'd become. She was victim and villain.

Was she worse than Zack Barrow, a greedy, power-seeking traitor to his country, or just a mirror image?

He couldn't answer that because he didn't know Zack at four years old, but he had known Sophia. And the part of him that loved his sister—and who would love her to his dying day—didn't want to believe that girl was the worse villain, even though what she'd done to him had been vile.

A cry from the bedroom brought Ivy to her feet. Julian was awake and crying for his mother.

Ivy turned to him before running to the bedroom. "Do you want to meet him?"

Dimitri touched the bruises on his face as he considered his answer. He wanted to meet his nephew more than anything, but his needs came second. "My face might scare him."

Ivy nodded and headed for the bedroom. She left the door open so he could glimpse inside as she entered and picked up the four-year-old. Her face blanched with pain, and she adjusted her grip so her cast arm didn't bear his weight. "Hey, buddy. Ivy's here."

Julian asked for his mom in perfect Russian. It surprised Dimitri to realize Sophia had taught him the language.

Dimitri didn't know which the three of them cried harder as Ivy stroked his hair and held him, whispering words of love to the boy she'd just met.

Epilogue

Grand Cayman, Cayman Islands
10 months later

*A*ccent: German. Age: late thirties. Attitude: interested, too interested.

Ivy never should have let Hazel talk her into this vacation. But getting away to take a break after Patrick's very public conviction had seemed like a good idea, and her sister Laurel had offered to take Julian along on her family's annual trip to Orlando. Now Ivy wished she'd gone to Disney World instead. How could she have passed up the opportunity to see Julian's delight as he rode Dumbo for the first time?

Instead, she was at a posh resort on Grand Cayman, playing wing woman to Hazel in the crowded hotel bar. That part she didn't mind; it was when men set their sights on her that made her uncomfortable. Funny that all it took to become desirable was to put out "not interested" vibes.

Hazel thought she was still off all men thanks to Patrick, and that was what Hazel would always have to believe. The FBI had drilled into her the importance of silence, or her adoption of Julian would be in jeopardy, and the chance for a future with Dimitri would be impossible.

She hadn't heard a word from him since they'd said good-bye in her Koror hotel room. Not his fault, she knew, but still she ached with the uncertainty of their future.

In her mind, she wrote him long letters. The first would have told him of her mixed feelings when she learned she wasn't pregnant. Disappointment, but also relief that Dimitri wouldn't miss the experience of being by her side as she carried his child. And the adjustment for Julian would have been harder if she'd been pregnant too.

She'd wanted to tell Dimitri everything about those first months with Julian, holding him as he cried for his parents. But she didn't dare commit the words to paper. If found, they could ruin the life she was trying to build.

Strings had been pulled to make her his foster mother, but that was only the first step. They'd needed to be certain Rudy Fredrickson had no living relatives, and that the couple had no will with provisions for their son.

A handwritten letter by Alyssa Fredrickson listed an unnamed brother to be appointed as guardian should anything happen to her and Rudy. The letter was locked away in FBI files and couldn't be used to support Ivy's claim.

In the meantime, she and Julian built a relationship. It wasn't smooth or easy, but the love was there, and it was enough to build on. Julian was learning to find joy again as he settled into his new life. It was all Ivy could ask for.

Now Hazel was dancing with the friend of the German man who was hitting on Ivy, while Raptor operative Sean Logan watched them both from the corner of the bar.

Alec had insisted a bodyguard accompany them—while threats to Ivy had ended with Patrick's conviction, traveling outside the US was still deemed a risk. But Hazel and Sean had clashed from the start because Sean intimidated any man who approached her.

Two days into a seven-day vacation and Ivy wished she'd gone with Laurel and Julian to the Magic Kingdom.

Beyond the open-air nightclub was a stretch of beach, and beyond that the turquoise Caribbean Sea. She longed to be out on the water, or better yet, on a deserted island with a certain reformed Russian spy. Island life was only fun with the right company.

She apologized to the man who'd asked her to dance and crossed the room to Sean's side. "I'm going paddling," she said. She'd feel better on the water. Calmer.

"I need to go with you."

"I really want to be alone. You can watch from the beach. I'll stay within sight of the resort."

Sean's mouth pinched, then he gave a sharp nod. As one of Raptor's top operatives, she knew he hated this kind of babysitting duty. He was usually off in foreign lands guarding much higher-risk targets than the boss's cousins, and with CAM firmly in the hands of the Pentagon, Ivy was in no danger here.

She headed for the exit, only to find Hazel, hands on hips, planting herself before her. "Oh no, you don't, big sister. You *promised*."

"I just want to go paddling."

"We paddled all day. Tonight you said you'd dance."

She shrugged. "I'm not feeling it."

"So you didn't like the German guy. That's fine. There are a dozen other nationalities to choose from. How can you possibly resist a Jamaican accent?"

Ivy puffed out a breath. "I'm just not in the mood, okay?"

"Ive, you need to get out there and dance. It doesn't have to mean anything. Just have fun. Cut loose. Hell, pick up a guy and have a vacation fling. No one will judge you."

She hooked her arm through Ivy's and pulled her back to their table, waving to the cocktail waitress as she passed. The three of them arrived at the table simultaneously. Hazel ordered two fruity tropical drinks with Ivy's favorite coconut rum. After the woman left, Hazel asked, "When was the last time you got laid? Please don't tell me it was Patrick, because the thought of that makes me want to hurl."

Ivy usually accepted comments like that without a word, but something inside her snapped in that moment. Maybe it was the melancholy of missing Julian. Or the awkwardness of being in a bar ostensibly to pick up men, when there was only one man she wanted, or even Hazel's offhand reminder of the last time she'd had sex. Whatever it was, she couldn't be silent anymore.

"Hazel, I love you with all my heart, but you need to stop shaming me for the fact that I was in love with my husband. I carry enough guilt on that point myself without you piling on."

Adrenaline flooded her as she realized she'd said the *thing* that had been bothering her for years but which she'd avoided because, conflict.

Hazel was her best friend, and barbs from her hurt more than from anyone else.

Hazel sat upright, her eyes wide with shock. "Do I do that?"

Ivy cocked her head. "Um, yeah. Basically from the moment we got engaged."

Without warning, a tear rolled down Hazel's cheek. "You know how you can believe you're a good person, and in one moment you see yourself in a different light?"

Ivy gave a sharp nod. "Yeah. I've been in that neighborhood." She'd visited that street a thousand times in the months after Patrick was arrested, then again in Palau, and she'd set up permanent residence as she and Julian waded through the murky waters of establishing a parent-child relationship.

Nothing was easy.

The only way to approach Julian in those times was through the lens of love. He was a hurting boy. She was a flawed parental figure. If they held on to the love, they could navigate the heartache.

She called up that love to address her sister, who'd inflicted more pain that she'd ever realized over the years. "You've been better these last few months, but you still slip in these snide comments here and there, and I'm done with it. I don't need your judgment any more than I need the judgment of strangers. Less even, because from you, it *hurts*."

"Oh, Ive. I'm so sorry! Why didn't you tell me?"

She shrugged. "Probably because I felt it was my due to be shamed. But fuck that. I fell in love with a man and married him. He turned out to be a monster. But that wasn't my fault. And it wasn't my fault I didn't know, because he worked damn hard to hide it from me and the rest of the world." There. She'd said it. The feeble defense she hadn't bothered to express to the outside world. Because no one outside her inner circle would really give a damn, but also because in the long run, they didn't matter to her.

The waitress returned with their drinks. Hazel reached for Ivy's hand. "I'm sorry, Ive. I really—I didn't realize I was doing that. Please don't hate me."

"I could never hate you, Haze. You're my sister. Even when I'm mad as hell at you, I love you."

Her heart ached in that moment for Dimitri. She hated that she hadn't been able to be with him these last months, as he faced his sister's betrayal, which was infinitely more devastating than anything Ivy had faced—even when she added Patrick to the mix. She could only imagine how painful it must have been for him to come to grips with his sister's actions.

Hazel held up her drink. "Can we start this vacation over? I'll stop being a bitch and grousing about Sean."

Ivy picked up her drink. "And I'll try to relax and be more fun." They clinked their glasses together, pact made.

"Promise me you'll dance with the next man who asks."

"I don't think—"

"There's a man making a beeline for you right now. And oh my God, but he's hot. I saw him staring at you earlier when you were talking to the German guy."

Ivy shifted and caught a glimpse of the man with her peripheral vision. Her belly flipped, and her entire body flushed with heat and joy. She caught her breath and faced her sister. She couldn't let her reaction show.

"He's Death-Valley-in-July hot."

"If he asks you to dance, you'd better go for it."

She took a sip of her drink. "I think I might," she said softly.

☠

Ivy was even more beautiful than Dimitri remembered. He'd been watching her all evening, savoring the moment when he'd speak to her. He had to do this right. This would become their origin story, the story they'd have to tell everyone in her family except her cousin Alec.

Alec had been the one to suggest they use Hazel as a witness for their "first meet." Her presence would make it all the more real for the rest of the family. Alec had also suggested surprising Ivy. And the look on her face, the shock and heat, set Dimitri's heart pounding.

Ian had initially been suggested to play bodyguard, to set

up the meeting, but it was decided that he was too much of a friend to Ivy. His presence would be intrusive. Plus, Ivy would likely suspect something was up. Sean was the better choice, and he'd been brought into the loop and knew exactly who Dimitri was. He was also watching Dimitri's back, making sure no one was tracking him.

Today, at long last, Dimitri would claim his life.

He reached Ivy's table and she met his gaze. He saw the telltale pulse jump in her throat, the rush of joy in her eyes. She'd been practicing her poker face, but she wasn't quite there yet. Fine with him. He loved her just the way she was and didn't want any part of her to change.

Tossing out an awkward pickup line for her sister's benefit wouldn't work—Ivy would never fall for a guy who introduced himself with a cheesy line—so he simply said, "Would you like to dance?"

Ivy jumped to her feet, bumping the table and sloshing her drink. "Yes. Yes, I think I would."

Hazel laughed. "Have fun, Ivy."

"Your name is Ivy?" he asked, just loud enough for Hazel to hear as they walked to the crowded dance floor. "I'm Matthew. Matthew Dimitri Clark."

"Matthew?" she said as though she was testing the texture of it. "Do you go by Matt?"

"I haven't decided yet."

They reached the dance floor, and he pulled her against him. A slow song had just started, giving him about two minutes to hold her close and lay the foundation for their future.

He whispered in her ear, "It's my *real* name. The FBI tracked down my birth certificate in Berlin. They did a lot of digging and pulled a lot of strings, and it appears the GRU never knew that name, never knew who my mother was or where she was from. The FBI worked with the CIA and State

Department to get Matthew Clark citizenship. I've been given a past no one will have reason to question. Now I'm here to ask if you'll be my future."

He raised his head away from her ear and met her gaze. Her eyes had filled with tears. "Yes," she said softly. She cleared her throat. "But you should know, I've got a five-year-old at home I'm in the process of adopting. His name is Julian. We're a package deal."

His arms tightened around her. "I love him already."

He held her against him for the duration of the song, no words necessary until the music changed to a faster beat. "Keep dancing, or return to the table and play first meet for your sister's benefit?"

A glance toward the table showed Hazel chatting with Sean.

"Does Sean know who you are?"

"Yes."

"Table, then. The sooner we convince Hazel, the sooner we can escape and go for a walk in the garden…or go to your hotel room."

He flashed a grin. "You're propositioning me awfully fast."

"I don't do one-night stands very often, but I understand they can be quite empowering."

He laughed. "There's only one problem. I don't have a hotel room. I live on a boat. It's docked in the hotel marina."

"And this is a problem how?"

"Once I have you aboard *Steel Orchid* I'm liable to take you out to sea and have my way with you."

"It sounds like paradise."

*I*vy was strangely nervous when she stepped aboard the boat, *Steel Orchid*. Not about being alone with Dimitri—*Matt*—but more that this was too good to be true.

She'd been prepared to wait years before they were certain Dimitri was free of the GRU. These last ten months had been an eternity, but still, it was far sooner than she'd expected.

The first thing she saw when she stepped inside the salon was a framed photo. Ulai Umetaro, looking happy and healthy standing on the deck of a yacht that looked suspiciously like *Liberty*. A sign mounted to the rail indicated Umetaro Charters was open for business. "I didn't know *Liberty* had been recovered."

"She was found a few weeks after you left the islands, but it took months to get her ownership transferred to Ulai."

She grinned as she stared at the photo. Dimitri's arms slipped around her waist. His lips found her neck, and she wondered if it was possible to combust with joy.

She turned in his arms and tugged on his belt buckle. If she was going to explode with happiness, she'd take him along with her. He kissed her deeply as he scooped her up and carried her into his stateroom. They didn't even make it to the bed.

Her cocktail dress was pushed up and underwear brushed aside as he held her against the stateroom wall and thrust into her, hard and fast and everything she'd ever dreamed.

"Oh God. Dimitri."

"*Matt*," he corrected, then thrust into her again.

She laughed. "Matt. Matthew. Matt." She practiced his name with each thrust. Operant conditioning with the ultimate pleasure as the reward.

She came, hard. Intense. Euphoric. He came after she

did, then continued to hold her against the wall, kissing her neck. "I love you, Ivy," he whispered.

"I love you, Matt." She could get used to the name. A Dimitri by any other name was still the hottest, most incredible man she'd ever wanted. She cupped his face. "How is it you're even here? That this is even possible?"

He pulled out of her and deposited her on the bed, lying down beside her. He pulled her against his side.

"Ian had the idea of switching Zack's and my dental records. The Coast Guard had mine, and the CIA had Zack's. After the switch was made and they identified Parker Reeves as dead, the FBI closed the book on him. The GRU had never confirmed that I was their man, but there had been information shared when Parker disappeared. Through those existing channels, the GRU was presented with evidence of my death. Given that Sophia died in the jungle too, there was no reason for them to doubt the evidence.

"Between the shock of how deeply Sophia had betrayed the GRU and their scrambling to figure out how much she'd compromised them, they took my death in stride. An insider said I was even labeled as loyal and never having defected, because they found proof I'd reported in to Sophia and was working for her—who I believed to be my official handler with the GRU."

Ivy traced his cheek, which had been reshaped and scarred thanks to the blast in Palau. He looked different, but not too different. "Because Rudy didn't have any living relatives," she said, "the FBI and Child Protective Services entered Julian into the system under a false name, to protect him from being monitored by the GRU. Officially, Alyssa, Rudy, and Julian Fredrickson all died in a boating accident in Palau last April. Julian won't know the truth, unless we decide to tell him when he's older."

Dimitri's eyes clouded. "It feels wrong not to tell him, and yet…"

"He needs to have the memory of the mother who loved him very much. She sacrificed herself for him."

"I have trouble…even thinking about her," Dimitri—Matt—admitted.

"I know." She ran her hands over his freshly shaven cheeks. So much like that first night they'd met. The entire world had changed in the intervening months, yet here they were, meeting again for the first time. "I know."

She sat up and pushed him onto his back, straddling him and gazing down on his handsome face. He was no longer blond—even his eyebrows were dark—and he wore colored contacts. Those changes added to the broken cheekbone, new scars that wrapped around his eye, and a broken nose that now had a prominent bump, and his face had been subtly transformed. But he was still hotter than Death Valley in July.

She traced all the changes in his face, and then touched the familiar lines of his smile. She still wanted to see creases at the corners of his eyes, for joy to be stamped into his skin, indelibly. "I've spent a lot of years hating myself for loving Patrick once upon a time. But over these last few months, I've realized I need to stop beating myself up about that. Stop feeling ashamed. I loved him, and my feelings were real, and I need to honor and respect the woman I was then instead of holding her accountable for things she couldn't possibly know. If I can't do that, I'm no better than all the people I've met who've accused me of awful things. I'm a good person. I don't deserve that."

She ran a fingertip across the new scar on his cheek and over the bump on his nose. "You are a good man. You've spent your whole life trying to protect the only person you could. She did horrible things to you, and made you do terrible things to others. But at your core, you're a good man. I want you to know it's okay that you loved your sister, and it's okay, even now, to want to love her in spite of what she did. I won't judge you for it. She was your baby sister and you were in an untenable situation, put there by people who didn't actually give a damn about either of you. Sophia was a victim just as much as she was a villain. Just like you."

His eyes teared. "I still hate her sometimes. And then I remember the years right before our parents died, and I love her and wonder who we could've been. Siblings, like you and Hazel, taking a vacation together." He paused and cleared his throat. "I met Alec several times in the last few months."

"You did? He never said a word." But then, she knew he couldn't.

Matt smiled. "It's obvious you're close to him. I love what I've seen of your family, Ivy. I want to be part of it."

"You already are. Julian, he's going to love you. And someday, you'll be able to give his mother to him. He's going to need stories of her childhood. The good times."

"I can't wait to see him."

She jumped from the bed and picked up her purse, which she'd dropped on the floor as soon as they'd entered the stateroom. She pulled out her cell phone. "Laurel sent me this picture today."

She showed him the image of a grinning Julian on a ride in the theme park. He'd just lost his first baby tooth last week, leaving an adorable gap in his smile.

"He'll be starting kindergarten in the fall," Matt said.

She nodded. "He's so smart. So ready for school."

"I have a plan. After our whirlwind romance and I get to 'meet' him, we'll date for a bit and it will become clear to your family that we're serious…I'm going to suggest that we take off this summer, three months on my boat, before Julian starts school. It will give us a chance to become a family away from prying eyes. Give me a chance to get to know Julian quickly, without having to play a role for others."

"I think that's an amazing idea." Living on a boat with the two most important males in her world sounded like a slice of heaven.

"You can take the time off work?"

She nodded. "I'll take a leave of absence. CAM has been handed over to the Pentagon, I'm in the final stages of refinement and training so others can operate the system, then I'm out. I have no interest in being a spy, and won't dare risk using the system again myself now that terrorist groups are after it. I've got money saved and can afford the leave. But what about you? I assume you're working for the CIA now. Are they going to let you go?"

"They have all the intelligence I could give them, and in the future, I'll be called in to evaluate new intelligence as it comes in, but it will be consulting mostly. Dimitri Veselov saved every penny he could to set up his sister and her son with a new life. I'm going to use that money now to take care of Julian, like I always wanted."

"So this is really going to happen? We can really sail off into the sunset together?" Just the idea of it made her heart race. Once upon a time, Dimitri had told her there would be no happy endings for him, and they'd both believed him.

"It will, and we can. Just like I predicted, Russian spy Dimitri Veselov died when the AUUV was handed over in the jungle. But it turns out, American CIA analyst Matthew Dimitri Clark has an amazing future."

Author's Note

Archaeologists have been quick to adopt technology often used in intelligence gathering for finding and recording sites. This has resulted in some amazing discoveries, including locating entire villages and buried pyramids.

The technology of intelligence gathering is rapidly changing. Archaeologists and many other scientific disciplines are adapting in sync with the expanded abilities of drones and satellites. Ivy's inventions, CAM and RON, along with the Air/Underwater Unmanned Vehicle (AUUV), are fictional in the way they are used in this story, however they are based on technology that is being developed and could possibly already be in use. Sleeper surveillance drones, artificially intelligent mapping drones, Lidar mapping that works seamlessly above and below water, and vehicles that can autonomously transform from swim to flight are all in development stages (if not already in use) and the role of drones in espionage could well eclipse the traditional role of human intelligence gathering.

Thank you for reading. The Evidence series continues in *Silent Evidence*. Two things haunt forensic anthropologist Hazel MacLeod: the bones of victims of genocide she examines for her work, and former SEAL Sean Logan's rejection in Grand Cayman. But within days of moving to her cousin's estate to take a much needed break, she finds herself faced with both.

Visit Rachel Grant's website at www.rachel-grant.net for more information on *Silent Evidence* and her other books.

Acknowledgments

Thank you so much to the readers who write me and say my work brings you joy. Knowing my work brings pleasure at a time when we are bombarded with so much negativity is the light in my day.

Other people who bring light to my day are my author friends who are always there for me when I'm struggling with a scene, character, plot point, or real life. Gwen Hernandez, Darcy Burke, Jenn Stark, Elisabeth Naughton, Serena Bell, Toni Anderson, Bria Quinlan, and Gwen Hayes. Thank you ladies, for always being there for me. I'm pretty sure Ivy and Dimitri would still be stuck on that island if not for you.

Thank you to Dr. Stefan Groetsch for answering my questions about traumatic brain injury and medical facilities in Guam and for helping me find a way to give a secondary character a happier ending.

Thank you to my children for being exactly who they are. I am so proud to be your mom.

This book would not have been possible without input from my husband, who recorded archaeological sites in Palau for four months and shared with me the wonder and beauty of the islands. Thank you so much, Dave, for the story ideas, and for sharing this life adventure with me.

About the Author

USA Today bestselling author Rachel Grant also writes thrillers as R.S. Grant. She worked for over a decade as a professional archaeologist and mines her experiences for storylines and settings, which are as diverse as excavating a cemetery underneath an historic art museum in San Francisco, survey and excavation of many prehistoric Native American sites in the Pacific Northwest, researching an historic concrete house in Virginia (inspiration for her debut novel, CONCRETE EVIDENCE), and mapping a seventeenth century Spanish and Dutch fort on the island of Sint Maarten in the Caribbean (which provided inspiration for the island and fort described in CRASH SITE).

She lives in the Pacific Northwest with her husband and children.

For more information:
www.Rachel-Grant.net
contact@rachel-grant.net

www.ingramcontent.com/pod-product-compliance
Lightning Source LLC
Chambersburg PA
CBHW021235190726
48289CB00005B/1328